Osiris

Jeffrey Thomas

Published by Theatre of the Mind Books, LLC. in 2019

www.theatreofthemindbooks.com

Osiris /Jeffrey Thomas, 1st ed., Book 1 of the Derek Cross Series

ISBN –978-1-7336557-0-5

For author updates, visit Jeffrey Thomas on the web!

www.jeffreythomas.net

www.twitter.com/penfiction

http://www.goodreads.com/

Cover Design by Ryan Schwarz at

www.thecoverdesigner.com

Acknowledgements

I would like to say a special thanks to John DeChancie and to the late Ardath Mayhar, both of whom I worked with on the early drafts of this novel. Without their constant encouragement during the development of this story, it likely would never have been completed.

I would also like to thank my editor, P.D. Tovh, as well as beta readers Jess Angers, Jennifer Bourgeois, and especially Kayla Davenport, who provided wonderful thoughts and insights into every aspect of this book.

I would also like to say thank you to the staff at NaNoWriMo (National Novel Writing Month), who every November, poke, jab, push, prod, and encourage aspiring writers to push themselves to achieve the incredible goal of writing 50,000 words of fiction in that single month. The first draft of this manuscript was written during NaNoWriMo, as were three other manuscripts I currently have in development.

Last, but not least, I'd like to thank my wife, Denise, who has done more in support of me than she'll ever know.

This book is dedicated to the memory of my brother, Jerry. We miss you.

TABLE OF CONTENTS

Chapter One

Ganymede

The black void was shattered by the dull grayness of the ship. Like some massive leviathan splashing in the sea, the starship fired its braking thrusters as it approached the planet-sized moon. Red lights along the hull began to illuminate. The ship settled into orbit roughly a hundred miles above the pockmarked surface.

"Make sure your men keep their fingers off the trigger. I don't want anyone accidentally hitting a non-combatant," Captain Derek Cross told the three sergeants who stood before him. "I don't want any firing unless it's being returned toward a hostile. There are dozens of women and children down there. Make sure your men check their targets. You got me?" he bellowed.

"Yes sir!" the three men said in unison.

"Once you've made contact with the miners, let *me* negotiate this time, Sergeant De Silva," he said, glancing at one of the men. "Let's get this over with quickly. I'd like to find out what's bothering these people and make sure somebody fixes it, so they can get back to work. This disruption in ore shipments is costing a lot of money."

The three sergeants stood like statues, facing the empty wall behind Captain Cross.

"Alright, then. Let's light 'em up," he said with a slight nod. The three men gave quick salutes, and moved toward the door, their heavy boots thumping on the floor.

"Sergeant Cook," Captain Cross said.

One of the men turned back to Cross as the other two left the room.

"Yes, sir," Cook said, scratching his freshly shaved head.

"You up for a little golf when this is over? I bet I can drive two thousand yards here," he said, nodding toward the moon, visible through a small porthole.

"I got fifty that says I can top your best shot."

"Deal," Cross said with a smile and a slap on the back as they walked out of the room.

Along the side of the ship facing the moon, two large doors slid open, revealing a series of holes, from each of which projected a white cylinder. From a distance, the eight-foot long cylinders looked like needles bristling along the side of the massive ship. Behind the ship, Jupiter's massive bulk dwarfed the ship and moon. The planet's surface, brilliantly striped with shades of red, tan and even the occasional blue, stood in stark contrast to the dark gray of the tiny moon and the miniscule spacecraft.

"I want you men to remember why we're here. We are to negotiate and get the installation up and running again. It has to be back to full production before we can go home," Sergeant Cook yelled at the men in front of him.

Twelve men stood there, all outfitted in armored environment suits.

"If we start taking fire, remember your non-lethal striking points. The Captain wants no kills. Remember your training. Keep your eyes open for hostiles, but keep your fingers away from the triggers. I also don't want to hear any excuses why someone's pickup *accidentally* got blown up," he said, rolling his eyes, then glaring accusingly at a young Hispanic soldier. The soldier looked down at his boots, smiling.

"I also want you men to act like adults this time. Especially you, Jiminez!"

"Come on Sarge. I blow up one truck, and everyone thinks I'm trigger-happy."

"Shut up, Jimmy. I'm talking about the way you men are going to treat these people. I want you to watch your mouths this time. There are going to be women and children down there," he said. Pointing at a tall, slender soldier whose ears seemed to stick straight out from the sides of his head, he barked, "You too, Radar!"

The skinny soldier had been given the nickname during basic training because his drill sergeant said his ears looked like radar dishes.

"After we take the station, I want you men to stay clear of the local female population."

The men laughed.

"Remember your low-G combat training. Ganymede has a gravity field comparable to Luna, so stay low to the ground, lean forward, and for God's sake don't jump. If you're in the air, you're an easy target," he said, turning his back on them. Several seconds passed as he stared out a small porthole at the moon's rocky surface.

"What a desolate fucking wasteland," he muttered. "And to think, I had to get out of bed to come here and tell a bunch of miners to get back to work. Why couldn't we have been called out to go to Luna? At least they've got biodomes filled with trees and grass. They haven't got shit here."

Cook turned back to his men and took a deep breath.

"Alright, ladies. I'll see you on the ground. We've got a job to do, and we're going to do it. Can anyone tell me why?" he asked, his voice just above a whisper.

"Yes sir, Sergeant," they yelled. "Because we're marines!"

"Goddamn right we are! Let's do the Captain proud," he said as he picked up his environment suit helmet. He snapped it on with a loud click. The soldiers began putting on their helmets as well.

Along the underside of the ship, forty radar-like dishes slid into view, aligning themselves with their targets on the surface.

"Receivers firing," chimed a human-like electronic voice. "Stand by for departure."

Silently, the cylinders began hurtling toward the moon in a wave that started from the front of the ship, working its way toward the rear. In ten seconds, all forty of the cylinders were in flight.

"Receivers away. First wave enter transport chamber."

Thirteen soldiers entered separate, phone booth-sized pods. With a clang, the doors slammed shut, committing them to their duty.

"Receivers at fifty miles and decreasing."

The tips of the white cylinders began to glow a light shade of orange as it easily pierced the planet's almost non-existent ozone atmosphere. With a flash, the white casing blew apart into four sections. From inside the casing, a shiny, six-foot long titanium javelin sped toward the surface of the asteroid, accelerating from the lack of resistance. The rod was unadorned, except for a series of slots near the tail.

"Receivers at twenty-five miles, prepare for transport."

Like spears thrown by some ancient warrior, the receivers began to hit their mark. The titanium lances began slamming into the asteroid in a pre-designated pattern. They landed in three groups, forming the corners of a triangle around the mining station. Each lance had a space of fifty feet between it and the next. Of the six-foot long spear, only about eighteen inches was exposed above the ground; the rest was buried beneath the surface.

With a flash of green light, the receiver was activated. These pulses were signals sent out in a circle from the lance, to verify that there were no obstructions within a twenty-five foot circle surrounding it.

"Landing zones 100% clear, transport commencing."

The red lights along the outside of the hull began to dim. More brilliant than the distant sun came a wave of lightning from the dishes along the underside of the hull. Each bolt silently connected with a lance on the surface of the planet, depositing its cargo. Again came a flash from each of the lances, rechecking the landing zone. From the slots on each lance, a light green glow began growing brighter and brighter, illuminating the area around the lance for several feet. Another brilliant flash blasted across the barren landscape, as an arc of energy was fired from the tail of the lance, hitting the ground a few feet away. Now standing on the charred dirt was an armored soldier.

Upon realizing that transport was complete, the soldiers instantly threw themselves down on one knee and scanned the horizon to get their bearings. They first scanned the area, verifying that it was clear of enemies. The soldiers got to their feet and began working their way toward their objective.

"First wave transport complete. Alpha team is feet dry," came a voice over Captain Cross's radio. He stood in the ship's command center, listening to the communications. "Beta team, prepare for transport. Alpha team, move to rally point," came another voice.

On the planet, a young soldier looked up at the inside of his helmet. The helmet's internal display showed his location marked with an "X". The alpha team rally point, marked by an "R", was only fifty meters away. Numb from adrenaline, he was already moving before he made the conscious decision to start running. His environment suit was heavy, but its weight was more than manageable under the low gravity conditions on Ganymede. On his screen, the

"R" turned green as it was "touched" by his "X". He crouched and pressed a yellow button on the side of his rifle, activating his communications system.

"Marshall in position at rally point," he said, scanning for the enemy.

"Jiminez approaching your position," came a reply. To his right, he saw Jiminez sprinting toward him, his black environment suit bouncing up and down as he ran.

I don't care what anyone says, I'd take a high-G assault over this bouncy shit any day, Jiminez thought to himself.

Transmissions began to come all at once, as more soldiers began to near the rally point. Sergeant Cook had counted only nine when the hills and sky to the southeast lit up with lightning as beta team was transported.

"We've got to move," said Sergeant Cook. "Stragglers regroup at Op Point Able, over." The sergeant looked over his squad to recheck his numbers. His men were huddled together, still shielding their eyes from the blast of light to the southeast.

"Call off," he ordered. There were nine replies.

"Marines not currently at the rally point call off," he said. There was no response.

"Call off!" he barked. He waited a few seconds, but still there was no reply.

"God damn it! They should have sent us down here in transports. This electronic shit pisses me off! I need to shoot those engineers! Alright, saddle up ladies. Let's move to Op Point Able. The Captain will be down in a couple of minutes, and I want to be the first squad in position. Keep your eyes open, and check your targets. We have families down here."

The squad began moving in groups of two, in a leapfrog fashion.

"Squad, hit the dirt!" ordered the sergeant. "Gamma team comin' down!"

The troops barely had time to shield their eyes before the flash of brilliant light came from the east.

"Thanks for the warning, Sarge," Jimenez mumbled.

"Cut that shit out, Jimmy! I give you as much warning as they give me. Keep moving," Cook scolded.

"Gamma team is feet dry, sir," Corporal Tanaka said, his voice cracking.

The control room's three-dimensional display showed the moon's topography in green, wavy lines. Moving slowly across these lines were three groups of dots, each designated by a different color. Sergeant Cook's team was displayed as a set of nine blue dots, and Cook himself as a yellow dot. There was also a cluster of six white dots and Sergeant Hunter's yellow dot to the southeast of Cook's men. To Cook's east, seven green dots were being followed by Sergeant De Silva's yellow dot. In the center of the three colored groups was a white outline of the mining facility - the objective.

The individual dots seemed to be moving in zigzag patterns, stopping for a moment and then moving again at random intervals. The dots in each group were moving roughly parallel to each other. The yellow dots, however, were moving in a straight line behind the groups they followed. On the left-hand side of the screen, Tanaka noticed that four of the blue dots, as they went through their leapfrog and zigzag pattern, were slowly getting farther and farther away from the next nearest pair on the screen.

"Captain?" Tanaka said, pointing toward the four blue dots, his finger shaking.

Although Corporal Tanaka had been through all the required training and simulator time for his position, Captain Cross had seen that even the smallest deviation from mission protocol had caused him to show signs of nervousness, if not outright panic.

"It's alright Corporal, relax. I see it." Captain Cross rested his gloved right hand on the Corporal's shoulder.

Captain Derek Cross understood that many of the men under his command felt intimidated by him, and he assumed that Tanaka was no different. The men knew that if a soldier under Cross's command didn't give everything during a mission, that soldier would find himself reassigned. Much of this idea had been created in the minds of the soldiers themselves, and then perpetuated by their sergeants.

Captain Cross reached his gloved hand in front of the Corporal to the screen. His thick, stubby finger touched Cook's yellow dot, and waves emanated from it as if the screen were made of liquid. The dot began to flash.

"Sergeant, tighten up down there. You're getting a little sloppy."

"Yes sir. I'm..." a crackle of static interrupted the transmission. "Op point...fifteen...rally point..."

"What the hell is going on, Corporal?" Captain Cross demanded.

"I'm checking it out sir." In a flurry of movement, Tanaka's hands moved across the control station, pressing various buttons. The screen above his head showed a cut-away version of the ship in the center, and to the right was a three dimensional representation of Ganymede. A small red dot appeared, slightly above the asteroid, and was sending out red circles in waves.

"Sir, we're being jammed by a small satellite in orbit."

"What?" Captain Cross demanded, squinting at the screen.

"It's right there, sir! Sensors didn't pick it up earlier. It must have been on the backside of Ganymede when we arrived. It's sending out a jamming pulse." Corporal Tanaka appeared on the verge of tears.

"Alpha team approaching Op Point Able, sir," came a voice from across the room. "Beta team has reached their rally point."

Information was coming at him in waves, seemingly from all directions. Although his pulse was only slightly elevated, he was getting nervous. His left hand was in his pocket where it had been for at least ten minutes. Around his left wrist was a beaded silver chain, on which hung a medal. He rubbed the medal between his thumb and fingers, his finger slowly moving across the five points of the star, one at a time. Although he had been trained on them and how they worked, he had never actually encountered a jamming system. Cross noticed that the medal in his pocket felt warm and damp, and he realized he was sweating.

"Sergeant," he leaned his head to the side listening. "Sergeant, please respond, over." He was answered with static, and an occasional bit of a word here and there.

"...op...ess.... Repeat, alpha team...awaiting..."

"Fire control? I've had enough of this. Target that satellite. Take it out as soon as you get a lock," he said, through gritted teeth. He shifted his weight back and forth, his thickly insulated environment suit weighing heavily on him.

"Target acquired, sir. Firing," responded the weapons officer. A blast of white light erupted from a small hole at the front of the ship. The satellite was hit by the blast, and bits of molten metal sprayed in a cone from where the satellite had once been.

"Sir! What the hell is going on up there, over?" Sergeant Cook yelled at them.

"Calm down, sergeant. Everything's under control. Give me a Sit-Rep."

"Sir we're at Op Point Able."

Captain Cross looked at the screen in front of Corporal Tanaka noting that the blue dots were all clustered around a small, flashing "A". He noted that De Silva and his men were slowly approaching a "C" from the north.

"That's where I'm going in, Tanaka," Cross said, pointing to the south of the flashing "B".

"Sir, I only received nine men," Cook interrupted. "Please tell me the other three are still with you, over."

"Yes, sergeant, your men are still alive. There was a malfunction with a few of the lances. Your men, six from

Sergeant Hunter's squad and 5 from De Silva's squad are standing by in case they need to come down as an additional wave."

"God damn electronic shit!" echoed through the situation room.

"Uh, sergeant?" Captain Cross said smiling.

"Sorry sir, I thought I switched off."

"I think we all appreciate how you feel." he paused for a moment, squeezing the medal in his palm until it hurt. "Have your men hold at Op Point Able. I'll be down in a few minutes."

"Roger."

"Lieutenant, radio the Colonel. Let him know I'm dropping in through one of Sergeant Hunter's lances, as planned. Tell him I'll be in contact when I reach the facility. You're in command. I'll be radio blackout for about three minutes. I'll report in when I'm down," he said, as he reached down and picked up a helmet sitting just behind Tanaka's console. He turned and headed toward the door.

Captain Cross walked down the long hallway. The white walls were awash in pink from the red lights, indicating the ship's red-alert status. His boots felt unusually heavy as he approached the transport station. The black plasma rifle bounced against his back with repeating thumps, which he could hear emanating from his chest as he exhaled.

Stepping into a long room, he began patting all of his pockets, double-checking the presence of all of his equipment. He paused for a moment and pulled his rifle down from his shoulder. With a click, he pulled his primary power cell from his belt pouch and held it in his hand, staring at it. He pressed a small button on the top of the cell, activating the cell's 'self test'. After a few seconds, the display showed a green light and read '75', the number of rounds the cell's charge held.

"I've got a bad feeling about this," he muttered.

Cross almost never felt the need to have a magazine in his rifle when he dropped into a landing zone, and actively resisted the urge when he'd had it. He served more as a negotiator than a fighter, although he was well suited to both tasks. He slowly placed the cell back in its belt pouch then and placed his medal and beaded chain in a zippered pocket on the chest of his environment suit. He put on his left glove and then slung his rifle back over his shoulder. When he put his helmet on, the latches clicked and the suit's air system began to hiss as it filled the helmet with breathable air. He reached down toward the pouch containing his secondary power cell, but stopped.

"Oops, almost forgot," he said, reaching toward a plaque on the wall. He rubbed his gloved hand across the plaque. A swath of dull bronze was worn down the face of the plaque from all the soldiers who had passed this way before. The plaque, rubbed by the soldiers for good luck, gave the history of the ship's name – *USS Valley Forge*. The plaque read:

<u>USS Valley Forge</u>

The *USS Valley Forge* was named for the United States Revolutionary War location where George Washington's soldiers weathered several months of winter in 1777-1778. The camp was marked by the bloody tracks of barefoot soldiers in the snow, around the nearly 1000 small shacks that made up the camp. Nearly 3000 men died in the camp from a variety of ailments, including starvation, disease and exposure. The leadership and training instruction of General Washington and his officers burned away the cold in the hearts of his men, and after the winter's chill had abated, his men, now well-disciplined and well-trained, marched on. Five years later, these men helped win the American Revolution.

The name *USS Valley Forge* was first used during World War II. A Boxer Class amphibious assault ship (CV-45) was the first to bear the name. This ship also served as an assault aircraft carrier (CVA-45), as an anti-submarine warfare vessel (CVS-45), and as an amphibious helicopter assault ship (LPH-8). After a long career, this ship was decommissioned in 1970. The USS Valley Forge served its crew valiantly in Korea and Vietnam, earning the ship eight and nine battle stars in these two conflicts, respectively. Overall, three Navy Unit Commendations, two Meritorious Unit Commendations, and two National Defense Service medals were earned prior decommission.

USS Valley Forge was reissued in 1986 for the Ticonderoga Class Aegis Cruise Missile ship (CG-50). The *Valley Forge* served in Operations Desert Storm, Enduring Freedom, and Iraqi Freedom, and served in anti-drug operations in the Atlantic and Pacific Oceans, as well as the Caribbean before being decommissioned in 2004.

The current designation (CV-192) was commissioned on May 18, 2128. A Daedalus Class Assault Ship, this ship carries on the proud heritage of the name:

<u>USS Valley Forge</u>

Below the history, pressed into the bronze plate, were replicas of the awards the name had earned throughout its history.

"Step on the pad, please," came a human-like electronic voice.

"Yes, mother," Cross said sarcastically, stepping up to the shiny steel plate outside the chamber door. He looked down the wall at the row of small booths that lined the wall. They looked similar to telephone booths, and each stood empty.

"Checking landing zone, stand by," the voice said. Captain Cross had always joked with his sergeants about the psychological meaning of having a woman's voice, or at least the resemblance of one, played to them before they were deployed. Psychiatrists were consulted on all aspects of design for the *Valley Forge*. They had decided that a woman's voice would stimulate a primal instinct to fight for a female. Whether that female was a mate or a maternal figure was irrelevant. One man would fight for a mate, while another would fight for a mother-figure. Some men would call the voice "Honey", some "Dear", while others called it "Mother".

"Standby for departure. Please enter the transport chamber," said the voice. His pulse began to race. The transport chamber door slid silently open. He stepped into the chamber, turned to face the door, and looked down at his equipment for one final check. Seeing his secondary power cell pouch still open, he closed it.

Derek took a deep breath and looked up as a gray-haired, barrel-chested man came into the room.

"Come to see me off, Captain Gregory?" Cross said loudly in his helmet.

"Yes, sir. You and your boys have fun down there. I'll have my Ex-Oh get the galley to make something special for you guys for dinner," he said, his voice barely audible inside the transport chamber.

"Thank you, sir," Cross said. "Cook and I have eighteen holes scheduled when this thing is over. How 'bout you?"

"I'll bring one of my officers, and we'll make it a foursome."

Captain Gregory flipped him a relaxed salute, but Cross drew himself up and fired back a very stiff salute in return. Gregory turned and left the room.

"Receiver at twenty-five miles. Prepare for transport." Cross took a deep breath and exhaled loudly in his helmet. The clear faceplate fogged over, and then slowly cleared. He looked back down at the belt pouch that contained his secondary power cell, and realized that he had forgotten to run the self-test on it. As the lights in the transport bay began to dim, the realization that it was too late to check the cell washed over him. The hairs on the back of his neck stood on end as a chill ran down his spine.

"Landing zone clear, transport commencing," chimed the voice. "Stand still." The hair all over the rest of his body began to stand on end, as the chamber was filled with an electric charge. The white light in the room began to grow brighter. Suddenly, there was a flash of brilliant light, and then he was plunged into darkness.

Captain Cross was suddenly disoriented. He felt as though he were being pushed down into his boots.

Tremendous pressure had suddenly built up around him, although there was no pain. He began to hear a buzzing in his ears. Suddenly, the pressure faded and he felt as if two people were trying to pull him apart. It felt as though someone was holding his feet, while someone else was holding his head, trying to stretch him like saltwater taffy. He felt as though he had been smashed into nothing in the booth, and was now being stretched back into shape. The buzzing in his ears grew louder and louder, until he could make out voices. They were screaming.

Chapter Two

Assault

Awave of terror washed over Cross as he suddenly realized he was on the surface, and the voices he heard were his men. He threw himself to the ground and rolled onto his back, fumbling for the power cell. His eyes struggled to rid themselves of the after-image of the light, as he pulled out the primary cell; it felt slippery in his hand. He squinted at the cell, and saw that when he had dropped to the ground, the cell had been crushed between his body and a rock. Electrolytic solution was all over his glove.

"..right there! Jesus! Right there! Get him!" someone screamed.

"Jimmy, where the hell is Jimmy! Jiminez, please respond, over!" a soldier screamed.

Cross pulled his secondary power cell out of the pouch and ran the self-test. Several seconds that seemed like years passed, and suddenly the display showed a red light. He looked at the display, which read "Discharge", and saw that the counter was at 47. He paused, trying to comprehend what he saw, and then watched in horror as the counter dropped to 46, then 45.

"Captain! Please respond! We are taking fire, over!" Sergeant Cook yelled.

"Roger sergeant, I'm here! Give me a status report!" he yelled, as he slapped the power cell into his rifle. He rolled onto his stomach, aiming his rifle in the direction of the rally point. He saw flashes of light on the dark horizon. Yelling continued to pour through Cross's helmet "...target, zero-five-two...twenty meters..."

"I'm hit! My arm! God, Jesus Christ my arm! I need help! Somebody help me!" came another voice. "God it's bad, my arm, please somebody!"

"We've...ambushed, Captain! I...three men hit...pinned down...over!" As Cook was speaking, Cross could hear intermittent sounds of weapons fire, cut off by bits of static.

"Watch the comm-chatter! Call off!" Cross yelled. He listened as the static-filled yelling continued.

"Call off, goddamn it!"

Captain Cross opened a small forearm-mounted display that showed a similar view to the one he had seen on the large screen in the control room. He saw blue dots arranged in three groups. One group had three dots, the second group had four, and the third group of two blue dots was being followed closely by a single yellow dot. This group was closer to the station than the other two.

"Sergeant Hunter, do you read?

"Yes sir, loud and clear."

"Give me a Sit Rep, over!"

"Sir, we are pinned down about a hundred meters due north of our LZ. We started taking fire just after you went into blackout, over."

Captain Cross began pressing buttons on his display panel. The view zoomed in, showing the two dots standing beside the yellow "Sergeant" dot. The two dots began to flash alternating yellow then red.

"Sir, I have three men down, two of them are hit bad."

"I'll see if I can get you some help. Corporal Tanaka, get those other men down here, now!" he yelled.

Static was the response.

"Tanaka!"

"...no...get the ..." Captain Cross heard, garbled in his helmet.

"Hunter, I'm south of your position, about five-zero meters. The cavalry's on its way, over."

"That better be one fast horse you're on, we're in some serious shit here!"

Captain Cross, his eyes now fully adjusted to the dark, scanned the horizon toward Sergeant Hunter's position for several seconds and saw no movement. He was about to stand when a chill went down his spine. He froze, his eyes wide. He slowly reached up and pressed a button on the side of his helmet. His face was bathed in red light, as his infrared night vision was activated. Lying in wait beside a large rocky spire was a prone figure with a rifle. He took aim at the enemy's head. For several agonizing seconds he gritted his teeth. Beads of sweat began to form on his upper lip.

Shit, he thought to himself. He struggled for another option. His eyes moved to the rocky outcrop. He smiled as he took aim at the rock. With a barely audible thump, a burst of red light flew from his rifle, hitting the outcrop. At the site of the impact, the base of the rock exploded.

"Timber," he said, smiling.

A large piece of the rock fell on the enemy's upper back and neck, knocking him unconscious. Cross scanned the area and, not seeing any other danger, jumped to his feet. He darted back and forth from one rocky area to another, as he made his way toward Sergeant Hunter.

Cross approached Hunter's position from the south, scanning for the enemy. He saw several flashes coming from a large plateau. Just ahead he saw the source of the flashes. Two men, both holding heavy plasma cannons, were perched on the side of a mesa-like hill, firing toward the north.

"Nice toys," he said sarcastically.

The two men were dressed in military-style environment suits. They both had ablative chest and back plates, thigh pads, and armored environment helmets. *A bow and arrow would be nice right now.*

Cross knew that their armor offered protection against energy weapons, but only to a point. It would wear away with each direct hit. This would allow the enemy soldier to be hit several times in the chest, back, or wherever the armor was worn, before a breakthrough. This type of armor was useless against a blade or some other types of weapons.

One of the soldiers, about twenty feet behind the other, was perched on the side of the plateau some twenty or thirty feet above the ground. Seeing an opportunity, Captain Cross slowly worked his way up along a slight rise, just out of sight.

Standing below the soldier, Captain Cross watched him fire several times as he took aim. He took a deep breath and fired. The small ledge the enemy was standing on shattered beneath his feet, leaving him temporarily weightless. The soldier flung his arms wildly as he fell and hit the ground. His heavy plasma rifle hit a large rock a few feet away, landing directly on the power cell. With a flash of energy, the rifle blew apart, the force of the blast slamming the enemy into the rock wall.

Captain Cross approached him cautiously. The enemy writhed in pain on the ground, his leg broken and twisted beneath him. Cross knelt on one knee beside him and scanned for the other soldier, while he reached into a pouch on his belt. The soldier, in a daze from the intense pain, was unaware of his presence. Cross pulled a small medical pouch from a pocket, placed it on the ground next to the enemy and opened it, removing a small vial. Sticking out from the end of the vial was a needle. He stuck the needle through the soft, flexible section of the environment suit between the hip and thigh armor plates, and into the soldier's flesh. A flash from the North caused Cross to flinch and duck his head.

"It's going to help the pain," Cross said quietly. "It's a sedative." He squeezed the vial and, almost immediately, the soldier stopped moving.

Up ahead, the second soldier was apparently unaware that his partner was no longer behind him, as he continued to fire toward the horizon. Captain Cross stood and worked his way along the side of the rocky plateau until he was standing just below the enemy. Standing fully erect, the soldier's feet were level with Cross's chest. He looked his enemy over for several seconds.

These aren't miners. He knelt down in the dark in a small crevice, weighing his options. An idea flashed in his mind. *Another sedative.* He quickly reached for his pocket, and his stomach dropped when he realized that he'd left the medical kit on the ground beside the other soldier.

Oh well, he thought to himself. He instantly went into action. In one swift motion, he stood and swung the butt of his rifle across the enemy soldier's legs. The soldier's feet were knocked out from under him, and he hit the ground, hard. Cross saw the enemies head slam against the back of his helmet, and his eyes immediately rolled back in his head before closing. The soldier, unconscious, slid down the side of the hill and into a shallow crevice. Cross picked up the heavy plasma cannon and checked its ammunition load.

Only five rounds left. This isn't going to help me much. The last thing I need is someone else picking this up and using it on me or my men, and I can't carry both weapons. I'm better off with my rifle, at least until the power cell dies. I'll find a replacement. He removed the heavy plasma cannons power cell and dropped the weapon beside its owner. He threw the cell into the air and with a well-placed shot, blasted it with his rifle. The flash of the cell exploding lit the area with a warm, blue light.

"Captain Cross!" blasted in his ears. "You had better watch your step as you approach! I don't know what the hell they're using, but it's damn serious!" Sergeant Hunter yelled.

"I'm here - that was me. Your friends are no longer a threat. What is your status?"

"I have three dead and two wounded. Cortez is pretty shaken, but uninjured. I need immediate evac of my wounded, over." Hunter's voice was filled with rage. "I have some business to take care of, sir."

"Negative. I want you to fall back to your LZ. If Tanaka got my signal, the remaining troops who mis-dropped the first go 'round will be down soon," Cross told him. "That means you are going to have a second go with some fresh troops."

"Now you're talking! But what about my wounded?" Hunter asked. "I can't just leave them lying here, over."

"I don't see any more bad guys out this way. There are a few to the northwest and maybe some to the northeast, but Cook and De Silva should be dealing with them right now. I'll have medics drop in as soon as I can. When you get back with the reinforcements, you can mop up anyone that's left."

"Aye sir. They don't call me 'The Hunter' for nothing," Hunter told him.

"I've got to figure out why our transmissions aren't getting to the rest of the men," Cross said under his breath, looking toward the mining station. He started toward the north when he heard a mumbling coming through his earpiece. He paused to listen and realized it was Hunter saying a prayer for the three men who had been killed. Cross stopped, looked around for enemies, and then dropped behind a large rock. He closed his eyes and bowed his head.

Cross approached the location of Hunter's troops and found the two wounded men were conscious and alert. They were taking turns scanning for the enemy, while the other would tend to his own wounds. He began checking the plasma burns on the two men. After apprising them of the situation, he moved to the three dead soldiers, who were lying side by side on the ground, their pockets open and empty, and their weapons gone. He knelt down beside them.

"Is that Jones?"

"Yes, sir," one soldier said. "He got hit first. He never felt a thing. We didn't even see it coming. Caught him right in the back of the neck. Round barely missed his air-line and helmet power line. That would have been a bad way to go."

"Jesus. I just saw him at chow this morning." He shuffled from one knee to the other.

"His birthday was last week," the other soldier interjected. "He just turned 23. Got a letter from his girlfriend back home and everything."

The soldiers, who had been consumed by watching for the enemy, began to fight to maintain their composure.

"I've got to put a stop to this," he said, turning to face his men. The lighted display in the closest soldier's helmet illuminated his face with a reddish glow. In the light, he noticed a tear on the soldier's cheek. He quickly looked away.

"Stay alert. Hunter will be back in a few minutes with the rest of the platoon. You'll be topside shortly." He turned toward the station but stopped mid stride.

"What's your ammo status?"

"Fifteen rounds left on my backup mag, sir," one said.

"I've got twelve," the other said. "I'm using Jonesy's spare clip. I ran out already."

"Any extra ammo with the others?"

"No sir, I think Sergeant Hunter picked 'em up during the firefight. He must have them with him."

"Damn," Cross said under his breath. "Thanks, guys."

Cross sprinted from boulder to boulder, ducking and peering around periodically. He huffed deeply as he approached the last large boulder between himself and the facility. Dropping to his knees, he scanned the horizon to get his bearings. On the top of the main building, he saw that another transmitter seemed to have been hastily installed on the facility's communications tower. Bundles of cables were wrapped around a small dish, holding it onto the tower. A red light on the dish was illuminated and pulsing, which meant the dish was active and transmitting. *A jamming pulse?* He jumped to his feet and pulled an antimatter grenade from his belt. Without so much as a thought, he turned the knob to arm the grenade, and lobbed it onto the roof beside the base of the tower, before he quickly ducked behind the boulder. Several seconds passed, and he started to question whether the grenade was defective like his power cell when an explosion rocked the boulder in front of him. Several pieces of shrapnel bounced uncomfortably close to him.

"Captain Cross, please respond," Corporal Tanaka said. "What is your status, over?"

"I'm receiving you, Corporal. What's our situation?"

"Sir! We lost all communication with the elements on the ground the instant you left the ship!"

"Tell me what we have, Corporal," he demanded.

"Well, it's not good. Someone was waiting for us. We have several KIAs."

"Get the rest of those troops down here. Send them in using Hunter's lances. Hunter will be there waiting for them. He'll be in command of the mixed squad. I've left them an open door to approach the facility from the south."

"Yes sir," Tanaka said, exhaling loudly. "Sir, that's not all. We have..." A flash of white light blinded Cross, and the shock hit him like a heavyweight boxer. Temporarily dazed, he fell to the ground. He shook his head from side to side, trying to get his bearings. In his ears, all he heard was static. He looked up in his helmet and saw that all his electronics were damaged. His infrared system was out, so he could no longer see in the dark. He rubbed his glove across the right side of his helmet and looked at it. The palm of his glove was covered in charred resin from the blast point. His helmet had been hit.

"Shit!" he said as he rolled behind the boulder. He scanned the area, looking for a place to run. Glancing toward the station, he saw an opportunity - an open airlock. He struggled to clear his mind from the shock of the blast and come up with a plan to get inside the airlock. He patted his pockets to survey his equipment, and then looked at his weapon to determine how much energy his power cell had remaining. His stomach dropped when he saw that it read "empty". *How the hell did I manage to get a defective power cell?*

Cross slowly craned his neck around the side of the boulder, trying to determine the enemy's location. He quickly pulled back as a blast of plasma hit just above his forehead on the rock, chiseling out a trough in the stone. The shot was all he needed. Now that he knew the approximate location of the enemy, he quickly pulled out his last grenade and checked the open door again, making sure there wouldn't be another soldier waiting for him when he entered. He turned the knob and started counting backward from five. When he got to two, he threw the grenade straight up. When he got to one, he bolted toward the open door. The explosion sent out a shockwave that made the soft gray soil around the boulder jump, creating a cloud that masked him from the enemy. Knocked off balance by his own grenade, he slammed into the inner airlock door. He punched the outer airlock door button with the butt of his rifle. The door slowly closed, and air began filling the small room.

Once the room was filled with air at standard atmosphere, the inner airlock door opened. Cross quickly stuck his head into and then back out of the airlock vestibule, making sure there was no one inside. He tapped a button on his forearm display and brought up a floor-plan diagram of the facility. He knew that he was out of contact with his men and his ship, but the data system on his forearm was still working. The only thing he could do was to try and find out who was in command of these troops and capture them. He had the data system's map online, and that would be a big help in navigating the station. He felt extremely uneasy about entering the station without a charged plasma cell, but he told himself that he would try to find a replacement weapon inside.

Cross scrolled to the area on the station diagram that represented the airlock in which he was kneeling. The next chamber was a large room for storage and maintenance of the various environment suits the miners wore. The suits were extremely dirty, and looked to be nothing like the armored suits he'd seen on the men outside. There was only one exit from the vestibule, other than the airlock. He quickly moved into the room and stood against the wall inside the door. Listening for the sounds of footsteps, breathing, or the hum of a charged plasma weapon, he pressed his back hard against the wall. He could barely hear anything over his own heartbeat, pounding in his ears. He unlatched his helmet, and without a sound, quickly set it on the floor. Again, he tried to listen, but still heard nothing.

He knew, as all soldiers did, that the biggest drawback to fighting in close-quarters battle, using plasma weaponry, was the crackle or hum of energy that the weapons emitted when the ion coils were charged. The higher power models had more coils, and thus produced a louder noise. The average foot soldier knew to 'duck and cover' when he or she heard the furious buzz emanating from a heavy plasma cannon.

Inside, the main complex was filled with heavy machinery. Closest to him was a large moisture condenser that removed moisture from the air and recycled it into water pure enough for drinking. This unit, with several large air ducts leading into it, was specifically designed to condense the moisture expelled when people exhaled. There were a myriad of hiding places around it and all the ducts that led to and from it.

His heart pounded in his chest. He could feel the staccato thump in his temples. His head throbbed, but he had to concentrate on the mission and ignore the pain. Because his plasma rifle's power cell was out of power, he now carryied it by the barrel - a club of sorts. His only advantage was stealth.

He sat, silently crouched behind the moisture evaporator's main housing. The six foot wide steel casing would provide plenty of cover from enemy fire. He craned his neck, listening for enemy weapons. His eyes went wide as he heard a footstep. Several seconds passed in silence, and he began to dismiss it as his imagination, when he heard a light hum. He listened again; trying to determine how far away the weapon was when he heard another footstep - much closer than he'd thought. It was so silent that it had to be a plasma pistol, or an older, lower-wattage plasma rifle. Another muffled footstep assured him he was right. When the next footstep came, he had the realization that the enemy was standing just around the side of the evaporator. He squeezed his gloved hands around his rifle near the end of the barrel.

In one smooth motion, he stood up, and with every ounce of strength, swung the fourteen-pound rifle toward the unwary enemy. The blow sent the enemy careening backward as the air rushed out of his lungs. He landed on the steel grate and crumpled to the ground, dropping his pistol. Cross turned to see his enemy's weapon sliding toward a grate in the floor. He dove, just in time to see its handle disappear into the deep waste trap below. "Shit," he said under his breath.

Captain Cross suddenly bolted upright, thinking he'd heard another footstep. He paused, listening; his eyes moving in random directions. His concentration was broken by the enemy behind him, gasping for breath. He looked back at the enemy lying on the floor, curled into a ball on his knees; his forehead on the cold steel floor, holding his ribs tightly.

Cross felt a burning rage welling up, as he looked at this person he'd never met; this total stranger was ready to kill him without a second thought. Reaching down, he picked up his rifle by the barrel, ready to finish his enemy with a quick swing. His eyes stung with sweat. Gritting his teeth, he raised the rifle over his head and prepared to strike, when the enemy raised his head to look up at him. Cross stopped, mid-swing, staring into the blue eyes of a teenage boy.

Jesus Christ, it's just a kid, he thought to himself.

A loud boom and the shock like a mule kicking him in the chest sent him to the ground. He was suddenly disoriented, lying face down on the floor. He felt a searing pain and the sensation of liquid, which he knew had to be blood, running down his left side. His ears were ringing from the noise he'd just heard. Then he realized what had happened. It had been a trap to draw him out; another assailant was nearby with a "boomer" – an old ballistic weapon.

Every breath made his entire body burn with searing pain. The pain in his side was unbearable, and with each breath he nearly lost consciousness. He came to the realization that he'd nearly lost control and killed someone. Not just anyone, but a child. He now understood this, and his penance, his price, was death. He'd killed a man on a mission once before, and he'd never forgiven himself. Even though he'd had acted on instinct and training, the act of killing had changed him that day.

The room got slightly darker and blurrier with each shallow breath he took. He watched through the growing haze as the second enemy ran to the boy and reached around him to help him to his feet. The boy groaned as he was lifted off the floor. He squinted, and was barely able to make out the second man as he began taking the young boy away. His sluggish mind pondered why someone would be wearing slacks and a button-up shirt at a mining colony, just before he lost consciousness.

The cool dampness of early-morning dew hung heavily in the air. The alley had not yet come awake with its daytime level of activity. With each passing vehicle, the two men ducked behind a large trash bin. Mostly dark, the only lights in the alley were small porch lights that hung above the back doors of the restaurants and other shops that shared it. The light above them was a bare bulb in a rusty fixture, casting two evil shadows across the reeking garbage that lay strewn about.

"Where the hell is he? He said he'd be here at quarter after," one of the two men said to the other, looking up and down the alley. "I got to be at work in forty-five minutes."

The man was heavy around the middle. The jumpsuit he wore was several sizes too small and had spots around his belly where the fabric was starting to become thin from the abuse. A patch on the right chest pocket read, *Wastewater Processing Plant 4.* The patch on the left pocket read, *Tiny.*

"I ain't sure where he is, but he'll be here. I trust him," a tall, slender Hispanic man replied. "I trust him now."

The slender Hispanic man was dressed in an old t-shirt that had once been white but now bore stains under the arms and had a long beard-like stain drooping down from the neck. His jeans were tattered around the ankles and had stains on both knees.

"I don't trust anyone, Jose'. Neither should you. You'll live longer. Just look what happened to his buddies on Ganymede."

Jose' was about to argue when they both heard the sound of footsteps coming down the alley. Instinctively, Tiny put his hand in his jumpsuit pocket, palming a small knife.

"Relax, gentlemen. Your date for the evening has arrived," said the silhouetted figure approaching them. "I apologize for being a few minutes late. I was," he paused, "detained."

"Let me do the talkin'," Tiny mumbled, his head cocked toward Jose'. "I was starting to get worried, boss." Tiny squinted at the darkness, trying to see the man's face.

"I'm flattered that you care so much for my well-being," said the shadow. "Now, down to business." The man stepped into the cone of dim light. He stood as tall as Tiny, so he was easily six feet tall. Tiny thought the dark suit he wore also made him look very important, and that his slightly balding scalp made him look very distinguished.

"Was my little demonstration enough to satisfy you and your friends?" he said, his hands clasped behind him.

"Si, señor!" Jose' replied, just as Tiny opened his mouth to speak. "I don't know how you did it, but you got the mining union's number one colony to revolt. Fantastica!"

"Shut up, Jose'!" Tiny said through gritted teeth. "Okay, so you've proved to us that you can incite a bunch of miners to revolt. Those poor bastards didn't last too long against the army. What gives?"

The suited man unclasped his hands from behind him and took a slow, deep breath. He began rubbing his hands together in front of him. "Our deal was for a revolt, nothing more. I didn't expect them to last long, those fools. I did expect them to put up a pretty good fight, which they did with the help of the equipment I brought them."

"I'm still a little bit skeptical of your plan. It sounds far-fetched. How do you know it will work?"

The dark man dropped his hands to his sides and clenched them into tight fists, several of his knuckles cracking. "As long as you two idiots do as you're told and don't keep asking me stupid questions, everything will be taken care of." He took a long, deep breath and slowly blew it out. "If I could get the union's top colony, the colony that has been given more awards than I can count, to revolt, don't you think I can make this happen? It's mine! I built the ship in *my* factory. I've worked hard for this, and I will do whatever it takes!" He stared at Tiny and let out another long breath, his fists beginning to relax. "We're only talking a few hundred people who won't even be awake to see anything happen." He took another deep breath. "Just make sure your friends are as trustworthy as you say they are. I would hate for something bad to happen to them, or to their families," he said, matter-of-factly.

"Don't worry, boss. I trust them all," Tiny said, wide-eyed.

"I thought you don't trust anyone," Jose' said.

Tiny hit Jose' in the shoulder. "Will you shut up!"

"You just make sure you and your friends are ready when I need you. I've taken care of everything else. Make sure you know where their loyalties lie," he said, stabbing a finger at Tiny. "I don't have a problem with adding a few more names to the obituary column."

Chapter Three

Recovery

Colors and lights swirled in Cross's head. He felt no pain. Was this heaven? He was numb and felt as if he were floating. Suddenly, stars began to swirl before his eyes. A buzzing sound filled his ears, threatening to envelop him. Cross was about to concede that he was dead when something that felt like fire shot through his chest. The intense burning led to warmth that seemed to wash all over him. Slowly, the warmth, as well as all the other senses, faded and he was plunged into darkness.

A dim light slowly grew in the darkness. He could barely make out something moving in the gradually-growing light. He strained, but the harder he strained, the more difficult it was to make out, so he relaxed and watched the light grow. The shapes, he could now see, were moving around him, seemingly at random. He realized that the buzzing sound he'd heard before had returned. Suddenly, he became aware that he could feel cold. His toes were cold. His feet were cold. He felt an overwhelming joy because his feet were cold. He could actually feel them. The buzzing in his ears became words. He couldn't understand them, but he knew they were words.   Growing angry at all these 'half sensations', he began to try to move. Maybe this would help.

"Oh damn, the sedative's wearing off," came a voice from the haze. "Get the Captain some more."

"Call me Derek," he mumbled in a raspy voice. "My feet are cold."

"I can't believe no one was watching the monitor. You idiots. If he's ripped any of these stitches, I'm going to beat you senseless! And someone cover his feet."

He suddenly felt warm all over and tasted something metallic in his mouth.   Almost immediately, all his sensations were gone again, and he plunged back into darkness.

A piercing blast of light shot into his right eye, then his left. The light felt like a laser cutting completely through his head.

"Looks like you're well on your way to recovery," the light said.

Cross reached his hand toward it, and something slapped him on the top of the hand. The light went out, and he was plunged into a murky haze. He began blinking his eyes furiously, trying to see where he was.

"Where am I?" he asked. He tried to move his legs but couldn't. It felt as though something very heavy was lying on top of them.

"You're at Pearsall Station, sir. You're in recovery. I'm Dr. Pratt," a voice said.

"Pearsall Station? That's in Earth orbit. How the hell did I get here?" He tried to sit up, but numbness in his chest told him he'd better relax and get his bearings.

"A few friends dropped you off here," came another voice, this one somewhat distant. The voice had a bit of a slur, like someone who had been drinking. *I know that voice.*

"Who's there?" he asked.

"An old friend. Just dropped in to check on your progress, and they told me they were going to let you wake up today. Seems you woke up once a few weeks ago, before they were ready for you to. Scared the hell out of 'em."

"Is that JT?" Cross said. "I can't see anything."

With a click, the light dimmed and his eyes began to adjust to the room. He saw that he was lying in a small white bed. To the right of his bed were several large pieces of medical monitoring equipment Derek wasn't familiar with. Standing on the other side of his bed was a man dressed in a white jumpsuit. He could also make out several dark forms a few feet away from him. Two of them seemed to be standing, while a third was sitting.

"Don't try to take in too much at once," the man in the jumpsuit said. "You haven't used those baby browns in a few weeks. Don't take things too quickly."

"What do you mean, a few weeks?"

"Hey, Doc? Why don't you let us talk to him and tell him what's going on?" another voice said.

"Sure. I'll leave you gentlemen alone then. Press the yellow button there if you need anything," he said as he started away. A moment later, Derek heard a click as the door closed behind the doctor.

Derek lifted a heavy arm and rubbed his eyes. He looked back at the three shapes, and now he could tell who they were. The two men standing were Sergeants Cook and Hunter. He turned to the man who was sitting. His heart fluttered as he verified who it was. He felt a combination of joy and dread at the sight.

"JT," he said smiling. "It's been a while. You been drinking?" Derek asked him jokingly. Derek knew JT's voice always sounded as if he had been drinking when he was sober but seemed to sound normal when he actually *had* been drinking.

"It's been too long. I'd ask how you've been, but I can kinda see for myself," he said with a laugh.

Derek laughed. The laugh felt strange. His chest was numb, and felt as though it were being constricted by a giant snake. It felt that if he were to take a deep breath, he would split open. He looked down at his chest and saw why. It was wrapped with several layers of thick, white bandages. There was a thicker square bandage near his left shoulder.

Derek looked JT up and down. He hadn't changed a bit. He was still a burly, overweight black man who had a perpetual five-o'clock shadow. Derek had always said that JT looked like he needed a shave, even five minutes after he'd had one. His hair was mostly brown, with a few flecks of gray in it. Aside from being large in the chest and stomach, JT had thick arms that were covered in a mat of curly, dark brown hair. On his right arm, Derek could see a streak of what could only be grease.

"You haven't changed a bit," Derek said.

"Yeah, I do still look pretty good, don't I?" JT said, wafting his hair like a model, unknowingly smearing grease in it.

"What happened to me?" Derek asked.

"You were hit with a boomer, sir," Hunter said. "You're lucky I got there when I did. You might not have made it home."

"A ballistic weapon? Jesus, that's like being run through with a damn sword! Nobody uses them anymore. Nobody even has them except maybe collectors."

"Well, this was a real cluster-fuck all around sir. We looked at some of the men you neutralized, and..." he was silenced by a quick slap from Sergeant Cook.

"Sorry, sir," Cook said. "The whole mission is classified," he said, looking at JT. "We aren't even supposed to talk with you about it. You'll be briefed when you get back on your feet."

"I don't understand. You're my men. Why can't you tell me what happened?"

There were a few seconds of silence before Cook spoke up. "Actually sir, we aren't your men anymore."

The emerald green limousine slowed and made a leisurely turn onto the side road that went through a break in the thick trees that lined both sides of the main road. The trees stretched for several miles in each direction up and down the main road, hiding the factory by acres of dense forest. Unknown to the casual observer, various electronic security sensors were located throughout the trees.

A commuter driving past would have never known that sitting nestled in the middle of the trees was the Samson Industries factory complex. A small sign bearing only the corporate logo sat on the right side of the small entrance road that went into the complex. The corporate logo, which was comprised of a blue and green earth and a three-dimensional spacecraft that seemed to move out of the globe and toward the observer, was the only indication that anything sat somewhere down the side road.

The entrance road purposely curved after only thirty feet or so to prevent corporate spies from having direct line-of-sight with the factory from the road, thus preventing the use of the most common types of surveillance equipment. The curve would also allow the guards at the guard station to hear an approaching vehicle before the occupants were able to see the guardhouse.

The limousine meandered around the lazy curves until the trees began to thin, and the road straightened. As the vehicle moved farther from the main road, a fence twelve feet high loomed out of the ever-thinning forest. Crossing the road directly ahead of the limo was a large gate flanked by two guardhouses. A guard dressed in a light blue uniform stepped out of the guardhouse on the right and waved to the driver of the limo as the gate began to open. The car passed through without slowing.

The man's black leather dress shoes made a rhythmic, "click-clack, click-clack", as he slowly walked through the large open foyer of the building. With his head down and his hands clasped behind him, he could have been mistaken for a monk, were he not wearing a dark blue business suit.

"Mr. Samson. Your father is looking for you," a receptionist echoed across the entryway. "He's called down here twice looking for you. He wants you to go to his office as soon as you get settled in."

Frederick Samson, head of corporate security for Samson Industries, continued walking as though he hadn't heard the woman call out to him. The receptionist, having gotten used to his demeanor, didn't repeat herself.

He continued across the foyer toward a security door, checked his watch, and then retrieved an ID card from his pocket. He swiped it, and a man's voice said, "Samson, Frederick E. Please state title and department for voiceprint identification." Samson placed the ID back in his pocket and clasped his hands behind his back.

"Vice President, Security," he replied.

"Please wait." There was a several second pause. "Voiceprint confirmed for Samson, Frederick E., Vice President, Security. Please check today's calendar, as your schedule has changed. Have a nice day."

The door slid open with a hiss. He stepped through, pulling a small electronic device from his breast pocket. He opened the credit-card sized device to reveal a screen on one side and a small keyboard on the other. The screen flashed the word "Updating." The screen flashed again and began to list his daily schedule. He glanced over it and noted that all the events of the day were in yellow, with the exception of the one that had been added, which was in red. The new entry read, "Meeting, immediate. Samson, Jonathan. CEO."

"Jesus Christ, what the hell is so damn important? Next he'll start sending smoke signals, carrier pigeons, or flaming arrows," he muttered.

He reached his office and found that his door was slightly open; his office lights on. He peered through the crack in the door and saw a man sitting at his desk. He had the same receding hairline as Frederick, only the old man's hair was blue-gray. He looked tired. More tired than Frederick had seen in a long time. He rubbed his eyes and kept taking deep breaths. Frederick Samson glanced at the nameplate on the door. Between the name, "Frederick Samson" and the title, "Vice President, Security", he noticed an oily smudge. He wiped it clean with his thumb. He took two deep breaths and watched the man for several more seconds before opening the door.

"You wanted to see me, Dad? I figured I would just come to *your* office."

Jonathan Samson sat in his son's office chair, looking as though he had been there for some time. His gray hair was slightly ruffled, as though he had been running his fingers through it, the way he always did when he was under a lot of stress. The large bags under his eyes told Frederick that his father hadn't slept in at least a day or two.

"That engineer from the base called me again this morning, Son. This is the third call this week. Why do you keep putting them off? They paid good money for this research. We can't delay them forever."

"My staff is almost finished making sure there aren't any security holes in the reports, Dad. I don't want any of our intellectual property that they didn't pay for going to them by mistake. That would be a major setback for this company. You know the lengths we have to go to in order to protect our secrets from our competitors, especially now. This project is much too important for anyone to leak information."

"I understand the importance of that as well as, if not better, than you do. Six months. We can be there in six months, while those monkey-dicks at Kerey Star Drives won't be there for twelve years with even their fastest systems. You think I'm all peachy about this?" the elder Samson said, a loose flap of skin under his chin jiggling back and forth. "Hell no. I know the importance of security. I've worked on this project since it began. I'm just sorry that I'm too old to actually go with them."

"I'm not. I wouldn't want to see you run off to some paradise without me," said Frederick, smiling. "Listen, there were some indications that we might be able to remove part of the flux-field data from the reports we're delivering to the military engineers. Some of the..."

"What are you talking about?" he said, slamming his fist on the desk. "That data is theirs. The government funded this whole project. Our engineers came up with that technology after the government contract was signed, using their money. It's their data! Do you want them to come shut us down?"

"Alright, alright," he said, throwing up his hands. "I'll gather the reports and deliver them myself. Happy now?"

"I just want this whole thing to be over and done with. I'm tired of looking over my shoulder all the time. If your mother were still alive, she'd have gone over to that base and given them hell. I can hear her now, 'You boys will just have to wait on whatever it is you want. Johnny hasn't been getting enough sleep lately, and you know how that affects him.' Sometimes I felt like she was more my mother than my wife. But we sure did have it good together." A serious look came over his face. "That's why this is so important. If this rock weren't in such bad shape, she'd have lived another five years," he said glancing out the window. "Lots of people are dying just like she did because mother earth has reached old age, and all the wear and tear of her life has caught up with her."

"You mean," Frederick paused. "Mother earth has reached menopause?" They both smiled. "Hell, before long the earth will start growing a moustache!" Frederick said with a toothy smile. Both men began to laugh loudly.

After the two had stopped laughing, Jonathan stood and walked over to Frederick.

"You know, when I retire this complex will be yours. Hell, the whole company will be. When I started this company, I wanted to leave it to you and your sister, God rest her soul. Think of how much money..."

"Money has never been important to me, Dad," Frederick interrupted. "You know that. When Jocelyn and I were on Mars..."

"Not this politics nonsense again! You know I was a senator for four terms, and I don't want you to subject yourself to that life. Only two kinds of people want to be politicians. Those who want to change things, and those who are power-hungry. Neither of those attitudes is a healthy one to have. And don't forget that you lost the mayoral election on Mars, and on Titan. And that Outer Rim Colonial Council seat you held almost got you killed. Those people are always on the edge of rebellion. You were lucky that they listened to you and didn't kill you and that mayor. You're just not cut out for politics," he said, clasping Frederick's shoulder. "I didn't sleep well for a year when those rebels were executed and you started getting those death threats. You should stay here and be happy."

"You're right. You know me and my flights-of-fancy. Always the dreamer. Besides, being rich has its advantages."

"Now that's the spirit!" the elder Samson said, clapping his hands together. "The ship is scheduled to be completely loaded with equipment and stores by the end of the week, and departure is still scheduled for the 25th of next month. With the departure date only about five weeks away, I can't imagine that the military engineers will wait much longer before they come over here with troops and take what they want. You don't want that, do you?"

"No, sir. Like I said, I'll get everything together and haul it all over there in one of the delivery trucks."

"Excellent. I'll expect a call from that General by Friday letting me know how pleased he is with all the information you've brought him," he said as he turned to walk out of the office. "We're making history here, Son," he said as he walked out the door.

Frederick watched him walking away down the hall. "You have no idea," he said quietly. "Soon, you'll be one of the most famous dead people around."

Jeffrey Thomas

Chapter Four

Fallout

Derek lay there stunned, while he pondered why his command would have been taken from him. Maybe it was only temporary because of his injury. It had to be only temporary.

"Who's in command of the unit?" he asked.

"Captain Simms, sir," Sergeant Cook said, appearing extremely uncomfortable. "I guess he's doing a good enough job."

Sergeant Hunter quickly looked at Sergeant Cook, and then quickly looked away. Derek saw this but acted as though he hadn't.

"Well, at least he's keeping the unit together," Derek said, probing. His suspicions were confirmed when both Sergeants began to fidget.

"So tell me, how many men have resigned?" Derek asked.

"Six of the men, sir," Cook said.

"That's not bad, I guess. Something like this could shake a volunteer unit to pieces," Derek said.

"Well," Cook paused, looking at his feet. "It's worse than it sounds. We had six of the *remaining* men drop out, but only twenty-four of us left Ganymede with both of our dog tags. There were also two Sergeants that dropped out," he said, glancing at Hunter.

"Jesus, we lost fourteen of the men?" Derek asked, his chest flooding with an intense heartache.

"Actually, thirteen men, one Sergeant, sir."

"De Silva? How?"

"I'm sorry sir, that part we can't discuss here. I'm sure the General will tell you all about that when you're debriefed."

Quiet until now, JT began to stir in his chair as if it were becoming increasingly uncomfortable. He exhaled loudly enough for everyone in the room to hear.

"You got ants in your pants, Staff Sergeant?" Cook asked JT.

"God, don't call me that. I couldn't even stand it when I was in the service," JT retorted. "Will you guys quit beatin' around the bush and tell the man what you can? Stop lettin' him ask all the damn questions."

"Alright, alright," Cook said. "I'll tell you what I can. Well, when you dropped in we lost contact with you, at least until the blast on the roof. I assume that was you?" he asked, his left eyebrow raised.

"Yeah, chalk that one up to me," Derek said glancing at JT as if expecting him to berate him for it.

"Anyway, it seems your helmet took a shot, and we lost you again. The rest of the troops dropped in just after you went inside the station. Then, *The Hunter* here busted ass to get to you, fearing the worst. I mean, when your helmet got blasted, your medical monitor showed you as a flat-line. Let me just say, you had everyone scared shitless!" Cook stepped forward, and sat down on the foot of Derek's bed. "We didn't know what to think when we saw your position tracker start moving around with your medical monitor showing nothing. Good thing position trackers are on your wrist and not in your helmet."

"We breathed a sigh of relief when I found your helmet in the airlock," Hunter interjected.

"Well, someone got the drop on you with a boomer and Hunter showed up a few minutes later. He found you on the floor bleeding like crazy. He had the medical team drop in directly outside the airlock doors. They did what they could to patch the holes, but you were hit real bad. Apparently, the slug went in through your back, and almost hit your heart. It messed up a lot of stuff in there, and nicked your aorta. Since military doctors don't do much of this stuff anymore, they got some guy named Nakamori in Japan to walk them through the surgery with the VirtuMed system. Since our docs mostly deal with plasma burns and stuff like that, we needed the best, and that's Nakamori, apparently. Nakamori said it was pretty strange because of the time delay of the transmission from Earth to Jupiter. Every time he would tell them to make an incision, he would have to wait for a while for the medics in the ship to actually do it. Then shortly thereafter, he got to see the incision on his screen! Anyway, they kept you nearly frozen to slow your metabolism down, minimize blood loss, and head off most of the risks with the time delay."

"That sounds pretty inefficient," Derek said, looking at the mass of bandages.

"Yeah, well, because of this, the *Valley Forge* is in drydock having a faster-than-light comm. System added to the medical bay. Apparently, fleet's using this as justification for a budget increase to upfit every ship with one."

"Hmm," Derek replied not looking up.

"Anyway, the doctors on the *Forge* are pretty good, so we weren't worried about you for a minute. Once the surgery was done, they put you in a high-oxy chamber on one of the high-speed medical evac ships and brought you back here. They said that the increased oxygen will help you heal faster, but you've lost more than a few pounds of muscle and bone mass. The medical staff released you to this facility four days ago. Apparently, somewhere along the way your meds wore off before they wanted them to, and you started talking to them. You didn't have a tube down your throat anymore. I tell you - It's a good thing you didn't look down. They had you in a wet bag, just in case they had to go back in at a moment's notice. When you woke up, they had your chest open checking how your internal stitches were healing! They said that if it weren't for getting to you as quick as we did, and keeping you almost frozen, you'd have bled out. They said that no one has survived getting shot the way you did. It's why you were under for so long."

After another twenty minutes of conversation, Derek began to tire. He yawned a few times, and his eyes began to droop. JT was the first to notice, and decided that they should leave. As they were leaving, Hunter laid a thick, brown envelope on the table beside Derek's bed. He told him to open it when he had time, then he and Cook stepped out of the room. Derek's eyes drooped closed, and popped back open just in time to see JT place something else on the table. JT turned and stepped out the door just as Derek fell asleep.

The thick report landed on the top of the tall white stack with a thud. Frederick Samson was leaning back in his office chair, all but his feet obscured by stacks of paper on his desk.

"Sir? Are you back there?" an office courier asked.

"Just leave them on the top. I'll get to them when I get to them," Frederick Samson replied. "If you're afraid they're going to collapse, start a new pile on the floor over there," he said, raising his hand above the pile and pointing to the space next to a large bookshelf.

"Yes, sir. There are a few more loads of them coming. I'd say about another three thousand pages." She craned her neck around the piles, trying to see him. "Are you sure you don't need some help? You could tell me what you're looking for and I could help you."

"No. Don't you have other errands to run?" he asked, not looking up. "I'm sure there are much more important things you can be doing than bothering me," he said, peering around a particularly tall stack.

"Yes, sir. I'm sorry to have bothered you, sir." She started walking out the door, and looked back over her shoulder. After she had verified that he could not see her, she raised her middle finger toward the tall pile of papers and the pair of black dress shoes sticking out from them. She turned, and silently strode out the door.

"Sam! Can you come in here?" Frederick called out. A few seconds later, a young man stepped into the office.

"Sir?" Sam said.

"I need you to make a call for me. Call this General." A hand rose above the sea of white, holding a business card. "Tell him that because of security concerns associated with the project, I am his contact from now on. If he asks why, tell him that we've had an unconfirmed report of a break-in at our facility."

"Jesus! Someone broke in here?" Sam said, taking the card. "I'm surprised they didn't get shot! When was this?"

"I'm not at liberty to say. It's still being investigated," he lied. "Tell him that if he has any questions, he can call me. Also, tell him that I will be delivering all the technical data early next week." Sam heard the sounds of fingers tapping the top of the desk, and then a document being printed, coming from behind the pile of papers.

"Yes, sir. I'll let him know.

Frederick, leaned back in his chair and skimmed through reports page-by-page. The holographic computer screen on his desk displayed the electronic copy of the report he was reading. A holographic keyboard was illuminated on the open section of desk immediately in front of him. His hand quickly moved across page after page. Suddenly, something caught his eye, and he stopped. He flipped forward several pages in the report, and then dropped his feet to the floor with a thud.

With the speed of years of experience, his fingers quickly pressed various letters on his holographic keyboard. The open report went from the cover page directly to the section of the report he was holding in his hand. His hands slid back and forth while he pressed various keys. The section he had picked out in the printed copy was now highlighted on the screen. He reached over with a smile and pressed the "delete" key. Ten pages were deleted from the report. A few keystrokes later, the report had been resaved.

He reached over and removed the copy from the printer. Frederick slid the original report through a slot on the front of a large plastic bin, the door of which was locked with an electronic keypad. The papers fell into a plastic tub, and on top of several hundred pages of other reports he'd already looked over. A small label on the bin read "CONFIDENTIAL DOCUMENTS TO SHREDDER. DAILY PICKUP."

Derek awoke to a flurry of activity. His bandages were being removed, and new ones were being readied. There were four people in the fray, all in white jumpsuits. He tried to ask someone what time it was, but he was ignored. After a few moments, he looked down and saw the wound on his chest.

Derek felt the contents of his stomach trying to escape. He swallowed hard and kept it down. Just below his left shoulder was a mass of purplish flesh with bits of dried, black blood. Holding this together was a neatly sewn strip of stitches. The mass traveled like a lightning bolt from his collarbone to about three-quarters of the way to his sternum. Covering the wound was a clear, yellowish slime.

A nurse began wiping the gooey substance off his chest until it was nearly gone. In a series of swift but deliberate motions, she reached into a pocket of her jumpsuit, pulled out a tube, removed the cap, and deftly applied a new layer of yellow ooze without missing a drop. She pulled a flat, wooden stick out of a clear plastic package and used it to smooth out the slime until it was evenly spread over his wound and a little of the surrounding skin. A few minutes later the nurse was finished with his chest and he was rolled over onto his stomach so that the entry wound on his back could be dressed as well.

The next two days went by quickly. The pain was light because of the painkillers he was given, and the dressing changes became less and less frequent. Because of this, he had spent most of it sleeping.

In all the chaos of the various nurses, doctors, and orderlies that had been constantly in and out of his room, he'd forgotten about the things that Sergeant Cook and JT had left for him. He looked around the room and found that at some time while he was asleep, someone had moved them out of the way. The envelope was lying on top of the package JT had left him in the chair beside his bed. Derek tried to find something he could use to reach them with. He saw nothing, so he began to push himself up, when he felt a pull in his chest. A sharp pain took his breath as he rolled onto his side. Using his leg, he threw the heavy blankets off of him and onto the floor. He shifted his weight, and found himself sitting with his legs dangling off the side of the bed. The yellow button on the console beside the bed beckoned to him, but he dismissed calling for help. He pulled some slack in the wires and tubes that were connected to his forearm and stood.

Derek found that his legs were very weak, but still strong enough to carry him to the chair. He reached down to pick up the items when he felt another sharp sting in his chest. After waiting for the pain to subside, he scooped the packages up and slowly made his way back to the bed. He lowered himself onto the bed with a thump, dropping his back against the pillow. A more intense sting caused him to grab a fistful of the sheets. As the pain abated, he relinquished his grip, centering his attention on the items in his other hand. He threw the envelope onto his lap with a heavy thud and discovered what JT had left him.

The small paper bag was unusually heavy for its size. Derek opened it and found that it contained a picture frame. He flipped it over and saw that the picture it contained was one of himself as a child standing next to JT. Derek remembered when the picture was made. His father had taken it one day behind their house in Huntington, Oregon. JT and Derek had been playing basketball all afternoon, and both were very dirty. Derek, who looked much worse than JT, had a skinned knee and a torn shirt.

Derek's thoughts drifted from the picture to his father. He stared off into space, a half smile on his lips.

A study in duality, his father had taught Derek discipline at a young age yet tried to be a friend to him as well. Ultimately, Derek's father was the influence that pushed him into military service. His father had been a soldier as well, and following his father's death, Derek decided to join.

Derek's father, even though trying to be a friend to Derek, unknowingly kept him at arm's length by being an overly strict parent. JT, however, had served as his outlet for fun. JT was only twelve years older than Derek, so Derek looked up to him like an older brother. JT had served in the military as a vehicle mechanic, and Derek's father had been his commanding officer. They had met when Derek went to visit his father on base one afternoon, two weeks after they had moved to Huntington.

One thing Derek hated about the military was the fact that once you got settled in somewhere and made a few close friends, they moved you to another base.

"Share the wealth, son," his father had always said. "You and I are so cool, we have to give as many people as possible a chance to know us." He would then poke Derek in the ribs, always a little too hard. He had always joked around about moving, although Derek knew his father didn't like it much either.

Derek's eye was drawn back to the picture. It had been taken at their house off base when his father was stationed at the Snake River Marine Corps Air Station (MCAS). Behind the basketball goal, Derek could make out several of the spiky, cactus-like shrubs that grew all over Huntington.

A cool dampness drew Derek's attention to his chest, where a dark reddish spot had appeared on his otherwise clean bandages. He gently laid the envelope on his bed and then pressed the yellow button.

After the bandages had been removed, and the extent of the damage Derek had done to the stitches on his chest had been repaired by a nurse, the doctor he'd seen when he first awakened came in and scolded Derek for nearly ten minutes. Most of that time Derek wasn't listening; his gaze had fixed on the envelope that was now sitting, along with the picture, on the table beside the bed.

Eventually, when he felt Derek had had enough scolding, the doctor left. Derek immediately reached for the envelope and placed it in his lap. He opened the top, reached inside, and pulled out a stack of papers. Something heavy was still in the bottom, he realized. He turned the envelope upside-down, and with a sound like a mass of coins being dropped, something metallic landed in his lap: A mass of dog tags, held together by a beaded, silver chain. The dog tags, ones that had been hanging around the necks of the soldiers who'd been killed, were splayed out like fingers on a hand pointing accusingly at him.

He could feel the sorrow of fourteen families who would never again see their loved ones. Why had he survived? *If I had trained those men properly...* he stopped. *I trained those men to do their jobs, but to preserve life,* he argued with himself. *But what good does it do someone to hold life sacred, when they're dealing with someone else who doesn't give a shit?* His pulse quickened as a rush of emotions filled him. Anger, fear, frustration and sorrow billowed up inside him like a coming storm. They grew until he snatched up the dog tags in his clenched fist, held it to his face, and began to sob.

Tired and puffy-eyed, he went through the tags to see exactly which soldiers he had lost. He knew there were fourteen, but for some reason unknown to him, he counted them.

As a tradition in the service, one of the two tags was left with the soldier who had died, used for identification. The other one, as a matter of tradition, was given to the dead soldier's commanding officer.

Some in the Corps said that it was to remind the officer that he had lost men, to use it as a reminder next time he went into battle. Many officers, rather than having to deal with the constant reminder of men they felt they had killed, would send the tag with a letter to the parents or spouse of the soldier who was lost. Derek debated this and decided that he would keep the tags himself. He needed a reminder that people had died needlessly, that he himself had nearly killed a young boy, and he wanted never to forget that. *I will never take another human life,* he thought, squeezing the tags in his hand. *Those men are dead because of me.*

Later that day, Derek took the stack of papers he had removed from the envelope and began going through them. The first sheet was a letter addressed to Captain D. E. Cross – Commanding Officer, 609th Counterinsurgency Force. He glanced down at the bottom to see who had written the letter. In large bulky letters, the signature read "Major General Lee R. Durus, USMC."

Derek took a deep breath and slowly exhaled it, very loudly. He began to read:

> Captain Cross,
>
> I hope your condition is steadily improving. I trust you have heard that your unit has been placed under the command of Captain Simms. Simms is making the best of a bad situation, but I can't go into any details in an uncontrolled letter, as everything associated with your mission is classified. I'll explain everything later.
>
> Unfortunately, I can't wait for you to get completely healed, because I need all the details from you regarding your mission. I've gotten after-action reports from everyone else who took part in the mission. I can wait a few more days for yours. I'd like to debrief you on Friday of next week. Also, your

orders are in this envelope. Your orders take
effect as of 0800 on Monday, August 17, 2136,
so you've got more than a month to
recuperate before reporting back for duty.

Everyone at HQ is pulling for your speedy
recovery. I'll see you in my office next Friday
and we'll discuss things.

P.S. From all the intelligence I've
received, you handled yourself very well on
Ganymede. Your father would have been
proud of you.

Derek looked at the date printed at the top of the letter. *Next Friday,* he thought to himself. He scanned the room, looking for his belongings. There were none that he was able to find, so he looked through the small window in the door and saw a nurse smiling, apparently talking on the phone. He waved his arms in an effort to get her attention. After a few tries, he gave up and pressed the yellow button. A moment later, he saw the nurse slip her phone into her pocket and she strode to his room.

"How can I help you, Captain?" she asked, looking annoyed.

"My things, where are they?"

"Mr. Towson has them, sir. He has agreed to take you home and look after you for a while there."

"Oh he has, has he? And why didn't someone ask me if I wanted to be taken to Mr. Towson's home and be looked after?" he said with equal insolence. "I've never known JT to be able to take care of himself, much less anyone else."

"Because you were comatose," she said. "I'll ask Mr. Towson to bring you some clothes - you're being discharged into his care in the morning."

Derek sat, his mouth agape. *I don't need JT's help. I'm in excellent shape,* he thought, looking down at the bandages on his chest.

The doctor came bounding into the room half an hour later. For the first time, Derek noticed his name stamped onto the left side of his jumpsuit. It read, 'Dr. Pratt'.

"I guess you must be ready to go home, hmm? Well, guess what?"

"JT is coming tomorrow to pick me up?" he asked touching two fingers to his temple, as though he had just read the doctor's mind.

"Your friend JT is..." he broke off. He opened his mouth and began to speak when Derek cut him off with a wave of his hand.

"The nurse told me earlier. I don't need someone to take care of me, doctor. I'll be fine by myself."

"I'm sorry Captain, I'm afraid your release is dependent upon your having home care. I assume that you don't have a room-mate who's a nurse or something, do you?" He stared at him for a moment. "I didn't think so. Anyway, your friend JT's business is based out of his home, so he will be there twenty-four seven, and being that he's former military, he has basic medical training."

"Great," Derek groaned.

Chapter Five

Old Wounds

The next morning, Derek awoke with a start as a duffel bag landed on the bed between his legs.

"Up and at 'em!" JT barked.

"God, you're so lucky I'm not armed," Derek said half asleep, his voice deep and scratchy.

"Thought you'd be up runnin' around or doin' pushups or somethin'," JT said. "You know, soldier stuff."

"You're nuts."

"Oh yeah, I'm sorry. You're an officer. You'd be tellin' other people to run around or do pushups or somethin' like that," JT said smiling.

Derek pulled the blanket over his head as if JT would disappear when he did.

"Come on. It's checkout time. Here," JT said holding a tube of antibiotic like the one the nurse had used on his chest. "Dr. Pratt gave me this in the hall. You are supposed to put this on every other day until the stitches disappear," he said tossing the tube on top of the duffel bag.

Derek uncovered his head and, nodding toward the duffel bag, asked, "What's in there?"

"That sweet man, Sergeant Cook, gave me the clothes and stuff out of your locker from the *'Forge*. The rest of the stuff that was in there is at my house."

Derek tried to stand on his own, refusing JT's help. After several minutes of trying, he finally conceded and JT helped him to stand and then to dress. Derek stood in front of a mirror, staring at himself. He looked a lot like that skinny kid in the picture JT had brought him. He'd apparently lost more than a few pounds of muscle. Derek noticed that something else was different as well. Derek first thought it was the lump of bandages under his shirt, but no, that wasn't it. It was something he couldn't put his finger on. He tried to put it out of his mind as he grabbed his duffel bag, and he and JT left the hospital.

Reentry was no more bumpy than normal, yet for Derek it was extremely painful. JT's shuttle was an older model, a Kerey Star Drives S43, but all shuttles rode the same during reentry, even newer ones on the market. This model was first produced in 2114, and JT had purchased it used when Derek was a kid. Even then it wasn't in the best of shape. There were several spots where the shielding was rusted, and it had more than a few dents. JT purchased the shuttle when he was in the military, so Derek had always said that all the dents and rust were camouflage.

"We're going to burn up," Derek mumbled as he glanced out at the shielding.

"I'm taking it slow so atmospheric friction will be low. We'll be fine. I just haven't had a chance to replace the old shielding. KSD shielding isn't cheap, and I'm not going third-party."

Bouncing up and down on the thermal currents in the atmosphere sent waves of pain through Derek's chest and back, causing beads of sweat to form on his forehead and upper lip. He gritted his teeth and tried to ignore the pain as he and JT exchanged small talk.

Derek dreaded getting into the conversation he felt they needed to have. After all, it had been almost three years since he had seen JT and their last conversation had been very uncomfortable, consisting mostly of one-word answers to JT's questions. Derek didn't really remember what was said. He had thought about contacting JT several times, but hadn't. He was about to say something to JT about having wanted to call him, when he realized that JT apparently hadn't tried to contact him either. He suddenly didn't feel quite as bad about his long silence.

The shuttle swooped down from the sky just above the Baker County Skyway. Four panels opened on the underside of the shuttle, and four shoddy-looking black tires descended into view. With a "chirp" the shuttle softly kissed the dark gray landing strip section of the roadway. JT slowed down and switched off his ion drives. This procedure switched him over to ground-transportation mode, and the ride got bumpier than it had previously been. The shuttle hit an uneven section of road and Derek let out a grunt.

"Damn, I'm sorry about that," JT said to Derek as he slowed the vehicle down and began to avoid bad spots in the road.

"We should be back to my shop in about fifteen minutes. Can you hold out until then, or do I need to stop and get out your meds?" he asked with genuine concern in his voice.

"I think I can make it, just try not to drive off into the Grand Canyon again."

The remainder of the trip was uneventful. Derek looked out the window, watching rows of buildings flash by. He was startled at how the area had grown since he and his father left when he was a kid.

The Skyway, a reinforced section of highway designed for spacecraft landings and takeoffs, had been completed shortly before Derek's father had been reassigned to another base, so the area hadn't really started growing before they left. Derek remembered that many people who lived in the area hadn't wanted the strip going in near them because of the constant threat of sonic booms as spacecraft reentered the atmosphere. Another issue was the fact that statistics showed a higher rate of spacecraft crashes around areas with Skyways because of the increased amount of space-to-surface traffic. As is the case with airports, most accidents occur within twenty miles of either the origination or destination airport. So, too, was the case with Skyways. If there were going to be a mechanical malfunction with a shuttle or other ship, it would generally occur either on takeoff or landing at the Skyway, or nearby.

Ultimately, the Skyway was built here because the area was sparsely populated, and the risk of ground casualties in the event of a crash was lower than the other areas that were considered. This, and the fact that the other fifteen areas of the United States where a Skyway had been built had seen dramatic drops in property values, had set the stage for several large protests during the proposal hearings.

Derek had taken part in one of the protests. When his father found out he was there, he left work, picked him up and took him home. Expecting to be grounded or whipped, if not both, Derek was suspicious when they sat down at the kitchen table.

His father began asking him questions about the protest and why he was there. Derek couldn't answer very many of them. Derek decided that he didn't really know why he was there. Derek's father told him that it was a cry for attention, as he had been working a lot of long hours and not spending much time with him.

The two of them decided to make a schedule that included days and times that they would do things together like they did when Derek was younger. They wrote the schedule together, and posted it on the refrigerator. Until his father's death, the two of them followed their schedule doing things like going hiking, playing basketball, and going to the movies without fail - spending as much time together as his father's schedule would allow.

JT and Derek exited the Skyway, and moved onto the regular highway with a slight bump. JT looked in Derek's direction but said nothing. Derek continued to look at the changing face of the town. He watched as the view changed from the ubiquitous 'Welcome to Earth' signs posted outside fueling stations and trinket shops to department store billboards and other smaller signs in front of numerous other stores.

A few minutes later he saw several tall office buildings and then two sprawling manufacturing and distribution centers. Derek remembered when this area, only fifteen years ago, was nothing but fields and rolling hills. It was far enough from the urban sprawl to have been a nice place to be a kid. He was disappointed at the level of expansion that had taken place in his absence. This was a necessity, of course, given the need for space in the world. He knew this. Deep down, he had hoped that off-world expansion would help to ease the hunger for more raw materials, but this was not the case.

If anything, the off-world colonies had spurred the growth and expansion of the area. This was because of the large amounts of raw materials that were shipped to Earth in order to be processed. Many of the ores mined in the asteroid belt needed to be processed in the presence of oxygen, which wasn't feasible anywhere except on Earth. Oxygen was easy to remove from a dozen different ores, but not in the quantities needed for smelting and other manufacturing or purification processes. 'Oxygen stripping' as it was called, was sufficient for producing the breathing oxygen for the colonies, but immense oxygen strippers would be needed to produce enough oxygen for these processes, so they were primarily on Earth.

The landscape continued to change as they moved farther and farther from the Skyway. They had reached an area that appeared to have been dilapidated for some time. There were old warehouses that looked empty; many of their windows broken. JT turned onto a side street, and began to slow down. He approached an old steel fence with several holes rusted through it. Derek could make out a three-story warehouse building about twenty yards behind the fence. JT pulled the vehicle up to the fence and stopped.

"Here we are! My house is on the third floor, above the shop." JT jumped out, and walked toward a hinged section of the fence that obviously served as a gate.

Derek stared, taking it all in. He hadn't even thought about what kind of place JT must have lived in, but this wasn't really a surprise.   JT had always had shabby apartments and houses when he and Derek were close.

Derek suddenly had an image of Amanda, JT's ex-wife, putting flowers in a pot on the front porch of a run-down house that didn't even have any grass in the yard. Derek smiled. His smile grew wider as he remembered JT asking her, "Why are you trying to make this place all pretty? You can't put a shine on a turd!" Derek began to laugh to himself.

His smile vanished almost instantly when he remembered the day JT called him, telling him that Amanda had left him. Amanda had told JT that she didn't love him anymore. JT had tried to pretend that it didn't bother him, but Derek was able to see that he was hurt. He and JT spoke nearly every day until the divorce was finalized. They chatted about minor things, but even at sixteen, Derek knew that it was important for JT to have someone to talk to.

JT opened the gate, got back in the transport, and pulled through the fence. Derek said nothing about his thoughts of Amanda. It was an old wound that he didn't want to reopen.

As JT drove between massive hulks of antiquated technology feelings of anger suddenly welled up in Derek from deep down where he'd pushed them five years ago. He'd thought the whole idea of what JT wanted to do with his life was stupid, and the argument that ensued had nearly severed their friendship permanently. His sudden flash of anger was replaced by feelings of guilt for his behavior way back then, and a lump formed in his throat.

The fenced in area looked like a junkyard, except it was filled with military vehicles and piles of parts. Everywhere Derek looked he saw pieces of every imaginable size and shape. As they drove toward the building, Derek saw an old Huey UH-1 helicopter that was missing the entire tail section. On closer inspection, it appeared as though it had rusted through and fallen off. Most of the windows were missing, and he had no idea what color the fuselage had once been. It was now a dark reddish-brown from the rust that was caked on it.

Sitting off to the side of the building was an armored personnel carrier that was missing all six of the tires. Derek was surprised to see this particular model, because it was one that was still in use in the military. He noticed several large holes in the armor that appeared to be from weapons fire. His thoughts drifted to his pocket, where the bundle of dog tags resided. A large overhead door opened as they approached. With a squealing of brakes, they pulled to a stop inside the building.

"There's my baby!" JT said with pride, pointing toward a helicopter at the back of the shop. "It's a Blackstone Beowulf! Almost done, too. I've been workin' on her since last Christmas. She's gonna fetch me a mint when she's done. Got a collector up in Seattle who wants it," he said.

The black skin of the Beowulf had a mottled look to it. Derek could make out 'bubbles' of dark gray in the black paint. This was used as a camouflage and RADAR absorbent coating.

"Is that a 'B' model?" Derek asked, wide-eyed.

"Yep, only 52 made before they lost their contract with the Air Force. I been havin' some trouble findin' some of the parts for this pup. I had to have the LIDAR custom built by a guy in Phoenix. Nobody had one for sale."

With JT's help, Derek got out of the transport and walked around the helicopter for a closer look. Derek remembered that JT was a good mechanic, but he was surprised to find the helo in such good shape. The exterior was complete, and the interior was nearly finished. The only things missing inside were the seats and a section of instrument panel between the pilot and the copilot. He had seen an 'A' model in a museum when he was a kid, but the B models were so rare that he had never seen one. Blackstone had gotten a government contract to build 400, but there had been a scandal of some sort, and the contract had been canceled before they could be delivered. The 52 that had been produced were stripped of weapons systems, anti-RADAR coatings, and were sold off to collectors and wealthy businessmen who wanted a new toy.

Because these were around twenty years old, much of the technology was now commonplace. This was evident in the anti-RADAR coating on the fuselage. This had once been a closely-guarded secret but now was available in many automotive shops. People purchased it, thinking that you could avoid getting speeding tickets if your transport was coated with it. Unfortunately, this wasn't true, as Blackstone also produced police RADAR equipment that was able to thwart the speeder's efforts to evade it.

Derek walked around the shop for nearly half an hour, looking at the many projects in various stages of completion. None of them were even close to being as complete as the Beowulf. A few were nothing more than piles of parts, sitting off in a corner. The more he looked around, the guiltier he felt. He felt a dull ache in his chest and fought to suppress it.

Derek absentmindedly put his hand over the mass of bandages on his chest. He walked around several flight consoles, tapping one with his boot. A plume of dust rose up to meet a second tap.

"You need to sit down?" JT asked him.

"What?"

"Are you in pain? You're holding your chest."

"Oh," he said, dropping his hand to his side. "I guess I didn't even notice. I was just..." he paused, "admiring your place."

"Uh huh. Wait 'til you see the house. It's probably a bit more your style," JT said with a toothy smile.

They stepped out of the large freight elevator into an open area on the third floor. The area looked like a lobby in an office building. There were paintings by unfamiliar artists hanging on the walls, and several chairs sat around the room. On one wall was a table with a lamp, and several magazines artistically strewn about.

"The dentist will see you now," Derek said looking at JT. "This doesn't look like you. Not at all."

"I like to sit in here and read. It's comfortable, and quiet. It's in the center of the house, so there's really not any noise from the road. Occasionally, an aircraft will fly over, but that's rare."

They stepped up to a leather chair that sat a few feet to the left of the only door in the room. Derek could smell the leather. *Real leather. Expensive.* JT opened the door and motioned for Derek to enter. Derek stepped into the flat and his jaw dropped. The large open space had been converted into a one-level apartment with freestanding walls. The floors, made of hardwood, were clean and shiny. In the center of the room was a large oriental rug. The air wafted around him gently with a light scent of flowers. Derek looked for the source of the breeze but was unable to find it.

Derek looked up, taking in all he could. The ceiling of the building was about fifteen feet up, but the walls were only about ten feet high. This gave the illusion of immense space. The ceiling and all the pipes and ducts that were suspended from it were painted black and didn't stand out, thus broadening the sense of space

The room they were now standing in was a study or library. There were six tall bookshelves, each filled with books. Derek looked closely at the books and noticed that they were not cheap paperbacks but thick, leather-bound classics. In one corner was a three-foot tall vase, filled with eucalyptus and several other dried plants Derek didn't recognize.

Without saying a word, Derek walked through to the next room, the kitchen. JT followed closely behind him. The kitchen was long and narrow with a stainless steel countertop along one wall that reflected the morning sun around the room. There was one large cabinet mounted on the wall, directly above a small dishwasher. Derek absentmindedly opened the cabinet, revealing a collection of flat, black ceramic disks of various sizes. He let go of the door, and it closed without a sound.

Derek continued through the kitchen into a small dining room. There was a large dark brown rectangular table with eight chairs sitting around it. He looked closely at the ornate carving on the table and noticed tiny chisel marks. Hanging above the table was an immense, almost gaudy chandelier. Derek wiped his finger across the table and looked at it. It was clean.

He walked to a window and looked out. In the yard below was a massive pile of discarded metal scrap. Metal garbage was strewn all about as far as he could see to either side. He turned back to the ornately hand-carved table, then back to the garbage.

"What the hell is going on here? Are you sure this is *your* house? You didn't steal it, did you?"

"Yeah, it's mine. Nice, ain't it? Besides, how the hell do ya steal a house?"

"Mmm hmm," Derek said eyeing him suspiciously. "This just doesn't look anything like *you* at all."

"I'm hurt," he said, hands clamped to his chest.

Derek stared at him for a moment, then cupped his hand around his ear and made a face as if JT had started speaking, but too quietly to be heard.

"Okay, okay. I met this woman..."

"Ah ha!" Derek blurted, pointing an accusing finger at JT. "There's always a woman, isn't there?"

"Well, she opened my eyes to a lot of things I never would have experienced. I actually went to a museum!" JT said. "We broke up when she had to move because of her job. We still keep in touch now and then, but things ain't really the same."

"I'm sorry to hear that. It appears as though she had quite an effect on you," Derek said, waving his arm in a wide arc.

"She's a good soul. So, what about you? You seeing anyone?" JT pried.

Derek turned away, pretending not to hear the question. JT understood immediately. Derek had never had much luck dating. He was always gone, either on a mission or training. This, coupled with his inability to open up to others, had ended several relationships before they ever really started. JT had known this about Derek ever since he was a kid. He had always assumed that it was because Derek never had a female role model in his life; Derek's mother died only three days after he was born, as a result of an opportunistic infection.

Derek's father had also never dated. He had told Derek once that he had married the perfect woman, and that no one could ever replace her. To date someone else, he had told Derek, would be an injustice to his mother's memory. As a child, Derek didn't understand this. As he matured, he began to understand his father's unwillingness to let go of his wife.

"Are you hungry?" JT asked. Derek didn't answer. Instead, he continued walking toward the next room, groping for a new subject to talk about.

"Hungry! Are you hungry?" JT repeated loudly.

"Sure, the hospital breakfast consisted of what looked like runny eggs. They looked worse than what we had on the *'Forge.* I was afraid to try them."

"Good. I'll get somethin' for lunch started, since it's after eleven."

For nearly an hour, they walked around the rest of his house with JT stopping to explain the things that, to Derek, seemed most out of place. With each item JT explained, Derek' began feeling more and more as he had when he was much younger. He was awash in the feeling that JT was a very impressive person, the salt of the earth, but he could still surprise you with the breadth of his kindness. Derek knew this simply because he was standing in JT's home. After nearly three years without speaking to each other, JT came to pick him up from the hospital, knowing that he was going to have to take care of him. Derek had never had another friend like him.

Derek realized that his face was starting to hurt. He rubbed his cheeks and realized that it was because he hadn't stopped smiling for nearly an hour. He hadn't smiled like this in a long time. The last few years he had missed JT, but this was the first time he actually admitted it to himself. The smile faded from his face with the realization.

Over lunch they sat and talked about old times, both purposely avoiding the topic of the argument they'd had five years ago. Whenever something that should have triggered that topic came up, they both started to fidget with their food. After several seconds of silence, the subject would then change to something far from their falling out.

"So somebody else is runnin' your unit while you're away?" JT asked, his mouth full of sandwich.

"Yeah, Simms," Derek said, swirling his fork in a pile of baked beans. "He's wanted my unit for a long time. Ever since I killed..." Derek stopped without looking up. JT stopped chewing and watched Derek intently.

After a few seconds Derek said, "He's wanted my unit for a couple of years now. This is just the thing to put him in charge." Derek took a bite of his sandwich, chewed it rapidly then swallowed. "As bad as I got hit, I can understand why they put someone else in charge. I need to start getting back in shape if I'm going to pick it back up in a month or so. As a matter of fact, I need to get started right away. I need to show General Durus, when I see him next Friday, that I'll be ready on the 17th to resume command of what's left of my unit."

JT, still staring at Derek, began to chew again. Derek continued to stare at the shapes he was making in his beans.

"When are we gonna to talk about what happened? It ain't gonna go away by itself, you know? You have no idea how scared I was when I heard you been hurt. I was afraid that you wasn't going to make it, and I wouldn't ever have a chance to say I was sorry."

Derek looked up at JT, who stared back at him. Derek felt the same dull ache building steadily in his chest. He felt as though his guts were going to spew out across the table at any moment.

"I'm sorry too," Derek said, gingerly placing his fork on his plate. "I was angry that my father was gone. I always wanted to do right by him, you know? Then one day, he's just gone. Closed-casket funeral. No chance for me to say goodbye to his face. How could someone out there hold other people's lives in such disregard? Jesus, three people died in that explosion, and the fourth is paralyzed for the rest of his life! How could anyone do that?" Derek took a deep breath. "I felt like I had to do the best job I could for my dad. I still had all that anger floating around in me when you came to my commissioning ceremony and told me that you were leaving the military. I felt like I was being abandoned again; first my father, then you. I had worked hard for four years at the academy after my dad died, and I felt like you were going to be there for me when I graduated. I thought the whole idea of you being a mechanic outside of the military was stupid. I didn't understand what you wanted to do with your life, and thought that the military could provide you with everything. I think I might have even said that to you way back then. But looking around here," he said waving a hand in the air. "What you've done with this place, hell, with your life, is...." He trailed off.

JT, looking down at his plate said, "You know, Derek, your father never wanted you to join the military." Derek's jaw dropped. "I wanted to tell you that a long time ago, but you were so driven, I didn't want to stand in your way. Even so, I know he'd be real proud of you. I know I am," JT said with a smile. "You've done great things with that unit. I still have friends in the service, so I've been keeping tabs on you over the years. How do you think I found out that you were hurt, anyway? There are a lot of people who wouldn't be alive today if it weren't for you. If there had been someone else in charge of that unit, they would have gone in shootin' on every mission."

Derek looked down at his plate.

"You know, having you around again, reminds me of when you came to stay with me after your father passed. I know it only lasted a few months before you went off to the academy, but them was some good times."

Derek blushed.

"It felt good when you called me three years ago, too. I know the situation was bad, you killin' that colonist and all, but I sure was glad to hear from you." A serious look came over JT. "You understand that it wasn't your fault, don't you?" JT asked, stabbing a finger at Derek. "If you hadn't shot him, he would have killed that full-bird."

"Yeah, I know. That Colonel gave me a medal for saving his life. Did you know that? A medal. A medal for killing someone. What an insult to that man's widow," Derek said, grabbing his fork angrily. "Then they promoted me to Captain, for Christ's sake."

"You know, not every man is good, right? He was gonna shoot somebody else, right? If you hadn't done what you done, he would have killed that Colonel, and somebody else would've done it instead of you. You just happened to be the fastest on the draw."

After a long pause, Derek decided to change the subject again.

"So, where do I sleep? I'm going to need to clean this," he said, pointing to his chest, "and find a quiet place to read this packet from the General. You know, it's confidential. You remember that concept, don't you?" he said smiling at JT.

JT showed Derek a spare bedroom he had gotten ready for him the day before. The room would have been deemed too small by most, but Derek thought it was larger than his stateroom on the *Valley Forge.*

Derek sat at the foot of the small bed, and unloaded the duffel bag into the dresser that sat across from it. After emptying the bag, he tossed it into a wooden chair that sat in the corner. He leaned back on his hands and felt a searing pain in his chest, then collapsed onto his side and curled up into a ball.

As he lay on his side, the pain began to ebb. His quick, shallow breaths began to slow, and he relaxed. After only a few minutes, Derek fell asleep.

The bedroom door creaked lightly as JT walked in.

"Derek I dug these out..." JT stopped and stood there for a moment, holding a handful of old photographs. He began to close the door, when he stopped and looked back at Derek. Images flashed in his mind of Derek, at age 17, sitting on the very same bed, playing cards and talking about whatever they felt like. JT smiled, and silently closed the bedroom door as he stepped out.

Chapter Six

The Other Shoe Drops

Derek awoke from a fitful sleep. Still fully clothed, he rolled himself over, letting his feet dangle from the side of the bed. Instinctively, his hand rubbed across the mass of bandages on his chest. He felt a dull pain deep within his chest as he slowly pressed inward. *Not as bad as it was,* he thought to himself. Glancing over at the dresser, he noticed a pile of photographs he hadn't seen when he first came into the room. He stood and looked over at the door, as though expecting JT to walk in at any moment. After waiting only a second, he reached over and picked up the photos.

Derek scanned the images, pausing every so often to soak in the emotions the pictures brought out in him. Many of the pictures had been taken while his father was still alive and included both himself and his dad. Occasionally, there was a more recent photo of himself, and a few with JT. Photo after photo filled him with a stream of conflicting emotions. One photo would bring him to the verge of tears. Then, his eyes still filled with tears, the next one would start him giggling. A picture of Derek at the age of ten wearing his father's huge combat boots, a big smile on his face, brought about a long fit of laughter.

Derek's heart sank as he came to a photo of himself, standing in front of a podium. From the look of the photo, Derek was in the middle of speaking when it was taken, as his mouth stood open and his right hand was engaged in some unknown gesture. In his left hand was a pair of gold rank insignias. He stared at it, feeling a rush of sadness, like storm clouds billowing within him. He remembered how good it felt at the time. Happiness filled him so much that he thought he'd burst. He was graduating from the academy and had just received his Second Lieutenant's bars. His 'butter bar' they called it, as the Second Lieutenant rank's bar was gold and looked like a stick of butter.

Standing in front of the group of families, he had given a speech. He had graduated as a member of the 'Honor Guard', the top five students in the graduating class. Each of them had been allowed to give a speech. He had waited for the valedictorian to give his speech, and then he gave his. He didn't remember a word of the valedictorian's speech, as he was poring over his own in preparation.

In his speech, he had thanked three people for supporting him. He had thanked a woman he had never met, yet she had given her life for him. He told the crowd that mother had passed away while in the hospital shortly after his birth. He told them he had double-majored in the academy. In addition to the standard Military Science major, he had also chosen Biochemistry, which was his mother's field when she was alive. He told them that when he was a child, he had gotten into his father's study while his father was away and found a large box of biochemistry books that his father hadn't gotten rid of. He began reading them and almost instantly developed a love for science. Later on, the box had been given to him by the second person he wanted to thank, his father.

Derek told the crowd that his father was the most dedicated man he'd ever known. He would purposely avoid anything that would take away too much time from his son. His father had missed a junior-league baseball game because of a last-minute meeting, and he had taken part in a protest to get back at him. Derek's father then vowed never to miss Derek's functions again. The crowd learned that Derek's father had worn his wedding ring, even though his mother had died many years before, and he had placed fresh flowers on her grave twice a month. His father had died while on duty, working on a classified military project that, as his father had put it, was for the benefit of not just his country but of all mankind – not something a military man said very often.

Three other men had been riding with Derek's father when he was killed. One of them was a General, one was a member of the General's staff, and the other was an executive from a starship manufacturer. His father's death had come only three months before his eighteenth birthday. The third person he wanted to thank had received guardianship rights over Derek.

James Towson, or JT as Derek called him, was Derek's best friend. He had been a friend of Derek's father, having worked for him at a base where they were stationed several years before. He explained that JT and Derek had become such good friends; the two of them were nearly inseparable. Derek's father had initially been against their friendship because of the large difference in their ages, but later came around because of how well they got along.

Derek looked into the image of his own face, seeing the happiness that beamed out over the crowd like a lighthouse beacon. The sadness in him began to boil as he stared. When the picture was taken, he'd had no idea that only a few minutes later he'd have a fight that almost cost him his best and only friend.

Derek piled the photographs back onto the dresser and walked out of the bedroom. Coming from somewhere below him, he could hear a light humming noise. Ignoring it, Derek walked aimlessly through the house, again taking in all the things that just didn't fit. He couldn't believe the changes in JT that living in this house seemed to indicate.

After a few minutes of walking, Derek's stomach made its presence known by growling ferociously, so he made his way to the kitchen and began searching the cabinets for something to eat. Not finding anything that didn't require preparation, he opened a small, refrigerated vegetable keeper. He pulled out a bag of mixed greens and dropped it on the counter.

He looked around the kitchen for a clock but didn't see one. He looked up at the ceiling; seeing a small black box with a small red light on it, he said, "Time?"

A rather jovial-sounding male voice said, "It is currently four forty-two, PM."

Derek opened the cabinet above the counter, revealing the flat disks he had seen the day before. He picked up one of the larger ones from the pile and scanned the edge of the disk until he found what he was looking for.

He placed the disk on the counter, and turned it so that a small rough circle that appeared to be etched in the ceramic, as well as the NanoTech company logo, was facing him. As he touched his finger to the rough circle, the completely flat disk began to change shape. The edges slowly rose, leaving the center flush with the counter. He looked at the shallow bowl then the bag of greens, then shook his head and touched the rough circle again. This time, the edges of the bowl curled upward so that they were perpendicular to the counter. Now sitting on the counter was a bowl that was deep enough for a salad.

Derek reached into the bag and grabbed a handful of moist greens, dropped them into the bowl, and then put the bag back into the vegetable keeper. He opened a drawer and pulled out a small metal bar. At one end, was a rough circle similar to that he had pressed on the disk. He pressed it, and the metal began to change shape until it had become a spoon. One more press, and the spoon split into four sections, and then became a fork. He tossed the fork into the bowl with the greens and picked up a bottle of salad dressing from the countertop. With a shake, Derek splashed the fork, the greens and the countertop with dressing.

The humming noise, now growing louder, began to pique Derek's interest. He stuffed a large mass of salad into his mouth, then headed for the elevator. Inside the elevator, the noise was amplified, sounding like someone scratching on a microphone that was currently set to 'On'.

Stepping out of the elevator on the first floor, Derek was bombarded by the volume of the noise. The deafening sound was coming from the shop beside the Beowulf. Stuffing another bite of salad into his mouth, Derek walked over to the helicopter.

"Is this thing almost finished?" Derek yelled. There was no response. He stepped around the side of the cockpit, into view of JT, who was using a large hand tool on the black skin of the vehicle.

"Is this thing almost finished?" Derek repeated. JT, having just noticed Derek, shut down the tool.

"Hey there, bright-eyes. I didn't wake you up, did I?"

"No, I was up. Salad?" Derek said, offering JT his bowl and fork.

"No thanks, you'll ruin my dinner. Hey! You're gonna ruin *your* dinner! After gettin' hurt like that, you need protein, not salad." He took a deep breath through his nose, smelling the air. "Smell that?"

Derek took a few small breaths of the air. "All I can smell is ozone from that thing you're working with there," he replied. "What am I supposed to smell?"

"Maybe it's best you don't smell what I got cookin' out back. It'll be a good home-coming surprise!" A devious grin came over JT's weathered face. "You go on back upstairs and bring me the big platter in the cabinet beside the sink."

After a few minutes, Derek returned, carrying a large stainless steel platter akin to those his food had been served out of when he went through basic training. *The platter looks like it would be at home in a prison, or maybe a school*, Derek thought to himself. He stepped around the helo toward JT and noticed a door he hadn't previously seen. He followed JT out the door and was immediately treated to a wonderful smell. Thick smoke was billowing from a cooker that was sitting between two large piles of scrap metal. A fire had been built on the ground, and a metal frame stood over it. On the top of the frame looking like a large bowl was one side of a large jet engine housing.

Derek immediately looked at JT, wondering what was cooking.

"Smells damn good, don't it?" JT asked. "I bet you don't even remember that smell, do you? Last time you smelled it, you was about thirteen."

"Are you cooking ribs in a jet engine?" Derek asked, his voice cracking. "That is a jet, right?"

"Sure is. And those ain't no ordinary ribs neither. Those are buffalo ribs. Damn long ribs too. They got a buffalo farm about twenty miles from here now. Real nice folks out there, too."

Derek slowly approached the smoking cauldron, and looked into it.   The bubbling sludge in the bottom completely covered anything that could have been mistaken for ribs. If it hadn't been for the delicious smell, Derek would have sworn he was staring into a bubbling cauldron of tar.

"Buffalo, huh? I haven't had buffalo in a long time. It's too expensive for me. Aren't you worried about getting fined for this fire?"

"Nope. Went downtown yesterday and got me a permit after you dozed off," JT said smiling. I could set fire to the house if I wanted to."

"Yesterday?" Derek asked.

"Yep. You slept all night and most of the day today. You needed it."

"Ah," he paused. "Well, those smell good anyway," Derek said, sniffing the air lightly. He tried to take a deep breath of the vapors rising from the bubbling mass, but a dull pain in his chest told him that it wouldn't be a good idea.

"They should be ready. Hand me those," JT said, pointing to a pair of tongs sitting on an instrument panel behind Derek.

JT retrieved the ribs from the bubbling goop, nearly dropping a full rack on the ground. After putting out the fire with a blanket of dirt, they went back into the house, and up to the kitchen. Derek set the remainder of his salad on the dining room table alongside the two-foot high pile of ribs. JT and Derek sat down, and ate until they both felt miserable.

For nearly an hour, Derek and JT sat at the table, discussing where their lives had taken them over the last couple of years. Neither of them mentioned anything particularly good happening to them. Derek realized this, but kept it to himself.

"I missed you," Derek said under his breath.

"'scuse me?" JT replied.

"I said, I missed you, you old bastard," Derek repeated loudly.

"I know that's what you said. Just wanted to hear you say it again!" JT said, reaching out and giving Derek's hand a squeeze. JT abruptly stood, and grabbed the large platter and piled up the mass of rib bones.

"I gotta get back to work. I need to finish this job if I'm gonna get paid. I'm supposed to deliver this thing in about a month or so. I just hope this guy's got the money. I'm chargin' him extra for the stealth skin I'm electroplating on it. It wasn't exactly standard when this was built, but she sure is state of the art now! I think he'll like it," JT said, a broad smile spreading across his face.

"You never did know when to quit, did you? Well, I guess if you're going to go back to work, I'll go read my orders and whatever else they might have given me."

Derek tried to help clear the table, but JT refused his help. After a minute of arguing about Derek's current state of health, Derek conceded defeat. He picked up the packet containing his orders and walked JT to the elevator.

After JT had gone downstairs, Derek sat down in one of the chairs in the elevator lobby and opened the packet. The first thing he pulled out was the letter from General Durus. He dropped it on the small side table, and pulled out the rest of the contents.

The pack of paper, clipped together with a paperclip, seemed thicker than it should have been. A small yellow piece was clipped on the top. Derek looked at the paper; scrawled in barely legible handwriting was,

'Derek, make your choice on this. I want you to know that whatever the decision, I'll stand by you. In light of all that's happened with you, your father and me, it's the least I could do for you. There were some people who didn't want to give you the choice I'm giving you.' It was signed, 'Lee Durus'.

What the hell is he talking about? Derek thought to himself.

Derek removed the paperclip, and dropped it and the yellow note on the table beside the letter. He looked at the papers, and realized that there were two sets of orders instead of one. *This was what the General was talking about, my choice of duties, not a bad way to come back from R&R. I guess they aren't angry about what I did on Ganymede.*

Derek's elation was short-lived when he saw the document ID number at the top of the first packet. The paper, a form DD-214, was a military discharge form.

"Oh my God!" Derek said out loud. He looked over the form, which had him listed as an 'Honorable Discharge'. There was no other information regarding the circumstances surrounding the discharge. The form's effective date was August 17, 2136. "I thought I was supposed to report back for duty on that date," Derek mumbled.

The elevator door flew open, and JT jumped out.

"Are you okay? I heard you yell," JT said, his breath coming in short, panting gasps. "What's wrong?"

"I'm not really sure what's going on here. The letter I got from General Durus says that I'm supposed to be back on duty the 17th of next month, but right here is a DD-214 dated the 17th of next month. The same date. Hang on a second," Derek said, dropping the DD-214 in his lap and examining the other set of papers.

"Jesus Christ!" Derek yelled.

"Alright, I'm gonna piss all over myself if you don't tell me what the hell's going on!" JT bellowed, his hands now resting on his hips.

"Just a second," Derek said, poring over the form. "I don't believe this. Now I understand what's going on. I'm being given a choice." Derek held up the form so JT could see it, then picked up the discharge form and held it up as well.

"Not really much of a choice, though. I'm being given the choice of either being reassigned," he said, shaking the second form in the air, "or discharged from the military."

The large box landed on the loading dock with a thud. Several engineers, who had shown up to watch the files being unloaded, had been coerced into helping carry the boxes into the building.

"This data is the culmination of about twenty year's research in physics and metallurgy," Frederick Samson said, picking up another box. "You're very lucky to be getting this."

"We're just glad to finally be getting our hands on it. We've had twelve people sitting on their hands for weeks waiting for this stuff," a tall, slender man with dark hair replied. Sweat dripped off the tip of his nose, making a dark spot on the lid of the box he was holding.

"Now we can get to work on some designs of our own," he grunted, walking into the building through the open overhead door.

"You guys aren't going to be able to do anything right away. This data will take six months to sort through,"

Frederick said, looking over his sunglasses at the man's back. He dropped the box on the edge of the loading dock and turned to pick up another.

"Who's the lead engineer on this project?" Frederick asked the small crowd.

"I am," a barrel-chested Asian man said. "Sammy Tong, Lead Scientist." Tong instinctively stuck out his hand for a handshake, but withdrew it when he realized that Frederick was holding a large box of papers. He took the box from Frederick and handed it to another person standing beside him.

"If you're in charge, then this is for you," Frederick said, reaching into his shirt pocket. He withdrew a clear, crystalline data chip.

"It's the catalog of the reports. Don't lose this chip. You'd never get the reports you wanted in any order. The catalog is search-based. You type into the search what you're looking for by keyword, and it will bring up the relevant documents. We've set it up this way for security reasons. If someone were to just go and open a file cabinet somewhere, they'd never find what they're looking for without a document number from that chip."

Tong took the chip from him and dropped it into his shirt pocket. Behind the dark sunglasses, Frederick watched Tong's hand closely, his eyes coming to rest on Tong's shirt pocket.

After the remaining boxes were unloaded from the truck, Frederick took Tong aside.

Putting his arm around Tong's shoulder, Frederick said, "Don't hesitate to call me if you have any questions regarding the reports or the catalog. I'm at your beck and call," he said, grinning.

Tong picked up a box and started to turn. "Here's my card," Frederick said, holding out a business card. "Oh," he said, looking down at the box. "Here you go," Frederick said, placing it into Tong's shirt pocket.

Frederick closed the rear door of the truck and climbed into the driver's seat. He looked back in his mirror as he started the engine. Frederick slowly pulled away from the dock and toward the gate of the facility. Once he had cleared the gate, he looked at the object in the palm of his hand. *This is too easy,* he thought to himself. With a smile, he tossed the data chip he had just taken from Tong's shirt pocket, onto the passenger seat – a simple exchange when putting the business card in. *All too easy.*

"Why the hell would they reassign me? I just don't understand what's happening here!" Derek yelled.

"Maybe it's a temporary assignment," JT lied. "The military likes to do things like that. Maybe they need you somewhere else for a while," he reassured.

"No, that makes no sense. I bet it's that damn Simms. He's been waiting for something like this to happen, ever since I killed that colonist. Simms tried to have me removed then. He said I was unstable in the hearing. I was just lucky I passed all the psych evaluations. After that, he had no ammunition against me, so he dropped it. He never made it a secret that he wanted command of my unit."

Derek paced back and forth in the lobby, the envelope now crumpled in his hand. JT, unsure of what to say, sat down in another lobby chair.

"You know, the military does this sort of thing all the time," JT said calmly. "It's just what they do. They have to move 'resources' around where they need them. Maybe you should look at it that way."

"I won't! That's my unit. I selected them. I trained them. They're my men," Derek said pointing a thumb at himself.

Derek paused and looked down at himself. He was still standing, his thumb pointing directly at the wound on his chest. A realization washed over him. They were his men, and he'd gotten nearly a third of them killed, and nearly himself as well. As he slowly smoothed his hand over the bandages on his chest, he understood why he had been given the choice of reassignment or retirement. He was damaged goods, and would probably no longer be capable of performing his duties as he had before. JT watched as Derek rubbed his chest.

"Whatcha thinkin'?" JT asked.

"Now I understand," he said, looking up at JT. "This is why," he pointed at his bandages. "They've given up on me. I guess I'm no good to them anymore. I'm damaged goods."

Derek slowly sat down in his chair. Staring off into space, he felt as though he had lost his purpose for being.

"I'm a Saint Bernard without a barrel," he mumbled.

"What's that?" JT asked. "You ain't gonna start that feelin' sorry for yourself crap, are you?" he said, walking over to Derek. "Just because this happened ain't no reason they'd wash you out. Look, you got a meetin' in a few days with that General. Why don't you just talk to him about it then?"

Derek suddenly had an idea. A thin smile began to creep across his face.

"I know what I'll do." He looked up at JT. "I'll go back to General Durus, alright. I'll go back to him, and show him that I'm ready to take command of my unit!"

JT stepped back. "You ain't serious, are you?"

"Of course I am! I meet with him a week from Friday. That gives me 8 days to get this crap off my chest and try to put on some weight."

Derek's thin smile had blossomed into a full, toothy grin. JT, however, appeared less enthused.

"Look, you need rest, not exercise. I brought you here to make sure you got the rest."

"Great. You can help me, by letting me help you around here. I'll do some work for you around the shop. Your house might be neat and clean, but your shop is a mess!"

"I didn't bring you here to make a slave out of you or to have you end up hurting yourself worse. Remember the doctor's orders?"

"Look, I can either do it here with your help, or I can do it at my house without it," Derek said, the threat hanging in the air like a bad smell.

JT sat staring at Derek, his mouth slightly open. His face gave away the monumental struggle that was raging in his head. Derek knew that his threat of leaving would bring back all the memories they both shared. Nearly three years had passed since they last spoke to each other. Before that, they hadn't spoken for two years. Derek knew that JT didn't want to push him away again, not after he had gotten him back for such a brief period of time.

"Alright, alright. I'll help you, but the first sign that you're working yourself too hard, you have to stop. Deal?" JT said, holding his hand out to Derek.

"Deal," Derek said, taking JT's hand. "Let's get to work."

Derek spent the next two days cleaning the shop. He moved the components that were in the various piles, placed some onto shelves and hung others on hooks that lined the walls. Derek realized early that he had lost a lot of muscle mass and with it a lot of strength. Occasionally, he would feel a sharp pain in his chest, but for the most part it was just the dull throbbing pain that he had almost gotten used to.

Once the shop floor had been cleared, he swept it with an old broom he found in a corner. The sweeping had stirred up a large cloud of dust that made Derek's nose tickle. He fought back a sneeze, but eventually it got the better of him. As he sneezed a searing pain shot through his chest, feeling as though the fate of all vampires had befallen him; he had been stabbed through the chest with a stake. He dropped to his knees on the concrete floor, teeth gritted tightly.

"You alright down here?" JT asked as he walked out of the elevator. "What are you doing down there?" he asked as he saw Derek on his knees on the floor.

"Oh, I'm fine," Derek said as he stood up. "I just dropped the broom." He leaned over and picked up the broom handle and started to sweep, keeping his eyes on JT. A bead of sweat glistened on Derek's forehead, which was flushed a deep red.

JT eyed him suspiciously. "Well, if you don't need anything, I need to go out and get a couple parts for the helo."

"I thought you had everything to finish it. What else do you need?"

"Just a couple little things, but unfortunately I got to go to a supplier outside Portland to get 'em. I will be gone most of the day. You sure you're gonna be alright by yourself?"

"Yeah, I'm almost done here anyway. I think I'm going to mop the floor here, then I'll call it quits."

"Alright," JT said. "I'll see you in a few hours."

When Derek had finished sweeping the shop, he mopped as much of the floor as he could, as well as under and around the large items he wasn't able to move due to his level of pain, and restriction of movement from the bandages.

His whole body ached from the exertion of the last two days, but he kept going. After finishing the floor inside the shop, he moved outside and began moving things around in the yard, trying to organize things to make them easier for JT to find when he needed them. Not being as familiar with the equipment as JT was, he had difficulty placing it, so he made several assorted piles around the yard with the items he didn't recognize.

As the sun began to set, Derek decided to quit for the day. He worked his way into the house and up to the bedroom, shedding his dirty, sweat-soaked shirt and leaving it on the floor outside his bedroom. In the mirror, he saw his reflection, complete with grungy bandages. He carefully removed the bandages, showered, and then replaced them with new ones, adding a fresh coat of yellow goop.

JT returned home to find that Derek had worked in the yard, and much of it had also been cleaned and organized. The larger components of vehicles were the only things that hadn't been moved. He went upstairs and found Derek asleep in his room.

Over the next several days, Derek and JT worked together to move the larger pieces in the yard. The two of them worked to arrange the yard into sections that made it easier for JT to find all the components associated with a particular project. In one corner of the yard was the old Huey helicopter. In another corner was an old troop transport dropship, and in still another was a military staff transport. Several of the vehicles appeared as though they had seen combat, although it looked as though it had been many years ago.

Derek also began to do some basic calisthenics exercises in order to build up his aerobic tolerance. He worked out twice a day, doing exercises like sit-ups and jumping jacks. He had tried to do a pushup, but a pain in his left chest told him it was too soon to try it.

By the time Friday came, Derek and JT had completely rearranged the yard. JT had neglected his work on the Beowulf, but because so much had been done in the yard, he told Derek that he wasn't upset about the lack of progress on the helo. He and Derek had both enjoyed the time they had been spending together. The last few years apart seemed to have dissolved, and it was as though they had been friends the whole time.

Derek stood in front of the mirror. His neatly pressed uniform was draped over him. It hung off of him, showing him how much weight he had lost. He took a deep breath, and exhaled slowly. Now that he didn't have the bandage wrapped tightly around his chest any more, breathing came much easier. Now covering his wounds were several smaller bandages. He was no longer using the yellow anti-microbial salve, so the bandages he was using didn't have to be held tight against the wound. It was still slightly sore, but the stitches had disappeared, and it would only be a few more days before the bandages wouldn't be necessary at all.

Derek absentmindedly picked at lint that was stuck to the chest of his dress uniform. *I need a haircut, but there's no time for that right now.* He brushed a hand through his hair, then walked out of the room.

"Captain Derek Cross reporting as ordered, sir," he said, stepping into the General's office. He immediately stood at attention, his eyes focused on the wall behind the General's desk.

Taken aback, the General nearly dropped the papers in his hand.

"I apologize if I gave you the wrong impression, Captain," Durus said, pulling a soggy, unlit cigar from his teeth. "This isn't a formal proceeding. You aren't due back in uniform for a few weeks," General Durus pointed at Derek's oversized uniform.

"Sir, I'm ready to get back to my unit now, if I may," Derek said, his head held high, eyes staring straight at the dark oak paneling that lined the office. He took a deep breath, inhaling a deep lungful of the air that was thick with the smell of stale cigar smoke. Derek held his breath, keeping his chest pushed out.

"At ease, Captain."

Derek clasped his hands behind his back, and stood with his feet slightly wider than his shoulders.

"Didn't you read the orders I sent you?" the General continued. "I have a new assignment for you.

"Sir, with all due respect..." Derek started. "I read the orders, but I don't understand why I'm being reassigned. I've worked hard and gotten back into shape, so..."

"In shape?" the General cut him off. "I can just look at your uniform and see what kind of shape you're in," Durus said, pointing with the chewed end of the cigar. "Besides, even if I wanted to give you back your unit, I can't. My hands are tied. This came straight from the top. There are a lot of people who are outraged about what happened on Ganymede. Jesus son, I gave fourteen eulogies for those boys."

"Sir, something wasn't right on Ganymede! I don't know who we were up against-" He stopped as the General raised his hand.

"I have a lot of intel on Ganymede that we should discuss. If you want to discuss your reassignment, we can do that after the Ganymede mission debriefing," General Durus said, handing him a file folder. "Take a seat and skim over this for a minute, Captain," he said, placing the soggy tobacco stub back in his teeth.

Derek unbuttoned his jacket and sat down in a chair in front of the General's desk. He spent the next five minutes poring over the information in the folder. Contained in the folder were pictures of equipment that had been taken after the battle for inclusion in the After Action Report. Derek was astonished at the amount and level of technology of the equipment they had taken. In addition to several heavy plasma cannons like the ones he'd seen in the hands of the enemies he'd neutralized, there was another communications jamming system and two cases of grenades, all laid out in one photograph.

Derek flipped to the next photograph, and the hairs on the back of his neck stood on end. In the photograph, Sergeant Cook was standing next to a Mantis Anti-Aircraft Battery. The battery consisted of a small automated sensor pad and four long-range anti-aircraft missiles.

"Jesus," Derek mumbled. "If we'd dropped in using the transports..."

"You might have all been KIA," the General said, completing Derek's sentence. "You made a good choice using the lightning lances. I understand some of them failed, but most of your men came back alive because of them. I've got HQ tracking the serial numbers on the gear, but it's going to take some time."

Derek continued to sort through the photos until he came to pictures of several men from the opposition force who had been taken prisoner. In one photo, an Op-For prisoner was standing sideways, his shirtsleeve pulled up toward the camera. Tattooed on his upper arm, was an army tattoo. Derek furrowed his brow, trying to comprehend the meaning of the photograph.

He moved the photograph aside and found a dossier on the prisoner. Derek skimmed it and found that the prisoner had once been a soldier in the US Army. He had been dishonorably discharged following an altercation with another soldier. Following his discharge, he was employed as a mercenary until 2134, when military intelligence lost track of him.

"Mercenaries?" Derek asked, looking up at the General.

"Keep going," the General said, pointing at the file.

Derek continued reading and looking at photos until he came to a picture of a large number of colonists. Looking at the picture, it appeared as though they had all been hiding in a cargo bay or some other large room. Derek continued until he had finished going through the remaining pictures.

"Why would they hire mercenaries to help them revolt? It doesn't make sense."

"Back up a few pages," Durus said. "The photo of the large group. Take a closer look at it."

Derek looked closely at the picture and noticed something he hadn't before. In the photo, all the men had their hands behind their backs.

"Are these prisoners?"

"It seems as though our mercenary friends had the colonists locked up in a vehicle maintenance shed. This wasn't a revolt. We are still trying to figure out exactly what it was, but it definitely wasn't a revolt. It was meant to look like one, though. None of the Op-Fors were residents of the facility." Durus held a small red-hot lighter to the end of his cigar in a feeble attempt to light the now loose mass of wet leaves.

"Why make it look like a revolt, only to have the military come in and find out that it wasn't?"

"That's what intel is working on right now," Durus said, dropping the lighter into a desk drawer. "They're also working on the identity of a small ship that got by us," he said as he stood up. "It seems a small, high-speed shuttle took off after you were hit and activated a second jamming satellite. By the time we blew it, the ship was too far out of range to stop them or even ID them. We think they are the ones who did *that* to you," he said, pointing at Derek's chest.

Derek's head was spinning with all the new information. He began to work backward through the file, stopping for a few seconds on each photograph.

"Let me take my unit out. We'll find out what happened, and we'll find that other ship!" Derek said as he jumped to his feet.

"No, Captain," Durus said loudly as he threw the bunch of wet tobacco into a marble ashtray on his desk. Several small bits broke loose from the once proud Cuban cigar and landed on the desk beside the ashtray. "*This* is your new assignment," he said, snatching up a thick folder from his desk and shoving it toward Derek. "Now I'm sorry, but this assignment came down from the Joint Chiefs. They wanted our best man on this. I think that's you. They don't, but I do. Either you accept this mission, or your DD-214 will be processed. I did everything I could to keep them from simply discharging you! I put my reputation on the line on this one, only because your father was my best friend."

Derek looked at him, his mouth slightly open in disbelief.

"Oh yeah, you didn't know that did you, son? Your father worked for me just after he joined the Marines. I was his first commanding officer after he got out of boot camp. He was such a good friend of mine, and I was devastated when he died. I was the one who requested that he be allowed to put in his application for commission. You don't think they let just anyone who started without so much as a stripe become an officer, do you?"

Derek had never even thought about this before. His father had joined the military without a college degree, and it was extremely rare for someone without a degree to get a commission. One requirement was for recommendations from senior officers, and Durus had apparently given him one.

"I..." Derek paused. "I had no idea about you and Dad." A smile crept across his face.

Durus sat back down and turned his chair away from Derek toward the window behind his desk.

"Jim and I were friends almost from the get-go. He was hell-bent on making a name for himself in the service. He certainly made an impression on me, that's for sure." Durus swiveled back to Derek. "He moved up in rank faster than anyone I've ever known, including you. He was a good man." He paused for a long moment. "Read that information," he said, pointing toward the packet in Derek's hand. "If you don't want the assignment, that's fine. Just keep in mind that your father would have taken this and run with it. This is your father's mission – plain and simple."

Derek felt as though he had just been punched in the stomach. His insides squirmed within him, and he could feel his blood pressure rising, his pulse pounding in his head.

Noticing Derek's face turn red, Durus said, "Look, I need to know if I can count on you. Otherwise, I have to find someone else, and the timeline's tight. Skim that information over the next couple of weeks and give me a call. You aren't officially due back until the seventeenth of next month, but there's a meeting you'll need to attend on the fifth if you accept the assignment. There's a preliminary meeting in a couple of days, but you're currently listed as 'unavailable'," he said with a nod.

Derek looked down at the folder, which read,

> 'Confidential, Osiris Project.
> Viewing by unauthorized persons prohibited.
> Unauthorized viewing may result in up to a
> $1,000,000 fine, and/or 50 years in prison'.

Derek opened the folder and began to read the contents. A wave of disbelief grew, the further Derek read. Derek felt as though his mind were floating in space. He continued flipping pages, barely taking in the contents. There were several pages of diagrams and floor plans, but Derek kept flipping pages without even slowing. After he had gotten two-thirds of the way through the pack, when the absurdity of what he was reading reached a breaking point, he stopped and began to chuckle. Durus' eyebrows rose.

Since awakening in the hospital, there had been one gut-punch after another, and now this. Derek's laughter grew until he was laughing so hard he was afraid he would start having sharp pains in his chest. He kept laughing until streams of tears ran down his cheeks. With the sleeve of his uniform, he wiped the tears away. Slowly, his laughter faded. Once he had stopped laughing, he wiped his eyes again and closed the folder.

Looking up at Durus, he said, "So, you want me to babysit, huh?

Chapter Seven

Acquiescence

The words still echoed in Derek's head. 'Your father would have taken this and run with it. This is your father's mission – plain and simple'. *How could he say that to me? And about this babysitting mission!*

"I don't believe it! I just don't believe it!" Derek said, pacing around in the shop. "I'm not trained for this shit! I'm a soldier and negotiator, not a babysitter!" Derek absentmindedly kicked an empty metal can across the shop. "What the hell am I supposed to do on this mission?"

"Look," JT said. "Maybe you should just read all that stuff and at least give it a chance. Besides, didn't you tell me that he pulled some strings to get this for you?"

"Yeah, but..." Derek held the folder out toward JT as if he could read the information in it though the cover. "This is a crock!"

"Well, whether it's a crock or not, it's your only *real* choice, now, ain't it? Unless you want to get out of the service."

JT's words hung there in the air like the stale dust in the shop. No one spoke for several seconds. JT finally broke the silence.

"Can you tell me what the mission is? If you tell me, instead of havin' me read it myself, you go to jail instead of me!" JT said with a smile.

Derek didn't return his smile but said, "Yeah, they're starting another colony, and they want me to head up the military contingent. Sounds fantastic, doesn't it?" he said sarcastically.

"Can you give me any details? Why would they want you, as opposed to any other soldier?"

"I don't know. I didn't read it all. Hang on." Derek opened the folder and began to read, this time much slower than he had in Durus' office. "Wow," he muttered. "This actually *is* interesting." He continued reading, his brows furrowed.

"Well, what can you tell me?" JT asked. "Without either of us getting in trouble."

Derek looked up at him, a slight smile on his face. "Since when did you care about getting in trouble with the military?"

"Good point," JT replied, grinning widely.

"Well, let's see. I trust you can keep a secret." Derek cleared his throat. "There's a lot of stuff here. My orders, blah, blah, blah, military commander, blah, blah, blah, colony. Ah, let me go back and start with the background section." Derek skimmed down the page and began reading.

"In 2102, deep space probes were launched from Cape Canaveral, Florida, from the Marshall Islands and from," Derek paused and looked up, "a base that will remain nameless. Data was received in March of 2126 from the seventh and eighth probes. Jesus, that was ten years ago," Derek said, glancing up at JT. He looked back down at the packet and continued reading. "The probes, nicknamed 'Remus' and 'Romulus' by the some of the staff at NASA, were sent to analyze the Alpha Centauri system, a three-star system four point three-five light years from Earth. The data proved the existence of twelve planets in the system, four more than originally thought. One planet was shown to have a mass nearly equal to that of Earth, as well as a carbon dioxide, nitrogen, and oxygen atmosphere." Derek paused and looked up at JT, whose eyes were now wide with shock, and his mouth stood open. "The probe used ultraviolet, infrared and near-infrared to analyze the composition of the atmosphere. When the data returned showing an Earth-like atmosphere, the onboard computer re-tested by moving closer to the planet, dipping a scoop into the atmosphere, and directly taking a sample. This sample gave identical results." Derek began flipping through the next several pages in the file.

"There's some limited surface mapping data here based on the IR data. Weather and climate data, too. The different sets have increasing dates on them. The satellites must have remained in orbit around the planet for several years, all the while beaming it back to Earth." Derek flipped further into the folder, stopping on a set of diagrams.

"Here's the layout of the ship." He paused. "Whoa, this is a *big* ship! It's a converted cargo ship with a cryogenic sleep system. Four hundred person capacity." He continued flipping through the pack of papers until he reached the end.

"This looks like a pretty major undertaking. They have four hundred people going to start this colony. That's a lot of people to keep in stasis for twelve years!"

"Twelve years?" JT asked.

"Well, this says Alpha Centauri is four point three-five light years away, and the fastest ships we have right now are the Daedalus Class, and their flanking speed is zero point three-five of light speed. That would take just over twelve years to get there. Actually, about twelve and a half years. That's if the reactor didn't go critical from being pushed so hard for so long."

"Wow," JT added. "They want you to go away for twelve years?"

"You're not thinking," Derek said. "It takes twelve years just to get there! Then, I guess I'm supposed to stay there for a while. Then if I come back, that's another twelve years. You're talking twenty-five years by the time I got back! No fucking way! Not to mention relativistic time effects. It would be like a hundred years have passed on Earth." Derek flipped through the folder again, landing on a section with the ship's specifications. "I mean, I just..." he paused. "Wait a second." Derek skimmed over a ship statistics table and nearly dropped the folder. "Oh my God! This ship must have some radically-new propulsion design. This says the transit time is six months! This ship must be able to travel faster than light!"

Derek and JT sat stunned at what they had just learned. Neither of them spoke for several minutes. JT walked over and looked at the specifications himself. Derek watched JT's eyes move side-to-side as he read.

"Do you know what this means?" JT asked.

"It means that this place could be crawling with humans in only six months, that's what it means," Derek answered.

"No, it means a second chance for us. People, I mean," he said, gently nudging Derek in the ribs. "This planet isn't doing so well, in case you haven't noticed. So many people die every year from things that twenty years ago didn't even exist, and why? Because the air and water are so polluted that we're poisoning ourselves. Not to mention that we can barely feed ourselves anymore."

"We seem to be doing okay, I guess. I mean, people are always dying from something. Last year it was this, this year it's that, and next year will be something else. It's always been that way," Derek replied.

JT looked at him, a look of sheer disgust on his face. "You don't really believe that, do you? I mean Jesus, man, your own mother died because of the hell this place has become. I think you been spendin' too much time in zero gravity."

"Look, I understand that it's important for us to find new places for resources, but that's not my job, remember?" Derek said, one hand crushing the edge of the folder, the other balled up into a fist.

"Not your job! It's everyone's job to make sure we got enough food to eat and water to drink. It *is* your job to make sure the guy down the street has clean air to breathe. He don't have no damn environment suit he can wear like you do when you're on a mission!" JT said, his hands moving wildly.

"I am a soldier. Period. My job is to negotiate a peaceful solution to insurgency problems. If that fails, I fight. I may do that differently than some soldiers. I do it in a manner of my choosing. That is a privilege that comes with rank. You wouldn't know how that feels, would you," Derek said.

JT, obviously having felt the sting of the insult, said, "You may be a soldier right now, but you ain't gonna be one for long! Especially if you don't take that mission," he said, pointing at the crumpled folder. "Use that thing on your shoulders for somethin' other than a hat rack. Another planet!"

"You know what, I think I'm done here," Derek said, heading for the elevator. JT followed after him.

"Where are you going?" JT asked as he stepped into the elevator behind Derek.

"I'm going home. I need to think, and I don't think I can do that here," he said, pressing the up button.

"Look, take some time and think this thing through. If you don't accept the assignment, you're going to get booted. That's bad, right?" The elevator began to move upward.

"In your hand there, you got a chance to do somethin' good, right? Also, you got a degree in Biology, right?"

"Biochemistry," Derek corrected.

"Whatever. Do you think you could do somethin' with that if you got booted out of the military? Do you think you could get a job?" The elevator stopped, and the door sprang open.

"I don't know what I can do right now. This is all coming at me way too fast." Derek stepped quickly out of the elevator, and JT followed closely behind him.

"I just need to get away for a few days and think this thing over."

They got to Derek's room, where he snatched his bag off the floor beside the bed and filled it with his belongings.

"Look, all I can say is you got to do what's right for you, but what I know is this...If it were me, I'd do this thing," JT said, picking up the folder.

"Drop that!" Derek snapped. "That's classified information!" He quickly ripped the folder from JT's hand and stuffed it into his bag.

JT felt an invisible wall go up between himself and Derek. The wall was cold and hard, and unfortunately, familiar. He had seen this wall before. Five years ago, he had told Derek that he was leaving the military. Derek had told him that he felt as though he was being abandoned by his best friend, and almost instantly this wall went up. It had taken two years before Derek contacted him again, and then only because he had been involved in the fatal shooting of a colonist and needed JT's support. Contacting JT had been a knee-jerk reaction, and the contact hadn't helped Derek, who wasn't ready to let go of the anger he still held at JT. Now, three years later, they were back in each other's lives again, this time with JT coming to meet Derek who had been shot himself.

"Well then..." JT paused. "If I can make a suggestion, I think you should take this mission. Then when you get back, hand in that DD-214, and go off and be a Biochemist somewhere. You can help yourself and other people at the same time. Think what this could mean for mankind."

Derek zipped his bag closed and turned back toward JT.

"You sure are one to talk. You got out of the military just when I got in. I needed you, and you needed, well, whatever it was you needed," he said, brushing past JT.

JT stood in the elevator lobby and watched as Derek got into the elevator. No words were exchanged as the door closed and the elevator dropped out of sight.

Derek's keys felt cold and heavy in his hand. He stared at them, his mind on JT. *Is it going to be another three years before I talk to him this time?* Sudden deceleration of the commuter hovertrain jarred the keys from his hands. They fell to the floor with a crash that jarred him back to reality.

Derek realized that the train was approaching his stop. He quickly leaned over and scooped up his keys. With a hiss, the doors opened and Derek exited the train.

His walk home was done solely by memory, for his head hung low, his eyes fixed on the off-white sidewalk, only looking up when one vehicle's horn screeched a warning at someone else on the road.

His mind began drifting back to Ganymede. The image overtook him. Hate billowed up within him as he looked down at the prone figure, whose eyes were closed as he reeled in pain.

The boy looked up, the terror showing in his bloodshot eyes. His sweat-soaked blond hair hung in clumps around his face. Droplets of sweat shimmered on his forehead. The boy's gasping wheezes echoed in Derek's brain. The hate had that welled up in him was instantly shattered, and self-loathing replaced it. The memory of the deafening boom shook him physically, and he nearly dropped his keys on the sidewalk.

Derek took a deep breath and looked around. He was only three blocks from his house, but an average person would have never known it. Along both sides of the street were old storefronts, many of which were closed and abandoned. There were people sitting in the alleys between the shops, huddled together and talking. The rags they wore were an assortment of whatever they were able to find on the streets and in the alley trashcans. Derek glanced down one alley, just in time to see an old woman wrestling with a stray dog for a scrap of food.

Derek had always known this section of town was one of the worst areas for vagrants. He had seen them many times but had tried to pay them no attention. This was usually much easier, as he was normally in his transport going home, so the people on the street passed by his windows very quickly. He would feel bad for them for a few minutes, and then concede that there was nothing he could do to help them. There were just too many.

A bark behind him got Derek's attention so he turned back in the direction of it just in time to see the stray dog run from the alley, the piece of food in his mouth. Derek turned back and looked up the road ahead. A small shop, just ahead of him, was an antiques store run by an old Jewish couple. Derek approached the shop, and for reasons Derek couldn't explain, he stopped and looked in the window. He peered in for a moment, and then went inside.

Inside the shop, the sun shone through the front window, sending beams of light that illuminated the dust that hung in the air. The smell of dry rot overtook him for a moment, nearly making him nauseous.

Derek wandered aimlessly around the shop, stopping periodically to look at some of the old items. A clock, a gramophone, and a microwave oven were all interesting bits of history that stopped him briefly. Images of flappers and cowboys and knights all replaced the image of the young boy in his mind.

Derek moved toward the back of the shop where he came across a long, glass case. The case was filled with weapons from various time periods. The older weapons were on the left side of the case, while the more recent items were on the right. He slowly moved from the left side, dragging a finger across the dusty glass, leaving a trail of clean.

A heavy-looking axe sat on a blue velvet pillow, which sat next to a long sword. Beside the sword was a small shield that bore several deep gouges.

Continuing down the case, Derek came across a rusted flintlock pistol. He eyed it briefly before continuing past, and then glanced over a musket with a worm-eaten wooden stock. He continued past a nineteenth century breechloader, the manufacturer of which he didn't recognize when he stopped suddenly. Staring up at him from the case was a 'boomer' – a small handgun.

His heart started racing as he stared at the shiny pistol. A similar weapon was used on him and nearly killed him. His eyes scanned every millimeter of the weapon. In small letters engraved on the side was the inscription '.45'.

Part of him despised the thought of the gun, but he felt as though his feet were nailed to the floor, so he continued to stare at it. The heavy metal handle bore several scratches, which Derek traced slowly with his eyes. His gaze moved to the top of the case and a small bell. A sign beside it read, 'Please Ring for Service'. He glanced at the gun, then back to the bell. Derek's hand, seemingly on its own, swatted the bell, and it let out a ring in response.

An hour later, Derek reached a corner of the road that was walled-in by an eight-foot high wooden fence. He walked around the corner and pulled out his keys. He placed a key in a heavy deadbolt lock and turned it. A section of the fence that served as a gate opened with a slight hum. Derek stepped through and put his key in the lock on the backside, turned it, and the fence closed.

Once inside the fence, Derek saw that all the trees he had planted had been taken care of. He had been away for several months, and in the summer, plants can quickly die if not watered. *Mannie deserves a raise,* Derek thought to himself, as he pulled a hibiscus flower from the plant nearest him and took it.

Derek reached the door, and found that it was unlocked. *So much for that raise.* He entered his house and dropped his duffel bag on the floor. The paper bag he had gotten from the antique shop landed on the table with a thunk. Inside the house, the low hum of the air purifiers was the only sound.

A creaking floor-board told Derek that he wasn't alone. He slowly began to turn his head, but he noticed a reflection in a glass vase sitting on a small table. The outline of a person holding a pipe or bat came into focus.

The image just began to swing when Derek pivoted on his heel and, with a quick motion, grabbed the attacker's arms at the wrists. Using the attacker's momentum, he continued the swing downward toward the floor and quickly pivoted, pulling the attacker's arms to the side. The speed of the attacker's swing, plus Derek's redirection of the force, caused the attacker's arms to twist, and his feet were flung out from beneath him. He crashed to the floor in a heap.

Derek stood over his assailant, now holding the bat and the now crushed flower.

"Hey Mannie. Good to see you!" he said, smiling down at the boy on the floor.

Manuel Rojas lay on the floor, dazed. He looked up and, realizing it was Derek, he said, "No es bueno."

"You okay?" Derek said, helping him to his feet.

"Si. I got to stop sneaking up on you, señor. I live longer," he said in a heavy Spanish accent.

"You've done a good job taking care of the plants outside while I've been gone. That, and attacking would-be burglars, I should give you a raise. I didn't really expect to be gone this long, I'm sorry," Derek said, looking at Manuel's dirty shirt.

"No problemo. I take good care of you place. I only drink two of your sodas!" Manuel said, his face beaming.

"I didn't realize I had left any. You know you're welcome to anything in the fridge, right? Everything would be spoiled by the time I got back anyway," Derek said, walking toward the kitchen. "You want one?"

"Yes, please," Manuel said slowly, obviously trying to make his English sound perfect. He smiled for a second, then began coughing. Derek looked at him and watched as he continued coughing. When his coughing had subsided, Manuel wiped his mouth on the back of his arm. Derek watched him closely.

"How's your family doing? Are you giving them any of the money I'm paying you?" Derek asked, his hands on his hips.

"Yes. I have to. My sister is very sick. She goes to the doctor a whole lot. The doctor says she coughs too much. He says that her insides don't like it when she coughs that much. He gives her candy. Sometimes she has blood," he said, looking down at his feet.

Derek handed him a soda from the fridge, staring at the top of Manuel's head.

"I think I have something extra for you this time, Mannie. Especially since you are a good guard dog. Not to mention the good care you take of this place. And," he paused. "Because I missed your birthday!"

Manuel looked up in surprise, a big smile on his face.

"I no think you remember!" Manuel said. Another fit of coughing started but quickly subsided. Manuel smiled a toothy smile at Derek.

"How could I forget that the best housekeeper I've ever had turned twelve!" Derek looked at Manuel and noticed a faint red color on his teeth. A dull pain began to swell in Derek's chest. Instinctively, his hand went to the thin bandages over his wound. He suddenly realized that the pain wasn't coming from his wound.

"You drink that, and I'll go get you the money for watching the house and your birthday present." Manuel began to cough again. Derek started toward his bedroom and stopped in mid-stride, his back to Manuel.

"How would you like to earn a lot more money," Derek said, facing away from Mannie.

"Señor?"

Derek turned back and walked over to him. He knelt down in front of him, so that he was nearly eye to eye with Manuel. He looked at Manuel's lips, and saw that bright-red blood had pooled in the corners of his mouth.

Derek's thoughts went to Manuel's family. There were eight of them in the immediate family. His mother, father, and his two sisters and three brothers lived together in a large tenement building half a mile from Derek's house. Also living with Manuel were his grandmother and her sister. In his ten-member household, four of them had jobs, including Manuel and his older sister, Alicia, who worked for a barbershop cleaning the floors and doing odd jobs.

"I might be going away for a long time, and someone will need to watch the house for me while I'm gone," he said, putting his hands on Manuel's shoulders. "I might just need to hire you on permanently, which means I would have to pay you a good salary and give you some insurance for little things like medical and dental. And of course, every good employer keeps a fridge stocked with his employee's favorite blueberry soda! I might be going on a mission, and if I do I'll need you to accept this 'mission' for me as well."

Manuel threw his arms around Derek's waist, nearly knocking him over.

"I love you, Big D! You treat me like familia, I mean family. You treat me better than family."

Derek sniffed, trying to maintain his composure.

"Nah, I just know how hard it is to find good help these days," he said, letting go and standing up. "Stay right there, and don't peek. I didn't have a chance to wrap it before I left."

Derek stood and went into his bedroom, and a few moments later came out with an envelope in his left hand, and his right hand holding something behind his back.

"This is your pay for the work you did while I was gone," Derek said, handing him the envelope.

Manuel quickly opened the envelope, and his mouth fell open. His eyes, now as wide open as they could be, turned up to Derek.

"Señor, I...I can't take this much money. I only water plants, and clean up around the house. My papa makes less than this."

"Your papa isn't sick, either, is he? I know your sister isn't really sick." Manuel quickly wiped his mouth with his arm. "I want you to take this money, and go to the doctor. He will give you some medicine that will make that cough go away. Okay?"

Manuel moved as though to hug Derek again, but Derek held up a hand stopping him.

"Not yet, you haven't gotten your birthday present." Derek pulled his right hand around from behind him, a large box coming into view. "Tada!" Derek said.

On the box was a painting of a Daedalus Class Assault Ship. On the side of the ship, near the stem, were the letters 'USS Valley Forge.'

"Wow, is that *your* ship? The *Valley Forge*?"

Derek didn't have the desire to explain to him how he'd lost his command, and with it, his place on the '*Forge*.

"It sure is, and see that little window," Derek said, pointing to a small window on the front of the ship near the top. "That's my command center. And down here is my quarters," he said, his hand moving to the rear section of the ship.

"This is the best present I ever got!" Manuel said, hugging Derek tightly. Derek felt a dull pain in his chest; this time he knew it was from his wound.

Chapter Eight

Alliances

"Alright," Derek said, dropping the file folder on the desk. "I'm in, on one condition." Derek stared at the wall, his hands clasped behind his back.

General Durus looked over his glasses at Derek. "What's your condition, *Captain*?" Durus said, reminding Derek of his place.

"I want to pick two of the squad leaders that go. I think you know two of the men I want, Sergeants Cook and Hunter. I believe they are currently..." Derek paused. "Unassigned."

Durus held his hands in front of his face, tapping his fingertips together. He opened his mouth, but before he could speak, Derek cut him off

"And I want this Sergeant on the team as maintenance chief," Derek said, pointing at the folder on Durus' desk. "I think you'll see by his qualifications that he is more than qualified for the position."

"That's two conditions, Captain, not one." Durus picked up the folder and opened it.

"Whose service jacket is this?"

"Staff Sergeant James Towson, sir."

Durus skimmed through the pages of the military service record, stopping occasionally and glancing up at Derek, who continued to look straight ahead.

Durus mumbled as he read, "...Marine Corps field mechanic..." he continued mumbling. Durus pressed an illuminated button on his desk, and a three dimensional display appeared in midair in front of him. Glancing back and forth from the service jacket to the screen, he typed in a series of numbers.

Derek's eyes glanced down at backward image on the screen and occasionally looked back toward the wall, trying to avoid being caught reading.

"James Towson," General Durus said. "Is this the same James Towson who was reprimanded for discharging a five-thousand dollar plasma mini-shell while on temporary duty in Africa?"

"I think-" Derek started

"I understand that the camel was aggressive, son, but a *mini-shell?*" he said, his voice slightly elevated.

"Well sir, I-"

"Would this be the same James Towson who was reprimanded for using a maintenance bay for four months while working on a personal project?" he said loudly, his face turning slightly pink.

"Um, I think he thoug-"

"Would this also be the same James Towson whose commanding officer states, and I quote, 'shows a total lack of respect for authority and would be removed from military service except that no two marines currently serving in the corps possess his technical skills'?" Durus paused. The redness drained from his face, and his tone became soft. "Would this be the same James Towson who served under your father at Snake River?"

Derek nodded.

"Would this also be the same James Towson who acted as your guardian after your father's death?" he asked, his voice unusually soft and comforting.

Derek looked down at the General. His weathered face showed his years of serving the military. The years of stress, both physical and mental, had really worn him down. Thick, puffy bags drooped beneath his gray eyes. Derek had never noticed them before. He had always seen him as a 'tough as nails' man, and to hear him speak in such a soft tone made Derek feel very uncomfortable.

"Yes, sir. JT, I mean Sergeant Towson, did all of those things you said, sir. But I think whoever wrote that statement about his technical abilities knew him very well. You know that I'm a good leader of men, sir, and an excellent mission planner. I think that in order for this mission to be successful, we need the absolute best people we can get in every field. I think he is one of the best at what he does, sir. He can do amazing things with a pile of scrap. I mean, you should see what he's doing with this Beowulf. The thing..." Derek broke off as Durus stood.

Durus walked over to a large file cabinet on the wall beside his desk. Derek followed him and watched as he opened the top drawer, retrieving a small box. As Durus closed the drawer, Derek turned back to the wall.

"I wanted this to be done with all the appropriate military flair, but unfortunately, that wasn't an option." Durus held out his hand to Derek.

Sitting in the palm of Durus's hand was a blue box, four inches wide, by three inches long. Emblazoned on the lid was a large gold cluster.

Derek's mouth opened slightly.

"Congratulations, Major Cross," Durus said, saluting him.

Derek fumbled with the box, then stood at rigid attention. He saluted stiffly. Durus reached out, and they shook hands, Durus squeezing his hand tightly.

Durus smiled widely at Derek, who noticed the smile immediately. He couldn't remember Durus ever smiling at him before. Durus suddenly took on a grandfatherly manner. Derek felt even more uncomfortable. He smiled, a quiver curving the corners of his mouth.

"I don't understand, sir."

"This has been in the works for some time now," Durus said. "There was supposed to be a ceremony after you came back from Ganymede, but with what happened, there were some people who wanted to drop it altogether. Especially since you didn't know about it."

"But the usual promotion process, the hearings, reviews..." Derek said, waving his arm, the blue box still held tightly in his fingers.

"I was trying to get this through quietly. I wanted to make it a surprise for you. I filled out the proper forms while you were away. I've made it a battlefield promotion, partially out of necessity."

"Sir?"

"You see, the mission requires an Oh-four, or Major in the lead. If you had come back from the mission as planned, there would have gone through all the usual mess to get you promoted to Oh-four. Because of your hospital stay and the changing attitudes of some of our elected officials, that usual route was no longer possible. The only way to get you promoted, and thus qualify for the commander position, was to give you a battlefield promotion, to serve as a major temporarily. Of course, the mission being as long as it is, 'temporary' isn't really an appropriate word. I had to convince the powers that be to approve this. I had to call in a lot of favors, especially because this isn't actually a combat mission."

Derek looked down at the box in his hand. He opened the lid to reveal a pair of gold clusters, wrapped in plastic.

"Temporary, huh," Derek said.

"It's only temporary because it's a battlefield promotion. As soon as you return from the mission, we'd have to go through the normal process of promotion. The good thing is that the mission is lengthy, and you'll get experience as a major. This should make it an easy promotion, and with the time served under the battlefield promotion, you'd be halfway to an Oh-five."

"Lieutenant Colonel? Wow." Derek said, still staring at the gold clusters.

"Congratulations, Major," Durus said, returning to his desk. "You can have the three men you requested. I'll have orders drawn up for Cook and Hunter. I have a little trouble believing that Sergeant Towson has agreed to be reactivated and go along on this mission," he said rubbing his eyes. "From the look of things in here," he paused pointing to the service jacket. "He was damn happy to be leaving the corps."

"Well sir, he doesn't know he's going just yet."

Tong was frantic. He had already searched his office, the men's room, and his car, but to no avail. The chip was missing. He remembered what Samson had said, and he knew Samson was right. The files would take six months to sort through without the catalog.

"I know I had it with me when I was out on the dock. Did anyone check there?" he asked the three technicians who were helping him look.

"Yep. I've been out there twice myself. It's not there."

Tong searched his pockets again, and then dug through the pockets of the various lab coats that hung on hooks in the lab.

"Did I give it to anyone to run a search? I don't remember," he said, wiping the sweat from his forehead on his shirtsleeve.

Tong grabbed a box of storage chips and poured it out on the table in the lab. He spread them out across the table, quickly scanning the labels.

"It's not here, either!"

"Is this it?" came a voice from across the lab. A tall, thin lab technician handed Tong a chip. Tong took it and looked at the label. He realized that this wasn't the catalog, and flung it across the lab.

"Jesus, how am I going to explain this to the director? We are so far behind schedule as it is with all the delays in getting these reports from Samson. Now I've lost the damn catalog! Why the hell did they have to give it all to us on paper!" Tong ran his fingers through his hair, which was already sticking out in several different directions.

"Samson," he mumbled. "Samson!" he yelled. "That's it! I have his business card. Maybe I should call him and get him to bring us another copy of the disk. Hopefully he has another copy." Tong began patting his pockets again. "Now I just have to find his business card."

"You got to be out of your damn mind!" JT said, pacing around the kitchen. "I got too much to do here, like finish that helo."

"Look, the Beowulf will be here when you get back. I discussed all the mission details with Durus; we'll only be gone for two years. Six months there in cryo-stasis, one year 'on-planet', and six months cryo-stasis coming back."

"Sure, the Beowulf will be here when I get back, but the buyer might not be. I've been working on this thing for a hell of a long time. I need the money," he said, his hands outstretched. "Not to mention the other projects I have going on."

"Look, I've talked Durus into reinstating your pay at the current level for the rank you held when you left the corps. Staff Sergeant pay is nothing to sneeze at. All of your bills will be taken care of while you're away."

"And what about my social life? My social life will suffer, too," JT said, stabbing a finger at Derek.

"Your social life? You don't have a social life!" Derek said, laughing.

"Sure I do. I got young girls callin' me all the time!" He paused. "Well, I have some nice mature women callin' me occasionally." He looked at Derek. "Alright, alright. Some old lady might call, and I want to make sure I'm here!"

"Look, it was you who told me how important this mission could be to us, not just you and me, but mankind. After I left I did some thinking, and someone showed me how important this mission really is. I guess I just finally listened.   I always told myself that I couldn't make a difference. Well, in this case, one man really can make a difference." Derek smiled.

"I'm glad you finally heard something I said for once," JT said smiling back.

"Actually, it was a twelve-year old boy," Derek said, the smile leaving his face.

Derek told JT about Mannie, how he had looked after his house while Derek was away. He explained to JT that Mannie had tried to tell Derek that he had a 'sick sister' when it was obvioius that it was Mannie who was ill. He also told him he had given Mannie two months' worth of his military pay, which for Mannie's family was a small fortune. JT smiled broadly when Derek told him he had made Mannie promise to use half of the money to go to the doctor and get some medicine for his illness. The other half was his to do with as he pleased. Derek knew that a large portion of that remaining half would end up in his father's hands and would help to take care of his family.

"How did you ever meet a twelve-year old kid, much less have him start taking care of your house while you were away?" JT asked.

"Well, I was coming home one day with some parts to fix my gate motor. It had stopped working a few days before. I had also bought several plants, and was carrying them into the yard when Mannie walked up and told me, 'That's a nice Japanese maple tree, señor'. Of course, I stared at him for a minute, not really sure what to think. Then he starts telling me how to care for it, what kind of fertilizer to use, you know," Derek said, leaning against the wall.

"Then he started critiquing my other plants, telling me that my azalea is going to die unless I use this on the soil, but if I use this, my grass will die. So I started asking him about the different plants I bought, and he was a whiz with 'em. I ended up having him help me plant the maple and the azaleas I got. He talked me into getting an oleander too. I paid him a little bit for the help. He came back the next weekend, and I ended up taking him to the nursery with me. He told me he wants to be a 'plant person'. I told him all I could think about was leaves growing out of his head!" Derek laughed. "He wants to be a landscaper, or gardener. Honestly, I think if he had the opportunity, he'd make a great botanist. I just hope he gets the chance."

"Sounds like a great kid," JT said, eyeing him closely. "He remind you of anyone?"

"No, why? Should he?"

"No, just thought I'd ask," JT said, grinning widely.

Derek sat and thought about Mannie for a few seconds. JT watched him closely while he was deep in thought. He watched Derek's features change as the thoughts and memories flowed through him. Derek smiled, then his smile faded. Then he smiled again.

"So you think this is so important, that it needs my personal touch on it, huh boy?"

"I don't think it's the mission that really needs you, but I definitely think it would benefit from your wealth of technical experience. I do think that maybe five years is a really long time not to be around your best friend." Derek smiled at JT.

"Yeah, five years is a long time," JT added.

"Welcome aboard," Derek said, holding out his hand for JT to shake.

JT, bypassing the handshake went straight into a tight hug, which caught Derek by surprise. The tightness was comforting, not constraining at all.

"I'm sorry," Derek said, before JT had even decided to speak. "For everything."

"Me too. There are a lot of regrets I have in my life, but having fought with you is the biggest one I have."

"My biggest regret," Derek paused. "Is having never thanked you for all that you've done for me." JT and Derek released their grip on each other.

"Sure you did. I remember it like it was yesterday. You just thanked me in front of a room full of people, that's all."

"That wasn't a *real* thank you. I guess that's why I want you to go with me, so that we can spend some time together, and I can get to know you again."

"Sounds good to me! I only have one question: How do you pack for a two year trip?"

"I guess you get out the *big* suitcase!" Derek laughed. "And make sure you empty out anything perishable from the kitchen."

"No kidding!" JT said. He looked around the kitchen, his eyes stopping on the freezer. "Hey, you want some ice cream?"

Chapter Nine

Avalon

Tong found Frederick Samson's business card lying under a stack of monthly progress reports that were sitting on his desk. He was so nervous, that he mis-dialed the number four times, before hanging up to try and calm down. After several deep breaths, he tried again, this time successfully.

"Samson Industries, please state the name of your intended recipient," the computer voice said.

"Frederick Samson," Tong replied.

Several seconds passed, when the video system connected him. Flashing on the screen were the words, 'PLEASE WAIT'. A few seconds later, the screen flashed, and a young woman's face was illuminated on the screen.

"Frederick Samson's office, this is the Virtual Assistant, how may I help you?" she said with a smile.

"Yes, this is Sammy Tong at Aerospace Research. Is Mr. Samson in?" he asked, looking closely at the screen.

"I'm sorry Mr. Tong. He's out of the office right now, is there anything I can do for you?" she said, her fake smile still plastered to her face.

"It's really important that I talk to him. When is he due back?" Tong said, rubbing his eyes.

"He's out of the office for the next ten days, sir."

"Shit. Uh, sorry," Tong said. He looked back at the screen, and noticed her smile looked exactly the same. "Maybe you can help me. Mr. Samson dropped off a chip when he left the technical reports, and it seems to have turned up missing."

"You've lost the chip provided by Mr. Samson?" she said, her smile as bright as ever.

"Apparently," Tong replied. "Do you have a copy that you can provide me with?"

"I'm sorry sir, this Virtual Assistant has not been given security clearance, and cannot provide callers with confidential information. I'm sorry. Mr. Samson will be back in the office in ten days, I will log this call, and he can return your call then," she said.

Virtual Assistant, Tong thought. *Piece of junk if you ask me.*

"Thank you, I'll try him back in ten days then."

"Thank you for calling," she started.

Tong pressed the 'End' button and the screen went blank. He stood and walked out of his small office and into the lab. Sitting in a corner was the stack of boxes containing the technical reports Samson had left.

"Alright folks!" he said with a frown. "I want each of you three to start going through these boxes and writing down the titles of the reports and the report numbers. Samson is gone for ten days, so we can't get the catalog disk until then, but I think we can try to start one of our own in the meantime. We can at least get through a little of this stuff before then. Everybody grab a box; we've got to start somewhere."

The immense auditorium was filled with so many people that there weren't enough seats for everyone, so a large number of people were left standing against the sides, nearly blocking the aisles. A small group of people stood on the small stage at the front of the auditorium, their speech muffled by the murmur of the crowd. Several of them smiled broadly and occasionally laughed and slapped one another on the shoulder. Standing in the center of the stage was a dark wooden podium.

"Attention please," a man in a dark suit called out over the din of the crowd. "We have a lot to cover, so we might want to get started. I'm Dr. Evans. I'll be introducing the speakers today. As usual, please hold your questions until all the speakers have given their presentations. Please write your questions on the cards provided in your packets. There will be a wine social afterwards, and your questions will be answered there. If you'll look at the itinerary you received when you came in through the security check, you'll see that our first speaker is Dr. Ulrich McElroy, who'll be covering the ship's functionality. Following Dr. McElroy will be Dr. Heinrich Schtoller, who'll be giving us an overview of the mission, primarily focusing on the ship's layout and construction." Dr. Evans cleared his throat. "Following a short break, Dr. Phillip Mason will conclude with colony construction and the building timelines, as well as the long-term future of the colony." He paused for a few seconds, until a man off stage gave him the "OK" signal.

"Before our speakers present, we have a short project clip for you," he said, waving his hand in the air. At the back of the room, a tall blond woman bumped and pushed her way down the tightly packed aisle.

The clapping slowly died as people began taking their seats. The woman hunched down and slowly made her way along the aisle as she carefully scanned the crowd.

"Ladies and Gentlemen, this is Osiris," a prerecorded voice said. The room lights dimmed, and a large three-dimensional representation of the Egyptian god of the underworld appeared, hovering in midair. The woman stopped and blinked a few times as she tried to see in the dimly lit room.

"In Egyptian mythology, Osiris died and his body was cut into pieces. These pieces were sent to different parts of Egypt. When these pieces were brought back together, he became a god, and thus he was made greater than he had ever been in life. *This* is the future of mankind." The image slowly dissolved. In its place, a three-dimensional spacecraft began to form in the air above the crowd.

"This is *Osiris*, the first of many high-speed colonization spacecraft. *Osiris* has been constructed in orbit, thanks to help from several governments, and most importantly, Samson Industries."

The spacecraft on the screen was now fully formed. It resembled a grapevine, in that it had a long central tube-like section, which was studded with a large number of protruding spheres, cones and other shapes. At each end of the cylinder were larger elements of the ship. On one end was a large boxy section that was as wide as the entire ship, including the various other parts that protruded from the main cylinder. At the opposite end was a small spherical pod, not much larger than the central tube.

The image shrank to about a third of its original size. The screen now showed a blue-green planet, similar to Earth, that the ship was orbiting.

"Avalon," the voice said with an air of respect. "The legendary resting place of King Arthur of Camelot. Following the death of the great king, he went to paradise. The Earth itself is dying, and this, this is *our* paradise, our Eden."

"When the ship reaches Avalon, these pods will be released in orbit. Each one will enter the atmosphere and, under its own power, descend to the surface in a location currently being selected."

The image showed all of the small pods, except one of the cones, being jettisoned from the main core. Each one began to glow as it hit the atmosphere. The image zoomed in on the last cone as it was released from the ship. It followed the cone as it was buffeted by the upper atmosphere, and then watched as it rotated itself upright. Thrusters on the underside of the cone fired, and it slowly came to rest in a green field. The image swirled in a circle, taking in a three hundred sixty degree view around the landscape. Around the cone was a complex of pods that had just landed in a clearing. Surrounding the clearing was a vast expanse of forest and in the distance, mountains. The swirling view came to rest back on the cone, just in time to see a hatch open and several computer-generated people stepping out.

"Thank you very much, ladies and gentlemen."

The crowd began clapping again. The woman began scanning the crowd again now that her eyes were adjusted to the low light level. She swiveled her head back and forth until her gaze stopped on a man sitting in an aisle seat a few rows from the stage on the left side of the auditorium. She slowly made her way toward the front of the room, still crouched to allow the crowd to see the stage.

Dr. Evans stepped back up to the podium and said, "Ladies and gentlemen, Dr. Ulrich McElroy." He began clapping.

Several people in the audience started clapping, but a deafening silence emerged as Dr. McElroy walked onto the stage. The crowd stared at him, watching every step he took.

Standing just over three-feet in height, Dr. McElroy had been born with a genetic defect called achondroplasia. Achondroplasia was also called 'dwarfism' by many people, but this was an insult to people who were afflicted with the disorder. As it was customary for pregnant women to have the fetus undergo gene replacement therapy while in utero, 'little people,' as they preferred to be called, had become very rare. Having been born to a very poor family, Dr. McElroy hadn't undergone the treatment and was ultimately born with the disorder. He was well known in the scientific community as being one of the most brilliant physicists in the world, but his appearance still drew stares wherever he went.

He stepped up behind the podium and out of view of the crowd. Over the speakers, the crowd could hear the sound of a microphone being adjusted. McElroy stepped out from behind the podium, a lapel microphone now attached to his shirt.

"I would like to start with the end of the clip," he said, bringing back up the image of the *Osiris* orbiting Avalon. "Now, as we can see here," he began.

The woman slowly slid up beside the man and squatted down in the aisle. She paused for a moment and glanced up at the image of the spacecraft.

"Sir," she whispered. "A minute, please?"

"Can't you see I'm in the middle of something here, Doctor?" he said quietly.

"Sir, this is urgent," she said, grabbing his sleeve. "It concerns the cryo-stasis chambers. There's a problem."

She pulled out a small computer and flipped up the screen so that he could see it. It instantly dimmed in the low light of the auditorium. The screen showed the outline of a cone-shaped lander, and a two dimensional representation of the inside. The inside of this type of lander consisted of seven decks, the top five of which contained the cryo-stasis chambers, ten on each deck. The lowest deck contained the engines, and the one above it contained the lander's fuel, power cells, computer equipment, and storage. In small letters below the diagram the words, 'Colonist Lander D'. It was one of the eight passenger landers included in the mission.

He glanced at the image of the lander and nodded toward a door set into the left wall of the auditorium. The two made their way along the wall until they reached it. They stepped silently out of the auditorium and into a narrow hallway.

"Right here, sir," she said, activating a zoom feature on the computer. The screen zoomed in to the second deck from the bottom. A small square turned red as she touched the screen. "Sir, there's something wrong with the control system for the beds in this lander. It only affected the top four levels, so I've already had the techs replace the primary board and a couple of the secondary boards as well, but I keep seeing, well, weird things," she said, brushing her blond hair out of her face.

"Weird things? You're seeing weird things? Look, this ship cost more money than half the governments in the world make in an entire year, and you're telling me that you're seeing 'weird things'? Explain to me what exactly 'weird things' are," he said through clenched teeth.

In the auditorium, the crowd erupted with laughter that was muffled by the wall that separated the auditorium and the hallway.

"Well, I started running the test scripts that stress the system on this lander, Lander D. The accelerated scripts that make the computers think there are sleepers in the beds," she said over the laughter of the crowd. "On each run, after forty-four simulated days, the computers just shut down the beds. It shut down almost the whole lander – almost all fifty beds! I went back and checked the log, and it says that there were no people in most of the tubes. I had the programmers check the scripts first just to make sure it wasn't a problem with the scripts themselves, and the engineers are checking the lander's systems, but so far, they haven't found anything. The computers should have known there were sleepers in there. While the hardware was being checked, I started running the scripts on the other landers as well, but they found no issues, so it has to be a hardware problem."

"Look, they ship out in a month, so it's too late to replace the lander itself, so the only other option is to find out what's wrong," he said, his jaw still held tight. "Listen to me. That ship departs on schedule. Period. It's not going to be my head on the chopping block if this thing goes south."

"With all due respect, as flight physician on this trip, I have the final say in all matters relating to the safety of the passengers. I care about nothing more than making sure they, I mean we, get there safely. If I can't find what the problem is, this ship doesn't launch," she threatened.

The man, leaning close to her, said, "Listen to me, Doctor. You weren't the first flight physician we selected for this mission, and you can be replaced as quickly as the one before you. Do I make myself clear?"

She nodded.

"Find the problem," he said, straightening up.

She paused for a moment, weighing her options.

"Alright, sir, I didn't want to have to suggest this. I was hoping that the problem would be solved, but so far it hasn't been and my idea is becoming more of a possibility."

"What idea is that, Doctor Brown?" he asked, exhaling loudly and looking over her shoulder at the closed door separating him from the presentation.

"If necessary, the computers can be shut down and restarted en-route."

"How's that?" he said, turning back to her. "The computers are completely automated. We don't have a remote system onboard that'll allow us to restart them, much less the security issue of beaming commands toward the ship after departure."

"Someone onboard the ship can restart them."

"Excuse me?" he said, his eyebrows raised.

"Look," she said, pulling a slip of paper from her pocket. "I've done some calculations. A lone person could stay awake for the entire six months, monitor the sleepers, and if there are any problems they can restart the computers, or if necessary even replace computer components."

He stared at her, unblinking.

"I think that even if the computers were offline for a considerable amount of time, even up to a month, the sleepers would be fine because of their low metabolic rates."

Again the sound of muffled laughter echoed from the auditorium into the office.

"That would give the person plenty of time to either get the systems back online, or wake the sleepers altogether," she continued.

"So, if that's the case, why worry about the computers dying at all?"

"Because if the computers shut down the cryo systems on the beds part-way into the trip, the sleepers would die before they were awakened. And that's if the computer even tried to wake them up at all, which I doubt. The system said the beds were empty, so it wouldn't try to restart them. Four-and-a-half months is too long. They'd survive a month, tops. See here," she said, showing him the slip of paper containing handwritten notes and diagrams. "The person who stayed awake could use the living quarters in the foredecks of the ship. Also, they would only use about two percent of the ship's food and water capacity. Remember, this ship is built on a standard cargo vessel with a crew, so the galley stores a significant amount of food and water. Two percent is a negligible amount. Even if forty-plus people have to be awakened after forty-four days, we wouldn't starve. We might have to ration the stores, but no one would starve. Besides, I don't want to even consider this until there is one week to go before departure. If we're still having problems when we start the freezing process, then I'll consider it and put in the work order to get the galley stocked."

He placed his hand on his chin, pondering this new development. His head bounced back and forth, and then he smiled.

"Okay, give me a full *written* report of your idea next week. In the meantime, keep working on the computer problems. The best-case scenario is four-hundred people sleeping, not three-hundred ninety-nine. Besides, who would you be able to convince to stay awake in a completely empty spacecraft for six months, all alone?"

"Since I'm a doctor, I would be the most logical choice."

"That settles it, you really are crazy," he said, reaching for the door.

The two of them re-entered the auditorium while the crowd was still applauding Dr. McElroy. They drew no attention to themselves as they came back in and stood at the far end of the stage. Dr. McElroy, smiling as though he had just been given an award, strolled past them.

"Our next speaker for today, Dr. Schtoller, will give an overview of the mission, primarily focusing on the ship's layout and construction. He'll begin after we take a short break, but before we do..." He paused.

The room lights slowly grew bright again.

"I'd like to thank the representatives from Samson Industries who've decided to join us for part of the day. I understand they have to leave now, but before they do I want to acknowledge them. Would you gentlemen please stand up?"

A group of five men in dark suits stood up in the back of the room and looked around the auditorium. They all looked very uncomfortable with everyone staring at them.

"Samson Industries has met some very tight timelines in reaching the project milestones. Their staff has made incredible contributions to the success of this mission and I think they should be recognized." The crowd began clapping. Dr. Evans raised his hand, and the clapping subsided.

"Each of the milestones is important, but I think that after a year, the colonists will think 'day three-hundred forty', which is the arrival of their replacements, is the most important milestone!" He smiled as a few people in the crowd laughed. "The sister ship to the *Osiris*, the *Isis*, is currently under construction. The newly-built donor cargo ship is being readied, and all of the required propulsion components are currently being constructed in pieces at the Samson Industries factory complex. These will be transferred to the *Isis* in the Navy's orbiting shipyard. All the information and research data that went into constructing the two ships is being transferred from Samson Industries to the military engineers, so their designers can finish their work on the flux field portions of the second ship, the components of which are nearly seventy-percent complete. We're confident that the *Isis* will be completed in six months because the bulk of it is from the donor cargo ship. This is, of course, with the exception of the flux-field generators and field guides, and as I said, those are roughly seventy-percent complete. We have every confidence that Samson Industries will come through for us again, as they have so many times before."

Frederick Samson walked the long hall toward his study. The dimly lit corridor was decorated in dark mahogany paneling, and various pieces of art hung in a rigid line traveling down the hall. As he approached the closed double-doors for the study, he stopped, glancing at a painting on the wall beside the doors.

An original Monet, this painting always brought a smile to his face. His father had acquired it at Frederick's request, during the hostile takeover of SPD, a smaller, rival company. It had once hung in the CEO's office as a trophy of his and his company's wealth and power. After the CEO had been killed by a car bomb, the company's stock plummeted. This had opened the company up for a takeover by Samson Industries. This had also caused the government to close contract negotiations with SPD. They were the original company that had been chosen to build the ship for the Osiris project. With the company fighting to regain huge losses in stock price and investor confidence, the government had granted the contract to Samson Industries.

Frederick stood, taking in the thoughtful use of color. Reds, blacks and greens dotted the canvas. The *Garden at Sainte-Adresse* had been painted in 1867, and was one of Claude Monet's earliest works. In the foreground, brightly colored flowers stood in stark contrast to the gray ocean and the muted blue color of the sky. Samson gazed at the large number of ships on the painted horizon.

"Dad," a voice broke his stare. "You got a sec?" Samson turned to see his son, Thomas, walking down the hall toward him.

"I've always got time for you, Thomas," he said, taking one last glance at the painting as he pulled a set of keys from his pocket and unlocked the study doors.

"I wanted to talk to you about something that's bothering me," he said, looking down at his feet.

"Are you still in pain?" Frederick asked, gesturing toward the boy's chest as they entered the study.

The study was filled with dark oak furniture. A large desk sat in the center of the room, surrounded by bookshelves that lined the walls. The only window in the room was flanked by forest green curtains, making the room quite dark. The only other source of light was a small reading lamp sitting on the corner of the desk.

"No, it's not that. I'm fine. As a matter of fact, I'm ready to take this tape off my ribs," he said, rubbing his right side and underarm.

"Now, Thomas, everyone says you need to leave that on for another week. You need to listen to the doctors," Frederick said, sitting behind the desk. "That man hit you very hard, and you need to heal up, properly. I need you one-hundred percent."

"Yes, sir," he surrendered.

Frederick pulled out a small electronic key from his pocket and slid it into a slot on his top desk drawer. He paused, looking at his son.

"So, what's your problem?" His hand still rested on the electronic key, covering the electronic passcode that had already been typed into the small pad on the side.

"Well, it's about your plan."

Frederick released his grip on the key, leaving it sitting in the lock. He had feared that his son would end up losing his nerve and not want to go through with the plan. Frederick closed his eyes and took a deep breath. He slowly exhaled, then opened his eyes and smiled.

"Look, don't worry. We're helping these people. They don't know what they're going to need out there. I do," he said, clapping his hand over Thomas's on the desk. Thomas looked down at their coupled hands glancing at the key sticking out of the lock, and tried to read its code.

"Think about it. I've been to a half dozen colonies, and I've helped to run one of them. I almost became colonial governor of Titan, remember? And Mars before that. These people are going to end up billions of miles away from the Earth, and they'll be cut off from everything!" he said, raising his voice.

Thomas withdrew his hand from beneath his father's and sat down in a chair in front of the desk.

"I know, but don't you think they would have considered everything?" he asked. "I mean, they've done this before."

"They've never done *this* before!" he yelled. "They've built tree-houses before! They've camped out in their parent's backyard before! My god, they've never done anything like this before! They're like children, no, they're worse than children. At least children feel fear and understand their limitations; these people have no idea what they're getting themselves into. What happens if they get out there and find that there is nothing edible on that planet? What happens if they get there, and the water is contaminated with some poison making it undrinkable? Then what are they going to do? They *need* me! I've been working toward this for years!" he said, slamming his fist down on the desk.

The loud bang of Frederick's fist startled Thomas, who recoiled. "I'm sorry," he said. "I was just thinking that they..."

"That was your problem," Frederick cut him off. "You're trying to reason this out logically, but you don't have all the facts here. I do," he said, his voice suddenly calm.

"I'm going to lead these people out of the darkness and into the light. I'll be leading them out of the wilderness, like Moses leading his people. I'll be a king, and you'll be my prince. How does that sound to you; a prince?"

Thomas shrugged.

"Look Thomas, I need you to be a man now. I understand that you're only thirteen years old, but I need you to grow up for me. Part of growing up is knowing and learning as much as you can, but still doing what you're told, even when you think you might know a situation better than your superiors. Just remember, though, you can always tell me when you think you might have a better idea. That's fine. But I need you to do what you're told, no matter what you may think about it."

Thomas looked at him for a moment. "Alright, Dad. I'll do what you need me to. But can you do something for me?" He paused. "Even if I have to be a grown up now, do you think you can call me Tommy? Mom does. So do all my friends."

"Tommy, huh?" he said. "Anything else I can call you?" Frederick asked. Tommy gave him a look of disapproval. "Alright. Tommy it is."

Tommy smiled and got to his feet, his eyes lingering on the key code. Frederick saw him looking, and moved his hand to the key, covering the code.

"Thanks, Dad," Tommy said, turning toward the door.

"Tommy," Frederick called to him. "Think about it, we're going to do something no one else has ever done. We're creating a *civilization*. A new civilization on a new Earth."

Tommy looked at him and nodded.

Chapter Ten

Bad Intentions

Tommy spent the next week wondering what was so important that his father would keep it in his study, which he always kept locked, and in a drawer in his desk that was locked and could only be opened with a digital, encrypted key. He had tried several times to sneak into his father's study, but each time he had either been prevented by the appearance of the maid or his father. His mother rarely set foot in that wing of the house. She had always said it was too dark and dreary for her.

Tommy was awakened by the muffled sound of the small alarm clock he had placed under his pillow. He had put it there so that the chance of anyone else hearing it would be minimized. After silencing the alarm, he pulled it out from under the pillow and placed it on his bedside table. He rubbed his eyes, trying to rid them of the blurry vision his interrupted sleep had left him with.

Swiftly, yet silently, he put on a pair of pajama pants and slippers. He pressed his ear against the common wall between his bedroom and his parents. All he heard was a low rumble of the air conditioning rushing through the ducts in the wall. He paused, listening further, but heard nothing.

In the near-total darkness in his room, he reached under his dresser and pulled out a small white bag. Electronic components banged together, making him stop in his tracks. He paused for a few seconds, listening. Again he heard nothing. Slowly, he crept out the door.

Tommy worked his way down the stairs, and across the family room, all the while rubbing the sleep from his eyes. Moving toward the long hallway that led from the family room to the formal wing of the house, he bumped something in the darkness. Immediately, he knew what it had to be: the oak lamp table and ceramic lamp that sat just inside the family room. Because he was carrying the bag in his left hand, he shot out his right hand to try and keep the lamp from falling. His hand grabbed the edge of the lamp table as it tilted wildly, threatening to drop the lamp on the floor. His eyes were now cleared of the sleepy fog, so he was able to see clearly as lamp teetered on its edge, and fell.

Tommy's left hand was holding the white bag and his right hand was now holding the edge of the table, so with no other option open to him, he stuck out his slipper-covered foot. The ceramic base of the lamp landed on it with a low thump. He gritted his teeth from the pain as the lamp rolled off of his foot and onto the thick carpeting. Tommy quietly placed his bag on the floor. Gingerly, with both hands firmly around the base of the lamp, he lifted it from the floor and placed it back on the table. Letting out a deep sigh, he retrieved his bag, and moved into the hallway.

The hallway was pitch dark, and he found himself feeling his way along the wall until he reached the double doors of the study. He looked back down the hallway into the family room. Pressing the 'illuminate' button on his watch, he realized that what felt like an hour had actually only been three and a half minutes since his alarm had gone off.

Tommy tried the door handle, even though he knew it would be locked. It was, and he shrugged in the darkness. He reached into his bag, withdrew a metal hook fashioned from a piece of heavy wire, and knelt down in front of the door on the right. He knew that he would be unable to pick the lock in the handle of the door on the left, so his only option was to try and open the doors by capitalizing on the weakness of this set of double doors.

Reaching the hook under the right-hand door, he groped in the darkness feeling along the bottom edge of it. As he slid it toward the left, it caught on something. He moved the hook back and forth, trying to hook the bolt on the bottom of the door that slid down into a small slot set into the floor. The hook caught on the latch, and he began to work the hook up and down while wiggling the door. He wiggled the door harder, trying to release the pressure on the latch, making it easier to lift the bolt. With a metallic click, the latch popped free of the slot. Now that the latch that connected the right door to the floor was no longer holding it in place, he just had to push in on the two doors. Even though the doorknob was locked, the bolt that went from it into the door on the left wasn't long enough to prevent you from just pushing the doors open if the floor bolt wasn't pushed down into the slot. He'd discovered this once a year or two ago when their housekeeper hadn't re-latched the bottom, and he'd leaned against the doors inadvertently, pushing them open. Tommy glanced over both shoulders down the hall, and then pushed the doors open.

Now inside the study, he pushed the right door closed, and re-latched the bolt. He then moved quickly to the desk, where he poured out the remaining contents of the bag. Lying on the floor next to the desk were several pieces of electronic equipment and a digital key that was smaller than the one his father had used. The digital key had a long piece of wire with a plug at the end hanging from it.

Tommy stuck the key in the lock in the large desk drawer and plugged the other end of the wire into a small box. On the top of the box was a small display screen. He picked up a numeric keypad and slid the end into a slot on the top of the box, then plugged a battery pack into the box. A series of numbers began to flash across the screen. He pressed a key on the keypad, and a cursor began flashing. Because he had seen the code, he didn't need the decryption system to spend the time it took to decipher it.

Tommy listened to the sounds of the house, making sure he wouldn't be discovered, and then typed in the six-digit code. The screen read: 080126, his birth date. He smiled at the fact that his father had used his birth date as his combination as he pressed the 'star' key on the keypad, and with a click, the drawer was unlocked.

Tommy slid the drawer open, and what he saw made his jaw drop. The shock hit him so hard that he dropped the decryption kit he was holding. It landed with a clatter that jarred him back to reality. He quickly picked it back up and pressed the 'star' key again, re-locking the drawer.

He gathered his things, then quickly went out into the hall and pulled the right-hand door closed behind him, locking himself out of the study. He stuffed the electronics and the hook back into his bag as he stealthily took two stairs at a time. As he got back to his room, he kicked off his slippers. With a start, he nearly dropped his bag on the floor as his alarm began to blare.

Partly because of what he had just seen in his father's study, and partly because of the late hour, his mind was slow in taking in what was happening. He suddenly realized what had happened. He had pressed 'snooze' on the alarm, and not turned it off.

He swung the bag in the direction of his dresser and let it go. It slid across the carpet and under the dresser, slamming into the wall behind it with a thud. He leapt across the room and onto his bed, grabbing the alarm. Turning it off, he quickly stuffed it under his pillow and pulled his covers over his pajama pants, leaving his bare chest exposed.

He closed his eyes just as his bedroom door flew open.

"What's going on in here?" Frederick asked, his hair a mess.

"Wha," Tommy said, pretending to have been asleep. "What? What time is it," he said, sitting up and looking at a clock across the room on his bookshelf. He rubbed his eyes sleepily, then looked over at his father. His heart began to race as he saw the hook lying in the middle of the floor. He glanced over at his dresser and saw that a wire was dangling out from beneath it. *The bag came open!*

Several intense seconds passed while Frederick stared at him. He pretended to be half-asleep, letting his eyes droop and his head bob forward and backward.

"I...I'm sorry. I thought I heard something in here," he said, looking at the items in the floor. "Go back to sleep. And tomorrow you need to clean up in here."

"Alright," he mumbled, rolling over to face away from father and the open bedroom door.

He paused, his eyes swiveling back and forth as he listened. A moment later he heard a low thump as his bedroom door closed. He turned back over, and saw that he was alone.

He sat up, his mind blazing with thought. Why did his dad have them? What could he possibly need them for? In his mind, he still saw the image. The image of the green canisters with the small electronic keypads on them was forever burned into his mind. The wording on the labels that he'd never forget. They read:

GVX High Explosive

Break tab and press

button to activate.

Minimum Safe Distance – 150 meters

Remote Detonation Frequency - 180.24GHz

Property of US Army

Chapter Eleven

Preparations

Working diligently, Derek and JT had nearly finished packing up all the miscellaneous items from JT's house and shop. JT had asked Derek to help him pack and clean the house from top to bottom, since JT had no one he trusted to come in and clean while they were gone. JT had brought out all of his bed sheets to cover the furniture with. They knew that they would find a thick layer of dust when they got back and have to spend a lot of time cleaning again, but for some reason, they thought that they'd cover everything with sheets anyway.

In the shop, they had covered all the major projects with old military parachutes. All the chemical items JT had around the shop, as well as welding gases, were removed and disposed of to reduce the possibility of fire in their absence. The only project that wasn't inside the shop and covered was the Beowulf. The area of the shop once taken up by the helicopter now sat empty, as a group of military logistics officers had come to get it several days ago. Now in its place was a pile of mats Derek had been using for exercise.

When JT had asked him to help clean, Derek had said that he would, but only if JT would help Derek train. Not knowing what he was getting himself into, JT had agreed. After they had done some basic stretching and calisthenics, Derek mentioned CQB. JT began to look very uncomfortable.

CQB stood for close-quarters battle, which could entail anything from hand-to-hand combat, to close-quarters firearm training. In this case, Derek meant hand-to-hand combat training, and JT had lost count of the number of times he had been thrown, flipped, pulled, pushed, and in one case, bitten.

"Are you getting nervous about the trip yet?" Derek asked him, wiping sweat out of his eyes with his sleeve.

Derek and JT moved in a slow circle, sizing each other up. They were both squatting down, their gloved hands up to protect themselves from an attack by the other.

"Not just yet. I think I'll wait until I get in the tube and then I'll throw some kind of fit," JT replied, panting. "One thing I think…"

In one swift motion, Derek quickly stepped in and grabbed JT, and then spun around. JT suddenly found himself hoisted up onto Derek's back.

"This is gonna hurt," JT mumbled.

Almost instantly, the world lurched; with a thud, JT found himself lying on the mat facing up.

"Alright, I'm done," JT said, coughing. He looked up to see Derek reaching to help him to his feet.

As he took Derek's hand, he shot him a smile. Derek's eyes went wide as JT's foot collided with the side of his head. JT's other foot slammed into Derek's stomach, and he was lifted off the floor. Using Derek's own weight, JT pulled with his hand and guided him up and over. Derek found himself flying through the air. He came down on the mat with a thump that knocked the wind out of him. Coughing, he rolled over and looked at JT, who was laughing.

Derek, trying to catch his breath, began to realize that JT had been playing with him. He had been caught by a few punches as well as kicks, but at the time thought they were lucky. He now realized that JT, although a little heavy around the midsection, was still in good shape and very capable of defending himself.

"You old bastard," Derek coughed. "I thought you didn't remember any of this stuff."

"I lied."

Derek walked into the large auditorium to see that most of the seats were already taken. A seat in the back of the auditorium was empty, so he sat down. Glancing around, he saw that many of the people seemed to know one another and were smiling and talking. He looked at the man sitting on his right – an older, gray-haired man who seemed quite bored. He kept yawning and tapping his feet, as though he had somewhere else to be.

"Hi," Derek said to him.

"Hi," the man replied without looking at him.

"You going on this little trip?" Derek asked.

"No," the man said, still not looking at him.

"I am."

"Congratulations," the man said in a monotone, closing his eyes.

Derek turned to the man on his left. He was very small, and couldn't have been much more than three feet tall.

"Hi," Derek said.

"Hello," the man said, in a high-pitched voice that reminded Derek of when people speak after inhaling a lungful of Helium. Derek smiled at the man's voice. The man smiled back, kicking his legs, which were too short to reach the floor. "I haven't seen you around before. I'm Ulrich," he said, extending a stubby hand.

Derek took it, and gave it a light squeeze, afraid of hurting him.

"I'm Derek," he said politely. "Nice to meet you."

"This is simply amazing, isn't it? I've been working on this project for a long time. I don't know much about the parts of the project I haven't worked directly on. I'm really looking forward to hearing the talks I've been invited to attend. You know, government secrets and all."

"Yeah, I understand that all too well since I work for the government."

"Really? Me too. I'm an astrophysicist. What research group are you with?" Ulrich asked.

"Oh, I'm not. I'm a Marine."

Ulrich's smile faltered. "Oh. Don't worry". He smiled again. "I won't hold that against you."

"Thanks!" Derek said with a laugh. "I'm afraid I don't understand any of the physics of this thing. I skimmed through the packet I was given, but that didn't go into much detail."

"Well, unfortunately, most of the details haven't been released yet, but I can share the basics. It's mostly math," Ulrich said.

A man in a dark suit walked onto the stage and stepped in front of the podium.

"Ladies and Gentlemen, attention please. I trust everyone's had their coffee, so we would like you to go ahead and separate into your small groups discussions, which will be starting in a few minutes. Inside your handout are the room assignments where your discussions are to take place. It looks like you've got about fifteen minutes, so please start making your way to your conference rooms. As for those of you meeting in room 422, Doctor Elena Brown, Senior Medical Specialist, will not be with us today, so the mission medical briefing is canceled. You can just mark that off on the list of topics for your meeting. We're basically just moving the schedule up one slot to take the place of Doctor Brown's talk."

"Which room are you in, Ulrich?" Derek asked.

"I'm in *that* room," Ulrich said, pointing at the man who was now walking off the stage. "422, and you?"

"The same. At least we will both know someone there! Looks like we'll also get out early since that Dr. Brown lady didn't show up. I'm just upset that I missed out on the coffee. I didn't get here early enough."

"Yeah, that would be great to get out early," Ulrich said with a smile. "Don't worry about the coffee, though. They'll have some in our conference room, snacks too!"

"You sure are a happy little guy. Uh… I mean, person," Derek said. "I mean," he broke off. "Did I mention that I try to make an ass of myself at least once a day?"

Ulrich laughed. "Don't worry about it. I've heard them all."

They made their way into the conference room, Derek walking slower than normal to allow for Ulrich's short, hobbling stride. Derek couldn't help but notice the people staring down at Ulrich, and then up at him.

After they got to their conference room, they sat down at a large 'U'-shaped table. There were nearly fifty other people in the room, all engrossed in their own conversations.

"So," Derek asked. "Give me the basics here."

"Well, do you know anything about physics?"

"Not really," Derek lied. "Go slow."

"This ship has a drive system that breaks the universal speed limit."

"How can you break a universal limit?"

"TDCs do it all the time. Do you know how trans-dimensional communications systems work?"

"The signal is sent through another dimension, which somehow makes the transmission travel to the receiver faster, right?" Derek asked.

"Exactly. It doesn't take an incredible amount of energy to transmit something like a communications signal, but it's a wave not a particle. It's energy, and energy is relatively easy to work with. Matter is another story.

Derek frowned.

"Okay," Ulrich said. "How about gravity wells? Do you know what those are?"

"Those I know. Anything with mass creates a gravity well. It is what draws an object with smaller mass toward an object with more mass. The larger the mass, the larger the gravity well."

"Right, very good. Well, there has been a lot of research trying to create a ship that could create a massive gravity well, and thereby bend space-time to bring the origin and destination closer together. If you can imagine a sheet of paper with two dots on it, one being Earth, the other being Avalon, that might help you understand. You fold the paper so that the two points come closer together, then the ship moves from the Earth to Avalon. This way, you would only have to move a few feet, but you would travel a million miles. To someone watching, the ship would appear to accelerate and travel at incredible speeds. Rates of acceleration that would kill anyone inside the ship if it were actually traveling at those speeds."

"Wow."

"Don't get too excited. As it turns out, this can be done but we need so much power to do it that it just isn't practical at this point. This is where it gets really complicated. The drive system aboard *Osiris* uses what they call 'flux generators'. Now if you can imagine that same sheet of paper, bent the other direction, so that the two points are on opposite sides of the paper, facing away from each other. Now, what the flux generators do is allow the ship to pass through the paper, thus reaching the destination that way. I haven't seen all the technical details, but it seems that when the flux field is activated, the ship is somehow moved into another universe. You've heard of multiverse? No? Well, there are lots of universes. This much we know. Apparently, this universe either doesn't have the same speed limit we have, or maybe the distance between objects is smaller, I don't really know. This allows the ship to move incredibly large distances over a short period of time without the increasing mass becoming a problem."

Derek stared at him for a moment, and opened his mouth to speak, but no words came out.

"I guess a better way of looking at it is, say, an onion. It has lots of layers. Our universe is the outermost layer...or an inner layer. Anyway, we now have technology that can pierce that layer and move into the subsequent ones, each one being smaller. When we send trans-dimensional communications, we send the signal way down into the onion, where it's bounced back to the receiver. It's a bit more complicated than that, but you get the idea. It turns out that by going further into the onion, the distance is less than traveling around the outside of the onion. Now keep in mind that this is a simplified interpretation of the information, as it's all math, as I said. And, I still don't know anything about this 'flux field'. Like I said, government secrets. You know? I'll know more soon, once I get the complete documentation." He smiled.

"One thing to remember, though, is that during the early trials, they used the flux-field generators to push several test craft out of 'normal' space, and they were never able to retrieve them. It seems that if matter completely leaves our universe, you can't get it back. At least not remotely, anyway."

Derek frowned for a moment, then asked, "If that's true, how does this ship work?"

"This is where it gets really weird. From what I'm told, not all of the ship's mass will be pushed out of normal space. About a millionth of a percent will be still in our space. This way, when the field generators are shut down, the matter will return to our space. Even that miniscule amount of mass acts like an anchor in our universe."

"God, I sure hope it works," Derek said with a laugh.

"Me, too," Ulrich said. "I'd hate to end up in another universe. I just found a great apartment!"

"You're going too?"

"Sure. I wouldn't miss this for anything. Honestly, my apartment isn't that great," Ulrich said with a smile. Just the chance of seeing a place as beautiful as Avalon is supposed to be worth any price. I told the project director I'd do anything to get a chance to go, so he pulled some strings to get me assigned. I'm a VIP," he said, drumming his fingers on his tiny chest.

"Well," Derek said extending his hand downward. "Welcome aboard."

After nearly three hours of small group discussions and seminars, the meeting was adjourned, and Derek headed back to JT's. Derek and JT sat and stared at the house, filled with ghostly furniture covered in white bed sheets. They went out for a nice dinner and talked about their plans for the future.

"When we get back…" Derek paused. "I think I'm going to turn in my DD-214 and get out of the service."

With a smile, JT said, "I think that's a right good plan. What do you think you'll do for a job?"

"I'm taking all of mom's old books with me so I can do some studying. I have some of my books too. That way I can get caught back up and I can look for a biochemistry job. It'll be a little work, but I've got a whole year to do it, and the colony will have state of the art prefabricated facilities I can use to do some studying. They're going to be doing a ton of research, so I'll just have to ask nicely, and stay out of their way."

JT smiled at him and said, "I think that's a good decision for you." His smile faded as he began to look around the restaurant.

"What?" Derek asked, looking around as well.

"I'm thinking about closing my shop. I'm kinda tired of workin' for myself. Having to worry about every little thing. I just need some piddly job that pays the bills. I should get a job at a shop somewhere, workin' for some young buck like you!"

"You never could take orders from anyone, what makes you think you could do it now…" he paused for effect. "At your age."

"Eh, I don't know. I'm just tired of the monotony of it all. I go from one project to another, worryin' whether or not the rich schmuck will change his mind when I come to deliver and collect my fee. I'm too old for that stress."

"You're not as old as you're acting, young man! You should think hard about it before you do something rash."

"Yes sir," JT said with a smile and a half-assed salute.

The small Vertical Take-Off and Landing, or VTOL, transport dropped out of the clouds and with a cloud of choking dust, landed on the street in front of JT's house.

"Well, I guess this is it," JT said.

"Have you got all your things?" Derek asked him.

"Yeah, they took them up to the cargo lander this morning. All I need is what I'm wearin'."

"Yeah, my stuff is at the house. Because I wasn't originally slated to go, there wasn't room in the regular military landers. They're putting it in a different one. Somebody's supposed to come get it shortly before my transport comes to pick me up."

"Which passenger lander you in?"

"Uh, I'm in 'H'," Derek said, looking at the slip of paper in his palm. "I go up tomorrow."

"I'm in 'F'. Seems I got lucky and got a spot that opened up for me on one of the earlier landers that are gettin' filled up," JT said, an obviously fake smile on his face.

"Look, I'll see you in six months. Don't worry, it'll only seem like a couple of hours," Derek assured him. "Try not to let the dreams get you."

"I don't have no problem with a little hibernation. Bears used to do it all the time!"

Derek gave JT a hug, and then watched as he climbed into the VTOL and the doors closed behind him. The blast of wind and gritty, needle-like bits of sand made Derek cover his face as the transport lifted off. It zoomed up through the clouds and out of sight. Derek stared at the cloud where the transport had vanished, took a deep breath, and then exhaled loudly.

Chapter Twelve

Osiris

Derek spent the evening second-guessing the items he'd packed for the trip. There were so many crates and boxes that he was afraid some might be jettisoned into space because he had packed too much. He'd opened and re-taped several boxes during his search for something he could leave behind.

Lying on his kitchen counter was an envelope that contained information for Mannie. Included was the information for a bank account that Derek had opened in Mannie's name. He had set up an automatic monthly transfer from his account to Mannie's and had included this information in a letter. Also included was a note that a friend of Derek's would be by to check on the house to make sure Mannie was doing his 'duty' in keeping it clean and keeping the plants watered. Derek had no intention of having anyone keep tabs on Mannie, but he wanted to make sure that he would actually continue to keep working hard even though the money was guaranteed every month.

Derek re-checked several times before he finally decided to go to bed. That night he tossed and turned, not getting any real sleep at all. He pondered what he would see when he stepped out of the lander. He would be in the first group of people to actually walk on the planet because he was the commander of the marines in the group, and they had to make sure there were no hostile animals that could threaten the safety of the colony. He and his men would have to scout the surrounding area and make a threat assessment for the colonial mayor, who would also be in the initial group who set foot on Avalon. Part of him was slightly worried about the fallibility of their scanning equipment.

The primary sensor they would be using was a hand-held device that scanned for body heat and high concentrations of carbon dioxide. These things were common to animals and people on Earth, but how did anyone know if the creatures they would find on Avalon had similar metabolic processes and could be tracked by the sensors? The scientists back home had some basic data on the planet, but there were a lot of unknowns.

He finally got back out of bed at 5:30, knowing that the truck would arrive for his things in about three hours, followed shortly by his transport to the ship. He tried to go about his usual morning routine but got increasingly frustrated, as nearly everything he needed was already packed. He opened a small bathroom cabinet to retrieve his deodorant, only to remember that it too was packed.

Why the hell am I so screwed up? This is no different than any other mission I've been on. Oh well, I'm going to be frozen. It's not like I'll see anyone in my tube with me! I'll just put deodorant on when we get there, he thought to himself.

Derek ate a breakfast of whatever he could find in the pantry. He had disposed of everything that was perishable, including the condiments in his refrigerator, so he had been forced to eat a small can of beans and a large can of mixed vegetables. He had just washed his dishes and put them away when the VTOL truck arrived, landing in the street beside his house in a storm of wind and dust.

The truck that had been sent to retrieve Derek's belongings consisted of a pod-like cab in front of a flat section on which sat a large cargo container. As Derek walked out toward the road, he saw the truck's built in crane unload the container, placing it on the ground beside the truck. A burly man with a thick neck got out of passenger side and opened the container doors revealing a web of cargo netting. The man stepped inside the container and disappeared into the webbing.

The container was a larger size than he'd expected. Apparently, many of the colonists had packed quite a bit more of their things than Derek had. Derek, on the other hand, had taken all of his necessities, but very few niceties. He had packed all of his fatigues, which included urban, jungle, desert, arctic, and savannah patterns, as well as a low-light, night-vision invisible pattern. He had also packed one formal dress uniform, just in case. Several of his boxes were filled with books, and one box contained assorted electronic items, such as his personal computer, and some of his military electronics gear.

The driver of the truck got out and approached Derek.

"You all ready to go?" he said in a low voice.

"Yes, sir. I have all my things in here, follow me."

The burly man stepped out of the container, and ran up beside the driver. The two men followed Derek into the house, where he showed them the stack of boxes and crates in the middle of the living room floor. The men began carrying them out and stacking them in the netting.

"Oh, just a second," Derek said, running to his bedroom. One of the two men let out a low growl.

Derek came back into the room carrying the paper bag he'd gotten at the antique store. "I almost forgot this," he said, smiling. He opened the box containing the electronic gear, and gingerly placed the heavy bag on top. "There you go, all finished."

The two men gathered the remaining boxes, and carried them out to the truck. Derek followed them, still amazed at the size of the truck and container.

"There must be a lot of crap if everyone is using one of these carriers!" Derek said.

"There are only a few this size," the burly man said. "Most everyone got the small size.

Derek frowned. "What do you mean?"

"You're on the VIP list," the truck driver said. "Means you get special treatment. They apparently have a larger dormitory for you when you reach your destination, also."

Derek didn't really know what this meant, but he knew that he wouldn't be able to find out all the details until they were on Avalon, so he dismissed the questions that had popped into his head. "Okay," he said blankly.

The two men tied down the boxes and closed the webbing tightly. They closed the large door, and Derek saw that his name was stenciled on the outside of the crate. It read: Cross, Derek E. Admin. H404.

What the hell is Admin H404?

The driver got back into the cab, and began pressing buttons on a small panel. The crane lifted the crate high into the air, and Derek heard a woman's voice inside the cab say, 'Tare weight, six-hundred eighty five pounds'. Derek saw the driver typing in the numbers on a small pad in his lap. The crane then moved the container back over the flat section of the truck, and dropped it with a thud that made Derek cringe. The arm of the crane came down across the top of the container, holding it in place.

"Have a nice trip," the burly man said, climbing into the cab.

Before Derek could answer, the engines started and he was pelted with bits of flying dust and debris. He stepped back and the truck lifted off, moving straight up. After several minutes, the truck disappeared into the deep blue of the sky.

Frederick Samson shook hands with the chubby engineer, his toothy smile blazing.

"So Tong, you lost the chip, huh?" Frederick asked. Tong shrugged. "Well, I won't hold that against you. Here," he said, handing him a chip. "This is a copy of the original one I gave you.

A middle-aged, balding man came sprinting down the hallway, his pale face glistening with sweat. Just as he reached Frederick and Tong, all hell broke loose.

Red lights began flashing, and alarms started wailing. People began pouring out of every visible doorway, moving in all directions.

"Mr. Samson," the man panted. "There's been an explosion!"

"What?" Frederick said, grabbing his shoulder tightly.

"The factory, it…it's gone!" he said, wiping the sweat from his eyes.

"What do you mean, it's gone? What the hell happened?"

"A bomb of some kind. There are emergency crews there on the scene right now!"

"Oh my god, my wife and my father were both there working."

"I'm sorry, Mister Samson, the emergency crews said that they aren't expecting many survivors. They think it was a big bomb, or a number of smaller ones!"

"Oh god!" Tong said. "We've got to stop the launch!"

Panic took hold of Frederick. He squeezed the bald man's shoulder so tight that the man squinted in pain. He grabbed Tong with his free hand and guided them both against the wall to avoid the people who were moving quickly up and down the hall.

"No! We can't stop the launch!" he hissed. "That's probably what these bastards want! They want to scare us, so that we delay or even cancel the launch. We can't give in to them!"

"But your wife, your dad!" Tong said.

"They both knew what we were working on, and they knew the risks. They knew that if there were any security leaks and anyone found out about what we were doing, some other governments would have a big problem with it," Frederick said in a hushed tone. "This launch will go on time, alright?" The two men nodded, blank looks on their faces. "Now, I've got to go down to the factory. Maybe there's something I can do."

Frederick released his grip on the two men, and both of them made their way through the steady stream of people. Frederick watched them as they moved slowly away from him through the crowd. Things were progressing according to plan.

"I'm hungry," Samson said, a blank expression on his face. "How about I go get some lunch?"

Derek had just sat down in a chair in the living room when he heard a horn outside. He rose, and went to the window. Looking outside, he saw an old transport similar to the one that JT drove.

Well, I guess they spent the money on cargo shipping not my cab ride!

Derek closed and locked his door and took one last long look at his house. He had spent a lot of time working on his garden, and he was happy with his own little forest. He had spent many evenings in the spring and fall sitting in the garden reading, and he hoped it would still look this way when he got back.

The cab drove along the city streets until it got outside of town and moved onto the Skyway. The rear thrusters kicked in, pressing Derek back in his seat. A few seconds later the road ahead was no longer visible in the front window, and he couldn't feel the bumps in the road any more. Derek's body felt very heavy, pulled downward when the nose of the cab pulled up, and he knew they were becoming vertical. He sat, pushed back into his seat, for nearly five minutes; then he noticed the blue sky gradually darkening, and pinpricks of light began to twinkle as he left the atmosphere and entered space. The sky went completely black, and Derek began to see various space vehicles moving here and there, the purple glow of plasma emanating from the thrusters. He saw several vehicles start to glow orange as they dropped into the upper atmosphere.

A few minutes later, Derek saw the Navy shipyard in the front window. All around it was the usual flurry of activity. Derek was surprised that he didn't immediately see the ship. He continued to look over the driver's shoulder, but all he could see from this distance were several dozen ships in their dry-dock cages, each in various stages of completion or refit.

Once they entered the area of space designated as the shipyard, Derek noticed a massive congregation of large navy ships a few kilometers past the first grouping of dry-dock cages. There were several of the large carriers, at least twenty cruisers, and more destroyers than Derek had ever seen in one place.

Jesus, this must be the entire fleet, Derek thought to himself.

The cab moved toward the large mass of ships and headed through a small opening between the *USS Joseph Barnes* and the *USS William Harrison*, two of the new fast attack carriers. They weaved slowly around the hulls of the two ships, so close that Derek could peer into the portholes and see several people working. As the massive bulk of the carriers slid by, Derek began to make out the aft section of a ship.

"It must be behind that big cargo ship." Derek said.

The ship that had emerged was one of the largest cargo ships currently in use. It was longer than the two fast attack carriers end-to-end, and at least three times as wide. To gauge the scale, Derek looked back at the *Joseph Barnes* and realized that all these navy ships, along with the dry-dock cages, seemed to be blocking it from view from all sides. He looked back, just in time to see letters five stories high on the thruster section of the ship. The bright yellow letters read: 'Osiris'.

"Oh, wait, I guess that's it. It's a little different seeing it on paper." The driver ignored him.

They made a wide circle under the belly of the pod-studded central section. They worked their way down the length of the ship until they reached the small fore section. The cab slowed, and Derek saw their destination. Cut into the side of the spherical pod was a small shuttle bay. Derek felt a lurch as the cab slowed suddenly and then felt as it slowly thrust forward, into the bay. Silently, the bay door closed behind them. Derek saw two large red lights illuminate as they came to a stop. These informed them that the bay was not yet equalized to normal atmospheric pressure. After about a minute, the lights went out, and two green ones lit up. A small sign on the wall in front of the cab showed the words, 'Artificial Gravity Enabled'.

Derek got out of the cab and was immediately met by an older Indian woman wearing a gray jumpsuit.

"Right this way."

He followed her down the central corridor until they came to a hatch with a large 'H' painted on it. She pressed a button beside the door, and a moment later it slid open.

They stepped into an airlock, the door behind them closed, and she pressed a button similar to the one on the outside. The next door opened with a hiss.

"Wait in here for the others, and we'll be with you as soon as we're ready," she said with a smile. "Don't go wandering around; some of the ship doesn't have artificial gravity." She turned and walked back out of the bay.

Derek looked around the bay and saw that there were no other people waiting. He found that he was in the lowest level of a cylindrical seven-story lander. The top five levels contained ten cryo-stasis chambers and the large pieces of equipment that ran them.

Around the outer edge of this level, against the wall, was a series of large metal structures with pipes and wires running between them and around the pod. He knew from the diagrams he'd seen that these were the thrusters the pod would use during descent. He glanced up at the second level and resting just above where the thrusters were on the first level, were the large tanks that held the solid fuel.

Each thruster had its own fuel supply. This was a safety measure to prevent a disaster in case there was a problem during the descent. One problem the designers worried about was a fuel tank rupture inside the pod, or a rupture inside the thruster itself. This way, only the fuel from one thruster would be lost, not the entire fuel supply. The lander could safely descend with up to four of its ten thrusters non-operational.

The fuel used was a powdered solid that was fed into the thruster. The thruster then created an ionized plasma from the solid, which created pressure inside the bell of the thruster, creating the lift. The powder itself was non-flammable and non-toxic, which made it an ideal propellant.

Derek looked up to the third level and noticed that the cryo-stasis chambers were mounted directly above the fuel cells. His eyes followed the chambers up to the fourth level. Derek thought that the inside of the lander was oddly symmetrical. The lines of mechanical and electronic equipment seemed to reach into infinity. This was partially because the top levels of the pod were poorly lit, making each successive level darker. It appeared almost as though there was an eighth level above the seventh somewhere in the darkness, but Derek knew there wasn't.

The opening of the hatch startled Derek. A large group of people came in, guided by a different person than the one who had brought him in. Several members of the group seemed to know each other, as they were talking and smiling. None of them seemed as impressed with the layout of the pod as Derek was.

Derek saw Ulrich McElroy hobble in. Ulrich peered around the leg of an Asian woman and gave Derek a wave and a smile. Derek couldn't help but smile, thinking how childlike he looked and acted.

The group assembled in the bay included people of every imaginable description, men and women of widely varying ages. One couple even looked to be in their sixties. Ulrich McElroy stood just over three-feet tall, while one woman was a head taller than Derek and must have been close to seven feet tall. The most unusual member of the group, Derek thought, was a tall redheaded man, who from the looks of him must have been a coal miner. He appeared to have just come out of a coal mine, and was wearing blue jeans and a white shirt, both covered in black sooty dirt.

A gangly doctor walked into the bay carrying a small, blue plastic basket. Her blond hair bounced on the shoulders of her white lab coat as she walked. She stepped up to a steel control panel and quickly flipped the basket upside-down, leaving its contents in a neat, square pile. The pile, composed of small, white boxes, looked like a tiny building made of white bricks. She set the basket on the floor and stepped up onto it, making herself tall enough to be visible to people in the back.

"Listen up," she said, looking at the bottle in her hand.

The murmur died down as all eyes began fixing on her.

"I'm Doctor Elena Brown. I'm the mission's Senior Medical Officer. The people circulating throughout the bay are my staff. They will be walking you to your beds and giving you two injections." She stared at the bottle's label, not making eye contact with anyone. "If you have any medical questions or concerns, please direct them to me, not the staff. They're just here to administer the injections for me."

People began looking around at each other. A low murmur erupted from the crowd.

"The first injection is MATH. And no, it won't make you smarter," she said sarcastically. "MATH stands for Methoxy-Acyl-Thyroxine-Hemihydrate. The second injection is a solution containing Calcium Chloride, insulin, and a few other components. They're what makes this little nap of ours possible," she said looking up from the bottle.

"I don't understand," a man in a maintenance worker's uniform said.

Derek turned to see where the voice came from.

"You see," she exhaled loudly. "The problem with cryo systems is that when the body is reduced in temperature the cells freeze solid and crystals form. These crystals cause the cells to rupture and die. A way has been found to prevent this. If cells are saturated with sugar, this keeps the crystals from forming when we flash-freeze the sleepers," she said obviously annoyed at the question.

"So why the injections?" an Asian woman in the front asked.

"We'll be giving you an intravenous sugar solution called a cryo-protectant. If we didn't give you these injections, you'd go into shock and a coma, and possibly die, just like a diabetic goes into shock if their blood sugar gets too high. The calcium injection forces the sugar into your cells, and the insulin and other components prevent any sugar that doesn't go into the cells from causing any problems. Got it?" she asked.

"What is the MATH for?" a woman in blue coveralls asked.

"To prevent freezer burn," she said rolling her eyes. The crowd began to laugh.

"Enough questions. The technicians have a lot of injections to give in this bay, and we don't have time to waste. We've got a lot more people to see after we're finished here. Make sure you have your identification ready. We don't want anyone to get the wrong injections. The amount of each injection is tailored to you based on your body weight."

She stepped down from the basket, picked up the white boxes from the table, and tossed them into the basket. She then set the basket on the table, then looked at her watch. A member of her medical staff walked over to her and handed her two bottles. She read the labels to herself and then called out the name printed on them. A bald man stepped out from the crowd to receive his injections.

"Derek Cross," came a woman's voice from behind him.

"That's me," he called out looking around, not knowing which direction the voice came from. A tall, slender black woman approached him carrying a white box in one hand, and a handheld pneumatic injector in the other. She checked his identification card, and loaded the first bottle.

Derek looked across the bay and saw Ulrich pacing back and forth, waiting for his name to be called. The people around him, who were also waiting, were watching Ulrich closely.

"Which arm do you want it in?" she asked him.

"Left, please - I'm right handed," he said, turning his left side to her.

"With the pneumatic injector it won't really matter which arm you get it in, you probably won't be sore. But I'll give it to you in the left arm anyway. Lift your sleeve please," she requested.

He tried to pull up his sleeve, but because of its fit, he couldn't pull it up far enough to expose the muscle of his shoulder.

"You'll have to take off your shirt," she said.

He stared at her for an uncomfortable moment, then reluctantly untucked and began removing his shirt. He pulled his left arm out of his shirt while still wearing it around his neck and right arm.

"Jesus!" she said loudly. Several people turned to look at them. "What happened to you?" she asked, looking at the fresh, bright pink scars on his upper back and chest.

"Nothing," he said under his breath. "Just take me to my bed and give me the shots." He looked around and saw that many of the people close by were now watching them closely.

"Is there a problem here, Amanda?" Dr. Brown asked as she walked up.

"No, uh, doc. I, uh," she stammered, glancing back at Derek's scars.

"Start on the next row, I'll get this one." Dr. Brown said, swapping injectors with her.

"That's a pretty hickey you've got there. Been to the red light district, I see," she said smiling. She placed the injector to his arm.

"No, nothing like that," he said with a slight smile. "Occupational hazard."

With a snap that made him blink, the solution of MATH was injected into his arm. Derek glanced at Dr. Brown's face to see her give him a once-over, raking him from the tips of his toes to his eyes. When she saw him looking, she quickly looked back down at the things she was holding.

"Well, that's one occupation I think I'll steer clear of. What occupation might that be?"

"I'm part of the military contingent," he told her.

"Derek Cross, that name sounds familiar," she said, pulling the empty bottle out of the injector. As she read the label, her eyebrows went up.

"Major Derek Cross?" she asked. He nodded.

"You missed the first briefing...sir," she said in an accusing tone, loading the second bottle.

"And you missed the second," he said, turning away from her and looking up at the stasis chambers. He turned back to her and saw that she was ready to give him his second injection.

"At least you don't use needles anymore. God, I hate needles!" he said changing the subject.

"Actually, we do use needles," she said, a big smile on her face that told Derek she was obviously happy to be telling him. "We have to give the sleepers an infusion bag of sugar solution. Because of the large volume, we have to use an IV needle. It goes into the axillary artery under the arm. Don't worry, you'll be asleep shortly after we give you the sugar, so it won't bother you for long."

"That makes me feel better. The sooner I'm down, the better."

"You don't sound like most of these people. A lot of this batch are farmers and other laborers. They're really afraid. As a matter of fact, in the last compartment, I had to sedate one woman. Imagine that, sedating someone before you put them to sleep!" She laughed.

"I've done this a few times. It doesn't really bother me that much. I can deal with one needle, even if it is a big IV needle. I just can't do a bunch of shots in a row with needles. They give me the willies."

"Hey, why are you with this group, and not in the lander with the other soldiers or the one with the Administrators?"

"I wasn't, um, available for the initial briefing so I wasn't ready to go with the troops when they came up."

"Unavailable?" she asked with one eyebrow raised.

"It's a long story and we haven't the time right now, have we?"

"Right. You are in tube…" she read the label on his bottle. "404. Right up there," she said, pointing up toward the chambers on the middle level of the lander.

They walked side-by-side up the metal stairs, their feet clanking as they went. The clatter of the group below seemed to get louder as they got above it. Derek stepped in front of her to be out of the way as another doctor came down the stairs from the second level.

"There we go," he said turning back to her. "Right there."

They walked down the raised walkway to the fourth tube, which looked like a household upright freezer except for its large size and the fact that the door of the chamber was clear. Dr. Brown slid her ID badge through a slot on the side, and a green light beside the slot began to flash. Derek stepped over and slid his card as though she had asked him to. He knew this routine. He had done this a handful of times when he'd gone on long trips for Temporary Duty.

With a hiss of compressed helium, the door slid open. A wash of cold mist blew into his face and stung his lungs as he breathed it in.

A wry smile came over her lips as she stood behind him. She quickly extinguished it, and cleared her throat.

"I'll need your clothes," she said, her tone matter of fact. Derek whipped his head around to her.

"No sleeper-suits?" he asked, sounding shocked.

"Nope, too expensive. The people who write the checks thought to cut corners everywhere they could. This was one of many examples of cost cutting. Now come on, I'm a doctor. You don't have anything I haven't seen before, and we don't want those clothes freezing to your skin. I'd hate to have to use a scalpel to get them off when we thaw you out."

"That makes two of us."

The inside of the chamber, cooled to two-hundred seventy degrees below zero, began to crackle as a layer of ice formed on the insides of the chamber and cracked from the extreme difference in temperature between the inside of the chamber and the air temperature in the ship.

Derek reluctantly handed her his shirt, followed by his shoes. Looking over his shoulder, he saw that around the large chamber several other people were in various stages of stripping.

"Hell, if everyone's doing it..." Derek said, unzipping his pants.

Dr. Brown suddenly found herself embarrassed, which caught her off-guard. She looked away pretending as though she were looking for something in particular. She hadn't been embarrassed by a man undressing in front of her in a long time. Her attention was suddenly brought back to Derek as his pants hit her across the chest.

"Sorry. I thought you were looking," he said smiling.

"Nice shot," she mumbled, picking up the pants. "You can keep the underwear on."

Derek thought he detected an air of disappointment in her voice and suppressed a smile.

"What about thawing and scalpels? No way I want a scalpel anywhere down there."

"Don't worry. You'll be fine 'down there'".

"What about the socks? My feet are a little cold."

"They're going to get a lot colder!" she said sarcastically. "I'll let you decide. If your feet sweat, and your socks are even slightly wet, you need to take them off."

"I think I'll be okay."

Dr. Brown gave him a questioning look.

"I'll be fine. I have dry feet," Derek said as he stepped up to the open door, his hands crossed in front of his crotch.

"Step inside please."

She reached down beside the chamber and picked up a large plastic fluid-filled bag. Dangling from the bag was a length of tubing, at the end of which was a large needle.

"I'll need your arm," she said, looking down at his hands.

Derek's face took on a pink tinge as he presented her with his left arm. He briefly looked at her face and noticed a light pink in her cheeks as well.

"The cold in here is giving us both rosy cheeks," Derek lied. Dr. Brown smiled very slightly.

"Don't worry, the needle will retract inside the tubing once the end of the tube is in the artery. It'll only hurt for a couple of seconds."

She held his left arm above his head, and thumped along the large artery that ran under it. The vein grew larger and more visible.

The sharp pain and cold of the needle caught Derek by surprise. Derek got the impression that Dr. Brown hadn't tried to lessen the pain at all. If anything, he felt as though she were purposely being rough with him.

Almost immediately, the cold of the needle was gone, and the pain was receding.

"This will only take a minute or two," Dr. Brown said, hanging the bag on a small hook in the top of the chamber. She grabbed the bag with both hands and squeezed it, gritting her teeth. Derek felt his heart begin to beat faster. He knew this was a normal response to the flood he knew was entering his veins. She squeezed again, this time harder than she had before. The bag was now half empty, so she unhooked it and rolled the top of the bag down, like a tube of toothpaste. She squeezed the bag again, nearly emptying it.

"Are you feeling alright?" she asked.

"Roger. I mean, yes ma'am," he said, trying to get a rise out of her. "A little light-headed, but that's normal, right?" he asked, his voice slightly higher than normal; a side-effect of the helium gas in the chamber.

Dr. Brown rolled up the last bit of the bag and squeezed out its contents. She yanked the end of the tube out of Derek's underarm and placed a square patch of cotton on the small wound.

"We just have to wait a few minutes for the infusion to circulate throughout the body. You'll be underway in about ten minutes." She reached around him and tightened a thick, black strap across his waist, pulling him against the cold rear of the chamber.

She placed the pneumatic injector against his arm, and with a loud bang, the solution of calcium chloride and insulin was injected into his arm. Almost instantly his light-headedness faded. He watched as she gathered up his clothes and opened a small compartment beside his chamber. She tossed them into the compartment in a twisted wad of pant legs and shirtsleeves.

Derek began to shiver slightly. The cold mist from the chamber had stopped stinging his skin and lungs, but he knew he was cooling down. He reached up, and with a shivering hand wrote the words 'Derek Cross was here' backwards in the thin layer of ice that had formed on the inside of the door so that it was readable from outside.

He began to shiver thunderously and he gritted his teeth hard to keep them from chattering. All the muscles in his body flexed and fought, trying to generate heat in order to maintain his body temperature. He felt the cold mist of liquid helium continue to rain down on him. He felt as though his muscles would flex so hard they'd rip, when he suddenly relaxed. As if he'd walked out of the chamber and warmed up, he stopped shivering. His body felt very stiff, similar to how he felt when he had first gotten out of his hospital bed, only much worse. He knew this was a normal effect of hypothermia, but it offered him no comfort. He faintly remembered this feeling from the last time he'd been frozen but couldn't remember when that was.

His mind, too, seemed to be freezing, beginning to slow down. Memories and thoughts became clouded in a haze of cold. He moved his hand, but the impulse took an eternity to reach his hand, and by the time it got there he'd forgotten why he was moving it. He looked forward and saw a woman moving toward him so quickly that his eyes were having trouble following her. She was holding something long and white in her hands. *Wires.* She moved around his face and head, then down to his chest. She turned and walked away. He could feel something touching his head and chest, someone pressing something onto them. *Medical monitors.*

He watched as the clear glass door swung closed without a sound. There was something written in the ice that had formed on the door, but he was unable to read it. A large section of the door was not covered by the ice so he could still see out. He watched as the woman moved back and forth, moving too fast for him to keep up with. In his ears, he heard the sound of a door closing, and a hiss of air.

Something began falling past his eyes. Small round spheres moved past him, creating a dense fog inside the chamber. The rain continued falling, increasing in intensity until he could no longer see anything but the rain and fog. The fog grew more and more dense, a blackness forming somewhere out of sight. The darkness grew until it enveloped him completely.

Dr. Brown looked back at chamber 404. The medical monitor she had attached to him was sending information the small receiver she was holding. A small display on the unit showed the status of the sleeper. The chamber had just finished the flash-freeze using a heavy rain of liquid helium, and the soldier was in perfect hibernation. She placed the monitor in a small cradle beside the chamber door and glanced at the words written in the ice.

"Murderer," she mumbled as she turned and walked away.

Chapter Thirteen

The Journey

Elena Brown walked into the large stateroom and dropped her bag on the bed. If this section of ship had been in use on a transport as it was intended, this room would be the captain's quarters. She had decided to take it since it was the largest and most comfortable, and there was no one else on board who could object. Everyone else was an ice cube.

She sat down beside her bag, took off her shoes, and looked around the room. She took a deep breath and sighed loudly. There were several towers of boxes in one corner and a massive pile of books on the desk. The rest of the cabin was a clean slate for her to do with as she pleased.

The cabin was a rectangular room around twenty feet long by fifteen feet deep. One corner of the room had been walled in, making a bathroom complete with a toilet, sink, and shower. The living space housed a small closet, dresser, double bed, and a large entertainment unit that consisted of a video screen, media player, and two large speakers mounted in the wall above the video screen. There was also a desk, desk chair, and a file cabinet. Sitting on the desk was a computer terminal.

"You're in this for the long haul," she said aloud.

She stood up and took off her shirt, and tossed it into the corner of the room.

"Bad habit to get into," she mumbled. "What if someone drops by unannounced!"

She picked up the shirt, folded it haphazardly, and placed it on top of the dresser. Reaching into her bag, she withdrew a well-worn pair of gym shorts and a t-shirt. A few minutes later, she was dressed more comfortably, and her slacks were now folded beside her shirt on the dresser.

After she had unpacked her bag, she made her way down through the dimly lit decks of the ship, finally arriving at the bridge. She sidestepped several control consoles and looked out the front window at the mass of ships visible from the bridge. She stepped back and sat down in the captain's chair.

"Comm."

A light, airy tone rang across the bridge, indicating that the ship's communications system was active and transmitting.

"Dr. Elena Brown here. I'm settled in and ready to go."

"Dr. Brown, this is mission control. We're activating the ship's systems, stand by." There was a brief pause, and then she felt a light shudder in the deck of the ship. "Osiris, you are go. Prepare for flux, over."

"Uh, control? Do I need to strap in or anything?" she asked.

"Osiris, this is control. Negative. You'll feel some moderate acceleration, but that'll gradually decrease as you get up to speed. As long as you're seated, you'll be fine. Over."

"Thanks control, I..." she stopped. The other ships that were visible outside the window began to glow a deep blue. Looking around the fleet she noticed through a gap between two ships that even the stars were blue. Panicked, she ran to a large control panel and started pressing buttons. With a light hum, massive steel covers began sliding down over the window. She watched impatiently as the covers finally slammed shut, darkening the bridge.

"Lights."

The bridge was bathed in a cool, white light.

"Osiris, this is control again. Have a nice trip. Your relief will be along in about eighteen months."

"Thank you control, Osiris out. Comm. Off."

The outside of the ship glowed a deep blue that seemed to ripple from the rear of the ship toward the front, as if the ship was being bathed in a deep blue liquid. The main drives came online, blasting the ships behind it in a brilliant, shimmering silver glow. Several thousand crewmen aboard the ships watched as the *Osiris* began to fade, as if someone were dimming the light from the sun. The only things that didn't begin to darken were the plasma flares that emanated from the ship's drives. The ship continued to fade until it was barely visible. The *Osiris* began to move slowly forward toward the two large ships that blocked its way. The two ships didn't move. The *Osiris* continued to move forward until its nose passed completely through the hulls of the others. Like a ghost, the nearly invisible ship slid through, its speed slowly increasing as it went. The glowing tail of the ship moved into, through, and then out the other side of the ships as it continued to fade. Slowly, it disappeared completely.

Elena felt the ship accelerating. She felt it lightly pushing her into the seat. Suddenly, the speed began to increase at a dramatic rate, pressing her into the thick foam that cradled her body. The pull became so intense that her long blond hair was streaming straight backward behind her, around the sides of the headrest. She clenched the armrest with her right hand and squeezed a tight fist with her left. She found it increasingly difficult to breathe, as her chest was being compressed toward her back. The pain was becoming intense. Her left hand, which wasn't clamped around the armrest, slowly moved up despite all her efforts to stop it. Her clenched fist came to rest on the side of the chair next to her shoulder.

"God," she gasped. "Why couldn't I have been an 'A' cup," she groaned, feeling the magnified weight of her breasts trying to crush her ribcage.

She felt the pain grow so intense that she started screaming. She felt the warmth of tears streaming from her eyes, bathing her temples and wetting her hair.

Almost as suddenly as it had begun, she felt the pain start to diminish. With the pull against her slowly subsiding, she fought to retrieve her hand from the side of the chair. She pulled against the inertia and pressed her hand back down on the armrest, gripping it tightly. The grip of the foam in the chair relented as the pressure continued to weaken.

Using her neck muscles, and with incredible effort, she pulled against the force bearing down on her and drew her head away from the headrest. She let her head slap back into the cup it had made in the headrest. After a few more seconds, she tried again. This time, she was able to pull her head out with a little less effort. She lifted her arms, feeling their amplified, yet manageable weight. Leaning forward against the pull, she was able to push away from the seatback and stand up.

Suddenly the pull was gone, and she was thrown to the deck in front of the chair. For a moment, she lay on the floor, dazed. She curled up into a ball and began to sob from the pain. After the pain subsided, she stood up and looked around, trying to straighten her hair. She brushed the newly formed wrinkles in her t-shirt in a futile attempt to smooth them out. Wiping her tears with the palms of her hands, she left the bridge.

The deep cold had frozen Derek's brain, but not his consciousness. He continued to have thoughts and something akin to daydreams. These seemed to flow through him, out of his control. His mind and body were so cold that he had lost himself. He didn't know who he was, or that he even existed at all. It seemed he was in another world, another universe. He existed in a realm of pure thought, where there was no feeling, no pain. There were only the images that flowed through him.

Derek saw images of a group of men riding in a car. Moving incredibly slowly, the men laughed and talked, all of them smiling. Derek watched as the car moved slowly down the street, which was filled with other people and other cars. He could see that one of the men, a familiar looking man, wore clothes that were all one color. Green. The man wore green clothes with little shiny things on the chest and shoulders. His hair was short, his jawline strong. The man looked so familiar, but Derek still couldn't place him. Something about the man was very calming.

Derek watched as the car continued down the street, another vehicle sliding in front of it. He watched as the men slowly moved forward, one of them hitting the dashboard as they hit the vehicle in front of them with some force.

The driver of the car in front of them got out and slowly floated back to their driver's window. He stood there for a minute, his mouth making words with no sound. Derek watched as he stepped away from the driver's window and moved to the side of the street. The men in the car began slowly mouthing silent words to each other.

Derek continued to watch as the driver of the second car began to run away from the two cars. He was leaning forward so far, he looked as though he should fall, but he continued to slowly move forward. Derek saw him pull a small black device out of his pocket as he ran.

Oh Jesus! Dad! he thought, realizing who the man in the car was. *Run, Dad, run!*

The brilliant flash that came from the front car was blinding. Derek tried to scream, but no words came out of his frozen lungs. He tried to look away, but his face was in a frozen stare, unable to look away from the carnage that had been brought to bear on his father and the other men.

The flash subsided, and Derek saw pieces of the two cars flying out in all directions, followed by bits of glass and brick from the buildings that ran along the sides of the street. Pieces of car and building struck people who had been walking. Smoke and fire billowed from the crater that was left in the asphalt. Derek looked around at the remains of the car, but the men were gone. There was nothing left of them. He wanted to leave this place, and he found that he was able to move somewhere else in his mind.

The passage of time began to wear on Elena. Only a month had passed since she left Earth orbit and she had already finished reading nearly all the books she brought with her. The ship's main computer had an incredibly vast library, but she rarely spent much time in her stateroom, which was where the computer she used to access the library was located.

She preferred spending her time walking the length and breadth of the ship, dropping into any chair that she might pass along the way to sit and read. As there was no paper in the parts of the ship she had access to, she couldn't print out a story or textbook passage from her computer and take it with her. This, coupled with the fact that there were no printers onboard the ship either, seriously limited her choices of reading material.

She made periodic rounds, checking on the sleepers in order to feel useful. She checked to verify their vital signs, as well as the status of the computer system that kept them alive. She had occasionally made small adjustments in the oxygen level, but she didn't encounter anything that would have caused the passenger any harm if she hadn't altered it. Slowly, she got bored with the rounds, feeling that she wasn't really helping at all. She began to think that she should have been frozen with the passengers.

One day, when she was particularly bored, she went to the bridge and opened the metal window covers to see what was outside. Her boredom became depression when she looked out. The stars still had that blue glow about them, but this didn't really bother her. What upset her was how dark it really was in interstellar space. There were more stars than humans have numbers for, but in deep space, the space between stars, was incredibly dark. This was something that she hadn't been prepared for. She decided to close the window covers and not look out again until the ship was closer to Alpha Centauri.

She tried to keep her mind on the passing of the days. Since the computer simulations had failed on day 44, she knew that she had something to focus on; a goal of sorts to keep her occupied. It didn't help.

Derek floated over an endless field of tall brown grass that seemed to move lazily in a light wind he could neither feel nor hear. He looked around as he continued forward, but all he saw was the brown grass, and below him stretching off to the horizon, a road. Looking closer at the ground beneath him, he noticed that he was slowly getting closer to the road. He came down slowly and touched it, but continued to move forward. The road seemed to pass beneath him as he bounced lazily up and down for a while, continuing toward the horizon.

Derek looked around again, and found that he was sitting in a car that was being driven by a middle-aged black man. He felt a wave of relief in seeing the man, though he didn't know why. The black man seemed to be talking, his mouth opening and closing slowly.

Derek watched him, and felt at ease. He felt comfortable around this man; more comfortable than he had in as long as he could remember. His mind was moving so slowly, he didn't know why he felt this way, but knew that this man must be someone close to him. Derek watched him talk, then smile, and then talk again. He wanted to stay here where it was comfortable, but his mind began to move away. Derek fought to stay in the car with the nice black man, but the image faded completely.

Elena sat on the floor of Lander D at 11:59 on the evening of day forty-three, waiting for midnight. She sat, heart racing, waiting to see if the beds would shut down as they had in the simulation. Telling herself that she was justified in staying awake for the trip, she had been counting down the days, and now she sat, staring at the clock.

When the clock turned to 12:00, as she knew it would, the background hum in the lander suddenly dropped to an almost non-existent level. She jumped to her feet and ran up to the control panel for Level 5, the lowest level that contained sleeper tubes.

As in the simulation, all ten tubes on this level were online and functioning normally. She bolted for the stairs, and ran up to level 4, where she immediately saw on the control panel that the displays for all ten of the tubes read: EMPTY: OFFLINE .

"Son of a bitch," she mumbled as she went up the stairs to Level 3.

The Level 3, as well as the other levels 2 and 1 showed the same thing – all ten tubes showed the same offline status.

As she had practiced, she went level-by-level powering down the tube control systems, powering them back up, and reloading the system program, which started as though the mission were on Day 1. The tube control program recognized that there was a sleeper in each tube, and updated the display to show the tube's contents and status. Elena manually edited the program, one level at a time, to update the system date to Day 44 with the correct time. The total time the beds were offline was only about three hours, which was no threat to the safety of the sleepers due to their low metabolic states. She was so excited about having saved the forty passengers' lives that she wasn't able to sleep that night at all.

Three months into the journey, a deep depression had gotten a firm grip on Elena, and she found that she was spending a lot of time in her stateroom sleeping. She had waited until midnight every night for the first three weeks after restarting the system in Lander D, but the system had operated flawlessly. After the first three weeks, she visited less the fourth week, and only once after that.

Her regular routine was to get out of bed to eat, and then get back in. She did this several times a day when she awoke due to hunger, or the need to use the bathroom. There were rumpled clothes on every flat surface in her stateroom, and because she hadn't washed anything in a couple of weeks, the room had begun to smell. She had gained nearly twenty pounds since departure, and this added to her feelings of self-loathing.

During the system stress tests while in orbit, everything performed flawlessly for the rest of the simulated trip. She had realized that she could put herself back to sleep instead of enduring the continued stress of isolation, but she felt too afraid to do it, having never been in cryo stasis before. She knew the science behind it all too well, and her fear sent her deeper into depression.

A sound, like something moving in her cabin, woke her from a deep sleep.

She threw back the covers and yelled, "Who's there?"

She sat in the darkness, her heart pounding, listening for the sound she'd heard. *Was it a dream?*

"Hello?" she said.

She paused, waiting for a response. None came. Slowly, trying not to make any noise, she reached for the lamp beside her bed. With a click that was louder than she thought it should be, the lamp lit the room. The light abused her sleepy eyes. She took in the sights and smells of her room. It was empty.

"God this place is a mess," she said, looking around at the clutter.

She got out of bed and looked around, checking the bathroom and even looking down the corridor that ran past her room, but saw and heard nothing but the dull hum that was present throughout the ship. She went back into her room, and turned on the bathroom light. The bathroom light was very bright, so she pulled the bathroom door just until it touched the doorjamb, letting a thin beam into her room. She got into her bed and turned off the lamp.

She closed her eyes and dropped her head onto her pillow. Her heart was still beating quickly, so she took several deep breaths to try and calm down. After five minutes of this, her heart was still beating quickly, and she began to feel as though she wasn't going to be able to go back to sleep. She opened her eyes, and standing across from her in the room was the darkened silhouette of a man.

Her heart shot up into her throat as she stared at the shape, who seemed to stare back at her. She slowly reached under her pillow and grabbed it tightly with both hands. In a flash, she jumped from the bed and dove at the man, the pillow held high to cover his face. Slamming into him, she banged her knee on something incredibly hard. She wrestled and fought, trying to grab hold of him, but he must have moved, as all she grabbed was air. Elena jumped back and looked for the man, but he was gone.

She slid herself along the floor to the lamp and switched it on. The room was again bathed in brilliant light. She looked for the intruder, but saw no one. Looking down at the floor she saw him, or at least what she had thought was an intruder. Lying on the floor was a long black jumpsuit she had hung on the entertainment unit. The entertainment unit's plastic housing now had a long crack in it from the impact of her knee. She then realized that her knee was throbbing. Looking down at it, she saw the beginnings of a large bruise forming around her kneecap. She began to cry.

Feeling stupid, she stood up and limped to the bathroom and turned off the light. She picked up the pillow and fell backward into bed, covering her face with it. *Tomorrow I need to clean this place up and start exercising.*

The next day, she awoke to find that her knee was swollen and covered by a deep purple and black bruise. She limped to a small galley on the deck directly below the bridge, and picked up a bag full of ice. She took the ice back to her room, and spent the entire day going back and forth between standing in a hot shower and in front of her computer reading, the ice bag laid over her swollen knee.

Sitting in front of the computer, she pored over the status reports of the ship's systems. The cryo-stasis tubes were operating normally, and there was still no sign of computer problems after the computer reset in Lander D. She was glad that she'd stayed awake, as she'd saved all those lives, but she still had a long way to go until planetfall at Avalon, and that thought filled her with dread.

She was about to turn off the computer, when the hair on the back of her neck stood on end. She looked hard at the reflection of something unfamiliar in the computer screen. She could see that there was something behind her. She squinted, trying to make out what it was, when it suddenly moved toward her. She jumped out of the way, tripping on the chair. She came down hard, the bag of ice splitting open and spilling its contents all over the floor. She rolled over looking for her attacker, but no one was there. She came to her feet with a groan, looking around the room. As before, it was empty.

"Is someone there?" she asked, quickly scanning the room.

There was no answer.

Okay, I'm in another universe. Partially, anyway. This ship isn't visible in our universe, maybe it is here. Maybe we've been boarded by someone I can't see!

She began to flail her arms wildly in attempt to strike the intruder. She quickly began grabbing clothes and throwing them around the room. After nearly a minute of this, she stopped, panting. The room, now utterly destroyed, looked as though a burglar had ransacked it. Elena slid down the wall, and began to cry again.

Chapter Fourteen

Intruders

The next month sent Elena into a downward spiral of depression and self-doubt. She continued to hear and see things that weren't there. She began to question her sanity, and decided to read as much as she could about isolation and mental health. There were a number of studies in the ship's database, and she read them all.

Elena found herself going to the passenger landers, having conversations with the frozen passengers. Once, she found herself staring at the soldier in H404. 'Derek Cross was here' was written in the ice on the tube. Once, she tried to wipe it clean before she learned that it was written on the inside.

Elena felt a deep loathing for this man, even though they had only briefly met. She had visited the other soldiers' tubes as part of her rounds, but hadn't felt this way about them. This man was different. She didn't know exactly what it was, but there was something different about him. Maybe it was because she had thought him attractive until she learned about his occupation. She disliked soldiers in general because of what they stood for. How could someone choose to be trained as a murderer and think that it's an honorable profession? Was there anything in the ship's psychology database about that? There had to be.

This man went against everything she believed in. She had taken an oath to save lives whenever possible several years before she took the Hippocratic Oath in medical school. Her personal oath had been taken at the funeral of her high school boyfriend who had died in a car accident. The rescue attempt had also cost a local firefighter his life as well. The car had exploded as the firefighter was trying to pull the injured boy from the wreckage. She had vowed to spend her life trying to save the lives of as many others as she could, to prevent their families from having to endure the pain that she'd been through.

She only knew this man's name, yet she hated him. She hated everything about him. This man represented the worst part of humanity – the warlike part, and at the same time had this happy-go-lucky attitude. How two-faced.

They were going to a planet where man had never set foot, and they had brought the worst part of humanity with them. There existed the possibility of finding intelligent life on this planet, and these soldiers would ruin it. They might try to kill whatever intelligent life was found there. She hated that aspect of mankind, and she hated Major Derek Cross.

Elena sat on the foot of her bed, tying her shoes. The clothes that had adorned the floor and various other surfaces of the cabin had been washed and put away, and the foul smell that had permeated the room was now gone. She pulled her hair up into an elastic band to keep it out of her face. The studies she'd been able to read from the ships library had all indicated that in order to combat the effects of isolation, exercise and mental stimulation were best, so she did both – exercising, and going back to reading again.

She stood and leaned over, trying to stretch her legs. When she finished stretching her hamstrings she stretched her calves and thighs. Sitting down on the floor, she pulled her legs apart, and leaned forward to stretch the muscles that ran along the inside of her thigh.

When she felt that she had stretched enough, she got up and began jumping up and down on the balls of her feet. She bounced up and down, then side-to-side for several minutes until she began to sweat. Feeling that she had gotten warmed up, she moved toward the cabin door.

She grabbed hold of the desk chair, which was wedged under the door handle to keep out the invisible aliens. She gave it a forceful yank, and it broke free of its grip on the floor. She pulled it aside, slid it under the desk, and then stepped out into the hallway.

Her heart pounded thunderously in her chest as she jogged down the central corridor toward the rear of the ship. The rhythmic pounding of her feet on the metal decking made her legs numb. She had gotten used to running back and forth down this passage, and was lost in thought. She heard a voice from somewhere behind her calling her name.

"I'm not going to listen to you," she panted rhythmically, saying one word each time one of her feet hit the floor.

Elena continued toward the rear of the ship, increasing her pace. Her legs began to burn as she pushed herself harder than normal. She gradually slowed back down to her normal pace, and continued jogging until she had run all the way to the engineering section. She took the stairs in engineering two at a time, going down to the second, or mid deck. She jogged back up to the fore section of the ship, and up the stairs to her cabin.

Having started jogging for exercise two weeks before, Elena had already lost nearly ten of the pounds she'd gained. Her rapid weight loss struck her as something she should keep an eye on, but a self-physical showed that a third of the weight she'd lost was water, so she felt that the sudden weight loss wasn't something to be concerned about as long as she kept her electrolytes in balance.

She was sleeping less than she had been, and had been seeing and hearing things much less often than she had a month before. She had decided that each time she heard or saw something, she should ignore it, as it was just her mind trying to help her cope with isolation. She'd read that people who are isolated for long periods of time tend to invent 'imaginary friends', much like children do.

Elena had decided that this was fine for children to do, since they lived in the worlds of their imagination, but this was not acceptable for her. In about two months, the ship would enter Avalon orbit, and she would be working harder than she ever had before. She needed to be in good physical shape, and running was the best conditioning exercise she knew. It had been two weeks, and she'd run every day; she'd even run twice one day the previous week.

Elena moved from tube to tube, and lander to lander checking each tube's passenger. There were two months left in the journey, and she wanted to verify that all the passengers were still in proper stasis. She had gotten out of the habit of visiting the landers and wanted to start checking them regularly prior to orbital insertion.

She had decided that she would check one lander a day until she had checked them all, and then skip four days and then start over at the first lander, checking them all. She would repeat this before the ship would start the uncoupling procedure, during which all the landers would be released from the central section and would descend to the planet.

The central section consisted of three decks, and the landers were attached around the outside of the ship in a spiral pattern. Because of this, Elena found herself going to a different deck each day when she went to check the passengers. The entry hatch for passenger lander A was next to the doors for E and F, as well as several other landers. The hatches to most of the other landers were sealed, and door actuator motors hadn't been installed. They weren't made accessible from inside the ship, as there was no need to access the other landers until they were on the planet's surface because they only contained cargo, or other prefabricated materials for the colony construction.

She moved through landers A, B, and C without any difficulty. During her check of lander 'D', she noticed that the last three of the tubes on the lowest level were empty. She didn't remember any empty tubes in this lander, but since she had been focused on the upper four levels, the levels that had malfunctioned during the testing, she couldn't say for sure. She sat and stared at the tube for several seconds before deciding that the tube was supposed to be empty. There were no clothing items in the small locker next to it, and it didn't appear as though the tube had malfunctioned. If it had, she would have seen that when she performed the scans using the computer in her cabin.

She moved to the cradle, which normally housed the monitoring unit. She instinctively reached for it before she looked. Her hand grasped only empty space where the monitor should have been.

"Well that settles it," she said aloud. "Someone must have cancelled at the last minute and not made the trip."

She turned and moved to the next tube, the tip of her shoe pushing an empty injection bottle under the empty tube.

The next day, she entered lander E and immediately saw that there were two empty tubes twenty feet above her. She stood in the open hatch, staring up at the two side-by-side tubes. Her hand clutched over her mouth, she searched her memory for any recollection of empty tubes on the flight. She furrowed her brow, groping for an explanation.

"Okay, I've *really* lost it now," she said, shaking her head. "I need to get more sleep."

She proceeded into the lander and began checking the monitors on the tubes that contained passengers. When she got to the two empty tubes, numbers 503 and 504, she stopped. Both tubes had medical monitors in the cradles. The monitors were switched off, so she picked one of them up and turned it on.

The monitor came to life, and began to beep an alert. Because there was no input coming into the monitor, the computer thought that a passenger was in distress. Elena immediately silenced the alarm.

Elena pressed a series of buttons on the monitor, bringing up the data storage system. Information on the passenger came up on the screen, and Elena found that it contained basic information about a man in his late thirties.

She read all the information in the monitor, but since it had been switched off there was no stored history on the passenger.

"This guy must have ducked out at the last minute, too."

A sound from behind her made her jump and drop the monitor to the deck. She turned quickly around but saw nothing. She looked back and forth, taking in as much of the lander as she could see. She glanced down at the deck beside her. The monitor lay on the floor, the display screen broken. She looked around the darkened decks above her, trying to pick up the monitor without taking her eyes from the darkness above. With a quick jerk of her head, she looked down to locate the monitor. She scooped it up, slammed it down in its cradle, and quickly made her way out of the lander.

Elena pulled her shoes on and tied the laces in double knots. The sides of the shoes had a white, crusty film of dried salt that ran around them. She hadn't washed them, and each time she ran they got soaked with sweat. When the sweat dried, the layer of salt grew thicker and more visible.

She had been running now for about a month now, and she could easily run the length of the ship and back. Her goal was to be able to run the length of the ship and back twice, then walk around the foredecks of the ship to cool down afterward. This would be the equivalent of somewhere between two and three miles. She wasn't sure exactly how long the central section was, but she knew it to be over half a mile long. There was just over a month left until the ship reached Avalon, and at this rate she would be in pretty good shape when the ship arrived.

Elena stepped into the hall outside her cabin and began to stretch. She spent fifteen minutes stretching, and then jumped up and down to get her leg muscles warmed up. Once she had broken a light sweat, she began to make her way through the maze of foredeck corridors to the ship's central corridor.

Once she arrived there, she began to jog. Having altered her running style, she now bounced lithely on the balls of her feet, her calf muscles swelling in protest. She moved past the first few hatches that led to cargo landers and continued down the corridor past the colonist landers. She glanced at the hatches as she passed, as though expecting someone to walk out of one.

She continued past several other landers which contained mostly the personal effects of the passengers. She looked ahead, and saw that she was approaching her least favorite section of cargo landers. This area housed the military cargo landers, which contained various articles of military equipment such as weapons, uniforms, communications equipment and even vehicles. She gritted her teeth as she passed the hatches that led to these landers. Even though these landers were sealed and there was no way to enter them, she despised the fact that they had been brought along at all. She never understood why the mission administrators wanted the military on this mission.

As she neared the aft section of the ship she saw the metal stairway that went both up and down. She jogged up to it and, rather than taking her usual route down, decided to go up. She took two steps at a time, making little noise as her soft-soled shoes hit the steps.

She heard voices below her, somewhere in the distance.

"I'm not listening to you, remember?" she panted.

She continued up the stairs and then started back up the corridor. Several minutes later she reached the foredeck staircase and went down both flights to the lowest of the three decks, Deck Three. This deck was the most dimly lit of the three, and when she jogged it she always did it last. The rush of fear that she felt gave her a second wind that pushed up her pace, helping her to increase her endurance by training harder. "This deck is the carrot in front of *this* horse," she would say aloud, pointing a thumb at her chest.

Deck Three was long and dark, but the brightly lit bay at the end gave her a point to look at – a goal. She moved along, panting heavily, her feet hitting the deck she couldn't see.

The brightness coming down the corridor flickered several times in front of her. *Is the power fluctuating?* She squinted, trying to make out a reason for the flickering, when she saw it again. This time she could tell that it wasn't a power failure. She had seen several people pass in front of the darkened corridor between the light source and her.

"Oh this is getting ridiculous," she panted. "Imaginary friends go home."

Goosebumps rose on her arms, legs and even scalp. She moved closer to the brightly lit bay and began to slow her pace. Forty feet from the open doorway, she quit jogging and started walking.

When she reached the bay, as usual she didn't see anyone. She walked around several large pieces of equipment; then her heart leapt out of her chest. Lying all around the bay was an assortment of items she knew hadn't been there the last time she was here. There were several open crates of food and empty food packages, several stacks of papers, and sitting on top of a large crate was a pistol.

"Okay, this is weird," she mumbled, walking toward the pistol.

She took a quick swing at the crate with her leg, wanting to watch it pass right through the figment of her imagination. Much to her surprise, her foot hit it hard. The thud echoed throughout the bay. A lightning bolt of pain shot straight from her ankle to her brain, promptly dropping her to the floor.

She sat on the floor, rubbing her throbbing ankle, as a terrifying thought rose up from the depths of her mind. *I'm not alone.*

Several men's voices began echoing from the next compartment and seemed to be growing louder. She threw herself toward the open doorway to the dark corridor and limped into the darkness as a group of people entered the bay.

"I tell you I don't hear nothing," one of them said with a Hispanic accent.

"I don't care what you do or don't hear," another man said. "From now on, when I say 'check it out' you damn well better do it, or you'll find yourself walking home. Are we clear on this?"

"Si, clear."

"Look, Fred-," a third voice said.

"You be quiet, fat boy," hissed the first man. "I'm in charge here, not you. Do we have a problem with that?"

There was no verbal reply, but Elena was sure there were at least two men shaking their heads.

A dark-haired man stepped into the doorway. The light behind him gave him a shroud of darkness, so Elena couldn't make out what he looked like. He scanned the dark corridor, looking to see if he had actually heard something.

Elena held her breath for several excruciating seconds while he satisfied his need to be sure they were alone. Her heartbeat raged in her chest from her jogging, trying to force her to breathe. She was lying in the corner between the wall and the floor, perfectly still. Having been afraid that her white t-shirt might give her away, she had taken it off, revealing the black compression shirt she wore under it. The t-shirt was wadded into a ball under her chest. The top of her head was the only surface facing the man, and she was sure that he wouldn't see her if she didn't move.

She lay for nearly ten minutes, waiting for some sign that the men were moving away from the door. Only breathing when she felt as though she'd pass out if she didn't, her head was pounding, and she was shivering slightly from the combination of adrenaline and cold sweat on her half-naked body.

Elena slowly lifted her head and looked to the doorway. It was clear. She slowly got to her feet and moved to the other side of the corridor, trying to get a different view into the bay. She listened for voices but heard none.

Slowly, Elena made her way back to the bay and peeked inside. The bay was empty. The men had left it exactly as she had seen it, with one exception. The pistol was gone. *Shit.*

A muffled voice seemed to be coming from a doorway across the room. She slid behind a large crate and listened. Unable to make out what was being said, she slowly moved from crate to crate until she could see into the next room.

This was the secondary control station for the ship. There were numerous computer control panels, all of which were dark. Elena knew that this section of the ship had been disabled long ago, because it was known that it wouldn't ever be needed, since the ship would be on automatic navigation and control.

She looked into the room but didn't see the men, so she worked her way toward a door that led into the next room. She could tell that the voices were coming from there, so she knelt down under a control station and listened.

"...Tiny. Take this and break into the ship's database. Find out where the administrators are so I can eliminate them. The soldiers in Lander D who aren't in on our little plan should be dead already, so they won't interfere with us."

Elena's eyes went wide. A hand instinctively covered her mouth.

"You got it, boss. This may take a few days, though, maybe even a week. They're using some pretty sophisticated encryption technology here."

"Just set this up and it'll work non-stop until it finds the right decryption codes."

The voices were growing louder. Elena was debating on moving back toward the dark corridor when the men entered the room.

A tall, dark-haired man was in front of two others, one of them a slender Hispanic. The other was a heavy-set, bearded Caucasian.

Elena froze as the two men stopped in the center of the room. She looked down at herself and realized that she was in plain sight. She knew that if she moved, the movement would draw their attention. Whoever had that pistol would probably use it on her.

"We've got a month to make sure we've taken out the leadership of the colony. I want to make sure only administrators die. We need everyone else. If all goes as planned, I'll have my own little planet to rule!" He said, laughing. "And the best part is, when the colonists wake up planet-side, they'll all want me to lead them!" He laughed again.

The other men laughed as well.

"Your plan is flawless, sir. I love it," the fat man said.

"I've worked hard for a long time, and killed a lot of people to make sure it is," he said with a smile and a nod. "To think, this whole thing started with something as simple as a car bomb." He paused. "Anyway, we have a lot of work to do, but first things first. Let's go get the others."

Chapter Fifteen

Necessary Evil

erek had been frozen for nearly five months, but his mind continued to wander. He had been having waking dreams in which he saw several people he didn't immediately recognize. He'd figured out who they were, only to have the dream end and a new set of people float around into his head.

He'd noticed that slowly, he was becoming more lucid, and his dreams were more controllable. He'd begun to recognize the people in his daydreams more quickly, and they were more familiar to him from the outset. Occasionally, images flashed in front of him and then vanished. One image, a woman, had flashed so quickly that Derek had barely a chance to realize what he was looking at before she was gone. He hadn't recognized the woman, but somewhere inside the recesses of his mind he knew that he should have.

Derek continued to grow more awake and aware of his surroundings, until one day he realized where he was. He was still aboard *Osiris*, and he could make out some writing in front of him. He was very stiff, and was unable to move his arms or legs. His back was held tightly against the back of the tube and felt as though he were wet. Derek looked at the inside of the tube and noticed that the words he had written were nearly gone. A realization washed over him- he was thawing.

Derek's heart beat a single, painful beat. After being frozen for five months his heart had started beating on its own, which meant that he wouldn't be subjected to the jolt of electricity that awaited the sleepers whose hearts didn't. This had happened to him once before, and even his frozen mind could remember how painful it was.

Derek fought against the cold until he was able to move his fingers. He slowly worked them back and forth; the dull pain in them seemed to pulse throughout his body. His arms had become easier to move, and he began swinging them forward and backward, almost as if he were walking in place. He started moving his neck when he was able, making slow circles, warming and loosening up his muscles.

Derek didn't know how long he had been thawing, but from past experience, he knew the entire process typically took several days. *The cycle must be nearly complete.* He reached his hands forward and clumsily rubbed the last remnants of 'Derek Cross was here' away.

Derek reached up to the plastic buckle on the belt that pinned him to the back wall of the tube. Drawing his stiff arms in close to him took nearly all his strength. He managed to get a thumb under the flap, but when he tried to pry it up his thumb slipped off the wet plastic. Reaching across with his other hand, he fumbled with the flap until he managed to hook three fingers around the buckle. He reached over with his thumb and, using both arms, pulled the flap.

Derek's world spun as he felt himself falling. He landed with a cold, wet slap against the inside of the glass door. His legs, which hadn't been moved and warmed up, didn't want to function. He leaned against the door for a moment, the side of his face dripping with condensation from the door. His hands, slick with condensation, moved slowly up to push him away from it.

He pressed with all his strength, but his arms and chest were still too cold and weak to lift him off the door. Slowly, he began to wiggle his toes inside his wet socks. His feet, which had been numb, throbbed from the cold. He continued the movement, moving it up from his feet into his calves.

The heat generated in his lower legs radiated upward, warming his chest and arms. He took two deep breaths and with a groan gave a Herculean push.

His senses told him that he was flying. He saw the floor coming up at him quickly, but something moved in front of him and cushioned the impact. He looked up to see that he was in the arms of Dr. Elena Brown, who had kept him from crashing to the floor.

"Nice catch," he groaned.

"Shhhh!" she said quietly. "Keep quiet. Here, let me wrap you up in this. You'll warm up a lot faster." She wrapped him in a thick heated blanket and laid him down on the steel floor. She peered over the railing, looking toward the entry hatch.

"What's going on?" he asked, beginning to shiver.

"We've got company."

Elena explained to him what she had seen and heard. Derek's mind was still moving slower than normal, but he knew that their situation could prove very dangerous if the men were serious when they spoke of murdering the administrators.

"Do you have any idea who they are?" he asked.

"No, and I didn't hang around long enough to find out."

"Did they show any indication that they knew you were awake?"

"No," Elena said, running her hands through her hair. "The decision for me to stay awake for the trip was a last-minute change due to a problem with the cryo systems for one of the landers. It was decided that I'd stay awake just in case the system went offline, and it's lucky that I did. Just like the simulation showed, forty-four days into the trip, most of the beds in the lander shut down. I had to completely power down the system and bring it back up. It's been running like clockwork ever since. Anyway, I've been hiding in my cabin since I overheard those men in engineering. Nobody would know that I was here, but I wasn't taking any chances. It's been three days since I've eaten," Elena said, her arm trembling.

Derek paused, letting the situation sink in. He watched Elena closely, seeing her avoid eye contact with him. He reached a clammy hand to lift her chin, but she pulled away from his touch.

"Maybe we should get you something to eat before we do anything else. I don't think our friends are going anywhere. Besides, I'm pretty hungry too. I haven't eaten in five months!"

Derek slowly opened the cabin door and listened for footsteps or voices. The silence in the ship was unnerving, but it told Derek that the coast was clear, as people who think they're alone don't tend to worry about being quiet. The two of them made their way to the galley in the foredecks, stopping periodically to listen for the intruders. Once they reached the galley, they gathered several small food items and returned to Elena's cabin.

They sat in silence, eating. Derek, having rewrapped himself in the blanket, sat in Elena's desk chair while Elena sat across the room on the floor next to her bed.

"What are you going to do?" she asked, avoiding his gaze.

"I was just thinking about that. The first thing I need to do is find out how many of them there are. You said you saw three down in engineering, so that's where I'll start."

Elena raised a hand to him. "Look, I don't want to know the foul details of how you're going to kill these guys, and in what order," she barked.

Derek's mouth dropped open, revealing bits of partially chewed food. He swallowed with a loud gulp.

"I'm not going to kill anybody. At least I hope not, anyway. I'm going to sneak down to engineering to find out how many people are down there."

Elena glanced over at him.

"Okay," she said, looking back down at the food in her lap.

"Do you have any dark clothes I could borrow?" Derek asked. "I'd prefer something dark gray or black."

"You've got to be kidding!" he said, seeing her choice.

"It's all I have. If you don't want them to see you, this is the best set of clothes you can wear," she said, a cruel smile on her face.

She held out the clothes, and Derek took them. He went into the small bathroom and a few minutes later came out wearing Elena's long black skirt, and gray short-sleeve top.

"If you say anything about this to anyone..." he paused, implying bodily harm would come to her.

Much to Elena's surprise, Derek's face turned bright red.

Derek made his way down the darkened Level 3 corridor, heading toward engineering. He was thirty feet away when he began hearing voices coming from the large, brightly lit bay at the end. Pressing his body against the wall, he slowly made his way along until he was nearly at the open door.

"How do I get myself into these things?" he mumbled, looking down at himself.

Derek moved closer to the opening to listen to the conversation taking place in the bay. Listening hard, he heard a voice that was much higher than the others. He leaned just far enough to peer into the bay at the origin of the voice.

Sitting on a small box, wrapped in a multicolored blanket was a young boy. Appearing to be a young teenager, the boy looked vaguely familiar. Derek stared at him for several seconds before sliding back into the darkness of the corridor.

He sat in the floor, trying to place the boy. The only boy he could think of was Mannie. Was this one of Mannie's friends? Derek dismissed the idea. He moved across to the other side of the corridor, so that he could get a better view of the other side of the bay.

Silently, he moved forward and peered in the other direction. He immediately saw a thin Hispanic digging around in a large crate. His unkempt hair blended well with his unshaven face. Across from him was a very overweight man. Derek deduced that the fat man had been eating, because there were bits of uneaten food still stuck in his heavy beard.

Derek continued to crane his neck to see if there were any other people in the bay. A muffled voice came from directly behind the fat man. Another man stepped around him into view, well dressed, and clean-shaven. Derek was unable to hear what the man was saying, so he turned his ear toward the man. Derek's eyes moved randomly in their sockets while he listened. His gaze suddenly came to rest on a black strap that ran across the fat man's chest. He followed the strap with his eyes down to the man's underarm. Sticking out from under his arm was the handle of a pistol.

Derek scanned the rest of the men in the bay, and each of them, including the boy, was armed. The Hispanic man, the neat man, and even the boy all had pistols on them.

This isn't good.

Derek made his way back to Elena's cabin and changed back into his clothes. He paced back and forth in her cabin while she watched.

"What are we going to do?" she asked.

"I'm trying to come up with a plan. We've got at least four men on board, all of them armed. One of them is really heavy, so he wouldn't be able to give chase for long if they saw us. Another is a boy, a teenager. He looks *damn* familiar to me, but I can't place him," he said, shaking his head. "The other two are the ones that I'm worried about; a Hispanic and another guy. They would seem to be the biggest threats."

"Alright, alright. Enough of the killer, army-robot crap. Maybe we could go talk to them."

"Are you crazy, or just plain stupid? You told me these guys said they were going to kill the administrators as soon as they've figured out where they are. Do you think they would be the least bit bothered by killing us? We have the element of surprise right now. They don't know we're awake. That gives us an advantage that we lose as soon as we show ourselves to them."

Elena's mouth moved as though she were speaking, but no words came out. Her head moved back and forth as she groped for a response.

"I thought you'd say that," Derek said. "I think the first thing we need to do is get a message to mission control. We've got to let someone back home know what's happening. Maybe they can send some ideas."

Derek donned Elena's dress and top and made his way along the darkened Level 3 corridor toward engineering. This time, however, he had put on a pair of her shoes, because they were soft-soled and wouldn't make as much noise if he had to make a hasty retreat. Once he reached the opening at the end of the corridor, he lay down on his belly in the shadows.

He leaned in closer to the open door, craning his neck to see into the bay. Immediately, the young boy came into view, no longer wrapped in the blanket. Derek held his breath as the boy walked past the open doorway. After he passed, Derek let out a long, slow breath. *One down.*

Derek inched forward, undulating like an inchworm. Once he had gotten far enough to see across the right side of the bay, he saw the neat man and the Hispanic. *Two and three, one more to go.* He slid back slowly, melting in to the darkness. Once he was completely in the shadow, he moved to the other side of the corridor, trying to see across the left side of the bay.

Derek slowly worked his way forward and into the light. He'd started to move like a worm again when something caught his eye. Standing directly in front of him was the fat man.

Derek looked at the man's feet, only three feet away, and slowly followed them to his knees, then his thick thighs. He continued upward to his large round belly, and then his head. The fat man was reading a small booklet and hadn't noticed that someone was lying in the floor right across from him. *Well, there's four. That's all of them.*

Derek waited, unmoving, for nearly twenty minutes until the fat man turned and walked out of the bay through a door and out of Derek's view. Derek immediately began to slide backward into the darkness. Once completely shaded, he got to his feet. He listened for any signs that he'd been seen.

When none came, he turned and began to jog, the balls of his feet tapping softly on the steel deck.

"All four of them are still in the large engineering bay at the end of the Level 3 corridor," Derek said. "I think now is the best time for us to go send the message. They'll have no idea that a message has been sent, and we can set the computer to relay any incoming messages directly to the computer here." He waved his arm toward the computer on Elena's desk.

"Why are they staying down there in engineering?" Elena asked.

"Well, my guess is that Chubby's having trouble getting the locations of the administrators out of the computer. We're just lucky he doesn't have access to the database. If they did, all the admins would probably be dead already."

Elena frowned. "This mission is supposed to help save lives. I can't believe this is happening. It's just too easy these days. You just press a button or flip a switch and people die."

"I guess it depends on how you look at it. I don't think that I could even 'just press a button or flip a switch' if I knew someone would be dead afterward," Derek said.

Elena looked at him for a moment, and then said, "You're kidding, right? Aren't you the big, 'gung-ho, kill 'em all and let God sort 'em out' kind of guy?"

"I'm not sure those kind of people really exist," Derek replied, smiling. "At least, I've never met anyone who really thought that way. A lot of 'tough-guys' say that, but when the shit hits the fan, they really don't mean it."

Elena stared at him, her mouth slightly open.

"We need to get going so we can send the message to Earth," Derek said, reaching a hand out to Elena. She looked at it for a moment, then took it and pulled, lifting herself up from the bed.

Derek and Elena made their way to the end of the corridor that ran past Elena's cabin. The corridor ended in a 'T' junction, so Derek took a quick look both ways to make sure none of the intruders had made their way to the foredecks after he'd left them. He instinctively flashed a series of hand signals to Elena, who gave him a puzzled look in return.

"Sorry," he whispered. "Force of habit."

He started to explain the commands he'd been giving her when he noticed a power junction panel on the wall behind her. A toothy grin appeared on his face.

Derek pulled the panel open, revealing a series of knobs, switches and dials. He began tracing his finger along a series of buttons as if he were reading Braille.

"What are you doing?" Elena whispered.

"I'm going to cut the power to the lighting system. We will be able to move around without being seen if anyone comes up this way. Don't worry, I'll only cut the lights in the corridors that lead from here to the bridge. We'll be able to see down the other corridors. That'll give us an advantage."

Derek continued to feel his way across the panel, when he suddenly stopped. He flipped a switch, and the lights in the corridor went out.

Standing in darkness, Derek was still able to see by the light given off by the large number of small lights in the panel. Using them, he was able to find the other switches he needed to flip to shut down the lights in the remaining corridors that awaited them on their way to the bridge.

"Alright, let's go."

Derek and Elena moved silently through the dark corridors, stopping occasionally at the intersection of theirs and one still lit. Derek would peer around the corners, and when the coast was clear they would go on.

When they finally reached the bridge, Derek told Elena to wait in the corridor outside until he made sure there were no intruders there. He told her that, just because they had only seen four total, not to assume that there *were* only four. That was an assumption that would get you killed.

"Do you smell something?" Elena asked, sniffing the air, a look of disgust on her face.

Derek sniffed the air lightly. "It smells like burning plastic."

Derek moved into the bridge, which was also dark. The stench of burnt plastic permeated the room and burned his throat. There were thousands of little lights twinkling on the various control panels. Off to one side, Derek noticed a series of bright flashes. He squinted in the darkness, trying to determine the source.

Having decided that the bridge was clear, Derek said, "Lights." There was no effect. He moved back out into the dark corridor and felt along the wall until he found another power junction panel. He looked at the series of red lights that indicated the sections of the ship he'd deactivated earlier. His finger slid along the panel to the last red light and found the switch in the dark next to it. With an audible click, the light turned green, and light began to stream out into the corridor.

The two of them stepped onto the bridge, which was filled with a light smoke. Elena looked at Derek, a look of questioning on her face. Derek shrugged.

"Comm." Derek said. Again there was no effect.

"Where's the communications system on this ship?" Derek asked her.

"It's right over..." Elena stopped.

Her finger was pointing to a control panel on the right side of the bridge. Flashes of light emanated from the broken mass of wires and plastic, that was also the source of the wispy smoke that oozed from the console.

"Well, *fuck me*," Derek said before he'd had a chance to think.

The console had been smashed with a fire axe, which, in some twisted statement, was still sticking out of the wrecked control station.

Elena, realizing the gravity of their situation, began to break down. Tears began to grow in her blue eyes.

"What are we going to do?" she said in a barely audible whisper.

"I don't know. I *really* don't know," Derek replied, putting his hand on her shoulder.

Elena turned toward him and found herself hugging him tightly. She was filled with a hurricane of emotions. She hated this man, but she had entrusted him to keep her alive. Now, it looked as though there was no way he was going to be able to do that.

Her fear and frustration had come to a head, and she started to cry. She dug her fingernails into his shoulders, and clenched her teeth as her sadness was replaced with anger. She let go of Derek, and then pushed him away.

"This doesn't make any sense!" she yelled. "Why they hell did they do that!" she yelled, pointing at the smoldering mass of plastic and metal. "They don't know anyone is here, do they?"

"I'm guessing this is only a precaution. You know? Just in case."

"No! There wouldn't be any need for this. The tubes aren't supposed to thaw anyone until we reach Avalon. It just doesn't make any sense!"

Derek walked over to the control station labeled 'Operations'. He noticed that everything was covered with a thin coating of dust, but this station had several streaks where the dust had been wiped clean, as if someone had been working there.

"Have you been up here?"

"Not in a couple of months," she sobbed. "Why?"

"Someone's been here, look," he said, pointing to the clean streaks.

Derek followed the streaks, and found that they were centered around a small data interface port.

"Someone's plugged something in here. This is an uplink port."

Elena peered around him, trying to get a better view of the console.

Derek looked back at the smashed communications station, then over to the Captain's chair. He walked over to the Captain's chair and sat down.

Derek looked down at a small button on the right armrest. He pressed his finger to the button, and a display screen slowly rose out of the arm until it was nearly vertical. It then tilted backward slightly - angled to allow for easier viewing. Elena moved around behind the chair, so that she could see the display as well.

Derek scanned the menu of options until he found what he was looking for. He pressed the option labeled, 'transmission logs'.

The screen changed to a list of transmissions that had been made. They were all in order by date and time, starting at the beginning of the mission. Derek pressed a small arrow at the bottom, and watched as the dates grew closer and closer to the current date.

When they reached the last entry, Derek saw that it had been made two days ago. It wasn't the same type of entry as the rest. This entry was labeled, 'Ship Distress – SOS'. Derek pressed it.

The screen displayed the message that had been sent to Earth. It read:

06/18/2136 16.28.32GMT
Warning: Unknown gravitational anomaly
detected. High gravity field affecting
structural integrity.
SOS. Ship in distress. SOS.
Integrity failing.
SOS. Ship in distress. SOS.
Artificial gravity lost. Life support system
offline.
SOS. Ship in distress. SOS.
Hull breach, central corridor. Hull breach,
engineering.
SOS. Ship in distress. SOS.
Main power failure imminent. Flux field
unstable. Reactor containment failure.
SOS. Ship in distress. SOS.
Reactors critical. Reactors critical.
Reactor explosion imminent. Reactor
explosion in…

Derek stared at the entry. Those men in engineering had forged a telemetry transmission to Earth. A telemetry entry that described the destruction of the ship. *Why would they want control to think that the ship had been destroyed?*

Derek turned and looked up at Elena, who looked as puzzled as he did. Derek furrowed his brow and moved back to the communications console. Elena followed closely behind him. Derek began pulling on the axe until it finally relented its grip on the wires inside the console. The axe popped out with a shower of sparks that made the both of them cover their eyes.

Derek dropped the axe with a clang. Leaning in closely to the hole in the console, he raised his hand to protect his face from the occasional spark. He looked around the inside until his eyes came to rest on a silver cylinder.

"Son of a bitch," Derek mumbled.

Derek pulled his hand up into his sleeve, and reached into the smoldering hole. He wrapped his sleeve-covered fingers around the cylinder and pulled it out.

"What is that?"

"This is getting more and more interesting," Derek said, holding the broken and charred cylinder out toward Elena.

"What? What is that?" she asked again.

"It's a telemetry monitor."

Elena stared at him for a moment. Derek saw by the look on her face that she had no idea what that meant.

"This cylinder is called a telemetry monitor. It is installed in advanced communications systems, which sends the ship's telemetry automatically. They sent a false telemetry signal to control that said we encountered something and that the ship was destroyed. The problem is that the ship would continue to send the actual telemetry using this," he said, waving the fractured cylinder at her. "Actually destroying the comm. system, and this in particular, is the only way to make control think that the ship really was destroyed, or at least seriously crippled. The act of destroying the communications system and sending the message that was sent will make control think that the ship went down."

Derek paused.

"We're on our own."

Chapter Sixteen

Missing Persons

I don't think this is a good idea," Elena said.

Derek turned and stared at her. She looked him in the eyes for a long moment, then cocked her head to the side and placed her hands on her hips.

"We need the help," Derek replied, crossing his arms.

"Look, I don't want some kind of battle taking place on this ship. This is not a war-zone, and I don't want you people making it one," she said, jabbing a finger at him.

"Listen, I can't thaw them without you. I don't know how to start the thawing process." He paused, searching for more concessions. "Okay, maybe two or three guys, tops."

Elena rolled her eyes, and then started toward the door of her room, pushing Derek out of the way.

"Which lander are they in?" Elena asked over her shoulder.

"Lander D."

"Hey, that's the lander that had the malfunction a couple of months ago," Elena blurted.

Derek stopped walking, followed a second later by Elena. She turned back to see him standing stock-still.

"Malfunction?"

"Yeah, that's the lander that I told you about – the one where most of the beds shut down. The lowest level was the only one unaffected."

"That's odd," Derek said, rubbing his chin.

They made their way down the central corridor to the hatch for Lander D without speaking to each other. When they arrived, Derek opened the door and brushed past her.

"Anyway, we need some help. I told you those guys are armed, all four of them. We don't stand much of a chance without at least a few of the soldiers in here."

The two of them made their way up to the first level of tubes. Elena pulled a small electronic device from a cradle on the wall and began pressing buttons on it. On the small screen, a list of names, biographical information, and tube numbers began to appear.

"Here's the list of names and locations of your storm-troopers," she said, throwing the device at him rather than to him.

Derek caught the piece of equipment, nearly dropping it. He turned and looked down the row of tubes when something caught his eye. The last three tubes on the level stood empty.

"That's weird," he mumbled. "Look," he said, gesturing at it with his forehead.

Elena moved past him, hitting him with her shoulder as she walked to the nearest of the three tubes. She reached for the medical monitor, but the cradle that normally held it was empty. Derek absentmindedly opened the small locker beside the tube. It was empty.

"I don't understand," Elena said. "There's been something in there. See, look. There are scratches on the inside of the locker from something being put in here and then taken back out."

Derek walked up behind her and looked over her shoulder. He looked into the tube, and saw that the floor of the tube was wet. Derek began looking over the list, trying to find tube 508.

"This isn't good," he said. "This lander is only military personnel, right?"

Elena nodded. "Umm," she said, reading the information on her screen. "The top four levels are all military, and there are three more on..." she trailed off. "Those three tubes are listed as occupied with military sleepers." She pointed toward the empty tubes.

"Alright, let's go up and check the other levels," he said pointing at the next level up.

"What are we looking for exactly?"

"Missing persons," Derek said, rolling his eyes.

Elena and Derek checked the other levels and found that only the three they discovered on the bottom level were empty, and that they appeared to have been recently vacated, judging by the amount of condensation still in them.

"We're in deep shit," Derek said. "This means that whoever those guys are, they've probably got three additional men, soldiers, working with them."

Elena stared at him, not believing what she was hearing.

"That means they're going to have training in tactics, weapons, and hand-to-hand combat," Derek continued.

Elena's hand covered her mouth involuntarily.

"What really doesn't make any sense to me is this," he said, raising the electronic screen to her. "The three invisible men here aren't *my* men. I don't recognize these three names. They aren't the soldiers I selected for this mission. So the question is, who the hell are they, and how did they get here instead of the men I selected? General Durus gave me the final go-no go on all of them, so I've read all of their files."

"Whoever those guys in engineering are, they seem to be holding all the cards," Elena said, looking down at her feet. "That and their numbers keep growing. There are a total of seven of them now, including your three soldiers."

"Well, we do have one advantage. They don't know we're here." He paused. "Actually, we have two advantages."

Derek and Elena made their way down to the Level 3 corridor. They walked into the darkness until they came to a doorway hidden in the shadows. Derek felt along the hatch until his hand brushed across a large letter F.

"This is it," he said.

He pressed the button next to the door, and with a hiss the hatch opened. They walked into the lander and after the hatch had closed, Derek turned on the lights.

"Who are we looking for?" Elena said, looking at the passenger list for lander F.

"James Towson," Derek replied, glancing back and forth at the rows of tubes.

Elena pored over the list until she came to the name, 'Towson, James'.

"Here he is, 204. Right up there," she pointed up into the darkened heights of the lander.

They made their way up several flights of steps to the second level. Derek listened to Elena's breathing, expecting to hear her panting after the brisk five-story climb. To his surprise, she appeared to be breathing normally.

Derek stepped up to the tube and, seeing JT's frozen face, smiled broadly. Elena saw the smile on Derek's face and looked at the black man in the tube.

Only the man's face, neck and lower left leg were visible behind the frost inside the glass door. These parts were covered with small fluffy patches of white ice. The hairs on his legs looked like a forest in wintertime, the tufts of downy white on the tips of the hairs like clumps of light snow.

"Who is he?" Elena asked, still staring at Derek.

"My best friend," Derek replied, not taking his eyes off of the man in the tube.

Elena watched Derek looking at the frozen man. The contagious smile on Derek's face made its way to Elena. She found herself smiling broadly as she looked at Derek. She looked back at the frozen face.

"Well, I'd better start the thawing process. It's going to take 36 to 48 hours before we can come back and get him out."

Derek stepped out of Elena's way, and she began to press various buttons on the tube's control panel. The small display beside the tube indicated that the heaters had been activated, and that the slow warming procedure had begun.

"Here, take his stuff," Derek said, opening the small locker and retrieving the clothing and other items. "There might be something in here we can use."

Elena took the clothes, belt and shoes out of Derek's hands. Derek went through the various other items in the locker, but was unable to find anything that immediately gave him any ideas.

"Take these, too," Derek said extending JT's watch, ring and other personal effects to Elena. "I need to go through them more thoroughly, but I don't want to do it here."

Elena took JT's shirt, and used it to bundle the remaining items together. She tied the sleeves of the shirt together to keep everything from falling out, then stuck the bundle under her left arm and with her right hand continued pressing buttons on the medical monitor.

"He's in excellent hibernation," Elena said. "All his vitals are perfect."

"Good. Too bad he can't stay that way," Derek replied. "We need his help."

Elena began pressing buttons again. A moment later she hung the monitor back in the cradle.

"Alright, there you go. We just have to wait a day or two for him to thaw out."

Derek and Elena made their way back to Elena's cabin. They sat down on the floor and started eating the remainder of the food they'd gotten from the galley. Various empty food wrappers and plastic water pouches were strewn about the cabin.

"So how do you know that James guy?" Elena asked.

"JT," Derek corrected. "We've been friends since I was seven. He worked for my father in the Marine Corps. He was a mechanic. I always looked at him like an older brother, I guess."

Derek paused and took a deep breath.

"When my dad died, JT took care of me until I turned eighteen and joined the marines too," Derek elaborated.

"What happened to your mom?"

"She died when I was a baby. Just after I was born, actually. She never left the hospital. Some kind of infection she picked up there."

"I'm sorry to hear that. Those kind of things are all too common these days. You know, back around nineteen-hundred, seventy-five women out of every ten thousand who actually survived giving birth died shortly thereafter. That doesn't even count the women who died during childbirth."

"That doesn't sound too bad," Derek said.

"Well, here's where it gets interesting. In two-thousand, only around three women died for every hundred thousand. Then, in twenty-fifty, it dropped to one in a hundred thousand."

"Wow, that's really good."

"Well, that's where it bottomed out and started getting bad again," Elena said looking down at her hands folded across her lap. "In twenty-one-hundred it had jumped to nearly thirty deaths, and I read in a journal a couple of years ago that in the twenty-one-thirty census, the rate had jumped again. It's estimated that a hundred women die for every ten thousand babies that are born."

"That's crazy. I had no idea that things were that bad."

"It's actually worse than it sounds. Think about how many babies are born every year, and you get an idea of the total number of women who die. Of course, this doesn't take into account how many babies die as well."

"I guess I didn't think of that."

"I guess being a woman, I'm just more interested in these things."

The two of them sat quiet for several moments until Elena cleared her throat.

"You and JT have been friends for a long time," she said, taking a bite of a food bar.

"Well, actually we had a bit of a falling out about five years ago. We've only spoken once since then. This trip was supposed to be our time to reconnect. You know?"

"That sounds nice. So, what did you guys fight about?"

Derek sighed. "Well, I was receiving my commission just after graduating from the academy, and then JT tells me that he was getting out of the service. I took it as a personal insult. I felt like he was abandoning me. It had only been a few months since my dad died, and I guess I was still hurting from losing him, and it felt like I was losing JT also."

For several seconds, the only sound in the cabin was the sound of crackling plastic as they opened food bars, mixed nuts and other foodstuffs.

With a mouthful of half-chewed peanuts, Derek asked, "So why did you come on this trip?"

Elena's chewing slowed for a moment. She swallowed her mixed nuts and began to speak.

"Well, I've always worked hard to save lives. That's why I became a doctor. I wanted to help people. I guess *saving* lives is an alien concept to a soldier like you, isn't it," she said.

Derek looked at her as though she had punched him in the face. A vast array of nasty comebacks rifled through his brain. He calmed himself by taking several breaths.

"I've done everything I could to keep from taking lives," he countered. "I wish I could say I've never killed anyone, but I can't. I have killed one person, and it's haunted me ever since."

He turned away from her, sucking the water from a plastic pouch. Elena watched him closely, not sure of what to make of his response.

"What happened," she said, her voice as soft as velvet.

Derek proceeded to tell her about the mission where he'd been forced to shoot a colonist. During the story he kept his head down and never made eye contact with her, pretending to read and reread the labels of the food packages.

Derek described how, during negotiations, the colonist had become agitated and then combative, and when Derek tried to calm him down, he pulled a small laser pistol that he'd hidden in his pants. The colonist had taken aim at a Colonel, and Derek stepped in front of the Colonel and shot the colonist, killing him instantly.

"I got some shitty medal for it," he said, looking up. "They called it a selfless action saving the life of another marine. The truth is, I think they only gave it to me because that *other marine* was a full-bird Colonel. It was a reflex action from all the combat training. I spent a long time untraining myself, coming up with non-lethal combat techniques, and then retrained myself so that I wouldn't have another instinctive reflex that cost someone else his life."

Elena looked at Derek, not sure what to make of him. She found herself hating him less and less the longer she knew him. When she had first met him, she had instantly pegged him for the worst kind of human being, one who didn't care about the value of human life. She had felt that all soldiers were this way and that he was no different. She found it hard to continue to hate him, when he was trying to protect her from the men who were aboard the ship.

"So why did you become a doctor, fame and fortune?" Derek asked.

"No, it's personal," she replied.

"I apologize, I thought we were sharing," Derek said.

Peppered with guilt, Elena decided to open up to him.

"Well, when I was in high school, I had this friend," she stopped, emptying her water pouch with a slurp. "He was my boyfriend, actually."

She shuffled herself around, trying to get as comfortable as possible in an uncomfortable situation.

"Anyway, he was in a bad accident one day after school. He was pinned in his car until the emergency crew arrived. On my way home I happened to come along when a fireman was trying to cut the top of the car open to get him out. I could see him talking to the fireman."

She took a deep breath. Derek watched her closely.

"I stood back where the firemen made the crowd stand - they made me. I remember feeling so relieved that he was okay and talking, you know?" she said, not really expecting an answer. "Anyway, it all ended a minute or two later," she said, her voice cracking. "The car exploded. He died instantly, at least that's what they told us. The pneumatic cutters impaled the fireman who was trying to cut the roof of the car open. He died two days later as well."

Derek reached a hand across the pile of empty plastic and gave hers a squeeze. She looked up at him, and something inside them changed imperceptibly.

"Well, it was then and there that I knew that I wanted - no *needed* - to become a doctor. I wanted to do everything humanly possible to keep someone else from having to go through the pain I went through. I had never lost anyone so close to me, and I hurt for a long time. I guess sometimes it still does."

"Yeah, I still hurt when I think that whoever murdered my father is still out there somewhere."

Elena cocked her head to the side.

"He was murdered?"

"Yeah, a car bomb," Derek said. "It was back in twenty-six when we lived in California."

"I think I remember that on the news. Weren't there several other people killed also?"

"Yeah, two dead and one paralyzed. A couple of military men and the CEO from some company that builds starships."

Derek looked down and noticed that he was still holding Elena's hand. She looked down and realized it as well. Both of them quickly pulled their hands back.

"That's weird. That company was Kerey Star Drives. They originally had the contract to research and develop *this* ship! The guy leading this group said that he started this whole thing with a car bomb," Elena said, absentmindedly.

The hair on the back of Derek's neck stood on end. He stared at Elena, his mouth open wide.

"Oh my God! This whole thing is starting to make sense. Who would have known about the telemetry monitor?" Derek asked. "Who would have had access to the tubes and the passengers?"

Elena didn't answer.

"Someone intimately associated with the building of this ship! These guys in engineering have no regard for human life, right?"

She nodded.

"Would it make sense that these same guys might do anything to get the contract to build this ship, especially if they planned to steal the ship all along?"

Again, Elena nodded.

"These guys must work for the company that built this ship!"

"If that's true, then we're in real trouble here," Elena said. "They would know every nook and cranny on..." she trailed off, looking at Derek's face.

Derek's face was so pale that he looked as though he had been embalmed. His eyes were wide with a terrible realization.

"Are you okay?"

Derek's gaze came to rest on Elena's. His eyes narrowed to slits, and his hands balled into tight fists.

"General Durus said to me before I left, 'This is your father's mission – plain and simple'. These may be the same people who killed my dad."

Chapter Seventeen

Captured

Derek felt a lurch in his stomach. Stomach acid churned up within him, making his throat burn. He was unable to look Elena in the eye. It was as though there were a heavy weight on the back of his neck, keeping him from raising his head.

Elena stared at him in silence. She furrowed her brow, deep in thought. Her hands moved to her face, as her mouth slowly opened.

"Could that really be true?" she asked. "I mean, someone would have had to have been planning this for that many years. It would take someone cold and calculating, not to mention sociopathic!"

Derek felt as though he wanted to cry, scream or throw something, if not all three. He felt the dull pain of heartache pressing in his chest. Somewhere deep inside, he felt something else welling up beneath the heartache.

The new feeling continued to grow steadily until it suddenly flashed, overwhelming the pain he was feeling. The sudden rush of anger exploded out of Derek in a scream that made Elena jump. Derek's head tilted backward as though blasting this sudden anger out into the heavens. All the years of pain and self-imposed exile from JT erupted out of his open mouth and washed back down upon him, reflected by the high gray ceiling.

Elena, now recoiling from the sheer pounding in her ears, squinted as if to make the scream stop, her head turned away from the source of the noise. After several seconds, it stopped. She turned back to Derek, just in time to see a fountain of vomit erupt from his mouth. Bits of food, diluted by the copious amounts of water Derek had consumed, provided plenty of ammunition for his stomach.

"Oh God, I'm so sorry," Derek said, wiping his mouth.

Derek's face was now a deep shade of crimson. He started looking around for something to clean up the pool of vomit that was slowly spreading out across the floor.

"It's okay," Elena said as she ran to the bathroom. Several seconds later she returned and handed him a towel, another one just like it in her hand.

"I'm not going to catch anything if I clean this up, am I?" Elena asked, a smile on her face.

"What? No, I don't have anything, except maybe a stomach flu, you know?" he said, providing an alternative reason for why he'd thrown up.

"Yeah," Elena said. "That would explain the puke. It would have nothing to do with what you've just figured out." She gave him a half-hearted smile.

The two of them began to clean up the mess. Elena cleared her throat.

"Patients with gastrointestinal infections often regurgitate at regular intervals. For example, with *Salmonella typhii*," she stopped, looking up at Derek.

Derek's mouth was open slightly. His eyes had the 'glazed over' look.

"Sorry. Just trying to..." she trailed off. "Never mind", she said, her face turning slightly pink.

Neither of them spoke while they cleaned up the mess. Derek, whose stomach had settled down, didn't vomit again. He decided that their silence was because of embarrassment on both sides. Instead, he felt an anger that seemed to simmer within him. The feeling was like a low noise that, despite all the effort that's put into finding it, is never discovered. While they cleaned, he found himself continually taking deep breaths and noisily exhaling them. Elena kept a close watch on him but didn't say anything.

It can't be true about Dad. It can't be true. It's not.

Derek looked up several times while he was cleaning, and caught Elena watching him. At first he felt uncomfortable about the idea, but slowly the discomfort waned, and he began to enjoy it. The anger that pulsed through his veins began to fade away, replaced by a calmness he couldn't explain.

While he stared blankly at the floor, his mind was filled with an image: Elena was looking at him, smiling. Her hair was blowing in some unseen breeze. His mind cleared, and he realized that he had been rubbing the same spot with his towel. The spot had already been cleaned. He looked up to see Elena still watching him.

A droplet of sweat ran from his underarm and down his side, breaking his train of thought. Realizing he was sweating, he rubbed his upper arm across his side, trying to conceal it. Elena, having already finished cleaning the remainder of the pool, had been watching him wipe the already clean spot.

"Care to talk about it?" she said in the same soft voice he'd heard when telling her about his father.

Derek felt the familiar wall come up within him. His first instinct was to stand up and walk away from her, but he stopped himself. *I can't keep doing this. I have to stop pushing people away. She's a doctor for God's sake!*

Derek took a shuddering breath and said, "I guess all these years I've been in pain because of the loss of my dad. It hurt so much that, ever since then, I've always pushed people away from me when things got too emotional. I mean Jesus, you have no idea how hard it is for me to tell you this."

Elena's hand shot out and picked Derek's hand up.

"It's okay. You can talk to me," she said, her voice even more soothing than it had been.

Derek looked down at their entwined hands. He quickly pulled his hand away.

"Jeez," Derek said, looking at his palm.

"I'm sorry. I guess I shouldn't push you into talking to me. I mean, we're practically strangers."

Derek looked up at her, a look of confusion on his face.

"What? Oh, no that's okay. I just, well, look," he said, pointing at her hand.

Elena looked down, and saw that the palm of her hand was covered in a thin film of slimy vomit, studded with bits of peanut.

"Oh, now that's just nasty," Elena mumbled.

Derek laughed and handed Elena his towel. Elena wiped off the vomit without looking at Derek. After she had wiped her hand clean, she looked at him. He was watching her, a slight smile on his face.

Elena laughed through her nose, dislodging a short stream of gelatinous goo that hung down from her nostril.

"Oh my God," she said as she felt what had happened.

She quickly pulled her vomit soaked towel up to her face and wiped her nose with it. The acidic liquid burned the inside of her nose.

"Alright, can we start over? Hi, I'm Elena Brown. And you are?" she said, sticking her hand out as if to have him shake it.

Derek started laughing harder than he had in a long time. After several seconds of hard laughter, tears began blur his vision. Elena began to smile and eventually laugh. The two of them continued laughing for several minutes.

"I've got an idea on how we can handle these guys in engineering," Elena said. "You puke on 'em and I'll blow snot on 'em. They'd never see that coming!" They laughed again.

After the laughing subsided, they both went to the bathroom and washed out the towels. After they had washed their hands, Derek put his hands on his hips and looked at Elena, a look of disbelief on his face.

"What is it now?"

"Now that I've thrown up everything, I'm hungry," he said, as if he didn't believe it himself.

"No shit," she said, giggling.

The halls of the aft section of the ship were now dark again. Derek had gone to the circuit-breaker panel as he had done before, and shut off the sections they needed to travel through to get to the galley again. Because they had exhausted the food supply they had gotten on their previous visit, they needed to return. This time, Derek had decided to have Elena bring a small wastebasket that had been in her cabin. If they filled it with food and water pouches, they wouldn't have to make a return trip for quite a while. They also knew that they would be going to get JT shortly after their trip to the galley, and he would most likely be hungry as well.

Derek crept silently along the wall of the corridor. Elena, peering around the corner of the passage behind Derek, watched him closely. He reached a crossing corridor and slowly leaned his head around it. After he'd verified that it was clear, he motioned Elena forward. As she stepped around the corner, her wastebasket bumped the corner and made a dull thump.

Derek immediately crouched down on one knee, pressing himself against the wall. Elena swiftly ducked back around the corner, her teeth gritted. She waited for nearly a minute and then peeked around the corner. Her gaze met Derek, who was looking at her with a look of fury on his face.

Sorry, she silently mouthed to him.

He waved her forward again, and they continued off down the corridor. As they moved down the last passage toward the galley, Derek stopped dead in his tracks. Elena saw his head swiveling around, looking in all directions.

Did you hear something? he mouthed to her, his hand pointing to his ear.

Elena shrugged and shook her head. After a few seconds of listening, Derek moved on, Elena trailing behind him. When they reached the galley, Derek took the wastebasket from Elena and placed it on a small steel table.

"Alright, we're going to need to fill this thing up. JT's probably going to be hungry, and he's a big eater. We need high-calorie, high-fiber foods," Derek instructed.

The two of them began rifling through the small, locker-like cabinets.

"Don't forget water. We need lots of that, too."

"Yes, sir," she said stiffly, coming to attention.

Derek looked at her, and then smiled. Elena smiled back and resumed her search.

"What about this?" she said, holding out a can of lentil soup. "It's got lots of protein and fiber."

"Well, that would be fantastic, except for one thing."

Elena stared at him, waiting.

"Are you going to gnaw that can open or what?"

"Well, there's a can opener right there," she said, pointing to an electric can opener, mounted under a cabinet.

Derek looked at her, waiting for her to realize the folly of what she had suggested. She simply stared at him.

"Too noisy."

"Oh, yeah right," she said, placing the can back in the cabinet.

They continued for several minutes, the wastebasket slowly filling.

"You know, I have a question," Elena said. "Where do you suppose these assholes in engineering are getting their food?"

"I'll answer that one," came a voice from behind them.

Startled, Elena dropped a water pouch on the galley floor. Both she and Derek turned to see a man standing in the galley doorway holding a pistol pointed directly at them. The man, whom Derek didn't recognize, had a military haircut.

Derek instantly began scanning the room for exits, as well as improvised weapons. Various scenarios raced through his mind. He could grab a can of beans and hurl it at the pistol wielding man, or he could lunge for the weapon. He could even try diving behind the steel counter for cover while he came up with a decent plan.

His eyes, which had been moving rapidly around the room, stopped on the back of Elena's head. In all the scenarios that he had being contemplating, none had included a civilian. She would be helpless if he made a hasty retreat. Even worse, she might get shot if Derek attempted to rush the man and disarm him. He stepped out from behind Elena to get a better look at their opponent.

The man was nearly Derek's height and weight. He was wearing a pair of black military pants, and a gray shirt. Judging by the volume of the hum emanating from the plasma pistol he held, Derek assumed it to be fully charged. Derek looked at the floor sections, and, knowing that each section was a one-foot square, saw that he was standing nearly thirteen feet away.

Even on my best day I couldn't close thirteen feet before he got a shot off. I'd be dead before I even got to him.

"Keep your hands where I can see them, both of you," the man instructed.

Derek and Elena both held their hands out in front of them.

"I might just get a nice fat reward when I show those 'assholes in engineering' the two of you. Of course, my employer will want to know how you got on board, seeing as how everyone is supposed to be sleeping."

"We aren't going to say anything, soldier," Derek said in a monotone.

"Oh really? We'll see. This way," he said, waving the gun toward the dark corridor. "Ah, wait right there a second."

He reached around and opened the power distribution panel. He quickly scanned the buttons and switches and found the sections that were disabled. With a few clicks, the corridor lights all illuminated.

"Now then, where were we? Oh yes, right this way!"

He slowly backed out of the room as Derek and Elena approached him. As they got to a cross-corridor, he backed around the corner, and motioned them to continue on down the straight corridor ahead of him.

"Can't you order him to let us go?" Elena asked.

"I don't think he'll listen, but I'll try. I have an idea."

Derek stopped and turned on his heel. He stood stiffly upright, his hands down at his sides.

"Soldier, drop that weapon right now or I'll be forced to place you in the brig."

"Oh, really? And just who might I ask would be putting me in the brig?"

"I'm Major Cross. This is Captain Brown."

Elena looked at him, then back at the man.

"Major? Captain?" the man said, a look of shock on his face. "What are a Major and a Captain doing here?"

"Soldier, I'm not going to ask you again." Derek extended an open hand. "Your weapon. This is your last chance."

For a few seconds, the man appeared to ponder his situation. Derek stared at him, allowing him ample time to think about the consequences of either decision. The man's features softened, and Derek knew he was only seconds away from being handed the pistol.

Derek watched in anguish as the man's features hardened again. He knew the man had decided not to relinquish the weapon and surrender.

"I don't think so, sir," he said sarcastically. "I think we've pretty much got things under control here. We don't really need any officers screwing things up. Besides, you're all supposed to be dead already. Now, turn around and keep walking."

Derek slowly turned and started down the corridor. As they walked, Derek started consciously taking smaller and smaller steps, hoping that he could close the distance between them and the man with the gun. If they could do that, and he didn't notice, Derek could quickly grab the weapon and, if he were lucky, take it away from the attacker.

"You know," Derek said, turning back to the man, checking the distance. "We aren't going to tell your friends anything."

He noticed that the distance was still too great for him to be able to lunge out and get the gun. The man stopped, staring Derek in the eye.

"You might as well give it up, sir. I know you're trying to close the gap between us. It won't work. I know the same tactics you do."

Derek turned and started walking again, trying to come up with another plan. Because the corridor was now well lit, trying to run would make them an easy shot for a trained soldier.

"If that's true, you know that the Captain and I here have both been trained in resisting even the worst tortures during our POW training. We'll never tell you anything. We'll die first. If you know anything about officers, you know I'm not lying to you about that."

The footfalls behind them stopped. Derek stopped immediately thereafter, followed quickly by Elena. Turning slowly around, Derek saw that he had struck a nerve with the soldier behind them. His pistol pointed slightly downward, the man was obviously thinking hard on the situation, as he wasn't even looking at his captives. Whatever information he wanted, it was obvious he was convinced that he and his boss weren't going to get it.

"God, I don't want to piss him off," the man mumbled.

"That's right," Derek said, waving his arms. "He's not a very pleasant guy when he gets mad, is he?"

"No, he likes to kill people who make him angry. If I take you to him and you don't talk, he'll likely kill you. But he'll be angry for a long time, and I don't want to have to deal with that."

"Yeah, it would be a bad idea to take us to him," Elena added, glancing at Derek.

The man rubbed his chin, deep in thought. Suddenly, his demeanor changed. His eyes narrowed, and a slight smile crept across his lips.

"I think I have a better idea," he said, his grin broadening.

Derek and Elena found themselves backed into a cargo lander just down the passage from several of the passenger landers. The barrel of the pistol was pointed at Derek's chest.

"You can't do this!" Elena pleaded.

"I'm afraid this is my only option. If I take you to see my boss, you'll make him very angry, and then he'll kill you. That will be the end of your problems, but only the beginning of mine. If I kill you, then go get him, he'll be happy with me. Especially when I tell him that I snagged a Major and a Captain! And he'll realize that something happened with his plan to kill the soldiers automatically, and he'll start questioning the entire plan."

The man had a very sinister look about him, partly because of the gun he was holding, but also because he was standing just inside the open cargo lander doorway and was only partially lit. The darkened corridor behind him and the dim light that shone on him gave him a very forbidding, ghostlike appearance.

"Look, why don't you let her go? She can't hurt you. She's only a Captain because she is a medical doctor. You guys might even need her at some point."

"Move!" the man said, gesturing toward the blank wall behind them. "I'll make this quick, unless you keep this up, in which case I'll have to expend a whole power cell on the two of you."

Derek and Elena slowly backed toward the wall. Both of them kept their hands out in front of them, their palms facing the man.

"Don't we get some kind of request?" Elena asked. "People who get the firing squad always get a request."

"You're making an assumption," the man replied. "Condemned people get a last request in the old world; a world with rules and laws made by a bunch of assholes. On this ship, there are no laws, except the ones *we* make," he said pointing his thumb at his chest.

Derek moved slowly backward, until his heel hit the wall. He glanced at Elena, who bumped the wall just after him. She looked at him, and their intertwined gaze seemed to envelop them. Without thinking, Derek slowly lowered his hand and reached it toward her palm up.

Derek watched as Elena looked down at his outstretched hand, and with a light smile, reached out and took it. Derek stared at their joined hands, his mind racing. *Why the hell did this have to happen now?*

Slowly, Derek traced Elena's arm up to her elbow, and then to her shoulder. He continued up until he saw her neck. On the side of her neck, he could see the large artery pulsing and flexing as it filled and emptied rapidly. Derek realized how frightened she must be, and a wave of sorrow washed over him. Unconsciously, he cocked his head to the side and gave her a half smile, as if to show her that he was sorry this was happening.

Derek looked up at Elena's face and saw that she was still looking at him. She was pale, and the tears that were beginning to form on her lower eyelids stood in stark contrast to the smile she too had on her face. When she looked in his eyes, her smile broke wide, exposing her teeth, just as a single tear fell down her cheek.

Derek gave her hand a squeeze as he turned back to the man with the gun.

"Alright, we've made our peace. Get it over with," Derek commanded.

Derek stood tall, his back muscles tensed. Elena squeezed his hand so tightly that he could feel the circulation being cut off. Derek stared directly at the man, feelings of anger as well as sadness brewing inside him like a thunderstorm.

Derek stared at the man, waiting to feel the plasma bolt burn through his chest when the man fired. He stared, his heart pounding. The pistol in the man's hand began to shake. A look of grim determination began to grow on his face, as he appeared to fight a battle within himself.

Derek continued to stare at the man, while the shaking of the gun grew more and more violent. The man's lips drew back, exposing his gritted teeth.

"You can't do it, can you?" Derek asked. "You're more civilized than that. This isn't a firefight. This is murder."

"Shut up!" the man said, transferring the gun to his other hand.

"You can't look two civilized people in the eye and pull that trigger, can you?"

The man continued to wrestle with his emotions, the battle within him bringing out an array of sweat beads on his upper lip. Suddenly, the gun stopped shaking. The man smiled, and exhaled loudly.

"You're right. I can't look you in the eye and shoot you."

Derek and Elena both let out a loud sigh and smiled. Derek knew that because he had looked them in the eye, it would be very difficult for him to pull the trigger. He knew that it was easy for a soldier to shoot at a silhouette that was fifty yards away, but once combat got into close quarters, something deep in the human psyche told the rational mind that what was happening was wrong. Somewhere in antiquity, the human species evolved this instinct as a way to help continue the dominance of the species and reduce intra-species conflicts. Man had, of course, nearly eliminated this instinct with the advent of ranged weapons.

"You're right. I can't look you in the eye, so turn around!"

The smiles instantly vanished from their faces. Derek knew the only thing that had kept them alive was their stares. Once they turned around, he wouldn't have to see the life blasted out of their bodies, and see it reflected in their eyes.

"Please don't do this," Elena pleaded.

"Shut up and turn around, or I'll make this long and slow," the man said through gritted teeth.

Elena turned to Derek, and they both relinquished their grips on each other's hand. They slowly turned to face the cold steel wall. Derek took a deep breath, and then blew it out, leaving a sphere of condensation on the wall in front of him. He watched as the wetness slowly vanished.

Derek felt a light contact against his low back and looked around. Elena, who was facing the wall beside him, had reached her arm around him. He looked over at her, and saw that she was facing the wall, her eyes closed.

Derek looked forward again at the blank wall. He closed his eyes and took a deep breath. The seconds seemed to last an eternity as Derek waited to die. His heart was racing, and the underarms of his shirt were soaked with sweat.

He took another deep breath, and slowly let it out. He repeated the deep breathing until he felt his heartbeat slowing down. Death was only moments away, and he had accepted his fate. He felt Elena's hand on his back start to move slowly up and down, caressing him.

Derek tried to concentrate on her touch, and forget about what was coming. He found himself anticipating the movements of her hand, almost willing it to move upward, then downward again.

His mind wandered as he followed the hand up and down. He heard a thump, the hand stopped moving, and he was jarred back to the cargo lander. Another sound followed almost immediately after the first one. The second was like something heavy, yet soft, falling to the floor.

Derek opened his eyes and stared at the wall, examining its plain surface, listening and trying to figure out what the man was doing. He slowly turned to Elena, whose eyes were open as well. She turned to look at him.

Slowly, Derek and Elena turned to look at the man, but what they saw didn't make any sense, like seeing a dog riding a bicycle. The two of them turned to each other, and then back again, their minds racing to understand what was happening. The man lay in a heap on the dimly lit floor, the pistol still clutched in his unconscious hand.

Derek cocked his head and made a face of sheer bewilderment. He glanced at Elena, who just pointed, her mouth slightly agape. Her eyes suddenly opened wide, causing Derek to look back toward the man.

Something in the darkened corridor was moving toward the doorway.

"Alright," came a familiar voice. "What the hell is goin' on here?"

An overweight black man, who happened to be completely naked, stepped into the bay rubbing the knuckles of his right hand.

"And where the hell are my pants?"

Derek started to laugh. He glanced at Elena, who had turned a light pink.

"Man, am I glad to see you, JT," Derek said, trying to avoid looking at JT's naked body. "Of course, I would have liked to have seen a little bit less of you."

Chapter Eighteen

Defection

After Elena had checked the unconscious man's vital signs, she helped Derek and JT tie him up. She spent most of the time complaining about how tight the bindings were, as well as various other things that the two men were doing that were either wrong or cruel. JT had started complaining about his hunger while Elena was checking the bump on the back of the man's head to make sure his injury wasn't life-threatening. He didn't stop until Elena and Derek agreed to take him to the galley.

After they had gone to the galley and retrieved the food-filled wastebasket and as much food as they could carry in their hands and taken it back to Elena's room, Derek and JT went back to the cargo lander and carried the still unconscious man to the lander where JT had been frozen. Elena came in just after Derek and JT strapped the man's limp body into one of the three empty tubes.

"Plug this in for me," Elena said, handing Derek the cable attached to the electronic medical monitor. "I've encrypted the control so no one is going to wake this guy before we get to Avalon. I don't think those guys will even think to look here once they realize he's missing, but I'm not taking any chances."

Derek plugged in the device, and Elena began pressing buttons. JT stepped back several feet to be out of their way. Elena dropped a small pack on the deck at her feet and pulled out a pneumatic injector, two bottles, and a bag of cryoprotectant.

"I'm only estimating his weight, so I hope I get this right," Elena said, placing a bottle in the injector.

"Take this," Elena said, handing the bag of cryoprotectant to Derek. "I need to start the IV."

Elena took one of the man's limp arms and jabbed the needle into it.

"Start squeezing that bag," she commanded, putting the injector to the man's other arm.

With a bang, the solution in the first bottle was fired into his arm. Elena unloaded the empty bottle and slammed the second into the injector. A second bang echoed throughout the bay, as the second injection was given.

Derek, continuing to squeeze the bag, said, "Hey, I have a plan. I'd like your opinion on it, both of you."

JT stepped back up beside Derek while Elena packed the injector and empty bottles into her small pack.

"Well, I know that there were four guys in engineering when I did my latest recon. My initial threat assessment would put the dark-haired guy at the top of the list, followed by the Hispanic, then the fat guy, and then the boy. I never did see this guy, so I hadn't counted on him. That was a problem that nearly got us both killed. The problem now is that there are two more we haven't seen yet - two soldiers."

Derek squeezed out the last of the liquid in the bag, and then handed it to Elena.

"So there are two more grunts like this one running around somewhere?" JT asked.

Derek nodded.

"Doctor Brown is it? Do you got any more of that stuff you just gave that guy?"

"Yes, there are a few more doses left in the medical bay. It's lucky someone forgot to unload the cabinet. Why? I don't think it could be used as a weapon or anything."

"No, I'm talking about puttin' my ass back to sleep! That way, when I get back up, all this will be over."

Elena looked at Derek, a stunned look on her face.

"He's just kidding, don't worry." Derek paused. "You are just kidding aren't you?"

After a long pause, JT said, "Yeah, I'm kiddin'."

"Anyway, back to my idea," Derek said. "We were able to neutralize this guy by getting the drop on him. Maybe we can do that with the others as well. I was thinking that I could go back down to engineering. When one of them gets off by himself, I'll take him out."

Elena made a face. "I can't agree to killing anyone. There has to be another way we can stop them without murder!"

"I don't believe you! You keep jumping to these conclusions that I want to kill everyone I see. If I can use the element of surprise on these guys, I can use non-lethal means of capturing them one at a time," Derek said, his hands on his hips.

"He's right, doc. He wouldn't hurt nobody if he didn't have to," JT added.

"I'm sorry," Elena said. "It's just that, well, you're a soldier. It's really hard for me to think of a soldier as being someone who values life, that's all."

"Look, back there in the cargo bay when we were about to be killed, something happened between us. Didn't it? Believe me when I say I don't want to kill anyone if at all possible. We have a single plasma pistol, thanks to that guy. As a show of good faith, I want you two to keep it when I go to engineering."

Elena looked at JT, who gave her an approving nod. She turned back to Derek, a look of suspicion on her face.

"That's all well and good, but you're trained to kill with your bare hands, aren't you?"

"What do you want me to do, cut my hands off and leave them here too?"

"Yeah, that would be good," Elena said with a smile.

She reached out toward Derek, who slowly reached toward her. She moved toward him, and just before their hands met she brushed past him and picked up the freezing tube control unit.

Derek cleared his throat and looked at JT, hoping he hadn't seen what just happened. *She did that on purpose.*

Elena pressed the buttons that started the freezing process, and droplets of liquid helium started to rain down on the unconscious man as the tube's glass door closed.

The three gathered their things and made their way back to Elena's cabin. After threatening to do bodily harm to JT if he laughed, Derek walked out of Elena's bathroom wearing her dress and long sleeved shirt. After ten minutes of JT laughing, Derek made his way down to the Level 3 corridor and worked his way toward engineering.

Derek slowly approached the open doorway at the end of the dark corridor. As he approached he could hear voices talking loudly.

"Hurry up, chubby. I want to read the news and see if my stock has made any money," an unfamiliar voice said.

"I'm almost finished, and stop calling me chubby or I'll stop working on this right now. Everyone calls me Tiny, or one of two things happens. One, I kick the shit out of them, which in your case probably isn't very likely, or, two, I don't do jack shit for 'em."

"Well, I apologize, Tiny. Now hurry the fuck up! Jesus, the worst techs in the corps could have had this uplink hacked hours ago, and we're stuck with you."

A marine. A shiver shot down Derek's spine, making goose-bumps rise.

"Everyone be quiet," came a shout Derek knew had to be from the dark-haired man. "Conway, give Tiny some breathing room and he'll finish the uplink. I would like to catch up on the news from Earth from while we were sleeping, just as much as you do. Shouting at him isn't going to make things go any faster."

"But sir!"

"No buts!" boomed through the bay and down the corridor. "You are here for one reason and one reason only! To provide me with military support once we reach Avalon. If I find that you are going to become an impediment to my plan, I will have you blown out into space and I'll replace you with someone else, do I make myself clear?"

The other voices in the bay fell silent.

"Yes, sir," Conway said softly. "I'll make myself useful and clean up here, and then run up to the galley and gather some of the ship's food. This junk we're eating is giving me the shits."

"Hold off, Conway," the dark-haired man said. "News feeds are almost up. I'll give you the honor of checking your stocks before you go."

Derek slowly backed away from the door. When he was out of earshot of the men, he started jogging down the corridor.

I'll hide in the galley and take him out when he gets there.

Derek arrived in the galley and began searching for a place to conceal himself and wait for Conway's arrival. The galley was roughly square, so there were no corners he could hide around. Because he felt rushed for time, he finally decided to simply turn off the galley lights and crouch behind a steel table. When Conway entered the room and turned on the lights, Derek would know exactly where he was and could spring out and take him down before he knew there was another person on board.

Derek knelt down behind the table and waited. After a few minutes, he started shifting his weight back and forth from one foot to the other, as he felt his legs falling asleep. He checked his watch; it had been nearly thirty minutes since Conway had been told to come down to the galley. *Maybe he changed his mind.* Derek was just about to stand when he heard something in the corridor approaching the galley.

Light footsteps approached the galley and stopped when they reached the open galley door. Something about the footsteps didn't sound quite right to Derek. He couldn't put a finger on exactly what was wrong until he heard the sounds of someone sniffling.

Conway caught a cold on the way to the kitchen?

With a click, the galley lights came on, temporarily blinding Derek. He hadn't expected to be in the dark for so long, but he had been. He would have to make this quick, otherwise his opponent would have the advantage because of Derek's temporarily poor vision.

Derek caught a glimpse of a leg moving around the edge of the table, and he sprang into action. His weight on the balls of his feet, he put his hands down in front of him and spun around on his right foot, sending his left foot upward toward Conway.

His heel made solid contact, and Derek could hear the gratifying sound of the wind being knocked out of him. Derek took a step back and readied another blow as he watched his enemy crumple to the floor.

On his knees, holding his stomach, the enemy gasped and coughed. Derek saw only the top of his head, as he held his stomach tight. The blond hair hung down and touched the steel deck plate. Something about this felt vaguely familiar; déjà vu of sorts.

Conway raised his head, and to Derek's alarm he found that not only had Conway not come to the galley, someone he knew had. Derek stared into the eyes of the same young boy he'd nearly killed on Ganymede.

Derek gave the boy several minutes to catch his breath. Derek's own heart was racing, and he had started sweating. He noticed that the boy's nose was running heavily, and his eyes were bloodshot. *I don't think I caused that. All I did was knock the wind out of him!*

"Sorry about that. Hold your arms up over your head, it helps," Derek said softly, looking at the boy's eyes.

The boy nodded and held his arms up. His breathing slowly returned to normal.

Derek looked at the boy's shirtsleeve, and saw that he had damp streaks along the inside of the right forearm. Derek's gaze moved back to the boy's runny nose and bloodshot eyes.

"Have you been crying?" Derek asked.

The boy slowly nodded and sniffled loudly without looking up. He ran his right arm along his nose, wiping it clean.

"Are you alright?" Derek asked in a calm tone.

The boy nodded.

"Do you mind if I ask your name?"

"Tommy," he paused. "Well, actually it's Tom," he said, looking up at Derek. "I know you, don't I?"

"We've met once before. Rather briefly, actually."

"I don't remember your name," Tom said. "I'm usually really good with names, but I can't remember yours."

"We actually didn't speak to each other." Derek took a deep breath. "I did the same thing to you once before, only I hit you with a rifle. My guess is I bruised or broke a couple of ribs, didn't I?"

Tom's eyes went wide. A look of fear swept across his face, and he cringed slightly. He started looking around for an escape route.

"It's okay, Tom. I'm not going to hurt you. Not again, anyway."

Tom didn't immediately relax.

"Do you mind if I ask why you were crying?"

Tom took a deep breath.

"He killed my mom and my grandpa," Tom said, looking down at his hands.

"Who?" Derek said softly.

"My dad."

"Your dad killed your mother and grandfather?"

Tommy nodded.

"We just hacked into the data feeds from Earth so they could read the news briefs for the last few months while we've been asleep. Apparently he planted bombs at the factory where they all worked. My mom and my grandpa were both at the factory when they blew it up."

"I don't understand. Why would your dad kill your mother and grandfather?"

Tommy shrugged.

"They are all happy about it, like it's some great thing they did. He said we were doing this for good. He said that mankind needed our help and that we had to be strong. I had no idea this is what he meant. I guess I should have known when I found those bombs."

Derek paused, trying to take in what he was hearing.

"Bombs? What did the bombs look like?"

"They were these green, cylinder-tube things. They said something like 'one-hundred eighty gigahertz' and 'US Army GX something'."

"GVX explosive?"

"That sounds right," Tom said.

"How many of these were there, do you remember?"

"I don't remember, maybe six."

"Jesus, you could level a city block with six GVX HEAPs."

"What's a heep?" Tom asked.

"H, E, A, P. It's short for high-explosive anti-personnel. It's a common explosive used in dense terrain, like forest. The concussion blasts out all the trees, as well as anyone hiding in 'em. It's a really nasty, as well as a fairly new explosive. I'd like to know how your dad got his hands on 'em."

"I don't know. I just found them."

"What's your dad's name?" Derek asked.

"Frederick Samson."

"As in *Samson Industries*? He blew up the factory where the components for this ship were built?"

"Yeah, my grandpa started the company a long time ago. My dad is the VP of security. My mom is…," he paused. "My mom *was* a department director."

Derek began to piece all the information together. Frederick Samson would be privy to all the information on the colony project, since his company had designed and had built the ship. He would have had access to the crew records and been able to change the manifests in order to replace colonists with people who would follow him.

He must have got the colonist manifest before my name was added, otherwise he'd have known about me, and I'd probably be dead right now.

"I'm sorry about your mom," Derek said, placing a hand on Tom's shoulder. "I lost my dad in much the same way. I was a little bit older than you are now, but I know it doesn't make it hurt any less."

"How can you even say that you lost someone in much the same way I did! My own father murdered my mother!"

Derek pulled back his hand, and placed it on his hip.

"Well, if it makes you feel any better, your father may be working with the people who killed mine."

Tom looked stunned. He appeared to be searching for something to say, his mouth slowly opening and closing as if he were speaking in slow-motion.

"You don't have to say anything," Derek said. "To be honest, I'm not really sure that's right or not. I just..." he trailed off.

After a few seconds of silence, Tom stood and surveyed the galley.

"I'm afraid I can't let you go back to engineering," Derek said.

Without missing a beat, Tom said, "Don't worry, I don't want to go back. I want to get as far away from him as I can."

Derek looked him over, trying to decide what to do.

"I guess baby makes *four*," Derek mumbled.

"Pardon?"

"I was just commenting on where you can go. You can come with me if you want."

Tom looked Derek up and down. He then turned and looked around the galley again. Derek watched him suspiciously.

"Alright, I'll come with you on one condition. No, make that two conditions."

"And they would be?"

"First, you explain to me why you're dressed like a girl," he said looking at Derek's dress. "And second you promise me that I won't have to dress like a girl."

Both of them laughed.

"Done," Derek said. "I wasn't supposed to wake up until we got to Avalon, and this was all I could find to wear. What, you don't think black is my color?" he asked, smiling broadly.

Tom raised his eyebrows and stared at him.

"Never mind," Derek said. "It'll be interesting to explain this to Doc and JT."

"Who?"

Derek sat and explained the situation to Tom. He intentionally left out the part about Elena nearly losing her mind.

Derek continued up to the point where he had hidden himself in the galley to catch Conway.

"Conway's a jerk," Tom said.

"I got that impression, too," Derek said.

"When this is all over, I want Conway's jacket," Tom said with a smile. "It's really cool."

"Oh yeah, what makes it so cool?"

"It is a neat army jacket. It has this really cool patch on the side. It has a picture of a spaceship with lightning coming out of it striking a bird that's holding a sword."

Another chill ran down Derek's back and radiated down his arms.

"A lightning bolt coming down from a spaceship? Could it be that the bird is coming down from the spaceship, sort of riding the lightning down?"

"Yeah, I guess that could be what it is, why?"

"No reason," Derek lied, rubbing his arms to rid himself of the goose bumps.

"So there are four of us now?" Tom asked.

"Yeah, we should probably head down to Elena's room. They might be getting worried about me."

Tommy scanned the galley again.

"Are you okay?" Derek asked.

"I'm *really* hungry. Can we grab somethin' to eat?"

"We have some food back in the cabin, but go ahead and grab whatever you can carry."

Back at Elena's cabin, Derek lightly thumped on the door. After a few seconds the door clicked and opened slightly.

"Password?" Elena asked.

"What?"

"Password."

"Open the door before I kick it in and kill you both with my bare hands," Derek said.

"Uh, password accepted," Elena said, opening the door fully.

Elena had started to ask Derek how his recon had gone, when Tom stepped around the corner and into view. Her eyes went wide and her mouth fell open.

"There's a kid here." JT stated the obvious.

"Where the hell did he come from?" Elena asked.

"I'll explain later. We've got a major problem," Derek said in a serious tone.

JT, who had been across the room, walked over and sat down on the edge of Elena's bed, looking up at Derek and Tom.

"The guy who's running the show in engineering... Frederick Samson."

"You mean, like, Samson Industries, Frederick Samson?" Elena asked.

"That would be the one. At least now we know how they got those three soldiers onto the ship without raising an eyebrow."

"Yeah, those guys would have had free rein with this mission," JT added.

JT walked over to Tom and knelt down on one knee.

"Are you hungry or thirsty? We got plenty of stuff to eat over there," JT said, pointing at the desk where the overturned wastebasket was sitting, the food in a pile beside it.

"Thanks, but I grabbed some stuff when we left the kitchen," Tom replied, patting his pockets.

"Good," JT said, standing. He placed his hand on Tom's head, and mussed his hair.

Elena looked at Derek, who looked back smiling.

He's great with kids, Derek mouthed to her.

Elena smiled and nodded.

Derek turned and walked back over to the cabin door. He turned around to face the group, a serious look on his face.

"I'm going to need to borrow that," he said pointing to the pistol. "I think it's time we made our presence known."

Chapter Nineteen

Modifications

Where the hell is Tommy?" Tiny asked. "I'm starving."

"He hasn't been gone that long. Relax," Frederick said, looking at his watch.

Frederick was beginning to wonder what Tommy had gotten himself into that was taking so long. He knew that his son was prone to flights of fancy and was probably at this very moment sitting in the captain's chair on the bridge. *Spoiled little brat.*

"I'd *really* like some chow, too," Conway said. "What about you, Barney?"

A stocky man dressed in a navy-blue military uniform stepped out from behind a crate and said, "I could do with some grub, too. That kid of yours ought to hurry up, or I'll have to go get something myself."

"Will you all drop it," Frederick snapped. "He should be back any minute now."

The room was silent except for the engine noise, the continual low hum reverberating throughout the ship.

Conway stared at Frederick, who looked back and forth at the rest of the men. No one else looked him in the eye.

A crackle of static broke the silence in the room, and all five men looked up at the high ceiling of the bay. Another crackle echoed, and they fixed their eyes on a small black intercom speaker in the ceiling.

"That damn kid is lost and needs someone to rescue him," Conway said laughing.

"Shh! Tom wouldn't know how to operate the intercom system on the ship, much less where to find a control unit."

The five men got quiet, waiting for the person who had activated the intercom to speak. After several seconds, their wait came to an end.

"Attention. This is Major Derek Cross, United States Marine Corps to the men in engineering."

The men, with the exception of Frederick, all started looking around at each other. Frederick stared at the speaker.

"This is...the men in engineering," Frederick said, his tone eerily calm.

"I assume I'm speaking to Frederick Samson, correct?"

Frederick brought his head down and leveled his gaze at Conway. Conway, understanding the unspoken question, simply shrugged. Tiny, Barney and Jose' all moved in and clustered around Frederick.

"Very good, mister Cross. You've got our attention. What do you want?"

"It isn't what I want. It's what I have that *you* want. And it's *Major*, not mister."

"Touché, Major. So what is it that *I* want?"

"Well let's see. How about your son, for starters."

Frederick stared straight ahead at the blank wall in front of him. The other men all looked around at each other except Conway, who started laughing.

"You think this is funny, do you?" Derek said, his voice tinged with anger.

"No, Major. I don't find this funny. One of my associates seems to think it is, though."

Frederick turned and looked at Conway, who immediately stopped laughing and cleared his throat.

"So Major, how do I get my son back?"

"By surrendering unconditionally."

Frederick looked around at his men, and said, "And if I refuse?"

"Well, I've already neutralized one of your men and I'm not above taking out your son as well."

Frederick looked directly at Conway, as if looking through him.

"So be it, Major Cross. At this stage in the game, my son isn't a priority."

The long pause told Frederick that his calling of Derek's bluff had worked.

"Do you have anything else I want, Major Cross?" Frederick asked calmly.

"Just the ship," Derek said, pressing a button on the console in front of him.

Instantly, all of the doors that led out of engineering began to close. Conway ran for the nearest door, which closed just as he reached it.

"You can't really do anything if you're locked in engineering," Derek said. "I've also disabled all of the control systems and rerouted the ones I couldn't disable. You're trapped and helpless."

"Tiny," Frederick said calmly. "Please open this door, so that I may go and kill Major Cross."

"Yes, sir," Tiny said, moving toward the door nearest to them. "Give me a few minutes."

"Oh, and one more thing," Derek said. "I still have to kill your son."

Derek raised the plasma pistol, aimed it, and fired.

Frederick stared straight at the wall in front of him as he heard the sound of a bolt of plasma erupt from the speaker high above him. He heard a grunt, then something falling to the floor.

"Major Cross out," Derek said, turning off the intercom.

Derek stepped away from the console, taking a deep breath. He turned to walk out of the bridge, looking at the plasma burn he'd just created on the back wall.

What am I going to tell the kid?

Derek sprinted out of the bridge, jumping over the large bag of freeze-dried potatoes he'd dropped on the floor after firing the pistol. He ran as fast as he could down the hall toward Elena's cabin.

"What did he say?" Tom asked.

"You don't want to know," Derek said, sitting down on the bed next to Tom.

"What *exactly* did he say?" Elena asked, a frown on her face.

"Well, let's just say that Tom's going to be staying with us."

"What the hell did he say," JT said loudly.

Derek looked at Tom, a look of pity on his face.

"He said that Tom didn't matter to him."

Tom's head hung down. Elena knelt in front of Tom and looked up into his eyes, which were filling with tears.

"You can stay with us," Elena told Tom. "You can stay with us as long as you want to. We'll take care of you."

Tom nodded. Tears began to roll down his face. His hands moved to cover his face, and he started to sob.

Elena wrapped her arms around him, his elbows pressing into her chest as she pulled him close. JT took Derek's arm and led him out into the hall outside the cabin.

"You sure you're up to this?" JT asked.

"That poor kid. His father just threw him away," Derek said, looking into the cabin.

"Derek," JT said, patting Derek on the arm. "We don't have a lot of time. I disabled what I could down there, but still have a lot to do, so we have to get busy."

Derek turned and looked at JT. He blinked and shook his head.

"You're right. We need to keep our focus."

"Those guys ain't gonna stay put down there. I give 'em about four hours before they're through that door."

"I don't know enough about that stuff to make a decent estimate, but you're probably right," Derek said.

"What do you think we should do with the kid?" JT asked quietly, looking into the cabin.

"I think we need to find an out of the way place to put him until this thing is over. I think we need to make sure his father doesn't get his hands on him. It would obviously be a bad situation for Tom if he ended up back with his dad."

"Maybe I could find a nice quiet little corner and take him there. He and I could hang out and get to know each other," JT said with a smile.

"That sounds like a pretty good idea. Why don't you go and scope out the landers and see if there's one you guys would be comfortable in for a while. You can seal the door, and when this blows over, *if* it blows over, I can page you over the intercom system and let you know it's safe to come out." He leaned in close to JT. "If I don't contact you in three days, assume the worst.

JT began shaking his head. Derek held up a hand to silence what he knew was about to come out of JT's mouth.

"If I don't contact you in three days, assume the worst. Stay here, drop in with the rest of the colony, and pretend you know nothing about what happened. Then, try and hide Tom. If you can, quietly find some help in the population. Can you do that?"

"If I have to."

"Alright. Right now, we'll assume that this will only take a little while, and you and Tom will have a nice time getting acquainted with each other."

"Sounds nice."

Derek and JT stepped back into the cabin to find that Elena and Tom were sitting on her bed talking. His eyes were bloodshot, but he had stopped crying. Derek assumed that Elena must have been telling him funny stories, because he was smiling, and she was giggling.

"Okay Tom," Derek said, clapping his hands together. "Here's the deal. JT is going to go and scope out an 'out of the way' place somewhere. Then he's going to do some electrical work for me in the central corridor. After that, he's going to take you to the quiet little spot he picks out, and the two of you are going to hang out there together until this whole thing is over. How does that sound to you?"

Tom looked at Elena as if she were going to tell him what to say. He looked back toward Derek, and then to JT.

"Yeah, we'll have us a good time," JT added.

Elena looked at Derek, a look of bewilderment on her face.

"You see," Derek said, sitting on the bed next to Tom. "We need to put you somewhere that you'll be safe. After what you told me about the explosion on Earth, and what your father said to me when we talked, being with him is really not where you need to be."

Derek pulled out the plasma pistol and handed it to JT.

"JT will be a good person to have around. He can handle himself if things get out of hand. Besides, he practically raised me, and I turned out okay, I guess."

JT shrugged, a light smile on his face. Tom started laughing, followed immediately by Elena.

"What's funny?" Derek asked.

Elena and Tom continued laughing.

"Really, what's funny?"

"Well," Tom said. "Elena was just telling me about how you keep finding excuses to put on her evening wear!"

The laughter was joined by JT. His deep laugh echoed in the cabin and down the corridor outside. Derek cracked a smile.

"Yeah, well, black really is my color, don't you think?"

JT walked the length of the central corridor on each of the three levels, looking for hatches that were enabled. He found three on level one, and two on level two. Level three, however, was so dark that he had trouble finding them. After his search was over, he had found four enabled hatches on level three.

The enabled hatches on levels one and three were mostly colonist landers. There were two available colonist landers on level one, as well as one cargo lander. JT entered the cargo lander to see if it would be comfortable for a short period of time.

JT moved among the various crates and boxes that were strapped to the floor with spidersilk cables. The lander had several floors that were accessible using a set of stairs along one wall.

JT moved up to the second level and found that there were lots of small crates strapped to the floor. He absent mindedly started reading the contents of the crates, as indicated by small cards taped to the outsides.

Hmm. Laboratory equipment and laboratory chemicals.

He moved back to the stairway and up to the third level. As he stepped out onto the deck, something caught his eye. Against the back wall of the lander was a crate, unstrapped and open.

JT looked around, and not seeing anyone else on the level, walked over to the crate. He moved the lid lying haphazardly across the top and dropped it on the deck. Packed neatly in the crate were several rows of plasma rifles. *Son of a bitch.*

The hairs on the back of JT's neck stood on end. He picked up one of the rifles, turned it over, and saw that there was no power cell in it. JT began checking the rest of the rifles and found that none of them had cells in them.

He looked at the crates beside it and saw that one was labeled 'bacteriology supplies', the other 'nutrient agar'. He quickly searched for the label for the box that contained the rifles and found it labeled 'laboratory notebooks'.

JT quickly started searching the area for another crate with the same label as the rifle crate. He found only boxes that contained laboratory equipment.

Panicked, he began ripping the tops off several crates around the rifles and found that they contained the items listed on the labels.

Where the hell are the power cells!

JT stopped cold and began slamming the lids back on the crates he'd opened. Once he had put all of them back, he placed the lid back on the rifle crate the way he'd found it and moved quickly down the stairs, taking them two at a time. He slapped the door button as he ran out of the lander. The door slid silently closed behind him.

"You found what?"

"A crate of plasma rifles," JT said, panting.

"Um, that raises an interesting question." Derek said, and then paused for effect. "Why the hell didn't you bring as many as you could carry back down here?" he yelled, his arms outstretched.

"There weren't any power cells. My guess is that they have some kind of system that they used to smuggle the weapons on board and a different system for the power cells. I have no idea where they are. All I can assume is that they went to check on the rifles to make sure they were on board, and there's probably an open crate somewhere filled with power cells. If I'd taken any, and they came along after me, they'd sure as hell know someone else was here."

Derek ran his hands through his hair, which was greasy from not having bathed in several days. He paid it no attention.

"How many were there?"

"I don't know, at least one full crate."

"You mean there were none missing?" Derek asked, his eyebrows raised.

"No, it was full."

"Why wouldn't they take them?" Derek asked.

"No idea. I don't think like an asshole," JT said. "Would you want to carry around a rifle all the time when you didn't think anyone else was on board? Neither would I."

"Alright, this gives me an idea," Derek said. "While you're working on the wiring on level one, you'll need to cut into the surveillance system as well."

JT looked at him, a smile creeping across his face.

"You might just be on to somethin'," he said, the smile growing into a toothy grin.

JT removed the wall panel, revealing a mass of cables of varying thickness. All the cables ran from the front of the ship toward engineering, many branching off at random points in between.

God I hope they used the wiring color standard.

JT reached into the wall and pulled out a thick, black plastic-coated cable. He looked at it in the dim light. In small white letters, it read, 'Flight Control System'. He pulled a small knife from his pocket and slit the casing, revealing numerous other wires.

Reaching inside the plastic casing, he grabbed the wires and pulled them out of it slightly. JT pulled a rag from his pocket and wrapped the handle of the knife in it. He took the rag-wrapped knife in and, with a heave, cut the wires.

A flash of light issued from the wall and a shower of sparks flew across JT's face. Temporarily blinded by the flash, he knelt on one knee to wait for the after-image to dissipate. After nearly a minute he could begin to make out the wires inside the wall, so he went back to work.

JT pulled the two severed ends of the flight control cable out of the wall and placed them a fair distance apart. He began searching through the jungle of wires again, trying to find the surveillance system cables. Once he'd found them, he slit the casing and began searching the wires inside for one marked 'Lander 17'.

The wire he was searching for evaded him for nearly five minutes. Once he found it, he cut it, looped the end that ran to the bridge around itself, and stuffed it back inside the casing.

JT pressed his face inside the opening in the wall, searching for the last cable he needed. *A-ha! There you are!*

Reaching in deeply, he grabbed the thick wire labeled, 'Captain's Quarters Data System'. He pulled a foot of slack in the wire and began to work.

For nearly half an hour JT worked, splicing and joining, cutting and looping the various wires from the three heavy cables. Periodically, he wiped the sweat from his eyes. He knew their plan would work, it had to. There was no way he was going to let that bastard have Tom back, not after what he did to Tom's mother and grandfather.

JT's mind kept going back to the rifles in the cargo lander down the corridor. If he'd been able to find the power cells, none of this would have been necessary. He had found another cargo lander on level three, and he knew that when the time came he and Tom would go there. They would be safe with the door sealed, but that would leave Derek and Elena all alone against the men, if their plan didn't work. If only he'd found the power cells, they could make a stand outside the door of engineering when the men came through.

JT began to question his plan, to think he couldn't actually do what he was trying to do. His hands moved quickly, pulling and cutting the wires in the wall. He shook his head, as if telling himself that he couldn't do it, when he realized that he was almost finished. He paused, smiled, and then moved faster to complete his work.

After the wiring work was completed, JT cleaned up the bits of plastic on the deck at his feet and tossed them into the opening in the wall. He stuffed the cables back in, and then began to reattach the cover. Taking a step back, he surveyed the wall to see if there were any traces left on the wall or the floor that would show that someone had been working there. As he started to walk away, something caught his eye. Sitting several feet behind him was a small piece of black plastic casing. Written in white letters was the word 'Communications'. *Can't let anyone see that!*

JT picked up the piece, removed the cover on the wall, and tossed it in with the rest of the remnants. He looked around for more. Not seeing any, headed back to Elena's cabin.

"Alright, you're all set. The ship's circuit breakers should have automatically closed by now, so everything should be activated. All we need now is your computer, Derek," JT said. "Are you sure you want to go through with this?"

"We don't really have much choice. Those guys have been trapped down there for nearly two hours, and I don't know how much longer they're going to be there."

"Alright," JT said. "Here, take this."

JT handed Derek a short piece of wire with a plug on one end and several frayed wires on the other.

"You plug this into the device expansion port on your computer, and these go here," JT said, pointing to the various wires sticking out of the wall behind Elena's desk. "Don't worry, you won't get shocked. The circuit breaker's continuity test happens once every five minutes, so you'll have plenty of time to attach the wires before there's current going through the cable."

"That makes me feel much better."

"Doc," JT said. "You should be able to communicate with him from here using the Captain's shipboard comm system on the terminal here, so you can walk him through it."

"Okay, is the surveillance system tied in here also?" Elena asked.

"Yep, go ahead and turn on your terminal."

Elena turned on the terminal, which went through its normal startup. After a few seconds, the three-dimensional display showed the words, 'New Data Stream Added, Please Wait'. The screen flickered several times, and then the normal screen came up.

"It looks the same. It didn't work," Elena said.

"Sure it did, look down there."

At the bottom of the display was an icon labeled, 'New Data Stream'. JT reached across in front of Elena and touched it.

The screen zoomed in on the icon, which was actually a very small display screen. The small screen continued to grow until it became the full display showing a list of locations on the ship, each one shown by a small icon. JT touched one labeled 'Engineering I' and the other icons slid to the sides of the screen. A video appeared in the center.

The display was a top-down view of a large bay. There were several men in the bay, all clustered around a closed door. Tom, Derek and JT moved in around Elena, trying to see what was happening.

"I don't understand," Elena said. "If we can do this, then why can't we just set this computer up for everything?"

"This is just a data terminal," Derek said, pointing toward the system. "It only sends and receives data to and from the ship's database, and now, thanks to JT, the ship's surveillance system. The terminal doesn't have control capabilities for hardware, only software. That's why we need a different one. The only computer on board that I know of is mine, and it's in the cargo lander."

"They're further along than I thought," JT said, bringing their attention back to the display. "We need to hurry. See that," he said pointing toward the display. "They've gotten access to the emergency door release. They'll be out of there in a little bit."

"Alright," Derek replied. "You take Tom and head down to the cargo lander. You'll be safe there. It's out of the way and dark. Very dark. You keep that pistol in your hand the whole time, I don't care if you're in there for two days, you got me?" Derek said, sounding more like a soldier than ever.

"Yes, sir," JT said, saluting him.

JT realized how ridiculous he looked, old and overweight, saluting.

"If we get out of this alive, I'm going on a diet," JT said, patting his belly. "You ready, kiddo?"

"I'm ready," Tom said, picking up two big handfuls of food packets.

"Hey," Derek said quietly to JT. "You used to call me kiddo, remember?"

"I guess I did, didn't I?"

Derek smiled at JT. JT reached around Derek and wrapped him up in a bear hug.

"You be careful out there, kiddo. You haven't worked in space in a long time," JT said.

"I will, thanks. You guys have fun. I'll call you when this is over."

JT grabbed Tom by the shoulder and led him out of the cabin. Elena and JT watched as they moved out of sight.

"Are you nervous?" Elena asked.

"Not really. What's the worst that could happen?"

"Well, no one's ever done this before on a ship that's in-transit and surrounded by a flux field, so you could be incinerated, irradiated, even blown out into deep space...in another universe."

Derek, not expecting such a reply, grimaced.

"Okay, so that's supposed to make me feel better?"

"Sorry," Elena said. "Don't worry though, no matter what happens, I'll be sitting right here in my comfy chair, watching the whole thing on television!"

"God, you're as bad as JT," Derek said, walking out of the cabin.

Chapter Twenty

Flux

Despite the lack of fine dexterity, the thick gloves felt comfortable to Derek. The heavy environment suit he was now wearing was thicker than the suits he normally wore, but they functioned in much the same way.

The suit was designed for use in a zero-gravity, zero atmosphere environment, and were most at home in deep space, where their thick insulation protected the wearer from temperature that could be as low as two hundred seventy degrees below zero, or as high as two hundred fifty degrees Celsius.

The suit was made of a thick, white fabric that resembled canvas or burlap. During Derek's basic heavy environment suit training, or HEST, he made a comment to one of his fellow trainees that his freshly shaven head looked like a potato that didn't fit in the sack. From then on, he called men in environment suits 'taters'.

Derek pulled on the thin backpack that contained the suit's attitude control system, or ACS. The pack contained several tanks of a heavy gas that was compressed until it became a liquid. The tanks were connected to a control unit and a series of jets. When the control unit was activated, a jet opened, releasing a plume of the gas, pushing the suit-wearer in the desired direction.

The ACS was only designed to be used to reorient the suit, not for long-distance travel. Derek knew that he would only have enough control of the suit to help him stay oriented in during his spacewalk, and that was only a safety measure in case he lost his grip on one of the handholds that ran in various patterns along the length of the ship.

Derek pulled on the chest pack containing the suit's air handling system. This was nearly identical to the ones he used in his combat suits, except for the location. In combat, the pack was mounted on the soldier's back to reduce the likelihood of a weapons hit that might damage the unit, thus resulting in the soldier's death.

A crackle in Derek's ear told him that the communications unit he had put inside his right ear was now active.

"Elena, this is Derek. Do you copy?"

"I'm here," Elena replied.

"You're supposed to say, 'copy'," Derek corrected.

"Gotcha. I mean, copy. I hear you loud and clear."

"We're lucky they half-assed emptying out this cargo ship. They left lots of good stuff in here."

"Yeah, my luck has been fantastic lately, don't you agree?" Elena asked, her voice spiked with sarcasm.

Shaking his head, Derek picked up the helmet that was sitting on the shelf above the hook where the suit had been hanging. He pulled it up over his head and, with a click, locked it into place.

A female voice inside the helmet said, "Airpack, fully charged. ACS tanks, fully charged. Battery pack, fully charged."

"Hi, mom," Derek said with a toothy smile. "It's been too long."

"Who are you talking to?" Elena asked.

"It's a long story," he replied. "I'll tell you about it later. I'm suited up and entering the airlock."

Derek pressed his gloved hand against the large red button beside the door. Silently, the massive door swung open. He stepped aside as it moved outward, like a giant hand swatting slowly at a fly. The door swung completely open and beckoned him into the airlock. He stepped in, and pressed the red button on the inside wall.

The door slowly closed and sealed the room. Inside the helmet, Derek couldn't hear anything, but he knew that the air was being drawn out of the room. The light in the room began to dim, an effort to help the spacewalker's eyes grow accustomed to the dark he or she would experience outside the ship. He looked at a small pressure display mounted high on the wall and watched it drop from 1.0 atmosphere, to 0.9, then to 0.8. He watched it as it dropped to 0.0, and the dim white light was replaced by a red one.

"Atmospheric pressure is equalized. I'm proceeding outside."

Derek watched as the outer door of the airlock opened, revealing a sea of blue stars. He looked at them, not sure what to think.

"They're blue," he muttered.

"Weird, isn't it?" Elena replied.

"Uh, yeah. I didn't realize they'd be blue," Derek said.

"Yep. It's the flux field. It makes everything blue for some reason."

"It's pretty, but it's kind of creepy at the same time."

"It gives me the willies," Elena said.

"Alright, I'm proceeding outside. Wish me luck."

"Good luck," Elena said, crossing her fingers. She noticed that her palms were damp with sweat, so she wiped them on her pants.

Derek reached around the outside of the airlock to take hold of a metal loop handhold. As his hand moved outside the airlock, he felt a light tingling in his fingers that radiated down his arm.

"I sure as hell hope this is safe," Derek said. "Because I'm feeling something pretty strange."

"What do you mean?"

"Well, it feels like electricity on my fingers, but it's moving up my arm in slow waves. It's almost like reaching into the ocean and feeling the waves move up and down your arm."

"I'm not sure I like the sound of that," Elena said. "No one has ever done this before. We don't know anything about this 'flux field' thing."

"Well, let's look at is this way. Someone has to do it or we'll all end up dead, right?"

"Yeah, I guess."

"Well, if something happens to me, like radiation poisoning, it will only be one person who gets dead, not everyone. Statistics sound pretty good to me. How 'bout you?"

"I would rather it be someone else who ended up dead, not you," Elena mumbled.

"Say again? I didn't copy that."

"Yeah, the stats sound good to me, too," Elena said a little too loudly.

"Okay then. Here goes nothing."

Derek grabbed the handhold and pulled himself out of the airlock and instantly felt overwhelmed. He felt like an infant fighting a high tide. The massive waves slapped against him, receded, and then assaulted him again. The feeling of electricity, whether real or imagined, made all the hair on his body stand on end. It also buzzed in his ears, making it hard to think. He pulled himself tight against the handholds and stuck his feet into the ones below him.

"This is very intense," he yelled over the buzzing. "I can feel the flux field pushing against me. It feels like the ocean, only much stronger!"

"Are you sure you can do this?"

"Roger, I just need to get my bearings. The waves seem to come about once every two seconds. They seem to ebb and flow like ocean waves, so I can move when they start to relax."

"Alright, but if things get out of hand, you turn back. We can find another way to beat those guys."

"You got it, Doc."

Derek looked around. He hadn't noticed just how dark it was. He could see more stars than he'd ever seen before, but they were all so distant that there was very little light on the ship. He hadn't spent much time looking out the windows into deep space when he was on missions, so this was new to him. Even his zero gravity, heavy environment suit training was done inside an orbiting cage of scaffolding and metal panels that was designed to keep the new, untrained soldiers from drifting too far during the training.

He hooked his left arm around the handhold, and then pressed a button on his forearm-mounted control system. The hull in front of him was bathed in a dull, red light that emanated from the lights on the sides of his helmet.

Derek began to move, slowly at first, then faster once he got used to moving in a suit again. He would move one hand, then after the next wave would come, the other. After a minute or two, he started making several movements during each wave cycle. The buzzing seemed to be getting louder in his ears.

"I think I'm getting the hang of this. It isn't really that hard."

"Alright, if you think you can do it, move down the hull toward the cargo landers," Elena instructed.

"Roger, I'm moving aft."

Derek began making his way toward the rear of the ship. His body began to feel the effects of the tingling lessen. He realized that it was becoming less intense and started to say something to Elena but stopped. The sound of the waves was diminishing, and his ears felt as though he were wearing earmuffs. Hand over hand, he continued toward the central corridor of the ship where the landers were all attached. The effect of the waves continued to lessen. His body began to feel numb. He felt as though he were sitting in a huge vat filled with cotton. His hands were clumsy on the handholds he could barely feel.

Derek stopped when he reached the section of the ship where the central corridor was connected to the foredecks. He felt very relaxed and wanted to stop for just a minute. Sliding his left arm through the handhold, he lay back on the hull of the ship. *I've got plenty of time.*

Derek sat and looked out into the vastness of space. The beautiful blue stars winked at him. The constellations beckoned for his attention. His mind traced their outlines on the stars in several of them. Their forms began to grow from line-connected dots into the mythological figures they had been named after. He watched as Sagittarius galloped and fired his bow and Perseus held out the head of Medusa for all to see. Perseus turned and held out the head toward Derek.

"Hey baby," Derek mumbled, his voice a slurred drawl.

"Excuse me? I didn't catch that," a voice replied.

"Man, she's ugly," Derek said. "Medusa. Now, that's one ugly bitch. Perseus, put that thing away."

"Who the hell is Perseus?"

"Did I ever tell you how much I hate snakes?"

"Okay, what the hell is going on out there?"

Derek heard a voice in his head, but wasn't sure where it was coming from. He looked hard at the head of Medusa to see if she were speaking to him. Medusa's mouth moved and the snakes undulated around her face, but she said nothing. He relaxed against the hull again.

Derek's feet pounded repeatedly against the hull of the ship, moved by the waves he could no longer feel. His eyes began to feel very heavy.

"I've been up such a long time, maybe I should take a cat nap," he mumbled.

"Okay, I think you're losing it. You're talking about going to sleep in outer space. Can you hear yourself?" the voice said.

The voice was sounded pleasant. *Medusa has a pretty voice for such a nasty looking hag.* Derek took a deep breath, and slid his right hand behind his head to keep it from banging against the hull. He took another deep breath and closed his eyes.

"Derek," the voice said. "Derek, listen to me."

"Who's that?" he said, his voice sounding like a child.

"Derek, you have to get up. You don't have time for this."

"I just need a few more minutes of sleep, mom. Please?"

"No Derek, you have to get up now."

"Please, mom. I've got plenty of time before I have to get to... to wherever it is I'm going."

"Derek," She said softly. "People are going to die if you don't get up now."

Derek opened his eyes. *People are going to die?*

"You have to get up right now or we're all going to die."

Derek began feeling the waves slapping him against the hull. He started looking around, trying to get his bearings. He was hooked on a handhold, overlooking the central corridor. The cargo lander he was trying to reach was over a hundred yards down the central corridor from him.

"Oh my God! What's happening?"

"Worry about it when you get back in, just get moving."

He shook his head violently. "Yeah, okay."

"You mean roger, right?"

"Yeah. I mean, roger."

Derek moved down the central corridor until he reached the lander that contained his personal belongings. He continued to shake his head side-to-side to fight the mind-numbing buzz as he moved along the outside of it until he reached the external hatch that would be used to access the interior of the lander on the planet. After several minutes of wrestling with the mechanism, the door opened and he climbed through.

Derek noticed immediately that inside the lander the waves were gone. His mind was now completely clear, and he began to feel ashamed of what happened outside. He shook his head and began searching the lander. The lander, although inside the flux-field, had no gravity, so his searching was going to take more time than it would in the simulated gravity of the ship because his movements had to be slower and more precise to prevent him from constantly floating away from what he was searching.

Nearly fifteen minutes went by while Derek searched for the large shipping container that had his name on it. He floated around the lander, moving from container to container. He finally found his crate on the third level, against the outer wall. He unlatched the large doors and gradually forced them open.

Derek floated into the large crate and unhooked the straps that held his boxes tight against the bottom of the crate. The boxes sprang upward as the last strap was released. A small box rocketed toward Derek, barely missing him. It bounced harmlessly off the ceiling of the container.

Derek began moving his boxes. He searched the container, trying to find the box he had packed his electronics in. As luck would have it, it was on the bottom of the pile, so he had to move all the other boxes to get to it.

Once it was uncovered, he realized just how bad the dexterity in the suit really was. After a few seconds of groping for a grip on the edge of the tape, he punched a small hole in the tape with his gloved finger. He reached a finger into the hole and pulled hard. The tape ripped, and the lid of the box came open, spewing his belongings out. They bounced silently off the inside walls of the container. Derek saw his computer float slowly out of the box. He pushed off from the floor and slid quickly toward it.

As he snagged the computer out of the air, something below him caught his eye. Floating just above the open box was the paper bag he'd decided at the last minute to bring. *I forgot all about that.* He slid slowly toward the ceiling, debating.

After a few seconds, he reached the ceiling, kicked off it and moved back down toward the open box and floating bag. He swung his arm in a wide arc, just brushing the bottom corner of the bag, which spun quickly, and the top came open. A thick booklet slid partially out of the opening, revealing some text. 'TM-85: Care and Maintenance of M1911 .45' was all that was visible. Derek reached the floor of the container and kicked off again, this time grabbing the bag solidly. He stuffed the manual back into the bag, his heart pounding heavily. Seeing the title of the booklet caused a feeling of guilt to grow from deep in his gut.

After he had gathered up the mess of floating debris that was his personal effects, he closed the box and strapped it back down in the container along with all the others. He had retrieved a small backpack from another box and placed the computer in it. The paper bag drew his attention and he stared at it for a few seconds. He reached inside and pulled out a small box labeled, '.45 cal. Ammunition'. Gritting his teeth, he put it back in the bag and slid the bag into the backpack. A chill ran down his spine; He felt as though he were doing something very wrong.

Derek loosened the straps of the backpack in an attempt to make them large enough to fit over his environment suit. After several minutes of trying, he gave up and unhooked one of the straps that held the chest pack on. He ran the chest pack strap through straps on the backpack and then reconnected it. The backpack floated out in front of him, but it wouldn't get away.

Derek closed the shipping container, then moved outside. After closing the hatch, he quickly moved back toward the foredecks of the ship, feeling the intense push of the flux waves. The electricity tugged at his mind again, but he fought it by telling dirty jokes aloud. Periodically, after he told a particularly nasty one, Elena would groan, and this would help him to fight against the forces battering his consciousness.

"A blonde, a brunette, and a redhead walk into a bar," Derek said, giggling.

"Where are you?" Elena asked, exhaling loudly.

"I just got into the airlock."

"Good," Elena said. "Shut up."

Derek quickly removed the environment suit and dropped it on the floor outside the airlock. He quickly grabbed the backpack and threw it over one shoulder, running for the door. As he walked into Elena's cabin, he found her on the floor under her desk attaching the flayed out wires of the connector JT had given her to the corresponding wires from the wall. She was nearly finished, when Derek came in, panting.

"How's it going," he asked, glancing at the display screen, which showed twelve different surveillance monitors, one of which was in engineering. It showed the group of men, all still clustered around the door.

"Not too bad, I've gotten all but three of the wires connected, and I should have those done in a minute."

"Remember, time is of the essence on this. JT said that the circuit breakers automatically try to reset themselves every five minutes. How long have you been working on this?" he asked, kneeling.

"I don't know maybe..." Elena's words suddenly stopped, and her face contorted with a look of sheer agony. The veins along the sides of her neck began to bulge. Every muscle in her body contracted intensely, and her hair began to stand out in an aura of blond around her head.

"Oh Jesus!" Derek yelled, jumping to his feet. With all his strength he kicked at her hands, which were squeezing the wires as if she were trying to crush them into oblivion. Derek's foot knocked her hands loose from their grip on the wires. Elena, now free of the surge of electricity, slumped to the deck, her eyes wide.

"Elena?"

Elena didn't answer. She just stared at the ceiling, a look of terror frozen on her face.

"Oh Jesus, oh Jesus," Derek yelled, dropping to his knees beside her. He laid his head on her chest and found that Elena's heart was not beating.

"Don't you die on me! Don't you dare die on me," he yelled as he began pressing down with the palms of his hands.

"I do *not* give you permission to die here today, woman," he yelled as he pumped furiously. He moved his mouth to hers and breathed quickly into her, watching her chest move up and down with each of his two breaths.

"Oh please, God. Please."

He frantically continued pumping on her chest and stopped suddenly. He looked down at her feet, thinking he had seen her move. Again, he dropped his head onto her chest, listening for a heartbeat. A loud thump erupted from her chest as her heart began to beat on its own again. Derek began to laugh and cry at the same time, his head still on Elena's chest.

On the screen behind them, the door in engineering slid silently open, and the group of men disappeared through it.

"Oh my God, do I feel bad," Elena said in a raspy voice.

Derek lifted his head and turned to look her in the eye. He laid his head back on her breasts.

"Does this mean we're going steady?" she asked with a smile.

"Oh shit!" Derek said, jumping to his feet.

"Well damn, you don't have be like that," Elena said slowly rolling her aching body over.

Without a word, Derek pointed at the screen. The engineering bay appeared empty. As if on cue, several men ran by the third camera from the left on the top row of the screen. Elena groaned and lifted herself onto her knees.

"That is the camera at the top of the stairs on level one at the aft end of the central corridor. They must have just gotten out."

"Well, it's a good thing I looked up. A few more minutes and they would have spoiled my trap."

"Trap?" Elena asked, a look of suspicion on her face.

"Yeah," Derek said turning to her. He stopped and looked down at her hands.

"What?" Elena said looking down.

Elena's hands had bubbly fluid-filled blisters on the palms. She slowly closed them, noticing that there was no pain.

"Third degree electrical burns," she said, noticing her fingernails. "And blackened fingernails," she said, holding her hands up for him to see.

Derek knelt down beside her, placing a hand on her shoulder.

"Is there anything we can do for your hands?" Derek asked, glancing back at the screen.

"At some point, I need to put some anti-microbial lotion on them to prevent an infection." She paused for a few seconds. "It's going to be a long time before I go into an operating room," she said, her voice showing her displeasure at the thought.

"Nerve damage?" Derek asked.

"Yeah," she said, looking at her hands. "Third degree burns damage the nerves. That's why it doesn't hurt very much. I'm going to have to do some physical therapy when this is over."

Derek and Elena moved back to the display screen. Derek climbed under the desk and connected the last few wires, being careful not to bridge the circuit with his own body as Elena had apparently done. When the connections were complete, he slid out from under the desk and began pressing buttons on the keyboard.

"So, tell me about this trap of yours," Elena said.

"Just a minute, I want to go ahead and send this message. That's just in case the trap fails, and something happens to us. The people on Earth need to know what happened here, even if we don't make it."

"I don't understand. I thought you said that the communications system was destroyed completely to make it look like the ship was lost."

"The communications *control console* was completely destroyed, including the telemetry monitor to make it look like the ship was destroyed. Since the control console was destroyed, that means that we couldn't communicate with Earth from the bridge. I'm banking on the fact that the actual communications hardware is still intact. I can't imagine that they would have thought to destroy it as well. There would be no real need for them to do that."

Elena looked at him for several seconds, then began to smile. "So we tapped into the lines that run from the bridge to the hardware on the outside of the ship! That way, with your computer we can send a message to Earth?"

"Actually, we can send the message with the data access terminal right here," Derek said pointing to the display. "The Captain's console here has communications hardware built-in, so he can be reached from the bridge. We just switched some of the wiring around so that it now controls the 'ship-to-shore' radio, instead of the internal communications system."

"Good thinking. I'm glad you weren't one of *them*! I'd have really been in deep shit."

Derek gave her a nasty look as he began pressing buttons again. The screen changed from the stack of surveillance cameras to a communications layout. At the top corner of the screen was a flashing cursor, sitting in the large blank space where text would be entered to be transmitted. There were several buttons across the bottom of the display that indicated the functions of the system.

"Here goes nothing," he said, pressing a large button labeled 'transmit'.

"This is Major Derek Cross, Commander of the 609th." He paused, his words appearing behind the moving cursor. "I mean, Commander of the Osiris military forces. It is day one hundred fifty-nine of our journey and the mission has become compromised. I was awakened from stasis to find a small enemy force in control of the ship. The communications system and telemetry monitor on the bridge were destroyed to make it appear as though the ship was destroyed, as a means of covering up the hijacking. The enemy force is approximately 6 men strong, with one man already neutralized." He took a deep breath.

"I am attempting to capture the remaining enemies. If I don't send another message in three days, my attempt has failed, and I've been captured or killed along with Doctor Elena Brown, and possibly Sergeant James Towson and Tom Samson." He turned to Elena and saw that she had a sad look on her face.

"Because of this possibility, I have taken control of the ship's drive system, and, if we fail to capture the enemies, will be dropping out of flux. We are only a month away from our destination, and too far from Earth, so a rescue is not possible. If I'm successful, we will return to flux and continue our journey as planned. We cannot allow the enemy force to assume control once the ship has reached Avalon. So if we fail the ship will never reach its destination. I'll activate an emergency beacon so that once another ship is built it can be sent here to rescue the survivors who should still be in stasis." Derek took a deep breath, and exhaled loudly.

"We've also learned of the explosion at the Samson Industries factory on Earth. You have our condolences. We also want you to know that Frederick Samson is responsible and is leading the enemy force on-board. His son has joined us and told us that his father planted a number of US Army high explosives at the plant, knowingly causing the deaths of his own wife and his own father, not to mention the countless other people who were there that day. I'll do my best to make sure that justice is done." He glanced back at Elena and saw that her sad look had become one of apparent suspicion.

"Everyone there cross your fingers and say a prayer for us. We'll say a few for you guys, as well, for your losses in the factory explosion. Thank you, Major Cross out," he said, pressing the 'End' button.

Elena continued to look at Derek as though she were trying to figure out how to ask a sensitive question. Her mouth opened slowly, and before she got a chance to speak Derek cut her off.

"Unfortunately, we aren't on Earth, or even in an Earth colony. That means the system of justice has to be one of our own making. We can't sentence these men to five years in prison. We don't even have a prison. We can't afford the drain on our resources caused by keeping them locked in their quarters for the next year, either."

Elena threw her hands up. She shook her head and flailed her arms as she mouthed several silent questions. Derek simply turned away from her and back to the display. He began pressing buttons with one hand, while he picked up his computer with the other.

The large display screen read 'WORKING' for several seconds, so Derek turned his attention to his computer. He turned it on, and it began to hum as the internal drives ran their diagnostics. He lifted the computer's display and glanced at it, watching its diagnostics program as it displayed its status.

"Look," Derek said, not looking at Elena. "We have to decide how to handle these guys after we catch them. Keep in mind our options are rather limited."

Derek watched as the surveillance screens began to appear on Elena's monitor again, one after another. A few moments later, all twelve of them had appeared, filling the screen. He began pressing buttons on his computer again. The display on his computer began to show green skeletal schematics of the ship. He traced the ship's skeleton with his finger until it rested an inch above the displayed engineering section. He looked briefly at the surveillance screens.

Derek pressed the engineering section of the screen and it was magnified, taking up the entire screen. The display showed the various systems in engineering, as well as their status. He leaned in closer, reading the status of the flux field generators. The display read, 'ACTIVE, 98% CAPACITY, 98% EFFICIENCY'.

Derek pressed the 'Flux Field Generator' section of the screen. A small menu appeared. The bottom choice on the list, 'EMERGENCY SHUTDOWN', caught his eye. With a light tap, he pressed it. A small box appeared over the schematic with the text 'FLUX FIELD GENERATOR EMERGENCY SHUTDOWN, DO YOU WISH TO CONTINUE?'. Below it were two boxes, one containing a green 'Y' and another containing a red 'N'.

Derek looked back at the surveillance screens. There was no activity in any of them. He knew that the men had to be close to the cargo lander by now. They were running, and he knew that it only took about ten minutes to get to the lander at that pace.

"Look, maybe we should talk about their punishment before you do anything that we can't take back," Elena said quickly. "I mean, we need to know what we're going to do with them."

Derek ignored her and started pressing buttons on his computer's keyboard again. The screen split down the middle into two half-sized screens, the new screen showing the green schematic of the ship. He pressed the representation of a cargo lander, and the display zoomed in on it. The display showed the cutaway view, with its several decks. It also showed the status of the fuel and re-entry rocket systems, as well as its environmental systems. Derek pressed the schematic representation of the lander's hatch. A menu appeared.

"What are you doing?"

"Getting ready," Derek said, his voice monotone and almost robotic.

"Listen, soldier-boy, we *really* need to talk about..." she paused, "about whatever it is you're about to do."

Derek's head jerked up to the surveillance display screens as something caught his eye. Several men came running into the cargo lander, and past the camera.

"Damn! They're here already."

Derek watched the surveillance screen as the lander's hatch slid closed. He scanned down the menu and found the choice he was searching for. He pressed his finger on the words, 'ENVIRONMENTAL LOCKOUT'. The menu disappeared, and the image of the door now appeared in red. Derek pressed the button indicating the environmental system.

"Environmental system?" Elena asked.

"Yeah, I don't want these guys blowing that door open when they realize they're trapped in there and running out of air."

"What! Running out of air?"

"Yeah, it's the only way I could think of on such short notice," he said opening the environmental system menu. "We needed a way to neutralize them without weapons. This is the only way I know of to defeat a superior military force." He quickly pressed a menu choice, but his hand was covering the menu, so Elena didn't see what he pressed.

Elena watched as the schematic changed to red, and a bar graph appeared on the right side of the lander. The bar read '% ATM' and went from 100% at the top, to 0% at the bottom.

"What are you doing?"

"I'm evacuating the atmosphere from the lander," Derek said, looking at her.

"You son of a bitch! I trusted you, and now you're going to kill these people! She grunted as she got to her feet and reached for the display.

Derek jumped up and blocked her from reaching the display.

"You've got it all wrong," Derek began.

"You're goddamn right I have it wrong. I was wrong about you. I thought you cared. I thought you cared about me. Jesus, I thought I cared about you."

Derek took a step back, bumping into the desk behind him. He wasn't sure what to say. Staring at Elena, her face red, her breath coming in panting gasps, he felt as though she had just cut him to the bone. Before he got a chance to collect his thoughts into a coherent, and diplomatic reply, the words started flying out of him.

"You've got some nerve talking to me like that. If it weren't for me, you'd probably be dead already. I've been doing all this shit to keep you, JT and Tom safe, and this is how you repay me? You told me that you trusted me, and the first time I do something you don't understand, you think I'm killing off half the population of the Earth. You've got some Goddamn nerve!" he yelled, blasting a finger at her.

"Oh, so what am I supposed to think? I sit here," she said glancing at the display. "While you drain the life out of these men." She paused. Something about the image on the display struck her as odd.

Elena leaned around Derek, and looked more intently at the image. The 'ATM' bar, which displayed the level of atmosphere in the lander, now read 0.5, and was no longer falling. She turned and looked at Derek's face, which was now bright red.

"What's going on here?" she asked.

"I decreased the atmosphere in the lander to fifty percent. Low enough to render the men inside groggy if not unconscious, without killing them. If I hadn't done that, they would have blown the door, and we'd be worse off because they'd all be armed with plasma rifles and who knows what else. The atmosphere in there is about the equivalent to three-quarters of the way up Mt. Everest."

Elena looked at the surveillance screen and saw that three men were on their knees in front of the door, hitting it with their fists. The men, appearing extremely intoxicated, were obviously feeling the effects of the low oxygen level.

Elena looked back at Derek, and the color of her face, which was already slightly red, began to match his as she blushed heavily.

"God, I..."

Derek turned away from her and looked at the monitor.

"Shit! They're not all in there. Two are missing."

"Which two?"

Derek scanned the faces of the three men in the lander, and with a sigh said, "Samson and Conway."

Jeffrey Thomas

Chapter Twenty-One

Deceleration

O ur situation has not improved," Derek said, in a sarcastic tone.

"What do you think they'll do?"

"I'm not sure. Samson obviously sent those three to the lander to gather some more potent weapons like those plasma rifles. They obviously know where the power cells are," Derek said, pointing at the surveillance monitors. "Unfortunately, he and Conway are both carrying plasma pistols, so they're still a major threat. I'm not too worried about Conway at this point, but Samson worries me."

"Why do you say that?"

"I have some baseline information about Conway. He's in the special forces."

"Excuse me? Special Forces? How can you say that you're not worried about him when he's in the Special Forces? And besides, how do you know that? You said that you didn't recognize any of the names of the soldiers who weren't in their tubes."

"It's something Tom told me. He said that he really liked Conway's jacket because of a patch he had on it. Tom told me that it had a spaceship with lightning coming down from it, striking a bird."

Elena stared at him in silence.

"The patch he described is a Special Forces patch. The bird, an eagle, is actually coming down from the ship, riding the lightning. That's a rapid deployment system that we use for fast insertions. Most people don't even know it exists."

"Okay," Elena said shaking her head. "I still don't understand how you can say he doesn't concern you. He's a trained killer, just like..." She paused.

"You were going to say 'just like you', weren't you? Well, you're right. We've had the same training. That's why he doesn't concern me. I understand all his training, just as he understands mine. All I have to do is outsmart him. As a unit commander, I've had to go through a lot more training than the troops I command, so hopefully I can outthink him."

"Yeah, hopefully," Elena replied. "Okay, so you know a lot about Conway, and he doesn't bother you. So what is it about Samson that worries you?

"I don't know anything about him, that's what concerns me. At least with Conway, I can try to fight him in an unorthodox way. Hopefully he won't be prepared for that. He'll be expecting me to fight the way we were trained. Samson, on the other hand, I have no idea of how to fight, because I don't know how to assess the threat he poses."

"Hmm. I see your point."

Derek laced his fingers together, and pressing them out toward the surveillance monitors, cracked his knuckles.

"Well, we have to look at the possibility that we might fail," he said, not looking at Elena. We have to stop the ship."

Elena stepped up behind him and put her hand on his shoulder. "Yeah, we've done everything we can, but we have to look at that possibility," she replied.

Derek leaned in toward his computer and stared at the display. The schematic of the ship still glared at him from the display. The menu showed the 'FLUX FIELD SHUTDOWN' option, and the large 'Y' and 'N' were still awaiting input.

Derek slowly brought his finger up to the large 'Y', when Elena squeezed his shoulder tightly.

"Wait! I think we have to slow down first."

"What do you mean? Why would we have to do that?"

"Think about it: we're traveling at the equivalent of about ten times the speed of light, right?"

"Yeah? Yeah, so what?" Derek said, furrowing his brow.

"So, isn't it impossible to travel the speed of light, much less faster than it is in our universe, right?"

"Yeah, the closer to the speed of light you get, the larger your mass becomes. That's general relativity."

"So, if you turn off the flux field, we phase back into our universe still traveling ten times the speed of light. What do you think will happen to us when that happens?"

Derek thought about it for a moment, and then closed his eyes.

"Squish," he said, lowering his head.

"Big time," Elena added.

Derek quickly pressed the large 'N', and the menu vanished. He then pressed another button, and a detailed schematic of the engines appeared on the display. Small letters on the engines read 'Engaged'. Derek pressed the schematic of the engines, and another menu opened.

The menu that was now displayed on the screen had nearly twenty options, most of which had to do with engine maintenance. The last option in the list, written in a different font said, 'DECELERATION AND FLUX FIELD POWERDOWN'.

"Hey, this one looks promising," Derek said, pointing at the screen. "It must have been added during the construction of the ship. This control system is used in a line of cargo ships, so they probably just added the menu items that weren't in the original ship's control system."

"Yeah, the text is a little different, too," Elena said.

"I noticed that. So, do you think I should push that? Or should I keep looking through the menus?"

"I don't think we're going to find anything that looks any better than that one," Elena replied. "Go ahead."

Derek reached over and pressed the deceleration menu option. The screen displayed the words, 'SAFE DECELERATION AND FLUX FIELD POWERDOWN. DO YOU WISH TO CONTINUE?'. Below this were two boxes, a 'Y', and an 'N'.

"And away we go," Derek said as his finger pressed the menu 'Y' option.

"I'd like to know how this Major got on board," Samson said. "His name isn't on the passenger manifest, so where exactly did he come from?"

Samson and Conway slowly made their way along the Level 2 corridor, heading toward the foredecks of the ship. Both of them had their pistols out, and were moving very cautiously.

"I don't know, sir. I do know that we'll get him for what he did to Tommy. He'll pay good for it, believe me."

"Well put, Conway," Samson said, rolling his eyes. "If it's at all possible, I'd like him alive. I would like to sit down and have a little chat with the Major, if you don't mind."

Conway stopped abruptly and glared at Samson.

"You've got to be shitting me, right?"

"Although your mother did the day you were born, Conway, I am entirely serious."

"But this fucking guy, he..."

"I need to know how he got on board. If we have a spy among us..."

The threat hung there like the stale air in the ship.

"I doubt anyone would be stupid enough,"

Samson held up a hand, silencing Conway.

"Do you feel that?" Samson asked.

The deck plating below their feet began to vibrate slightly. Conway stepped over to the bulkhead, and placed his hand against it.

"The walls are vibrating. What the hell's going on?"

"That bastard. He didn't," Samson said.

Samson peered down the corridor toward the foredecks, and then back toward the engineering section. He slowly began to feel a light pull on his body, as though someone had grabbed him by the front of his clothing, and was pulling him forward. He and Conway both began to lean backwards, fighting against the pull.

"Jesus," Conway yelled. "What's happening?"

"We're slowing down you idiot!"

Derek and Elena began to feel the effects of the ship's heavy deceleration. Piles of food packets began sliding off of the desk and falling onto the floor as the pull grew more and more intense. Several books that had been on the floor slid across the room and hit the back wall with a thud. The chair Derek sat in began to slide backward. He splayed out his arms and pressed his feet into the floor, trying to stop it from moving, but it was no use. The chair continued to accelerate until it slammed against the wall, Derek's head leaving an indention and a small amount of blood where it hit.

"Shit, I forgot about this part," Elena yelled as she began to slide across the floor.

Derek, still seated in the chair, was pinned against the back wall, flailing his arms and legs, trying to free himself of the pull. Elena had grabbed the edge of the desk and was gripping it tightly. Her personal effects began slamming against the wall around Derek. A small bottle of perfume shattered beside his head, a shard of glass cutting his ear.

Elena gripped the desk tightly, but the pull was too strong. Her hands slipped, and she careened across the room, hitting her legs on the bed. The impact caused her to flip and spin wildly as she flew across the room toward the wall where Derek was pinned.

Elena fell the seventeen feet across the room and slammed into the wall. The impact knocked the wind out of her, and she hacked and coughed as she tried to regain her breath.

"How long is this going to last?" Derek yelled.

Elena coughed in response.

"Was the takeoff this bad?"

Elena continued to cough, trying to regain her breath.

Derek, about to ask Elena another question, looked back toward the desk where he and the chair had been. Dangling at the end of a cable was his computer, still showing the deceleration message.

"Oh shit! If that comes loose it's going to smash against the back wall! If that happens we're going to be stuck in the middle of nowhere for a long time!"

The computer hung directly in front of Elena, slowly spinning at the end of the cable that was pulled taut by the force of deceleration. Derek's heart leapt as the wires that been spliced together began to come unwound. Four wires, then five came undone with a sound like a guitar string being plucked.

"This may be it," Derek yelled. "If it falls, can you catch it?"

Elena, still coughing and holding her stomach, shook her head.

Samson and Conway found themselves hanging onto the metal floor of the corridor, their fingers laced into the regularly-spaced air holes in the metal floor plating.

"Conway," Samson yelled. "Unclasp your belt, and feed it into an air hole. Then you can reclasp it around your waist if it's long enough. It should hold."

Conway immediately followed Samson's instructions and held on with one hand, while undoing his belt with the other. He slowly worked the male end of the belt through an air hole, and pulled it out of the adjacent hole. Glancing over at Samson, he saw that his belt was already through the air holes, and he was in the process of re-attaching it around his waist.

"Got it," Samson yelled as he clasped his belt. "Now, when you get your belt attached, take the laces out of your boots. Be careful not to drop the laces."

"Okay, I got my belt hooked. God this hurts," Conway yelled.

"It doesn't hurt nearly as bad as falling twenty or thirty stories. That's how it would feel if you slipped and slid all the way down to the end of this corridor," Samson said, unlacing his left shoe.

"I see your point."

"Now, have you got your boots unlaced?" Samson said, putting his left shoelace in his mouth and dropping his shoe. The shoe fell away down the corridor without a sound.

"Not yet, I'm working on it," Conway said reaching for his left boot.

"When you get it, do the same thing, but this time tie it in two different places, making a foothold. Once it's tied, put your foot in it. Do the same thing with your other boot. You'll be able to take some of the weight off of your waist. It won't hurt as bad after that."

Conway and Samson finished making their footholds and sat in their homemade harnesses until the pressure of the ship's deceleration began to diminish.

"It's going away," Conway yelled.

"How perceptive."

Derek felt the inertia relenting. He pressed with all his strength until he was able to roll himself out of the chair and onto the wall. He looked at the computer, which was hanging by a single wire. It slowly began to curve downward toward the floor. On his hands and knees, he slowly worked his way to Elena, who was splayed out on the wall above him close to the ceiling.

"Are you okay?" Derek asked, tapping her leg. "If you can move we've got to get down toward the floor or we're going to fall when this wears off."

Elena grunted a response, and began to move toward the floor.

"I think we're okay," Derek said looking at the computer. "Talk about lucky."

With a twang, the last wire snapped and the computer flew directly at the wall where Derek and Elena were pressed. Derek's eyes grew wide as it flew toward him.

"Shit!" Derek yelled as he dove for the falling hardware. His arms slid across the wall, the friction burning the skin of his elbows. Just as he came to a stop, the computer landed in his outstretched arms with a slap.

Derek placed the computer under his arm and helped Elena the remainder of the way down the wall. Just as they reached the floor, the pull stopped completely, and they slumped down to the floor.

Derek moved to the frayed wires and reconnected his computer. The display blinked twice, and then updated the information in its memory. The screen now read, 'DECELERATION COMPLETE, FLUX FIELD GENERATORS OFFLINE, ENGINES IDLE'.

"Where the hell is my other boot," Conway asked.

"Keep looking, you moron. It has to be here somewhere."

Conway and Samson stood at the end of the central corridor next to the open hatch that led into the foredecks of the ship. Samson, whose shiny black shoes were back on his feet, paced back and forth, visibly impatient. Every few seconds, he glanced down at the spots on his expensive shoes where the shine had been scuffed away by their trip down the corridor.

"I'm not waiting for you any longer. Find your boot and join me on the bridge. I'd like to get this ship moving again. Hopefully Major Cross has stayed put there, so I can make this quick and get underway. I don't enjoy cat and mouse games," Samson said, his voice reduced to a hiss.

"I'll join you there as soon as I find my boot," Conway said, looking into an air vent that was much too small for his boot to have fallen into. "Do me a favor. If he's up there, hold him for me. I'd like the honor of taking him out myself for what he did to my buddy and your son."

"The honor will be all yours," Samson said turning on his heel and heading through the open doorway into the foredecks.

"Stop squirming," Elena said through gritted teeth.

"Stop doing that and I will," Derek said, trying to pull his head away from Elena's grip.

"Jesus, you're worse than a five year-old kid."

"Jesus, you're worse than a five year-old kid," Derek mocked. "Why don't we find a five year-old kid and let him save our asses. Maybe we could go get Tommy. He's probably twice the man I am. I bet you could even put that crap on *his* scalp without *him* squirming."

"Will you shut up and hold still!"

"No. You get away from me with that stuff," Derek said, touching his hand to the back of his head. He looked at his palm, and it was bore a streak of bright blood.

"Your scalp is bleeding pretty bad," Elena said looking at his hand. "I need to put some of this on it. This will stop the bleeding instantly and prevent infection. You don't want your scalp to get infected, do you? Have you ever seen an infected scalp? It swells up like a pumpkin. As much as I would love to call you pumpkin-head, I don't think you really want that. And besides, most of the medical supplies are inaccessible in one of the landers, so I couldn't treat a bad infection, anyway" Elena said, staring hard into his eyes.

After several seconds, Derek said, "Okay, but next time you slip and fall or whatever and get cut, I'm going to be there with some of that, whatever it is you're trying to put on me, and I'm gonna make sure I get a lot of it on you!"

"Deal," Elena said, reaching toward him.

Derek gingerly took her burned hand and they shook, sealing the deal. Several minutes later, Derek was getting ready to head to the only logical place to find the two remaining men on board who still posed a threat. They had to be going to the bridge.

"I want you to stay here. I'll take care of this," Derek said, stepping into Elena's bathroom. The door closed silently behind him.

"What are you talking about? You can't leave me here alone. You need me."

Elena listened at the door for Derek's response. She heard no words coming from inside the bathroom. Instead she heard the sounds of rustling paper.

"What are you doing?"

She heard several loud clicks, followed by the clatter of a number of small, metallic objects being dropped on the tile floor of the bathroom, but she got no response from Derek.

A minute later, the door slid open, and Derek stepped out, dropping a wadded up paper bag into a small recycle bin beside the desk.

"I have to do this alone. You'll be safe if you stay here. Just lock the door behind me. I'll be right back."

"You promise?"

"Yeah, I promise," Derek said with a smile.

"Promise me something else," Elena said, a serious look on her face. "Promise me that no one will get killed, especially you."

"I can't promise that, but I'll do everything I can," Derek said, moving toward the door. "Lock this behind me."

"What's your plan?" Elena asked.

"I have no idea. I'm making this up as I go along."

Elena closed and locked the door. She turned back to her room when something in the bathroom caught her eye. Lying just beside the toilet's base was something small and cylindrical. She knelt down and picked it up, rolling it in her fingers. The small item she'd found in her bathroom, was a bullet.

Conway made his way along the maze of corridors that led toward the bridge. His military boots clanged loudly on the metal deck plating as he kept up his brisk pace, his plasma pistol gripped tightly in his right hand. In the dimly lit passage, the open doorway to the brightly lit bridge slowly moved toward him as he took one slow step after another. He stopped in the hall outside the bridge.

"Samson," he whispered.

"Come on," came a whispered reply from the bridge.

Conway moved through the doorway and into the light of the bridge when something from just inside the door struck out at his hand, knocking the pistol out of it. The pistol clattered to the floor, and slid under a control console. Caught off-guard, Conway stepped back into a defensive fighting stance. Standing in front of him was a man who, oddly enough, was wearing a black dress.

Elena paced back and forth in her cabin. Derek had only been gone ten or fifteen minutes, but it seemed like an eternity. *He should have let me go. Maybe I could have helped him somehow.*

She moved around the room, looking around for something to keep her occupied. Her gaze came to rest on one of the books that had slid across the room during the deceleration. She walked over and picked it up.

Thumbing through the book, she moved toward the desk to get comfortable. She realized the chair was still sitting against the wall as well, so she walked back across the room and slid it toward the desk. She hadn't even gotten comfortable in the chair when there was a knock at the door.

"Derek!" she said, jumping up and running to the door.

She quickly unlocked the door and opened it. She peered into the hall, and the face staring back at her wasn't Derek's. The man standing in the hall was balding, dark-haired, and wearing nice, expensive-looking clothes. The pistol in his hand clashed dramatically with his clothes, Elena thought.

"Can Mister Cross come out and play," the man said in a wispy voice.

Chapter Twenty-Two

The Ultimate Evil

Derek and Conway circled each other, each sizing up the threat posed by the other.

"That's a *real* nice dress you have there, Major."

"It's all the rage in Europe," Derek replied. "That's a nice jacket you've got there, Sergeant."

Conway glanced down at the stripes on the sleeve of his jacket that had given away his rank. He took a step back, increasing the distance between them, and pulled the jacket off. He wadded it up in a ball, and tossed it into the Captain's chair. On top of the ball of wadded up fabric, the Special Forces patch was clearly visible.

"Special Forces, huh?" Derek asked. "Impressive."

"I'll show you impressive," Conway said, lunging forward.

Conway threw a tight fist toward Derek's face, but Derek had already anticipated the attack and slid to the left, blocking Conway's attack. Before Conway had realized that his punch missed, Derek had thrown one of his own, this one reaching its mark on Conway's right kidney.

Conway spun away from Derek, his right elbow covering his throbbing kidney. The look of pain on Conway's face was short-lived. It was replaced by one of sheer fury.

"Alright, you wanna do things the hard way, do ya?" Conway asked through gritted teeth.

Derek kept his eyes focused on the center of Conway's chest. A good fighter could trick his opponent if the opponent always looked him in the eyes. Derek knew this, and he knew that Conway knew it as well.

Conway swung his left hand at Derek's face. Derek, in an instinctive reaction, moved to block the incoming blow. His arm struck nothing but air as Conway realized his fake had worked. Derek, realizing the fake too late, clenched his teeth in preparation for the blow that was coming.

Conway's booted foot flew hard against Derek's chest, sending him backwards. Derek grunted loudly and fought to keep the air in his lungs by quickly tightening his stomach muscles. He took several steps backward, keeping his arms up to protect him against another blow that might follow.

"You're in real trouble here, Major," Conway said with a smile. "I served as the hand-to-hand combat instructor for my squad."

"That's good to know, Conway. A Special Forces hand-to-hand instructor for four or five guys, very impressive. Well, I do have some news for you as well. I served as a hand-to-hand combat instructor, myself. Only not for a Special Forces squad. I trained a platoon of thirty-six."

Conway's smile faded from his lips. Not even a second passed before he lunged forward again, his right hand coming down toward the top of Derek's head. Derek threw his right arm up to block the blow, which was exactly what Conway had wanted. At the moment Derek's arm impacted Conway's, Conway brought up his left arm and caught Derek's elbow. Conway stepped back, pulling Derek off balance and pulling Derek's arm out straight, locking out his elbow.

In a swift motion, Conway pushed Derek to the floor, using his straightened arm as a lever. Derek hit the floor with a thud, his right arm out straight, the elbow locked. Conway moved in to secure his hold on Derek's arm, but Derek flung his left fist behind him, catching Conway across the ear, causing him to release his grip.

Both men jumped to their feet, and were again facing each other. This time, Derek didn't wait for Conway to attack. He stepped forward quickly, the movement of his legs hidden by the black dress. Derek turned sideways, and kicked his right foot straight toward Conway's face. The sound of ripping fabric echoed through the bridge.

Conway raised his arm, blocking Derek's attack. Conway counterattacked with a punch toward Derek's stomach. Derek brought his left hand in and blocked the attack with his open hand as he started turning his body away from Conway. Using the momentum of the block, Derek continued to turn on his heel as he brought his right foot up, and thrust it straight into Conway's chest, lifting him off the floor.

Conway crashed to the deck with a groan. Derek immediately stepped in, attempting to kick Conway in the head, but Conway swung a leg and caught Derek off-guard. The world went topsy-turvy as Derek's feet flew out from under him. He landed on the deck next to Conway, who immediately swung out his arm, trying to catch Derek with the back of his knuckles.

Derek rolled out of the way as the blow struck solidly on the deck. Conway rolled up to his feet, clenching his left hand. Derek immediately jumped to his feet as well. The two men stared at each other, until Conway, still holding his hand, let out a scream like Derek had never heard.

Suddenly, Conway sprinted toward him, his arms outstretched. He grabbed Derek across the midsection, picking him up as he ran. The two of them collided with the back wall of the bridge, Derek taking all of the impact. Conway stepped back and launched a fist at Derek.

Derek, already disoriented from the impact with the wall, didn't see the punch coming. It landed solidly on the side of his face, nearly knocking him to the ground. He slumped onto one knee and blindly kicked out.

Derek felt his foot slam into something soft. He shook his head to regain his senses. Glancing over his shoulder, he saw Conway on his knees, his hands between his legs. Conway looked up at him and stumbled to his feet.

Again, Conway came toward him. This time, Conway's injured left hand stayed at his crotch, while his other hand swung wildly at Derek's face. Derek instinctively caught the incoming blow with his right hand, turned his body as Conway continued to move forward, and allowed Conway's momentum to carry him forward.

Conway's speed caused him to slam into Derek's hip, which was turned in such a way that Conway's legs were stopped cold, while the rest of his body continued forward. This caused Conway to flip over Derek, landing on the floor with a thud.

Conway slowly rolled over, getting onto his hands and knees. He pressed himself up onto his feet as he looked up at Derek. With a blur, Derek's fist flew toward his face, impacting his jaw. Everything went black.

Derek stumbled as Conway slumped to the floor. His entire body aching, he surveyed Conway's unconscious body. He wiped a forearm across his mouth and found that he was bleeding. Looking at the wall behind him, he saw a streak of fresh blood. He touched the back of his head, and found that the impact had reopened the wound Elena had just closed.

He began to walk toward the doorway when he heard a voice.

"Bravo, Mister Cross."

Derek looked in the direction of the doorway, and found Frederick Samson standing there with Elena, his neat dress pants and button-up shirt standing in stark contrast to the utilitarian industrial backdrop of the ship. In his hand was a plasma pistol that was pointed directly at Elena's back. Derek could tell by the hum that it was fully charged and that the ion trap was full - he was ready to fire.

"It's Major Cross. Why can't you get that through your thick head, Mister Samson."

"It's a matter of respect, you see. I have none for you, therefore, I care nothing about your rank."

"Maybe I should teach you a little respect."

"Mmm hmm. I have to say, *Major*, that is a lovely dress you're wearing, tear and all," Samson said, a toothy smile on his lips.

Derek looked down to see that in the fight with Conway, he had ripped open a seam on Elena's dress. He looked back up at Elena and Samson and saw that Elena had seen the rip as well.

"Sorry, Elena," Derek said.

"It's okay, it wasn't even my favorite dress. It can probably be fixed anyway."

"That's all well and good, ladies," Samson said, gripping Elena's arm tight. "You know, major, I should have killed you on Ganymede, or better yet when I killed your dear old dad. All those years ago. You see, our paths just keep on crossing," he said, shoving Elena toward Derek.

Elena collided with Derek, knocking him back against the damaged communications console. The two of them turned to see that Samson had leveled the weapon at them and was apparently waiting for them to attack him so he could gun them down.

"You see, I was able to find the updates to the personnel roster, while that fat slob was working to open the doors to engineering, lo and behold, there you were, family history and all."

Derek's legs were numb. He struggled to think of something, anything other than what Samson had just told him about his father. He had to be lying. He had to be. Derek shifted his attention to Ganymede. He tried to remember something, anything about the mission that could possibly validate Samson's story. *Tom was there, so maybe Samson's telling the truth about that part, but he can't be telling the truth about Dad.*

"Alright asshole, let her go," Derek spouted without meaning to. "Whatever it is you want, you name it and I'll do it, just let her go," Derek said in a voice much louder than normal.

"Oh I have no doubt that you will do whatever I ask, Major. I know this because if you don't I'll kill you both. You see, I have no qualms about shooting you two, so the longer you stall, the more likely I am to start shooting one of you in random places that won't kill you, only cause an awful lot of pain."

Elena and Derek looked at each other.

"Look," Derek said. "You aren't going to be able to restart the engines without us. We've taken the bridge controls offline. Without us, you're stuck here in deep space. Forever."

Samson pondered for several agonizing seconds.

"Prove it," he said, his voice barely above a whisper. He gestured toward the flight control console with the barrel of the pistol.

"Okay," Derek said. "Here, watch."

Derek began pressing buttons on the console. The screen slowly began to come to life. While it was warming up and reading the ship's systems, Derek struggled to think of a way to stall Samson.

"Why are you doing this?" Derek asked.

"You see, mankind has reached a juncture; a fork in the road if you will," he said as he waved the gun lazily in the air.

"If I don't intervene in mankind's future, he'll go this way," Samson said, waving the pistol to his left. "If I do intervene, as I have, mankind will go that way," he said, pointing the pistol toward the closed windows, and beyond them, Avalon. "Mankind has done so much to further his advancement, but all the while there has been a countercurrent of misuse of resources. A distortion of the plan that the universe has set for us," he said, his arms outstretched and his head back. "I'm here to lead mankind into a golden age of peace and advancement on a new world. I am Adam, and Avalon is my Eden. And believe me," he said, shaking the pistol toward them. "I'll take care of any serpents that stand in my way."

Derek and looked briefly at Elena in disbelief.

"I will lead us out of the darkness and into the light," Samson said, looking up at the ceiling. "I am the savior of mankind."

"You're the savior, huh? Look at the pistol in your hand, dumbass," Elena said. "You're fucking crazy, that's what you are."

"You have no idea how tired I am of hearing that," Samson replied, leveling a cold glare at her, his voice as cold as arctic seawater.

The display in front of Derek began to register a list of errors, all having to do with control systems being damaged and offline.

"See, without us, there is no way you can continue to Avalon and finish what you've started," Derek said. "You need us."

Samson's face turned a deep shade of crimson as he stared at the error messages on the display. His eyes began to dart around the bridge, moving from the destroyed communications console to Conway's unconscious body, and back to the pair of prisoners.

"Actually," he said. "I only need one of you."

Samson fired the pistol at Derek. A flash of brilliant light struck Derek. Derek spun around and fell to the floor, landing on his stomach. Elena screamed and threw herself down upon Derek to render some kind of aid, if possible.

"Doctor," Samson said in a calm voice. "Do come here."

Elena began crying hysterically, trying to feel Derek's pulse without turning him over. She reached around his neck, unsuccessfully trying to find his carotid artery.

"Doctor!" Samson yelled, his voice like the screech of a hawk. "Get up and come here!"

Elena turned and glared at him, a look of sheer hatred on her face.

"You bastard," Elena hissed. "You didn't have to kill him."

"Oh, of course I did. I needed to make a point. An exclamation point, actually," Samson said, his voice eerily calm. "Now, you will show me exactly how you disabled the flight control system, and then you'll help me repair it so I can get underway."

"I'll do no such thing," she said, her face scarlet with fury.

"Oh come now, doctor. I'll ask you one last time," he said, leveling the pistol at her head. "You will tell me, or you will die. My men and I will find the damage you've done and repair it, no matter how long it takes."

Elena's red face drained of color. The look of anger suddenly became one of desperation.

"I don't know where he cut them. You shouldn't have shot him. He could have shown you. I can't. I wasn't with him when he did it."

Samson gritted his teeth. He stepped forward toward Elena and Derek, and swung the pistol hard across Elena's face. The blow sent her sideways. Her feet caught on one of Derek's legs and she tripped and landed on the floor with a thud.

Elena lay on the floor, facing up at the ceiling. The world around her was hazy as she fought to hold on to consciousness. A man stepped into her view. He pointed a gun at her. She mind suddenly flashed back to where she was.

Samson looked at his pistol, checking its charge. He aimed the pistol back toward Elena's face and prepared to fire, but something caught his eye. Movement. He glanced over at Derek's body and saw that his legs were moving.

"Ah, it looks as though I don't need you after all. Your friend is still alive."

Elena rolled her head to the side, and saw that Derek was in fact, still alive. She watched as Derek pressed himself up to his hands and knees, his back to her and Samson. Derek slid his hands down the front of his dress, reaching for something.

"A tough soldier to the last," Samson said.

Elena furrowed her brow, trying to figure out what Derek was doing. She saw him pull something black out of his dress and press it to his chest.

"Goodbye, Doctor Brown. You've been a fly in my ointment long enough, and I'm going to enjoy seeing you die. Oh, don't worry though. Your friend over there will be joining you soon enough."

Samson placed the pistol against Elena's bloody forehead. Suddenly, a loud *'click-click'* sound echoed throughout the bridge. Elena flinched and closed her eyes. When she realized that she felt no more pain than she had a moment ago, she opened them. Samson was now looking at Derek, a strange look on his face; a look of fear. Samson still held the pistol, but it was slowly lowering toward the floor. Elena slowly turned her head to see what has Samson afraid of.

Derek was now sitting up, something black in his hand. Elena squinted to clear the haziness in her vision that Samson's blow had given her. She looked closer at the object and realized what it was - an antique pistol with a large patch of reddish rust on the side. Elena saw a slow smile appear on Samson's face. She glanced back and Derek, and watched his thumb slowly pushed down the safety on the side of the pistol, enabling the firing mechanism. It made a satisfying click. Samson's smile faltered.

For the first time in her life, Elena felt no sorrow for what she knew was about to happen. She had spent so many years trying to preserve life, but now she knew that the monster in front of her deserved to die. This man had killed so many people and felt no guilt at all. If he were not stopped, he would continue to kill indiscriminately until all who opposed him were dead. She and Derek couldn't let it continue. It had to end here and now.

Even though Elena knew it was coming, the boom and flash made her jump and close her eyes again. Her ears ringing, she opened her eyes and what she saw made her stomach lurch.

Staggering backward with a look of shock on his face was Frederick Samson, a large patch of blood growing on the front of his shirt. His plasma pistol fell to the floor with a clatter. Elena looked over at Derek, who sat surrounded by a thin cloud of smoke.

Elena turned back to Samson just in time to see him slump to the floor. She slowly lifted herself to her feet and looked into Samson's face. Blood had pooled in the corners of his mouth, which was slowly opening and closing like a fish out of the water. Elena found herself repulsed by the blood oozing from his chest – her medical training and instincts completely absent.

Elena moved to Derek and looked at his wound. The plasma burn was just below his collarbone on the right side and did not appear life threatening. She knelt beside him and took his hand. A raspy, gurgling laugh turned her attention back to Samson.

Samson was sitting up, the blood now dripping off of his chin. He had a bloody, demon's smile as he continued to laugh that disgusting, gurgling laugh. His hair, now drenched with sweat, hung in clumps around his face. He continued laughing as he slowly turned his attention to an object in his hand.

Sitting in the palm of his hand was a small electronic device. Samson flipped a switch with his thumb and then began to hack and cough. More blood issued from his open maw and trickled down his chin.

"Don't worry, ladies," Samson said, spitting out a mouthful of blood. "We all have to die sometime. I will still have the pleasure of seeing to your deaths personally."

Derek realized that something bad was about to happen. He struggled to get to his feet, then bolted for Samson's hand. Just as he reached him, Samson's thumb pressed a button on the device. Almost instantly, the ship's onboard alarm system began screaming, and all the white ceiling lights on the bridge turned red.

"What have you done?" Elena yelled, getting to her feet.

"I've ensured that you won't win," Samson replied. "I've set..." Samson's voice trailed off, and his eyes closed.

"What the hell did he do?" Elena screamed.

"I don't know," Derek said, taking the device from Samson's blood-spattered hand. "I don't know what this does. It just has a single priming switch and activation button."

"Warning, runaway fusion buildup detected," a female voice said. "Warning, runaway fusion buildup detected."

Elena looked at Derek, her mouth open.

"He set a reactor on overload. In a few minutes, it's going to go critical and explode, taking the ship with it."

"Seriously? Come on! What the hell are we going to do?" Elena asked.

"Uh, well, I'm not sure. We've got to find out which reactor it is, that's for sure.

Derek sprinted to the Captain's chair, and activated the intercom system.

"JT!" echoed throughout the ship. "JT, it's Derek. I need you on the bridge right now. We've got a major problem."

Chapter Twenty-Three

Critical Mass

JT and Tom came running onto the bridge, both of them huffing heavily, JT more so than Tom.

"Samson set..." Derek started.

"I know..." JT huffed. "A fusion overload."

"What can we do?" Elena asked.

"Well, obviously there's a few overload detectors on this ship," JT said. "So all we got to do is find which of these panels accesses the detectors, and that'll tell us where we have to go. It's generally the Operations station, but not being familiar with this configuration, I have no idea where to look."

"It's over there," Derek said moving toward the Ops station he and Elena had previously inspected. They quickly moved toward it. Tom followed them with his eyes when he saw his father lying dead on the floor.

"Oh my God," Tom gasped, turning away from the corpse.

"I'm sorry," Elena said, wrapping him in a tight hug. "He was going to kill us. He shot Derek.

"I know. I just," Tom stopped abruptly and began to cry.

Derek started pressing buttons on the console, trying to find any indication of the alarms, but wasn't able to find anything. Elena pulled Tom, who was now sobbing loudly, back by the doorway, trying to stay out of the way.

Derek and JT pulled up every screen on the console, but weren't able to find anything to do with warnings, alarms, or even shipboard errors.

"It must be on another console," JT said.

"Jesus, how many fucking guys does it take to fly this damn thing?" Derek asked.

They continued to move from station to station, activating the power for each of the consoles as he went.

"I think I got it," JT said loudly.

JT was standing in front of a chair surrounded by three panels, one in front, and one to each side.

"I think this is it," JT said. "It's still powering up, but it looks like the Systems station on the *J. Edgar Hoover*."

The displays came to life and ran their various system checks. After nearly a minute, the center panel displayed the message, 'FLUX FIELD OFFLINE, ENGINES IDLE.' Just below that was another message. 'WARNING, RUNAWAY FUSION BUILDUP DETECTED."

"Yeah, this is the Systems station," Derek said.

JT flung himself down at the station. He began pressing buttons on the console. A ship's schematic appeared on the screen. JT and Derek looked at the diagram of the ship, which showed the foredecks, the central corridor, and the aft section. The display was all green.

"What the hell? There ain't no buildup here," JT said.

"Now wait a minute, the alarm's going off! He pressed a button on that thing in his hand, and the alarms went apeshit," Derek said, his arms flailing wildly.

Derek stopped cold and turned to JT, who, having the same realization, turned toward him.

"The landers!" they said in unison.

JT began pressing buttons again. This time, the schematic of the ship shrank slightly, and various landers began to appear around it, starting at the front, moving toward the rear of the ship. Once the lander addition reached nearly three-quarters of the way to the rear of the ship, a lander appeared in red.

"That's it," JT said.

Derek turned and ran past Tom and Elena, and out of the bridge. Tom, now quiet, sat with his head on Elena's tear-soaked shoulder.

"Are you going to be alright?" she asked.

"Yeah, I just didn't want that to be the last image of my father I ever see. I guess it's fitting, though. I knew he was bad, I had no idea he was *that* bad."

"I'm sorry about that too. I'm sorry that you had to live like that for so long."

"Things are going to be better with you guys, won't it?"

"I hope so," Elena said stepping back and looking into his eyes. "One thing your father did that we won't do is lie to you. We don't know what's going to happen. Unless Derek and JT can do something, we're all going to die. Your father made sure of that."

Derek ran as fast as he could. His lungs burned and his shoulder ached, but he knew that he couldn't stop running until he reached the lander. It had been nearly three minutes since they discovered which lander it was, and he had set off at a run for it.

JT, on the other hand, wasn't as fast as Derek, so he was quite a bit behind. When he reached the hatch for the lander, he pounded the button beside the door as he took several rapid breaths. The door slid silently open, revealing a pitch-black interior.

"I'm here," Derek said aloud.

"I've got you on the screen in the hall outside the lander," Elena's voice echoed down the corridor from hidden speakers in the ceiling. "I can't see inside. I think the camera must be out."

"Hang on," Derek said, pressing a button on the inside wall of the lander. With a loud hum, various lights around the lander began to illuminate the interior.

"That's it, I can see in there now."

Derek surveyed the interior and found that it was not a large, open-aired lander like the ones for cargo transport, or the ones the colonists were in. This lander was nearly full of massive equipment that was built into the walls.

"Fuck," Derek said under his breath. "Elena, where is JT?"

"Uh, just a second. There he is. He's coming down the corridor now. He should be to you in about a minute. He looks really bad," she said, watching JT on the surveillance monitor, stumbling forward, obviously out of breath.

Elena watched as JT looked up at a camera he shambled past and raised his middle finger.

"Be nice, JT," Elena scolded.

"Elena? Can you call up schematics of a Tri-Centa fusion reactor on the Captain's data system?"

"Uh, I don't know. Why?"

"Because this lander is one of the two Tri-Centa fusion generators we are supposed to use for power on Avalon. Samson has done something to it, and it's on overload."

"I'll see what I can do."

Derek walked around, not sure where to start. He fumbled around in several cabinets at the base of the power station, but he was unable to find any manuals or books on the reactor.

"Where the hell are the books for this thing? Jesus!"

"They're probably in the lander that contains the library. The planners thought that keeping everything in one place would keep things well organized, and make it easier to find when we need it."

"Yeah, well, if I can't find one in a few minutes, they're going to have to search through wreckage spread across a couple of light years for all those books!"

JT stumbled into the lander, drenched in sweat. He huffed and swallowed, trying to catch his breath. Derek started toward him, but JT waved him away, pointing toward a small platform twenty feet above them. JT repeatedly stabbed his finger at the catwalk until Derek started toward the ladder that led up to it.

"Alright, I'm going," Derek said. "I'm not really sure what I'm looking for, but I'm going."

Derek hurried up the ladder and emerged onto the small platform. Once he was able to see the platform's contents, he understood why JT had sent him up here. The platform was a controller's station that consisted of several control panels and several monitors. One of the control panels had been removed, and a mass of wires was hanging out of it.

"Hey, Samson's been here! There's a bunch of wires hanging out of one of the panels."

JT coughed and sputtered at him. Derek rushed over to the panel, and saw that a small circuit board had been pulled out and was lying on the floor.

"There's a circuit board laying here," Derek yelled.

"Okay," JT huffed. "I'm coming up."

JT slowly made his way up the ladder and eventually to the platform. As he appeared, he saw what Derek was looking at and realized the gravity of their situation.

"Oh, no," JT said, covering his sweaty face with his hand. "We're dead."

"Whoa, whoa. What do you mean, we're dead?" Elena bellowed through the ship.

"Yeah, what the hell do you mean?" Derek asked.

"Well," JT said, flopping down on the platform. "These old TC reactors predate the standard reactors used these days," he panted. "I can't believe they were used in this ship. Must have been already constructed and sitting in dry-dock. Anyway, these reactors are real clean because they are fusion reactors. Their biggest drawback is that they have to have the cores cleaned out every once in a while. How often depends on how hard you run 'em. Basically, these reactors start out with hydrogen and make helium. The new reactors stop there and release the helium to the atmosphere on planet, or it's captured and sold. The geniuses who designed this reactor wanted to be able to get maximum bang for their buck, so they continued to fuse elements until they get to lead. They couldn't fuse any further than that. It's too heavy. Stars can't even do it."

"The lead has to be cleaned out of the core?"

"Yeah. They have a cleaning procedure that they can run on it that removes the lead buildup. The problem is, you can't run the procedure while there's anything other than lead in the core, or you'll start an uncontrolled fusion reaction and an explosion like the birth of a tiny star. The procedure fuses any remaining trace material that's not lead, so that there's no radioactive elements left in there, and the waste is safe enough to handle with radiation suits."

"It doesn't do that during the cleaning because the lead is too heavy to fuse, right?" Elena asked.

"Righto!" JT said, taking a deep breath.

Derek looked at JT for a moment and then asked, "Aren't there any safeguards to prevent it from running if there's material in the core?"

"Yeah," JT said, picking up the circuit board. "This is the fail-safe device. It's connected to a sensor that checks the core for lighter elements prior to the cleaning procedure.

Apparently, Samson removed it and set up some kind of remote to activate the cleaning procedure."

"What if we put the board back in? Will the system recognize the material in the core and stop the procedure?"

JT stared at him for a moment.

"Well?" echoed Elena's voice from the speakers in the ceiling of the lander.

"I don't know. Try it."

Derek snagged the board out of JT's hand and thrust it into the slot it had been removed from. The two of them got to their feet and looked at the display on the console.

The sensor began scanning the core, and registered the status on the display. Several seconds later, all the text on the display turned red and the display displayed the words:

WARNING, RUNAWAY FUSION BUILDUP DETECTED. UNSAFE CORE MATERIAL PRESENT DURING CLEANING PROCEDURE. FAILSAFE SYSTEMS OFFLINE. OVERLOAD IMMINENT. UNCONTROLLED FUSION DETECTED. CORE DETONATION WILL OCCUR IN 9 MINUTES, 48 SECONDS.

"I guess that answers your question," JT said, watching the seconds tick down.

"Anybody got any other bright ideas?" Elena asked.

"I'm working on it," Derek said. "I didn't go through all this shit, just to be blown the hell up!"

"Well, we got about nine minutes left. Anybody got anything they'd like to say? Now would *definitely* be the time for it if you do," JT said.

"I for one am not going to start saying eulogies for people who aren't even dead yet. That's a bit morbid if you ask me," Derek replied.

"Well, when my soul is released into the void, I want to have gotten a chance to get a few things off my chest first," JT said.

"First of all, about my ex-wife," JT started as he pointed a finger at Derek.

"Wait!" Derek yelled. "Released. You said released into the void! That's it!"

"What?" Elena asked.

"Come on JT, we have to get out of here."

"You wanna do *what*?" JT asked.

"We have to release the lander. If we make it think we've arrived at Avalon, it'll drop off and move away from us."

"Shit, you may be right!" Elena echoed.

"Alright, I'm coming back to your cabin, Elena. Get that computer turned back on, and get it ready!"

Derek sprinted away down the hall, JT trailing behind him. As he ran, Derek periodically checked his watch, trying to gauge how much time he had left. By the time he reached the cabin, his arithmetic told him that they had just under five minutes.

"Alright, here you go," Elena said showing Derek the computer. The schematic screen was up, so he jumped in the chair in front of it.

"Alright, here we go," Derek said as he began pressing buttons on the keyboard, followed by buttons on the display. "I'm overriding the program the lander is running that tells it when to deploy. I've almost got it," he said, gritting his teeth.

"There, the lander should be powering up for release."

They watched as the lander schematic began to change, showing the changing status. On the screen, they watched as the lander's power system came online, and the hatch seals were checked. Fifteen seconds went by, and the lander disappeared from the screen.

"What happened," Elena asked.

"I think it released," Derek said, as JT entered the room. "I think it's gone!"

"Well," JT panted. "We've still got to get to a minimum safe distance."

"Yeah, right," Derek said activating the engines.

The ship began to vibrate as the engines came to life. The quiet of the room was replaced by a dull hum. Derek pressed several buttons, accessed the ship's onboard tracking system, and displayed the position of the lander relative to the ship.

"How much time," Elena asked.

"About a minute," Derek said, turning to JT.

"We ain't gonna make it," JT added.

Elena looked at Derek, who shook his head, 'No'.

Tears welled up in Elena's eyes. She began to sob, as she wiped them away with her forearm. Suddenly, she gasped, and her eyes opened wide.

"That's it!" she yelled.

Elena pressed the schematic of the ship's engineering section. The zoomed in version was there, and where she pressed activated the flux field generator status screen.

"Oh my God, you're right!" Derek yelled. "The flux field!"

Elena reached out and pressed the button that activated the field. The ship began to vibrate as the generators came online.

"Everybody hang on," Derek yelled.

Suddenly, a blast of light poured into the room through a small porthole as the lander exploded. The blast of fire that erupted sent shockwaves in all directions, like a brilliant yellow bubble in space that grew outward at an incredible speed.

The ship, now in flux, was directly in the path of the oncoming shockwave. When the wave reached the nearly massless ship, it passed right through the hull, moving through it unimpeded. Derek, Elena, JT and Tom were all huddled together, holding each other tight, as the brilliant wave passed through the front wall of the cabin, them, and then the back wall. The four of them watched as the brilliant glow slowly faded away.

Chapter Twenty-Four

New Horizons

Derek and Elena sat in the darkened bridge, a relaxed silence around them like a warm blanket. Only a dim, blue light illuminated the two of them. Derek, sitting in the Captain's chair, reached his hand up to Elena who was standing behind him. Without a word, she took it. The bandages on her hands grated against the rough skin of Derek's palm.

They each took a deep breath, one after the other, and let out a pair of long sighs. They stared out the large windows at the field of blue stars visible from the bridge. In the center of the window were two massive blue stars, one directly ahead, the other slightly off-center. The star that was off-center had a dim counterpart, nearly invisible in the bright glare. Derek and Elena both knew that the star directly ahead of them was their destination. They would be there in a little over a month.

"So, what are you planning on doing over the next month?" Elena asked.

"I don't know," Derek said. "Maybe getting to know you."

"That sounds nice," Elena replied.

Both of them kept their gazes straight ahead at the three stars. Alpha Centauri A and B, the twins, seemed to wink at them, as if welcoming them to their new home. The darkest of the three stars, Proxima Centauri, seemed to hide in the brilliant protection of its larger brother.

Elena began to feel a dull pain in the blistered hand Derek was holding, so she gently pulled it away and laid it on his shoulder. She stroked her hand back and forth across the bandages that covered his plasma burn.

"Do you think Tom is going to be okay?" she asked.

"I think he'll be just fine. He has taken quite a liking to JT, and I think JT likes him too. I have to admit, I'm a little bit jealous. JT used to be my big buddy. Now Tom is there," he said, looking up at her.

She looked down to meet his gaze and said, "Don't worry, I don't think that anyone will ever be able to take your place in JT's heart. You two have had too many experiences together. I do think that they will make a good pair. JT is a good man, and I think Tom could do a lot worse looking for a role model."

"Yeah, I think growing up I chose the wrong role model. Don't get me wrong, I love my dad and all he did for me, but the role model that I chose didn't really exist. I made up this man I thought my dad was, and I tried to be like him, to please him. Look what it got me."

"Yeah, look what it got you. You have a friend who would go halfway across the galaxy to be with you. You also learned the skills that were necessary to prevent a terrible event from occurring. You saved a lot of lives. There's no telling how many of these colonists he would have killed."

Elena reached down and took his hand, bringing it up to her lips.

"You also got me," she said, kissing the top of his hand.

Derek stood up and moved close to her. She wrapped her bandaged hands around his waist as he drew her close to him. Standing taller than Elena, Derek leaned his head down toward her, looking into her deep, blue eyes. He slowly brought his face closer to hers, and watched as her eyes slowly closed and her head tilted back, extending her lips toward him.

Derek pressed his lips against hers, surprised that he felt nothing in the pit of his stomach. There was no nervousness; no butterflies. There was no racing heartbeat, no sweaty palms. He opened his eyes and looked at her, their lips still pressed together. Elena's eyes were closed, and she was off in another place. She seemed to feel as comfortable with him as he did with her.

Tom and JT walked up to the open bridge door. They stepped onto the bridge; seeing Derek and Elena kissing, Tom began to smile and blush. JT quickly placed his hand over Tom's mouth to keep him from making a sound. He took his free arm and wrapped it around Tom's waist, picking him up and slowly backing out of the bridge and down the corridor, leaving Derek and Elena alone.

Derek's mind raced as he wondered why he didn't feel any rush of emotions. For days he had wanted to be right here, and now that he was, there were no stars or fireworks as he had expected. It made no sense to him at all. He closed his eyes and started thinking about the conversation he and Elena had had in her cabin when he told her about his father, and about JT.

He realized that he had been able to talk to her about things he'd never discussed with anyone else, even JT. A feeling of comfort suddenly overtook him. It was as though he had been injected with a scdative. It was a sweet numbness that enveloped him completely. Going over the events of the last few days, his mind stopped on the two of them standing side-by-side, facing a blank wall. A soldier was standing behind them, about to kill them. He remembered thinking that he was angry with the soldier behind him for ending his life when he had gotten so close to someone for the first time.

Derek suddenly realized what love was, and that he was in love. He came to the conclusion that love was a complete surrendering of your emotions, all of your emotions, as a result of interaction with another person. There was no pain and no fear. These emotions caused the giddiness that people feel when they are first in love. They are results of subconscious fears of losing the one you want to be with, as well as a subconscious mistrust.

Derek knew that he felt none of these negative emotions. He felt comfortable, as he had never felt before. The other sensations he had expected, like euphoria, were also missing. He had decided that these emotions were a means of the subconscious mind to push the conscious mind into the understanding that you were in love.

Derek didn't need his subconscious to tell him. He knew it already. Part of him had known it for days. This was where he wanted to be from now on, for the rest of his life. His eyes popped open as he had a thought. *Elena is a part of me now. I can't imagine what it would be like if she weren't around.*

Derek pulled her in tighter against him, and kissed her deeply. Their tongues danced together, as they swayed back and forth in the blue light of the heavens. Their journey together had only begun, and that was what they both wanted.

Derek and Elena spent the next few weeks learning about each other. They told stories about their happy times, as well as their sad ones. They spent many nights lying on a blanket on the floor of Elena's cabin until early in the morning talking.

"It's funny," Elena said. "I ran away from everything on Earth because I was so consumed by mistrust. I ran billions of miles from everything I feared, only to find you." She fluffed the pillow behind her head.

She leaned over and kissed Derek lightly on the cheek.

"I guess we both were doing what we thought was right for ourselves. Maybe what we did wasn't for the right reasons, but the outcome has definitely been positive. I'll have to admit that I came out here to prove myself to the military, and maybe to myself as well. I've decided that I did prove something to myself after all. I proved that I don't need to be the stone cold robot they try to turn all soldiers into, always following every single rule that some bureaucrat has decided that I should follow. Bureaucrats don't get in the trenches with the ground-pounders, so they don't know what kinds of decisions have to be made there. Those people despise me for the way I ran my unit. I just proved that those same tactics prevented a disaster from happening." He shook his head and said, "I don't have to prove anything to them anymore. I'm done."

Elena smiled at him, stroking a tangle of his hair that hung down on his forehead.

"I've also decided something else," he said, looking deeply into her eyes. "I've decided that when this tour is over, I'm definitely getting out of the service. I thought about it before, but now I'm sure."

Elena smiled at him and placed her head on his chest.

"I've always known that life is precious, and the last few years I've done everything I could to protect people at all costs, but now I understand that there are evil people out there who'll stop at nothing to get what they want. I guess I learned that it's very difficult to stick to your convictions about holding life precious with people like that around. I understand that it's hard to know the good people from the evil ones, and that's not a decision I want to be forced into making."

Elena nodded.

"I regret that I had to do what I did to Samson, partially because now, because of me, Tom no longer has a dad. I'm one person who really knows what it feels like to lose your father."

"Do you really think he had one to start with?"

Elena's words hung in the air, like the stale recycled air in the ship.

"I guess not," Derek said. "Something else I regret is not being able to question Samson further about my father's death. I don't really know what I would have done with that knowledge, but I would have liked to have known the details."

"Honestly, I think he probably did everything he said." She paused. "It wouldn't really change anything, you know? You'd still be the same person you are today, whether Samson killed your dad or if he had died of natural causes. I think you still would have mourned his loss the same way," she said, her voice slowed to a drowsy slur.

For several moments, the bridge was quiet except for the ubiquitous hum of the engines.

"I'm glad you're getting out of the service," Elena said, her eyes closed. "Part of me thinks that you could do good things there if you could get others to value human life as you do, but another part of me understands that you will continue to be persecuted for the way you think until you are eventually driven out of the military. I would rather you leave on your terms than theirs. At least by doing this mission you'll know that you did some good, even if it wasn't by changing the way people think."

"This mission will be as good for me as it is for anyone," Derek replied. "I can impress my views upon the troops that are here, and maybe even the other colonists as well. I mean, we are going to be the first humans on this planet, so I think we should respect it the way we should have respected the Earth."

Derek waited several seconds for Elena's response. When none came, he glanced down at her, and saw that she was sleeping. Her chest was rising and falling softly. He took a deep breath, closed his eyes, and drifted off to sleep as well.

JT and Tom spent much of the remaining time in a cargo lander off of the third level of the central corridor. They had deactivated the artificial gravity and had been using it as a three-dimensional trampoline. Tom had also fashioned a ball out of packing foam and clear tape, and he and JT had been spending several hours at a time playing catch in zero gravity.

Tom had gotten very attached to JT, and vice versa. Tom enjoyed the time they spent together, and with all the extra activity JT had lost nearly fifteen pounds.

JT had mentioned to Derek that Tom reminded him so much of Derek that he felt as though he were twenty years younger. They both knew it was because Derek was about the same age as Tom twenty years ago. JT was reliving many of the memories from that time. Derek hadn't said anything because he thought Tom would be good for JT, who had spent much of the last few years alone, as had Derek. Derek also knew that he would be spending a lot of time with Elena, and he wanted to make sure that JT wasn't alone during these times.

The four of them stood on the bridge as they watched Avalon grow slowly larger in the window. The planet's dark side was toward them as they approached. As they watched, the sun slowly crept around it, slowly illuminating it for them to see. The blue oceans began reflecting the shimmering sunlight, which was periodically blocked by fluffy white clouds that hovered over the brilliant blue water.

They all stood in silent awe as they watched the sunlight reveal a large continent with colors so varied that not even a master painter could imitate them. Just in from the eastern coast, the partially visible continent was rimmed by mountains that appeared almost black from their view in space. To the west of the mountains was a vast area of browns and tans that stretched westward.

As the sun continued to move across the planet, the desert browns slowly turned into light greens. The light continued to move westward, revealing a forest of green so brilliant that Elena gasped. Derek traced the coast southward and followed the land until it moved out into a large peninsula. He followed it to its end, and then skipped from island to island down a long archipelago that must have stretched for a thousand miles.

"It's weird," Tom said, breaking the silence. "There aren't any space stations or anything in orbit. It looks like the Earth, without any people."

Everyone sat in silence, taking in the weight of what Tom had said. It was like Earth, without any people. They all knew the great responsibility they had taken on. To build a world the way the Earth should have been built was an incredible responsibility, as well as a great opportunity.

The four of them watched as the sun moved around behind the ship, completely illuminating the visible side of the planet. They stood in front of the window, hand-in-hand, staring at the planet for several minutes before anyone spoke.

Derek cleared his throat and said, "Looks like it's going to be a beautiful day."

For updates on the next book in the Derek Cross series, sign up for my email newsletter at www.jeffreythomas.net.

www.twitter.com/penfiction

At goodreads.com - http://bit.ly/2F7y6Nk